PRAIS...

"There's so much ...
it's great writing ...

"Spectacularly and spellbindingly perfect with high-octane action that keeps you on the edge of your seat and a romance that is surprisingly sweet and tender in a harsh and unforgiving setting . . . This is honestly one of the best SF romance series I have read." —*The Book Pushers*

"[A] fast-paced space adventure . . . A raucous tale of grit and gumption." —*Publishers Weekly*

"Ann Aguirre doesn't let up on the pace in this action-packed second installment." —*The Qwillery*

"If you like science fiction with plenty of action and drama, blood and gore, and sequences you can see playing out in a J. J. Abrams blockbuster, then pick up this series." —*Drey's Library*

Perdition

"Aguirre revisits the classic idea of survival within an anarchic, violent society, offering protagonists whose moral gray contrasts with the stygian dark of those around them. Sirantha Jax fans may be intrigued to see what befell Jael after his ill-considered actions there, and new lead Dred is a strong linchpin for a promising new series." —*Publishers Weekly*

"I didn't think Ann Aguirre could top the [Sirantha Jax] series, but she definitely did with *Perdition* . . . The themes of the book were thought-provoking and gripping because it really explores the nature of what it is to be human in a place like Perdition, but also the nature of good and evil . . . Overall, the fast, hectic pace, the intrigue, and the great characterization made this a breathless and amazing read." —*The Book Pushers*

continued . . .

"*Perdition* will give you no time to breathe, but it will make you appreciate your freedom . . . It will also make you care for its characters despite their awful and violent histories."

—*The Nocturnal Library*

"Definitely a must for fans of Aguirre's Sirantha Jax series or Joss Whedon's *Firefly.*" —*Vampire Book Club*

PRAISE FOR THE SIRANTHA JAX NOVELS
Endgame

"Infusing love and war together to make a pulse-pounding, heartbreaking read, the Sirantha Jax series . . . will remain on my keeper shelf for some time." —*Under the Covers Book Blog*

Aftermath

"Highly satisfying . . . *Aftermath* has all of the heart, soul, adventure, and sense of wonder that you could ask for in a characterdriven series like this." —*SF Site*

"Aguirre's writing is tight, and the characters have plenty of depth . . . [She] is quickly becoming one of my favorite writers, and *Aftermath* is a big reason why." —*ScienceFiction.com*

Killbox

"Fraught with action, farewells, and sorrow, fans of this series won't be able to put *Killbox* down." —*Fresh Fiction*

"An epic space opera . . . Five out of five stars!"

—*The Book Pushers*

Doubleblind

"One of my favorite aspects of this series is Jax. I love her as a heroine, and this book really allows Jax to shine."

—*Smexy Books*

"Ann Aguirre tells a good story, plain and simple . . . *Double-blind* was a fantastic installment in the series . . . immensely satisfying."
—*Tempting Persephone*

Wanderlust

"Fast-paced and thrilling, *Wanderlust* is pure adrenaline. Sirantha Jax is an unforgettable character, and I can't wait to find out what happens to her next. The world Ann Aguirre has created is a roller-coaster ride to remember."
—Christine Feehan, #1 *New York Times* bestselling author

"Aguirre has the mastery and vision which come from critical expertise: She is unmistakably a true science fiction fan, writing in the genre she loves."
—*The Independent* (London)

"A thoroughly enjoyable blend of science fiction, romance, and action, with a little something for everyone, and a great deal of fun. It's down and dirty, unafraid to show some attitude."
—*SF Site*

Grimspace

"A terrific first novel full of page-turning action, delightful characters, and a wry twist of humor."
—Mike Shepherd, national bestselling author

"An irresistible blend of action and attitude. Sirantha Jax doesn't just leap off the page—she storms out, kicking, cursing, and mouthing off. No wonder her pilot falls in love with her; readers will, too."
—Sharon Shinn, national bestselling author

"A tightly written, edge-of-your-seat read."
—Linnea Sinclair, RITA Award–winning author

Also by Ann Aguirre

Sirantha Jax Series
GRIMSPACE
WANDERLUST
DOUBLEBLIND
KILLBOX
AFTERMATH
ENDGAME

The Dred Chronicles
PERDITION
HAVOC
BREAKOUT

Corine Solomon Series
BLUE DIABLO
HELL FIRE
SHADY LADY
DEVIL'S PUNCH
AGAVE KISS

Cowritten as A. A. Aguirre

BRONZE GODS
SILVER MIRRORS

BREAKOUT

THE DRED CHRONICLES

ANN AGUIRRE

ACE BOOKS, NEW YORK

ACE

An imprint of Penguin Random House LLC
375 Hudson Street, New York, New York 10014

BREAKOUT

An Ace Book / published by arrangement with the author

Copyright © 2015 by Ann Aguirre.
Penguin supports copyright. Copyright fuels creativity, encourages diverse voices,
promotes free speech, and creates a vibrant culture. Thank you for buying an authorized
edition of this book and for complying with copyright laws by not reproducing, scanning, or
distributing any part of it in any form without permission. You are supporting writers and
allowing Penguin to continue to publish books for every reader.

ACE and the "A" design are trademarks of Penguin Random House LLC.
For more information, visit penguin.com.

ISBN: 978-0-425-25816-3

PUBLISHING HISTORY
Ace mass-market edition / September 2015

PRINTED IN THE UNITED STATES OF AMERICA

10 9 8 7 6 5 4 3 2 1

Cover art by Scott M. Fischer.
Cover design by Lesley Worrell.
Interior text design by Kelly Lipovich.

Penguin
Random
House

To Karen and Maja.
This book wouldn't exist without you two.
Thanks for everything.

Acknowledgments

First of all, thanks to Laura Bradford. We're heading toward eight years together, and that's amazing. Thanks for being a wonderful partner and friend.

Next I must mention Anne Sowards. This book heralds our second completed SF series, and it's been such a pleasure. I've learned a great deal and greatly appreciate all of her hard work, expertise, and dedication. Likewise, thanks to the Penguin team for all of their efforts. I need to tip my hat to Bob and Sara Schwager, who have been my copy editors. They do such a fantastic job; it has truly been a privilege and an honor.

Sometimes my friends are all that keep me going. This was a tough year, but because so many amazing people believe in me and encouraged me to keep going, I made it through. Words are inadequate to express how much that support means, but . . . Megan Hart, Lauren Dane, Vivian Arend, Bree Bridges, Donna Herren, Rae Carson, Veronica Rossi, Colleen Houck, Yasmine Galenorn, Courtney Milan, Kate Elliott, Sharon Shinn . . . thank you all so much.

To my beloved children, thank you for taking care of Christmas. Writing *Breakout* ransacked me, so I was too sick to do most of the things that I usually do. Because you guys are awesome, our holidays were still wonderful. It was touching, humbling, to sit back and see what competent, responsible young adults you've become. Thanks also to my husband, Andres, for making my dreams come true, no matter how difficult or improbable. I love you all.

Finally, thanks to my readers. My initial plan was to leave Dred and Jael drifting in space with a more open ending, so the reader could decide what happened—if they made it out or if they died together—but I decided that was a cop-out. Therefore, I hope you're as pleased with the end of their journey as I am. Truly, again thanks for staying with us all this while.

◄ 1 ►

Slaughterhouse Six

Chaos reigned in Queensland, and Dred was too tired to come down with an iron fist. There were occasions when even the Dread Queen couldn't salvage a situation. As Dred surveyed the damage in the main hall, she concluded this was one of those times. There were only twenty men left, and half of them were already wounded.

If they were in better shape, they'd probably argue about the alliance with Vost. But making a deal with the merc commander offered the best chance of surviving Silence's retaliation. She reflected that the chances still weren't good, considering that Vost only had two soldiers left.

Currently, they'd set up a microcamp on the other side of the room. Her own men gave them a wide berth as the unwounded ones tried to clean up. The smell of blood was overwhelming. *I'm so tired.* But she couldn't show her exhaustion as Tam strode up; over the past turn, she had relied on him for intel.

"Report."

"Casualties were steep, and our defenses are compromised. We can't hold here long term."

So they needed to consider a strategic withdrawal. Strange, not so long ago, she was struggling to hold the territory she'd claimed. Now she had to cede it.

"Any word on how Silence fared in the last battle?"

Tam shook his head. "I'm sure there are more than I saw on my last run, but many of her killers have gone to ground."

With a sigh, Dred beckoned the rest of her advisors though calling them friends was probably more accurate. Calypso reached her side first. The former mistress of the circle was bloodstained, but she looked as steady as ever, filling Dred with gratitude. Martine came next, a small, sharp-toothed woman that Jael called "bright eyes" because even Perdition hadn't been enough to break her. Jael strolled up last, and her heart twisted at how weary he looked. Somehow, his exhaustion was harder to bear than her own.

"We'll work on it more tomorrow," Calypso said, surveying the wreckage.

Jael glanced around the hall. "We've done what we can for now."

Martine traded looks with Tam, then said, "I'll leave a skeleton crew on watch. Tam, dismiss the rest. They need sleep, or they won't be able to fight later."

"On it," Tam said, moving toward the men who looked the worst.

Dred registered the way Vost watched, almost as if he could hear what they were saying even at this distance. "Warn the sentries to be wary of the mercs."

"Roger," Martine said.

"Everyone report to my quarters once you're finished here."

A series of nods came in response, then Dred headed off. She wanted first crack at the san. It felt like forever since she'd bathed, longer since she'd slept. Jael followed her, a quiet guard at her back that gave her more security than she'd cared to admit. Vost watched their departure with a laser gaze, but Dred didn't give him the satisfaction of turning.

That'd be like acknowledging he's a threat.

By the time she finished, the others had assembled. Dred checked the lock on the door, then she settled on the bunk. Jael flung himself next to her while the rest took turns in the san. She started a little when he rested his head in her lap, unaccustomed to his unfaltering affection. Dred stared down at his fair hair, then, slowly, she lowered a hand to rest on the nape of his neck.

"Sweet," Martine teased, but the other woman was smiling.

Tam sounded tired when he admitted, "I don't have a contingency plan."

The door chime sounded before she could respond. Keelah was outside, slightly wounded but bearing up better than Dred expected after the loss of her mate. "May I come in?"

"Of course." She stepped back and activated the lock again.

"I wanted to waste no time in lodging a protest against this alliance. Vost and his thugs cannot be trusted," Keelah said calmly.

Calypso and Martine were nodding.

"He has docking codes."

The debate went on for an hour, and Jael dozed off in the middle. Finally, Dred said, "Enough. The decision's made. I won't recant or apologize."

Keelah stirred, as if to leave, but Dred shook her head. "It's safer here. Get some sleep while you can."

Despite her own advice, she was the last one to doze off—and the first to awaken at the sound of shots fired.

Since there were so many people crashed out on her floor, it took longer than it should to arm up and stumble out the door. At first, she thought her men were attacking the mercs or vice versa, but in the corridor, she recognized the thin, silent shape of Silence's killers. Dred chased one down the hall, chains ready, but the man slipped away into the dark. Every which way she turned, the murderers retreated, refusing to do battle.

The others joined her, rubbing sleep from their eyes.

Vost and his men had chosen to sleep in the main hall, so they'd downed a few of the assassins, but the dorms . . . as Dred stepped in, her stomach turned over.

In complete silence, her people had been slaughtered. The tongueless killers had cut so many throats during downtime that the floor was awash in red. Most died clean, but a few held on for hours after, choking on their own blood. There was no medicine, nothing to ease their pain, and Dred moved among them with grim determination, performing so many executions that she thought her name hereafter must surely be Mercy-Killer.

I have lost everything.

When the dying stopped, there were only a handful of survivors. In this instance, Dred's favor had literally saved their lives, so Jael, Tam, Calypso, Martine, and Keelah lived while good armor, reflexes, weapons, and mods saved the mercenaries. *Everyone else is gone.* If she weren't so numb, she might be brimming with self-recrimination, but the sentries had no chance against such practiced stealth. Before, there were traps and mechanisms left from when Ike set defenses in place, but the mercs had destroyed or disabled them all. It was hard not to hate the surviving mercs when they emerged a few minutes later. She bit back a curse and went to do what she must.

The clanging of the pipes had never seemed so loud to Dred before. With so many voices permanently silenced, her territory felt cavernous. Dealing with the dead was excruciating, exhaustive work, and they struggled with it for hours. Many of the bodies, she shoved down the chute without knowing their names or stories, if they'd left families behind or whether those they'd known before had forsaken them when they were judged too dangerous to walk free.

Beside her, Jael swiped a trickle of sweat and left behind a dark streak that was part corpse blood, part grime from the murkiest seams in the station. "Almost done."

She nodded. There was a stack of ten dead Queenslanders behind them, and she heaved silently alongside him until the last of them disappeared. Dred dusted her hands, knowing she wouldn't feel clean even after she showered. Certain things crept down beneath your skin, leaving a stain that could never be scrubbed away.

"What now?" he asked.

It was a good question.

While they'd added Vost and his two mercs to their numbers, it was still laughable when she considered the scope of the turf she'd claimed. "We have to pull back. Find somewhere defensible while we're looking for parts."

"You think he really has launch codes for the secondary docking bay?"

Though Dred had spoken up for Vost in light of Keelah's objections, she lifted a shoulder. "If he doesn't, he'll die alongside us."

A wry smile quirked one side of his mouth. "That's scant comfort, love."

"Sorry, was I supposed to dip the truth in treacle for you?"

"Nobody ever has, can't imagine I'd enjoy it now."

"Then stop complaining." Though her words were sharp, her tone was almost . . . affectionate. That was the wrong word, maybe. She shied away from stronger ones.

For an instant, he looked as if he wanted to touch her, but she would've knocked his hands away. She knew exactly where they'd been, and she didn't want the decaying cells of a hundred dead men caressing her cheek. Exhaling slowly, she led the way back to where the others were camped out; nobody cared to separate after the bloodbath. That seemed like an invitation to let Silence's tongueless assassins pick them off one by one.

Dred found the survivors in what had been the common hall. From the holes blown in the walls showing tangles of wire along with scorched flooring, it looked like a war zone. Her gaze touched on the few she had left: Keelah, Tam, Martine, and Calypso. Vost and his men had retreated to the other side of the room, as if they didn't trust their new allies. She didn't blame them, as the converse was certainly true. Their situation was born of convenience and mutual need.

"How's everyone doing?" she asked.

"Tired," Martine answered.

"Hungry," Calypso added.

"I'd like to let all of you rest more, but we don't have that luxury. Pack as much food and gear as you can carry. Queensland is—"

"Lost," Tam said.

Not what I was going to say, but there's no point in playing the Dread Queen anymore. With a wider audience to impress, she once would've fixed a hard stare on Tam and rebuked him for interrupting her. But relief swelled when she realized that was done. Considering it came at such cost, that was unworthy of her, but she couldn't deny the truth. With only six people left from her former kingdom, including herself, there was no point in maintaining the persona. Vost and his men wouldn't be impressed by such chicanery, either. If she earned their respect, it would be through good decisions and martial prowess.

"Agreed," Jael said.

"I know somewhere that might be safe." Keelah's soft words were barely audible over the hum of aging mechanisms that kept Perdition in orbit.

"Show us, please." Dred wouldn't have added that a day before.

The alien female nodded. "Let's meet back here in a quarter hour. Don't bring more than you can carry through the ducts."

One of the mercs muttered, "Is she serious?" and Vost cuffed him on the side of the head.

"Guess that's our cue." Calypso shoved to her feet.

Walking down the hall toward her quarters for the last time felt so strange. When Artan was alive, this was the worst place in the world, but after she took Queensland, it became a sanctuary of sorts, space she'd carved out with blade and wit. *Now I'm leaving. It's funny how so little can come to feel like home.* Jael's hand on her shoulder drew her attention, and as she glanced back at him, she realized at once how dear and familiar he'd become, a necessity even in hell. A shiver went through her.

"We can endure this," he said. "We've been through worse, both of us."

"Done worse, too." She keyed in the code, and as the door swished open, he wrapped a hand around her arm.

"Are you saying we don't deserve to get out? Because that's a poor argument for anything, right? I never heard of anyone in this life getting what they have coming."

Dred smiled. "Except Artan."

"The way I hear it told, you did for him. That's not the same thing as being struck by lightning for your crimes."

"Let's not wax philosophical. The others are waiting for us to pack."

"It won't take long, I only have what I'm standing in."

"More than you had when you came in." She studied the charred spots on the merc armor. The damage told a compelling story about the pain he'd suffered, fighting for a few meters of rusted metal.

This place'll hurt you worse before it's done, grind you up and spit you out. Truth was, Jael wasn't invincible as he'd been when he arrived on station. Because Jael had given her a primitive blood transfusion in saving her life, Dred now had half his healing swimming around her veins, somehow, and while that was good for her, it also chewed a foreboding hollow in her gut. She suspected there would come a point when he regretted saving her because there was always, always a cost for kindness. Especially in a place like this.

In the end, Perdition always wins.

JAEL could tell something was eating at Dred, but she wasn't talking. Instead, she silently bundled some gear into a blanket and created a makeshift pack with enough proficiency to make him think she had experience sleeping rough. Now that was a sweet mental picture, imagining her free and easy beneath a night sky. The constellations wouldn't come into focus, but that didn't matter. The abstract was enough.

Once she was done, he followed her back to the others, keeping one eye out for an ambush. This would be the perfect time for Silence to finish them off, but he hoped she had been sated by the recent slaughter. *If I've any luck at all, she's reveling in her triumph.*

Everyone else was ready to go when they got to the common room, and Keelah led the exodus. They passed through what used to be the eastern barricades, now just a jumble of shrapnel. Blood spattered the walls, and biological material had dried in crusty chunks. The stench was similar to massacres he'd survived, and the smell carried him back to the killing fields on Nicu Tertius, where the marshes sucked at his boots and swallowed the dead. That fast he was lost, fog everywhere, separated from the few mercs who had survived the butchery some idiot noble called a battle, and a child's face leapt out of the whiteness. He bent to check for signs of life, but this girl was more than two days dead; her eyes didn't blink at his retreat, the mossy foliage, or the large, green-backed fly that landed to sample her remains.

He stumbled forward, and Dred was in front of him, eyes narrowed. "You sick?"

Only of the killing. The dying. The dead. Their ghosts were always with him. Sometimes it felt as if he had a spectral army at his back, and now it wasn't just the ones he'd murdered but also the ones he'd chosen not to save.

"Not exactly," he said.

She aimed a hard look at him and let him pass her before she fell in at the rear. *Guarding my back.* The idea filled him with so many conflicting reactions that he couldn't name the emotions, and it was enough that some of them were good. Keelah took them into the ducts before any of Silence's people attacked; that didn't mean they weren't watching, of course. But once they vanished into the walls, they could reappear anywhere.

The route was dusty and winding, and the lack of footprints made Jael think the aliens hadn't used these passages much. He lost all sense of direction along with concept of time; the narrow space, people ahead and behind, it hadn't seemed nerve-wracking before—when they had a whole settlement waiting for them to return. Now, everything was different, not a recon mission but a group of refugees fleeing for their lives.

At last, Keelah guided them into a small room hidden in engineering. At least, that was how it sounded, soon confirmed by a glance at a faded Monsanto sign, left from the days when this place was used for deep-space mining. There was machinery everywhere, but the noise came as a welcome change from the echoing silence in Queensland. Space would be at a premium in here, but he could see how heavy the door was across the room, and there were two bars across it, presumably to keep inmates from getting inside.

Keelah followed his gaze with her own and nodded. "They likely counted on the prisoners killing one another in the first turn. They didn't think we'd make alliances, take territory, and explore as deeply as we did."

"Your people charted the station far more than they fought," Calypso commented.

The fur on Keelah's neck puffed up. "What's that supposed to mean?"

"It's a big help now," Jael cut in.

Dred nodded. "If they stumble on us, we'll have time to prepare. That wall panel doesn't come off quickly or easily."

Tam crossed the room and knelt, inspecting the security door from top to bottom. "This doesn't seem to have a panel that can be hacked. It would take brute force or heavy weapons to break it down."

"This is a rat hole where vermin go to die," one of the mercs mumbled beneath his breath.

Jael had heard that particular slur aimed at Keelah's people before, so he took offense before she did. "Do we have a problem, mate?"

The merc took a step toward him. "Dunno. *Do* we?"

Vost spoke for the first time in what seemed like ages. "Enough. Think of this lot as your new squad."

The second merc spat on the rusty flooring, tipping his head at Dred. "And she's our new CO?" His tone said *Hell no*.

Jael tensed, but before the scene could turn ugly, she answered, "There are so few of us left . . . we don't really need one. An oligarchy makes more sense at this point."

The two mercs looked blank. Vost laughed. "It's a committee that runs a country, you idiots. Look at something besides porn-vids now and again, why don't you?"

"Can't even get porn, here," the taller one complained in an undertone.

Calypso smirked. "Welcome to *my* world." She took a step closer and scrutinized both of them. Then she tapped the side of the short one's helmet. "What's your name again?"

"Duran."

"You're with me. We'll stand watches together, and if I'm in the mood, you'll do for a warm body in my bunk."

The merc stared, openmouthed.

"She's not kidding," Tam said helpfully.

Deciding this could be fun, Jael put in, "She'll most likely kill you if you decline."

Calypso tilted her head, playing along. "I might do. Rejection is painful."

The merc took a long look at her, then grinned, his teeth white in a filthy face. "Done worse. I can muster up some enthusiasm for *you*, goddess."

"It makes sense to divide up the watches that way, one of us with one of them." Martine spoke low enough that only Jael could hear.

He nodded at the former mistress of the circle, now laughing with the merc she'd claimed. "I highly suspect that's her plan."

Bad enough that Silence is out there, but we also have to worry about having our throats cut in the dark by one of our own.

Come to think of it, that summed up every other night he'd spent in Perdition.

◄2►

Improv Rules

For the next two hours, Dred supervised the allotment of space and the allocation of resources. Really, that was deceptive. It wasn't like there were suites available or even bunks like employees would use. Instead, they had to set up camp and each of them claimed a section of the room. Tam and Martine chose a spot together, while Vost and his men went to the far corner. Dred should probably have been worried about that, but she wasn't here to turn this crew into a happy family.

No, we just have to survive long enough to get off Perdition.

Easier said than done.

She had taken enough from her old quarters to craft a comfortable nest, but she couldn't help think that it was poetic justice for the once Dread Queen to live like an animal in her final days on station. It might be nothing but intuition that told her this would end soon, one way or another. If Silence didn't kill them, it was only a matter of time before the conglomerate sent more troops to finish the job.

Jael watched her. She was aware of the weight of his regard, his gaze prickling on her skin. But she didn't say anything as she worked. The destruction of Queensland might just be hitting her harder than she'd expected. Though the place was a hellhole, it was one she had built from the ruins Artan had left behind.

"I think we're safe for now," Tam said, still studying the door.

Vost nodded. "Let's divvy up the watches and get some rest."

"We should eat first," Keelah said.

The alien had a point. Nobody had any particular skill in cooking, so they drew lots, and Tam won . . . or lost, depending on your definition. Martine helped him, and before long, they had a basic soup bubbling. Dred didn't know where they'd scavenged the hot plate, but it was a good thing. Without the Kitchen-mate and hydroponics garden, it could have been much worse. In this scenario, they could've ended up eating raw station rats until they died of internal parasites.

Conversation was sparse. That was to be expected. This was an uneasy alliance at best; it would be a miracle if it held long enough to construct a ship. Now that they had access to previously locked-down areas of the station, it should be possible to cobble a shuttle together, given sufficient time and expertise. Given their predicament, Dred was more worried about the former than the latter. Tam had predicted, and Vost confirmed, that if his team didn't return victorious, his employers would hire another band of mercs. For whatever reason, they wanted Perdition cleansed.

We can't withstand another tactical assault. Hell, Silence is likely to kill us before the second strike team arrives. She let out a near-inaudible sigh.

They drew straws one more time to determine the order of the watches. Tam and Martine took first, then Calypso and Duran got the second. Dred volunteered to work with Vost on third, which left Jael, Keelah, and Redmond on duty together for the last shift. While she didn't expect any problems so soon, it was best to be prepared. The merc commander apparently shared that opinion.

The corner she had chosen was behind a tall, rectangular machine, giving the illusion of privacy. Her head teemed with inchoate fears as she rolled up in her blanket. Jael didn't speak as he came in behind her, and maybe she should cut ties with him immediately because it was *so* unlikely that they'd both make it out of here. Better if she iced over now in preparation for that moment of parting. Yet she couldn't protest as his arm went across her side, and his heartbeat against her back was the only reason she could sleep.

Calypso woke her with a toe in the ribs. Dred was out of her bedroll with knives out by the time she realized why she was awake. The taller woman smirked at her. "Whatever time, and all's well."

"No problems?"

"Just Redmond's snoring," the other merc said.

"Vost is up already. We've been sitting near the duct-access panel, seemed like the most probable breach point."

Dred nodded and headed over to join the merc commander, who had a rifle propped across his knees. She frowned as she sat down on the other side.

"Something wrong?"

"You'll kill us all if you use that thing in here."

"Yeah, well, somebody stole my pistol." He aimed a pointed look at her, and she suppressed the urge to snicker.

She managed, "That's a shame. I don't know what this world is coming to."

He aimed a wry, green-eyed look her way. His hair was all spiky, salt-and-pepper dishevelment, and the lines about his eyes and mouth suggested he carried a heavy burden when he wasn't killing criminals. The icy shiver of curiosity felt like sensation returning to a long-paralyzed limb, and Dred didn't know if it was welcome or painful. She flexed her fingers and chose not to ask.

Best not to get personal.

"How long do we have?" she asked.

"Until . . . ?"

"The next squad arrives."

Vost shrugged, and his expression made her think he wasn't holding back. "I don't know what they want with this place, so I don't know how urgent it is. You know Conglomerate types."

"Not really," she said with a certain irony.

"I guess you didn't mingle in the corporate world much."

"Not unless I was hunting someone who had a desk job. Most monsters don't keep regular hours."

A few did, though. They had wives and children, almost like camouflage, and wore normal like a skin they could peel off to reveal the red and oozing truth, etched into the curl of sinew and meat. The worst of them listened when their inner voices told them to do terrible things. Turns ago, she'd nearly lost her soul as a vigilante, stalking serial killers that ran beneath the radar, not that society thanked her for it. Instead, the authorities clapped her in chains and proclaimed her the worst of the lot.

I never asked to be Psi. The thought came faintly flavored with bitterness since the empathic gift came at such a high price. It had driven her into the dark like the fiends she hunted.

For the first time since she'd made the deal with the merc commander, she opened her senses to take stock of the survivors and got only softly sleeping yellow from most of them and a muted blue worry from Vost himself. Of Silence's killers, there was no sign. No black of malice or red for impending violence, not even skimming the edges of her perception.

If I had been awake, I might have saved them.

He watched her with an inscrutable expression. "Sometimes you speak such madness with the saddest, sanest eyes I've ever seen."

"Yes," she said, unsmiling.

It was the last word from Dred for the rest of their watch.

* * *

ONCE everyone was awake, and they'd eaten, Jael mentioned what he'd remembered in the night. "Where's Ike's RC unit?"

A host of blank looks met the question.

Finally, Tam said, "I have no idea. I lost track of it in all the chaos."

Martine shrugged. "Is that important?"

"Aside from the fact that the bot is handy, you mean? It is indeed, bright eyes." He reminded everyone of Ike's message about the supply caches.

"Thank Mary." That wasn't an expression he often heard from Dred, and he appreciated the swift kiss she planted on him more. "There's no telling what it could be. Parts, food—"

"Both," Calypso put in with a palpable air of excitement.

Redmond stretched as he clambered to his feet. "What are we waiting for? We should hunt the droid down."

Dred shook her head before Jael could speak. "Best for all of us not to go. Too much movement, and Silence will find us for sure. You saw what she's capable of, and now we're certainly outnumbered . . . by what margin, I can't even guess."

"So who gets the mission?" Duran wanted to know.

"I'll go," Jael offered.

"I should as well." He was surprised to hear Keelah volunteer, but when he considered, it made sense. Her people had survived by sneaking around the ship longer and better than anyone else, and without her as a guide, he'd probably wander the ducts for days.

Dred's gaze met his, silently asking if he was okay with that. He inclined his head slightly. *I don't hate all aliens. It's only Ithtorians that get under my skin.*

They left shortly thereafter.

He didn't speak as they moved through the walls, like ghosts or rats or the ghosts of rats, eaten long ago by Mungo's ghastly horde. He focused on Keelah's breathing, and listening harder, found her heartbeat. She was nervous; it came in the rapid patter of her pulse, in the musk lingering on her fur. But he would be more surprised if she were completely calm.

That'd make me *nervous.*

They paused to take a break halfway, and Keelah produced a flask from one of her many pockets. She took a sip and offered it to him. Jael wasn't familiar with her customs, but it seemed best to assume a refusal might offend. Besides, he needed the fluids. The water was tepid and brackish, but no toxins prickled his tongue. That was a handy skill, one that had saved him from many a poisoning.

"Are you still seeking a good death?" he asked softly.

She'd said as much after her mate, Katur, died, but so far, she hadn't found one. Her alien eyes were wide and glimmering, looking at him and *not*, somehow, at the same time. At last she said, "That's what we're all waiting for, ultimately, and not all of us find one."

He thought of the dead children on Nicu Tertius and the bodies of the cannibals still rotting on the lower levels of the station. "Disturbing yet true."

"Come, we have a good deal more ground to cover before we reach Queensland again."

It felt like hours, but in the dark, Jael couldn't be sure. Eventually, she paused near a vent and cocked her head, ears swiveling. Her whiskers twitched.

"Problem?" he breathed.

She held up a small hand, motioning him to silence. A few seconds later, he heard it, too, no more than a whisper of sound. Straining, he translated it to the scrape of murderous feet, clad in grisly, real-skin slippers. He tilted his head and stared out through the slits in the metal, barely breathing. A company of five passed just in his line of sight, and from their movements, he could tell they belonged to Silence. It was unlikely there were other survivors though her men were probably sweeping the station, just in case.

So this is how it feels to be hunted. He'd been chased before, but with his abilities, he'd never felt like prey. No injury had been too grievous, no stunt too insane if it offered a chance at freedom.

Jael counted to a thousand after they disappeared from sight before risking a whisper. "Safe to move?"

"It should be, I don't hear anything. Stay close."

It was strange to travel with someone whose senses were sharper than his own; that almost never happened. But he merely nodded and followed her into the wreckage of Queensland. It seemed unlikely that—

The attack almost caught him off guard. *Almost.* But he smelled the killer before he saw him and sensed the stirring air behind in time to avoid the garrote. Likewise, Keelah had her shiv out and was crouched low, a small, ferocious target. Her front teeth were long and sharp, perfectly designed for gnawing, but they'd also sink deep into an assailant's flesh if the idiot got close enough.

In hand-to-hand, he had the advantage. His opponent excelled in sneak attacks, but he didn't have the strength or reflexes for a long battle. Jael rushed him and slammed him to the ground. *I know, mate. I'm stronger than I look.* Vicious anger rushed through him, and he crushed the asshole's larynx with his heel. Keelah opened an artery in her attacker's thigh, and he bled out while she darted away, whiskers flexing.

"This is better than a good death," she said with dark relish.

"We gave them better than they'd have offered us." Dead revulsion crawled over him, imagining what Silence might have in store for any captives she took. Death wasn't always easy or quick, after all.

"Come," Keelah said. "We don't have long before these two are missed. Let's find that RC unit."

◄3►

Scavenger Hunt

While Jael and Keelah were gone, Dred felt the walls closing in. The space they'd chosen was barely sufficient for their number, but it was well hidden and defensible. She inspected all the machines to see if there was anything worthwhile, but she didn't know enough about ship mechanics to be sure. Plus, stripping some vital part in here might compromise the station's systems, killing them before they were ready to take off.

Mary, I hate feeling useless.

So she was beyond relieved when the two returned . . . but Jael was *carrying* RC-17. That didn't bode well.

He handed it to her before climbing out of the wall panel, and she checked it for damage. The scorch marks on the casing looked like it had been shot, but she didn't think any of the prisoners, apart from her crew, had managed to steal rifles or weapons. Dred turned an icy look onto Vost and his men. The shorter merc, Duran, shifted uneasily. Both the grunts were younger than the commander, probably by as much as ten turns. Redmond had curly black hair and medium brown skin while the other was pale and freckled. Duran seemed to be the youngest of everyone, and he exuded a boyish air that was probably what drew Calypso.

"Something you want to tell me?" she prompted.

"Yeah, about that . . ."

"Spit it out," Vost ordered.

"Sorry, sir. When you sent us out to gather supplies a few days back, we ran across that unit. I thought it was scouting for our location, spying on us, so I blasted it."

"Why didn't you say something before?" Jael demanded.

Duran gave him a dark look. "You know how many cleaning bots I've run across up in this orbiting scrapyard? How would I know the one I shot is the exact droid you're looking for?"

Tam shifted through the bodies crowded around the broken unit to take a look, and Dred handed the metal carcass to him. With Ike gone, he likely knew the most about maintenance and repair. A few minutes later, he let out a sigh. "The battery's completely fried. I'll need to cannibalize another unit to get this one operational again."

"How's the memory core?" Martine asked.

That was the key bit. If that was damaged, too, they could forget about ever finding Ike's stashes. And that might mean the end of their escape plans. Dred leaned in, along with everyone else, until Tam motioned them to get out of his light. Sheepish, she fell back a step.

He poked around a little more before pronouncing, "It looks intact, but I won't know for sure until 17 powers up."

"So before we start scavenging for ship parts," Redmond muttered, "we have to find droid parts."

Calypso sighed at him. "Why is your brain so limited? There are nine of us. It makes more sense to figure out what we need, then divide into search teams."

"Like a scavenger hunt," Martine said.

Jael offered a twisted smile. "Serious sodding hunt, bright eyes. The prize is freedom, the penalty for failure is execution."

"I always liked a challenge," Vost put in.

Since the plan made sense, nobody argued with Calypso. Instead, with heavy input from Tam and Vost, she created a master list for the ship and a shorter one devoted to RC-17. Possibly fixing the bot would lead them to some caches that would tick some items off the other list, but they couldn't count on that. Dred knew that Ike had been a genius, but he couldn't predict the future. So his lifetime of accrued treasures would probably be random, gear he'd deemed too precious to use straightaway, but it might not help in their current circumstances.

"There's one small problem," Vost said, once they finished.

"What?" Dred tilted her head, thinking she already knew, yet she was curious if their minds worked in a similar fashion.

"Keelah is the only one who can find this room without fail. So every team moving without her will be handicapped and might not make it back, enemies aside."

"It's a problem," Dred agreed.

Keelah found an exceptionally dirty part of the wall and beckoned them over. "I'll map the route. If you can't remember later, it's not my fault."

Everyone paid close attention, memorizing the turns and landmarks she gave, most of which would be glimpsed through the vents. Keelah also listed some scent tells, but they would be of limited use to anyone but herself and Jael. By the time she was done, the mercs looked nervous. They were used to having the advantage of good gear and numbers; they had less experience in hiding, sneaking, and relying on luck and timing.

Dred decided to be blunt. "We don't have the food stores to sit around for another down shift. Ideally, Ike has some crates of paste hidden away."

Vost nodded. "Since we don't have to cook it, there's no scent to pass through ventilation and give away our location."

"Now we just need to decide on teams, split up the list, and move out."

"Same as our watches?" Calypso asked.

Duran grinned at her. "Fine by me."

Dred didn't want to go out with Vost, and he could probably tell, because the merc commander said, "Unless you object, we're better off together. He's used to me and vice versa."

Redmond agreed, "We've been fighting together for a while. We won't hide anything we find, guaranteed. Nobody's getting out of this hellhole unless we're square with each other."

"I'll go on my own," Keelah said quietly.

While Dred wasn't positive that was a good idea, she couldn't force the female to join another team. Plus, with her experience, Keelah *might* be safer alone, less likely to be caught by Silence's maniacs. So she only nodded. Unsurprisingly Tam and Martine partnered up, which left Dred and Jael.

Exactly what I wanted.

They staggered their departures to reduce the noise, so only Vost and Redmond were left when she and Jael slipped through the wall panel. The route back to safety burned in her mind's eye; wondering how long she could hold it there, Dred pushed forward into the dusty dark.

JAEL had always been good at navigation, one of the reasons he'd survived battles that annihilated everyone else. His uncanny healing was the other, of course. But it didn't hurt that he could glance at a map and orient himself instantly. So he led the way from the bolt-hole, with Dred close behind.

The route took them through their old territory, above it, anyway, and he paused the instant he saw Silence's men. Dred pressed closer, barely breathing, as they watched some kind of death ritual. *Those are the two Keelah and I killed. Now they definitely know some of us survived the Queensland massacre.* Five killers stood in black rags, adorning their faces with blood and ashes. In eerie quiet, they traced brow ridges and noses, mouths and chins, until their features were disfigured with the embellishment of death. Their eyes gleamed yellow at this distance, and they swayed as one, like ocean seaweed caught in a strong current. To Jael, it almost seemed as if they were dancing to unheard music, and they weren't grieving, either. This was a kind of awful ecstasy, a celebration, even. Everything about it made his flesh creep.

They're not human anymore. She's changing them somehow. It was a ridiculous, primitive thought, because Silence was *not* death incarnate, just a madwoman given too much power inside Perdition. But the idea rooted inside his brain, digging in like a barbed parasite to keep common sense from dislodging it.

He glanced over at Dred, but he couldn't read her expression in the half-light. Jael jerked his head, silently telling her they needed to move on. She agreed with a lift of her chin, and they both came away from the vent. He headed down, as they were bound for the recharge closet where the cleaning units went to power up. Their team had received the primary task of finding parts for RC-17, and in all honesty, Jael didn't mind. He looked forward to following the bot although it would be dangerous. Droids didn't think about opposition or danger; they just took the most direct route. So Ike's caches would probably be the riskiest mission.

Fine by me.

They didn't speak until they had put a fair amount of distance behind them, then Dred signaled her desire to pause by tapping his ankle. He couldn't turn fully because the ducts had narrowed, but he glanced over his shoulder.

"You all right?"

"Just . . . spooked." The somber tone told him he hadn't been alone in what he felt, watching those crazy, tongueless bastards.

"It's different now," he said.

"With what she did to Queensland . . . she seems larger

than life. I've been afraid before, but . . . not quite like this."
The words were barely a whisper, and they roused an
answering prickle of gooseflesh on his arms.

"I know. There's run-of-the-mill evil, like Priest and
Mungo. And then there's Silence."

"It's like she can do worse than kill me. Rationally, I
know that's not true—"

"But it's uncanny the way she's last one still standing,
moving through the carnage." He didn't say it out loud, but
he thought, *Like Death itself.*

Dred nodded. "I'm still here, too, but I'm not the Dread
Queen anymore."

"If it's any consolation, I don't miss her."

"Me either," she whispered.

There was no space to touch her as he wanted to, and it
wasn't the time anyway, so Jael continued on. They slid out
of the ducts near the closet, but when he opened it, there
were no droids plugged in. He choked out a curse. It was
impossible to predict when a bot would come back, and it
was dangerous to wait out in the open. They desperately
needed some intel about how many men Silence had left,
how often they patrolled, and where, but with manpower
as scarce as it had become on their end, recon had to wait.

"Back up?" Dred whispered.

He nodded. This time, they found a way in that gave
them vantage over their target, so they'd know when a bot
returned. He'd just finished fitting the vent panel in place
behind them when he heard the familiar, shuffling sound
of Silence's men. From her expression, Dred registered it,
too, and she practically stopped breathing. The fact that
her killers were roving freely must signify that she believed
herself the undisputed ruler of Perdition.

When they rounded the corner and came into sight, he
stifled a surprised sound. This group was huge, compared
to the usual numbers, ten this time, and horror jolted
through him like lightning when he realized they were
carrying a human-sized bundle. They'd wrapped their captive in dark fabric, so he couldn't tell anything about the

person, but the worst part was, he or she was still moving, thrashing against his bonds.

Who is that? And why the hell would Silence want someone taken alive?

Dred's eyes were wide with the same question. She tilted her head, asking with that gesture if they should intervene. *It might be one of ours.* Quickly, he calculated the odds. With a sneak attack, they could probably take them though Dred wasn't wearing her chains since this was supposed to be a secret, bloodless run. That meant her odds of being wounded were higher, but she'd recover. *So will I. And we're far enough from our hideout that an attack here won't draw them to us.*

Jael nodded and gestured, hoping she could figure out his meaning. *We have to get ahead of them. We missed our opportunity here.* When Dred fell in behind him, relief surged through. It was delicate work, scrambling alongside them light enough not to draw their notice, but the station sounds covered most of the movement though Silence's murderers glanced up now and then. Jael made out the occasional moan from their hostage, and his determination ratcheted up.

Silence won't have you, whoever you are, why ever she wants you.

Now, he mouthed at his partner. As one, he and Dred dropped out of the ceiling and onto their targets.

◄ 4 ►

Must Be a Hex

Dred landed on top of two of Silence's men and jammed her knife in the first one's neck before he could react. The other slashed at her, and she blocked instinctively with a forearm, half expecting her chains to mitigate the damage. Instead, the weapon sank in, almost to the bone. The pain screamed along her nerve endings as the bastard twisted; someone less accustomed to it might have folded. Instead, she clumsily tossed her weapon to her other hand while her attacker yanked the blade out for another strike.

The person they were carrying hit the ground and thrashed, but Dred couldn't do anything until she dealt with the four killers who wanted her head. Two male, two female, all dedicated to Silence's death cult. *They probably think they're doing me a favor.* They rushed her in a blur of spiked bludgeon, garrote, and knives. Fighting this many at once without her chains meant for every strike she dodged or blocked, she took a hit somewhere else. Soon Dred had slashes streaming on her arms and shoulders, bruises on back and thighs that trickled blood from the spiked weapon.

Silence's killers weren't tremendously strong, but they *were* fast.

Gritting her teeth, she changed tactics and slammed the club-wielder into the one who kept trying to get behind her. They stumbled but didn't fall, and she took the opening to stab the first in the kidney. Her knife went in clean, and she aimed a ferocious kick at the other's kneecap. It popped sideways with a satisfying twist, and the killer screamed. She cut the cry short by jabbing her knife through the man's eye socket. When she pulled her blade back, it was bloody, and she only had two women left to kill.

Their faces were both painted in the disturbing art of death they'd witnessed earlier, eyes ringed in blood and soot. Their teeth glowed a garish yellow against the white-ash paint that covered the rest of their faces. Both seemed at ease with their blades, and they came at Dred simultaneously. One sliced at her throat while the other tried to disembowel her. She swept the legs out from under the first while spinning away from the side strike. Dred came up off-balance, her right arm streaming blood, and the first woman slipped in it. She lashed out, spiking her blade up through the underside of the killer's jaw into her brain through her palate. That gave her last opponent the chance to stab her in the side. It was a good hit, nearly crippling.

Damn, I miss my chains. I've gotten sloppy.

She wrenched away before the woman could yank her knife out. *That'll buy me some time.* Clumsy from pain and blood loss, she circled. Her left hand wasn't as accurate as her right, but she had to take this last one out before she fell over. Before she could decide how best to do it, the fabric wrapped around the captive finally gave way to the frantic pulling, and a small person crawled out. Without hesitation, the hostage grabbed the bloody garrote and wrapped it with full strength around the nearest killer's knee. The wire bit through meat to the bone below, and the woman's mouth opened in a soundless scream. Dred ended her pain with one thrust of her blade. Breathing hard, she turned to see how Jael was doing, just in time to see him drop the last of his enemies.

He'd taken some damage, too, and was liberally smeared with red. He caught her eye, then they both turned to whoever they'd saved. On closer inspection, the person didn't seem to be human, but she'd never seen anyone quite like him . . . her? Before. Silently, she checked with Jael, and he shook his head. They'd rescued someone just over a meter tall and proportionately delicate, with long, spindly fingers that ended in tiny suction cups. The head was elongated, black eyes set pretty far on either side. No nose, flat features, and a small mouth, almost perfectly round. The alien was pale, somewhere between gray and blue, with lined, hairless skin.

It was also in a hurry. "We should get the hell out of here."

Jael nodded. "Introductions and stories can wait. The first order of business is getting away from Silence."

"No shit," the alien said.

"What about the droid?" Dred asked.

"I'll stay here, return with the battery whenever an RC unit comes back to charge."

"How? They'll be crawling all over this area—"

"I'll be fine," Jael cut in with a half smile. "I always am."

That was before. But she didn't say it aloud. While there might be emotional ties between them, she couldn't let them interfere with their escape plans. So she only nodded and limped back toward the access panel. It would be better if she could clean up, as the blood trail might give them away, but there was nowhere safe to stop for first aid. Her skin crawled at the idea of Silence's killers using it to track them.

The alien waited until they'd retreated to the ducts to say, "Did you know you have a knife stuck in your side?"

"Yeah. If I remove it right now, I might bleed out."

"Huh. But doesn't it hurt?"

"Like hell," she admitted through clenched teeth.

"Where are we going anyway?"

"Someplace safe, provided I don't pass out before we get there." And assuming this creature didn't eat her brain while she was unconscious. "What's your name?"

"They call me Hex."

"I'm Dred."

"I won't say it's nice to meet you, but I'm glad you came along."

"How is it you've survived on your own? Didn't you choose a faction?"

Hex shuddered. "Hell no. If I explain that, I reveal *way* too much to a complete stranger."

"Then I'll ask once you know me better," Dred said.

"Eh. Dunno how long I'll hang around though I will make sure you get where you're going. No offense, but there's trouble in numbers."

Famous last words.

"None taken," she said.

JAEL found a decent hiding spot farther along the corridor. The door had rusted shut, so he had to go in through the ceiling. This room was a scrap heap, with broken furniture and old electronics, probably left over from Monsanto's day. It didn't reek of biological waste, unlikely any prisoners had found their way in. Most wouldn't bother. A cursory inspection wouldn't reveal his location though if they did an exhaustive search, he'd have to bolt and run.

His wounds were barely clotted and still hurt like mad; once, they would've been healed already. Checking, he found the edges of his chest wound already puffy. *Those rotters like their poison, don't they?* He'd been paralyzed by one of them and nearly died, but likely not all of the grunts carried the most powerful toxins. Since his nervous system hadn't shut down, he should be strong enough to defeat it though it might get painful and dicey for the next few hours.

Hope I don't black out and miss the bot.

While he waited, Jael prowled through the wreckage and came up with a processor panel that might come in handy. After he had cashed out his last turn as a merc, he'd worked salvage for a while, so he had some experience in spotting overlooked junk. It helped that the other convicts had been looking for gear that could be weaponized or eaten, but ships required a lot more complex systems, and the idea that they could build one out of scrap seemed impossible.

But the alternative's waiting for Silence to pick us off.

The poison spiked him into a fever, so his perception skewed. Objects seemed too big and too close, and everything seemed painfully bright and loud. Shivering, he huddled against the rusted wall and rode out the pain of his joints knotting up. Whatever this was would probably kill anyone else. He blinked, and the station was gone.

The white walls of the lab formed around him and scientists in gray jackets moved about, making notes and consulting with one another. "Should we raise the voltage?"

He couldn't move, immobilized by the wires in his spine. *They* could stimulate his nerves and force a reaction while he hung helpless, but there was no way to fight, no way to free himself. JL489 had no choice but to endure.

Dr. Jurgin Landau moved closer to determine their next move. "Yes, do it. And time this, he's healing faster than the others. We need to document and discern why we're getting different results from the same batch."

The lab tech got a metal implement, electrified on one end. She hefted it casually, as if she wasn't about to maim. *I'm alive. I'm not a thing. I'm* not. He made a sound of protest deep in his throat, an animal noise, but he couldn't move his lips or tongue to form the words. *Why are you doing this to me? Wh*— His vision flashed red, and pain screamed up his arm where they burned him. Electricity ate through his skin and into the meat below; he couldn't writhe or thrash, apart from the involuntary twitches.

"Look at that," the tech marveled.

"Already regenerating. If this was manifesting in one of our more tractable batches, I'd be so elated right now. But I'm pretty sure this group is flawed."

"Maybe. Shall we see how much tissue it can replace?" Landau nodded. "Start with the eyes."

Jael came back from fever town with a scream choked in his throat. With trembling fingertips, he touched his face. *Cooler. I'm not dying today, it seems.* He felt weak and shaky, but the worst had passed. There was no way to be sure how long he'd been out; a few minutes after he came to, he heard two things at once: the sound of another group of Silence's men and the low-grade whir of an RC unit coming to charge up. It would take a while for the bot to power up, so it made sense not to move. He wished he could see what they were doing, but there was no vantage, and climbing into the ducts might draw attention.

I need some downtime before I fight again. Must be getting old. Wry amusement colored that thought since the Corp had tried to market their Bred creations as unstoppable, tireless killing machines with the added advantage of being biological, so they never broke down. Because the results were so unpredictable, however, they never did manage to sell the idea of mass production of Bred soldiers. Briefly, he wondered if there were any survivors out of the twenty that survived the escape run, if they'd ended up better off.

Somehow.

It seemed like forever that the dead heads lingered, probably performing their weird rituals. But eventually, they vacated the area, freeing him to shimmy up and out of the room. Pausing, Jael skimmed the scene below. The bodies were gone; Silence must have plans for those corpses. She used them for all kinds of grisly reasons, including home furnishings. He dropped from the ceiling, conscious of how liquid his muscles felt. The wound on his chest had sealed, but it was seeping yellow; the slice needed to be opened, cleaned, and drained.

Putting that aside, Jael crept down the corridor to the

charging cupboard. The RC unit was nearly powered up by this time. Any longer, and the droid would've disengaged and gone back to its cleaning subroutine. He picked the bot up and powered it down, then extracted the battery pack.

Finally. I better get back, so we can start the real treasure hunt.

◄5►

Salvation in a Can

Everyone stared when Dred got back to base camp, partly because of the alien but also because of the blade still lodged in her side. Breathing had become painful, and she probably had poison in her bloodstream, too. By the end, she was crawling even when she didn't need to. Hex helped her a good portion of the way, likely intent on paying off its debt. That gave her a sense of what kind of being it was since most inside Perdition couldn't give two shits about ideas like obligation and honor.

"Sod me," Calypso breathed.

"I need some first aid." Dred's knees gave out, dropping her on the floor.

But before anyone could respond, Vost churned into motion. His men seemed like they were trying to stop him, but he shrugged off their hands. He input a code and started assembling what had looked like spare parts in his bag. Dred watched with a mixture of confusion and interest until she realized he was putting together a medical droid.

"We broke it down to cannibalize for the ship," he

explained. "But the thing still has a little bit of meds and antibiotics."

"Not much," Redmond muttered. "And once it's gone, that's it. Your wounds—"

Vost shot him a sharp look. "Hers are worse than mine, guaranteed."

Dred wanted to say something, but she wasn't ready to confess, especially not when she didn't trust the mercs. Vost would frame insightful questions and might ask how the ability started, plus where it came from; she couldn't afford to give them the idea that she and Jael were more valuable drained of blood and used as heal packs.

The medical droid went to work on her, injecting her with medicines she hadn't used in turns. Hopefully, that meant the drugs would be more effective. *Holy shit.* A warm buzz stole over her, completely blotting out the pain. She felt nothing as the mechanical arm withdrew the blade, efficiently staunched the bleeding, and cauterized the wound with a laser. With a loopy smile, she touched the scar and felt nothing but the bumpy skin beneath her fingertips.

"Don't bust up the machine again," Martine told Vost.

Dred beamed at her. *I love these people.*

Tam nodded. "If we need the parts to finish the ship, then do it. But I have a feeling Silence may press us hard before we get to that point."

Hex paused on the way to the ducts and one of the mercs grabbed him. *Is the short one Redmond or Duran?* Dred couldn't remember, but she was smiling again for no reason. "No, don't hurt him. He helped me. Are you a he?"

"No," Hex said.

"She?" Dred tried next.

"Again, no. There's no gender binary. And why is that important?" The alien came toward the group, black eyes shining. "Did I hear something about a ship?"

Martine stepped forward, blades out. "How do we know you're not spying for Silence?"

"I was in a fragging bag when they met me. Knowing the crazy death lady, do you think it was a clever ruse?"

"Probably not," Martine admitted.

Dred couldn't think of anything coherent to add to the conversation. For some reason, everything was so funny. She choked the impulse to roll over on her side and laugh. Somehow, she kept a neutral expression, letting the conversation flow around her. The Dread Queen would've stepped in by now, imposing order or demanding fealty.

So much bullshit.

"It can't leave," Calypso said quietly. "If it decides to sell us out, and Silence descends on us here, we're done."

"Are you making me a hostage?" Hex straightened, as if readying for a fight.

Tam shook his head. "There's no need for that. You asked about a ship before. We're building one. If you want in on the escape, you should stay with us. Vost has the launch codes." He inclined his head at the merc commander. "Otherwise, you die on this station."

"Now you're talking my language. I noticed I can get to some areas that were protected by force fields before. Is that because of the cleaning crew? Nice work wiping them out, by the way. I had a blast watching that."

One of Vost's men snarled. "Just what I'd expect from a cowardly blue-faced shit bucket. Sorry, I mean Azhvarian."

"You think you can hurt my feelings?" The alien laughed. "Keep talking, I'll tell the story when I'm old and gray. By which I mean literally because the blue fades. But I bet you didn't know that because humans never bother learning shit about other species."

"I think we're getting off topic," Tam cut in.

Dred beamed at everyone. It seemed like she should do something, but her head felt like it was floating two inches off her neck. She thought hard, but no solutions came. *Damn, what did that droid give me?* But even forming that question took longer than it should have.

Redmond or Duran—she couldn't recall which he was— ignored the spymaster's intervention. "You got locked up in the worst shit hole this side of hell, and you have the nerve to lecture me? Get—"

"Asshole, you're dumber than you look if you think everyone in Perdition is equal." Hex shook its head with a faint sigh. "Look at what I'm trying to reason with. This thing can't even physically speak a civilized tongue, it's all vowels, glottal stops, and fricatives."

"We may be dumb monkeys to you," Keelah said with quiet dignity, "but we're the ones who have a means to leave this place."

That silenced Hex for a few seconds. When it spoke again, the tone had changed, no longer pugnacious and scornful. Instead, Hex sounded conciliatory. "True. I'll help you build the thing in exchange for passage when you go. In my solitary wanderings, I've found some supplies you'll find useful."

Keelah didn't wait for consensus, ignoring dissatisfied grunts from the mercs. "Happy to meet you, friend. We need all the help we can get."

WHEN Jael crawled through the access panel, everyone was asleep but Vost. Since Dred was supposed to be on watch with him, his whole body froze. "Where is she?"

"Relax," Vost said. "She's asleep."

"Why?"

"She was hurt worse than you knew, probably. The meds hit her hard, so I put her to bed."

Everything about that sentence rubbed him the wrong way, like they were literally made out of sandpaper scraping over raw skin. If he could take those letters and beat Vost to death with them, it wouldn't be enough to make up for how awful it felt. A snarl sounded low in his throat, a reminder that however human he looked, there was always a monster under the skin.

"Stay away from her," he said. "She might have made a deal with you, but *I* didn't. You'll put a knife in her back the minute it's convenient. I served with assholes like you, and I understand exactly how you think."

Vost smiled slightly and shook his head. "I don't think

you do. Is there something that you'd give anything to protect, anything at all? Life's blood, honor, soul, whatever you had. Can you even imagine what that's like?"

Once the answer would've been no, unquestionably. Nothing ever mattered more than freedom, saving his own skin. Didn't matter what he had to sacrifice or who he had to trample, as long as he cut free in the end. Some of the faces still haunted him, true, but even demons could have bad dreams. Yet his gaze cut across to the corner of the room he'd claimed with Dred. He was itching to go check on her, antsy with fear over Vost's "worse than expected."

"Yeah," he said softly. "I can."

The merc commander seemed surprised for a few seconds, then he nodded. "That's why you can be sure I won't turn on you. There's no way I can build this ship on my own."

He relaxed a little as he set down the part they needed for the RC unit. "You want this?"

Vost nodded. "I might as well try to get the bot working."

RC-17 looked like hell, and Jael had his doubts that anybody could bring it back from being fried. Yet Vost was clearly good with machines; that would prove helpful once they finished the scavenging portion of the process. The merc commander removed the old pack and slotted in the new battery. So far, nothing. Jael didn't realize he'd balled his hands into fists until the bot flickered and whirred. His knuckles hurt a little as his fingers unfurled.

"Looking good," Vost said.

17 spun in a circle, and Jael caught it with his foot. "Not so fast."

He knelt and checked the memory core. Two wires were burned out, probably impacting the connectivity. "Do we have any—" But Vost was already there, swapping them out.

"Should we wake everyone else up?" he asked.

The other man shook his head. "Better to find out if it's good news or bad first."

He ran through the interface to look at what survived the shooting. Jael didn't relax until he saw five coordinates programmed in the unit's memory. He patted the small metal unit. *You're salvation in a can, mate. Five caches. Five chances for Ike to rescue us from beyond the grave.* Jael bumped hands with Vost in celebration before he realized he was supposed to hate him.

Ah, whatever. Enemy of my enemy, right? One thing he was sure of: The merc leader would never team up with Silence.

"How much longer is the watch?" he asked.

Vost checked his handheld. "Couple more hours. Once we start the next cycle, we'll decide which location to check out first."

"Tam can probably tell us roughly where each is located. That'll help us plan, in terms of keeping out of Silence's way while we move."

"Depending on what it is and how heavy, retrieval might be dangerous," Vost said.

Jael smirked. "Breathing is dangerous."

"True. The oxygen levels are low, and station life support doesn't have long before the system's completely shot, and we all die anyway."

From the other man's expression, Jael could not fragging tell if he was serious. "You're a laugh riot, you know that?"

"So I've been told." Again, deadpan.

"Backtracking here, how bad do you think the transport will be?"

Vost thought for a second. "Depends on how big the items are . . . but if Silence hits while we're moving hover dollies down to the docking bay, we're screwed. I don't know if we can lock this stuff down, and if she destroys our salvage—"

"Then we're done," Jael said quietly.

"No point in speculating, though. We'll find out soon enough."

Vost fell silent, and before Jael could speak, a small gray thing slid out from between the machinery. His heart kicked into high gear, then he recognized it as the alien that went off with Dred. "Sorry, did we wake you?"

The alien shrugged. "I don't sleep much. So you got it

working? Let's nudge the rest of these lazy apes, huh? Time waits for nobody, or something like that."

While they probably needed the rest, he was also itching to get moving. So Jael went around poking everybody. Tam got up first, and the others followed, rolling out of their blankets grubby as hell. He could already smell himself.

Damn, I miss the san-shower. In a few days, we won't be able to stand each other.

The mercs were the last ones to get up, reaching for their weapons before they realized it wasn't an attack. "I hate you so much," Duran muttered, rolling away from Calypso, who came alert much faster, attesting to her prison-honed reflexes. "This better be good, pretty lad."

Jael grinned, letting RC-17 whir past him. "Oh, it is."

Redmond scowled. "I'll believe that when I see it."

Martine stared at the droid while rubbing the grit from her eyes. Then she brightened, apparently remembering what it signified. "Holy shit, put some pep in it, people!"

Finders Keepers

With the addition of Hex, they divided into five pairs, perfect to scope out each cache. Tam didn't love the idea of trusting Redmond to deal square, but since Keelah was watching him, it should be all right. He could tell that Jael was pissed that he had to let Dred go off with Vost, but it made sense not to let the mercs plot against them. The only way to avoid it was to divide and conquer. While the mercenaries had to be astonished at how well Dred was moving after twelve hours of rest, he'd seen her shake off worse. *Sometimes it's hard not to believe she's superhuman, just like the legend I crafted.* But he understood that her new healing abilities came from Jael, even if he didn't understand them. Plus, her physiology wasn't remotely the most important issue on his mind at the moment.

"We'll stagger our departures," Dred said. "Count it down, a full five minutes between each. We don't want too much movement nearby."

"Don't move anything," Vost instructed. "Just bring back an inventory. We'll compare notes and figure out what has to be relocated."

Calypso curled her lip. "I don't take orders from you."

Tam flicked a look at Dred, who said, "Then consider that it came from me. We have to be smart about this. With Silence in hunting mode, we won't get many chances."

Tam nodded. "Martine and I will go last."

Keelah and Redmond slipped out first, then Jael and Hex. Next Dred and Vost, who exchanged a significant look with Duran before he went. The merc only nodded, and with Calypso to keep him in line, Tam wasn't overly worried.

"I wish our comms still worked," Duran muttered.

"Too noisy. It would let Silence track us." Calypso was right about that. "And we'd sacrifice any advantage in being able to plan over distance."

Finally, it was their turn. He powered the droid down in case it started a cleaning subroutine and attracted unwanted attention. Afterward, Martine shimmied out, and Tam followed. He had the location fixed in his mind's eye; it would've been easier to use RC-17 as a guide, but the bot couldn't stay hidden.

With judicious pauses, Tam led the way. Once, this place was crawling with aggro, but now it was ominously empty. That didn't mean Perdition was safe, however. In his experience, the deadliest pitfalls were the ones that you couldn't see. The last leg of the trip was the most dangerous. He'd definitely seen Silence's foot soldiers patrolling this area, and that was *before* the carnage that gave them the upper hand.

He and Martine held still, listening, until he signaled the all clear. They dropped from the ducts because there was no access apart from open corridors. But despite the apparent lack of danger, his skin crawled with wrongness. Martine was close behind him, but she, too, froze, as if she sensed the atmosphere. Tam spun in a slow circle; there was nowhere to hide, which should have reduced the risk of an ambush.

Carefully, he crept forward, only to be yanked back by Martine. Silently she pointed at the trip wire. It was strung across the floor, not a few centimeters above it, and it would probably activate with the tread of a shoe. More alarming, they'd used wire that blended with the rusted-metal flooring. *Best not to imagine what that trap would've done to me.*

"Disarm?" she asked.

He shook his head and stepped over. That would tell the enemy that someone had bypassed their defenses. *Best-case scenario, they never find out that there's anything worth salvaging here.* Martine spotted two more snares on the way down, something that bothered him. *There's something here Silence wants to keep us away from . . . but what the hell is it?* They probably hadn't found Ike's stash, so what could it be? No answer was forthcoming as they reached a dead-end section of hallway.

"This is the place," Martine said, low. "Now what?"

"We start searching. Ike collected this stuff, it's up to us to find it."

Determination led Tam to check the seams and the wall plates. Ike had hidden the treasure on his own, so the concealment couldn't be too elaborate. Martine struck pay dirt when the next panel shifted as if it had been removed before. She shot an elated smile at him, and his heart turned over.

Mary, he thought.

It was an irrational place and time to develop such an attachment. The chances were good that one or both of them wouldn't make it. That was simple numeric probability.

Yet he smiled back, and said only, "Let's open it up, shall we?"

The subsequent blast put his lights out.

"DID you hear that?" Vost asked.

They were still in the ducts, heading toward their target. He hoped. The air quality wasn't great, walls were closing in, and the dark made it hard to be sure of their route.

Dred tilted her head. "Yeah. There was an explosion five levels down."

"How can you pinpoint it like that?" Sometimes the Dread Queen didn't seem entirely mortal. Possibly that was a psychological side effect of the bullshit shell game she'd been running on her entire gen pop, but it shouldn't affect Vost the same way. He knew damn well she was a predator, but a human one.

Her smirk rubbed him the wrong way, her drawl even more so. "I got skills, son."

"By which you mean you don't intend to explain."

"Why would I?"

"Point. Do you want to investigate the detonation?" He was prepared to vote her down if she did. Their mission parameters did *not* include search and rescue.

"If there's a problem, we'll find out soon enough. We'd better get our assigned cache."

"You know the station better than I do. Lead on."

"That's not saying much. You'd be better off with Tam or Keelah." That wasn't mock modesty. Vost could tell the difference, and Dred seemed completely at ease admitting she wasn't the best at everything.

Interesting.

"So tell me," he said, as she plotted their course from here. "Do you have any remorse for what you did?"

That earned him a hard green stare, sharp as glass. "What does that matter?"

"Call it curiosity."

"Mostly, no. They can say whatever they want about me outside . . . I know I left the universe better than I found it."

"By hunting monsters." That was what she'd claimed early on in her defense, before the barristers shut her down.

"Sounds like you don't believe me." He couldn't see her face, but he heard a wry amusement in her voice.

"That thing you did . . . when you read me. Is that how you found them?"

Dred flicked a surprised look over one shoulder, which he took to mean he'd guessed right. "Maybe."

"I need to understand what you can do."

"No, you don't. You tell yourself that, but really, you're

just dead curious. What kind of person sees demons in human skin? You're wondering if I'm crazy."

She wasn't wrong. Yet . . . "I'm positive you're not psychotic. The way you fought us told me that much."

"That's all you get, then."

Cagey, but he understood why. Public opinion hadn't been kind after she murdered a father in front of his two daughters. For some of her kills, evidence came to light after the trial, proving she was correct in her judgment. With others, there was no proof at all that she was anything but a bloodthirsty maniac.

Vost fell silent until a distant rumble clued him in as to their location. "We're down near the recyclers, aren't we?"

Dred nodded as she led the way out of the vents. "Do you know how long it takes to turn a corpse into usable organic material?"

"I can't say that I do." He wasn't looking to add that information to his general awareness, either. While killing a man in battle was one thing, it rang all his bells the wrong way to contemplate eating paste made from his processed remains.

They moved out of the corridor and down the ladder by one level. The rungs were rusted and scraped his palms. Small wonder they'd beaten his team. *I didn't even know how to access this part of the station.*

As she moved along the wall toward the churning groan of the recyclers, Dred sighed. "Mary knows how Ike came all this way on his own."

"He was one of the first to be sentenced, wasn't he?" Vost had definitely studied up on the prison's history before going in.

Not that it did much good.

"True. He was in here forever. I don't know of anyone who survived inside longer." Her tone was both quiet and respectful, a testament to her fondness for the old convict. "So possibly this gear has been hidden for a long time."

Vost nodded. The room they entered next was huge, an impossible amount of ground to cover for two people. So many nooks and crannies that he felt tired just taking stock. He ached all over, and the acid burns on his chest seemed to have a secondary pulse. But he staked out half the room nonetheless and set to work.

SILENCE watched. Death permitted few pleasures, yet she savored these blind moments wherein those she hunted had no idea of her proximity. It had been a long time since an adversary interested her enough to draw her out alone. The new Speaker had protested, but she silenced him with a single gesture. He knew all too well how careless she was with minions she no longer found amusing.

She could not recall why she had been sent to this place, but it had become more than home. This . . . this was death's dominion. The only way anyone ever left these halls was through him. Every murder, every quiet shiv in the dark, fed her hunger, but there was no sating it. Even should she stand alone on these decks, she would still need bones for the furnace.

On that day, she thought, *they will be my own.*

Since she'd always known her fate, even since before she could speak, the thought did not trouble her. It was only her devotion that had kept her from eternity all this time. *He sees my skill. He knows it's my life's work. Therefore, I survive when others fall.* She had no doubt that she would be the last one standing when the smoke cleared. *Then and only then will my work here be done.*

They were clearly searching for something.

She noted how methodical they were, how precise. The mercenary commander had joined forces with the Dread Queen, and now they both had a reason to fear. Wearing an expression that was *almost* a smile, she kept pace as they moved, just out of sight. It pleased her to glide into the shadows just seconds before the man's eyes focused.

He sensed her. Discomfort showed in the hunch of his shoulders—in the way he scanned the corners. She held still. *You know I'm here, don't you, prey?* As he brushed past, she silently sliced a lock of his hair and brought it to her nostrils. He hadn't washed recently, and there was a hint of smoke, oil. Silence curled a fist around the lock. The male paused. He said something to the Dread Queen, who lifted her head like an animal scenting threat on the wind. Except there was none, only the rumble of the recyclers.

Anyone with any sense of self-preservation would have slipped away. Instead, Silence moved in closer, stepping as they stepped, breathing as they breathed. So she was near enough to hear the male exclaim, "I found it."

Found what?

With the Dread Queen's help, he pulled a crate out from under an upended shell of a broken Peacemaker chassis. Then the other woman beamed. Silence would've liked to widen that smile at the edges, peel it away in a shining wash of red, until there was only slivers of bone. But she didn't move. Sometimes, information was more vital than personal satisfaction.

"We can't build a ship without this," the Dread Queen said, indicating something in the box outside of Silence's field of vision.

So that's your intent. You'll craft a vessel and sail away?

Considering, Silence mentally adjusted her plans. And smiled.

◁7▷

Hunting for Payback

A bad feeling plagued Dred all the way back.

The explosion might've been a failure in station systems, but she didn't think so. Something about the attack felt premeditated, and they wouldn't find out the truth until all members of the group were accounted for. Returning to base camp felt twice as long, and she couldn't relax until they popped out of the depths and found Jael already waiting, joking with Hex on the other side of the room.

A breath she didn't even realize she was holding slipped out in a sigh. Hex was unharmed, apparently unconcerned by the explosion. Jael must've heard it, considering he had the same acute senses as Dred, but he gave no sign. That was probably for the best, all things considered.

"Let's see your inventory," she said.

Jael pushed to his feet and crossed to meet her. He handed her a scrap of paper etched in what looked like charcoal. Dred skimmed the list with an appraising eye.

Vost came up to stand at her shoulder, reading along with her. "Looks like you found some good shit," he observed.

"What about you?" Jael asked.

Dred handed over the list. Before Jael was done inspecting it, Hex snatched it out of his hands. "Nice. I can't believe your friend stashed a power converter. That'll help."

"Where's everyone else?" Vost wanted to know.

Hex shrugged. "Not sure. We were the first ones back."

While they were waiting, Dred put together a meal. If the others ran into trouble, they would want some food when they got back. Sure enough, Calypso and Duran were hungry when they arrived about an hour later. Their inventory was the most promising yet, containing several parts that needed to be moved to the docking bay. So far nothing was big enough that it required a hover dolly, and most of it could be transported through the ducts.

Nice stroke of luck, that.

Another hour passed before Keelah showed up, with Redmond leaning heavily on her shoulder. They were both covered in blood, and the merc looked like he had narrowly escaped having his throat cut. Questions could wait. Dred sprang into action, using their precious and limited water supply to clean the man's wounds. As she worked, Keelah said, "The ambush came out of nowhere. I thought we were home free when they hit us."

"You didn't smell them?" Jael asked.

Good question.

She didn't pause for Keelah's reply. Redmond was still losing blood, so she tore his shirt into strips and bound his injuries as the female said, "No, it was too close to the engines. Everything down there is oil and hot metal."

"That's convenient." Duran wore a thunderous scowl. "It seems more likely that you saw an opportunity to thin us out."

Redmond shook his head weakly. "I'd be dead already if not for her. She's a ferocious fighter when she's cornered."

Since Dred had seen as much firsthand, that didn't surprise her though the mercs seemed startled. Vost leaned down, checking her handiwork, and she cut him a look that made him back off a few paces. Soon, she had Redmond bandaged up, but she didn't like his odds of survival without antibiotics, pain meds, and better treatment. By his commander's grim expression, he shared her dark outlook, not that they'd tell Redmond. He was pale-faced and sweaty, but he didn't seem to have processed the fact that the rents in his flesh would turn septic if poison didn't get him first.

It would be kinder to put him down.

Otherwise, dying would be slow and painful. But he wasn't one of hers, so that call had to come from Vost. On the floor, Redmond moaned. His cheeks were shifting from the pallor caused by blood loss into the ruddy splotches of fever.

The merc commander drew Keelah aside for a private conversation; he couldn't know that he'd have to leave the room to make it so Dred—and Jael too—couldn't overhear. She wasn't *trying* to eavesdrop. Recently acquired talents just made it impossible not to.

"How many were there?" Vost asked.

"Six, give or take. We got three, the others took off, like they were receiving orders." The female shook her head. "You don't understand how *strange* it was."

"They didn't have comm units."

"Of course not. But I swear it was like they heard something, all at the same time, too."

"Well," Vost said. "That's disquieting."

"You've no idea."

"Where did they come from?"

"Up above." Keelah's tone was neutral.

Vost let out a strangled sound, full of foreboding and frustration. "Which means they're scouring the ducts for us."

"Seems likely," she allowed.

"We won't be able to hide here long then." The mercenary commander spoke Dred's own thoughts. "We have to move quickly and set up in the docking bay, or they'll pick us off."

"I think we can get the force fields up again once we're inside," Keelah said.

Vost looked grim. "I hope so. At this point, fortification is our only hope."

He's right. We have to dig in and prepare for a siege while doing our damnedest to build something space-worthy out of scrap and salvage.

"Tam and Martine still aren't back," Jael said, drawing Dred's attention from the exchange across the room.

If Redmond and Keelah had run into trouble, the last pair might have, too. Unlike most of the other squads, Dred cared enough about them to risk search and rescue. She wouldn't stick her neck out for Duran, Vost, or Redmond. *Maybe* Keelah. Definitely not Hex since she'd just met the alien. Such emotional triage qualified her as an asshole, Dred knew. But that was how you stayed alive in Perdition—by calculating the odds and not taking stupid risks for people who wouldn't reciprocate.

"I'll go," she murmured.

"We're okay," Martine grunted as she popped through the access panel.

"Bit singed. And the stash was blown to shit." Tam was burned a couple of places, mostly his forearms.

"That doesn't sound like Ike," Dred commented.

Martine wore a permanent snarl. "Pretty sure Silence's crew raided our cache first and left us an exploding present to find."

Tam nodded. "There were traps all over the area. I should've been more careful."

"I'm glad you made it," Dred said. "Now we need to plan some payback."

Jael set his jaw, and she recognized the look from the last time when he'd gone rogue sniper, determined to take out the mercs. Since they only had one major enemy left to face, there was no question what he had in mind. *But maybe I can talk him out of it.*

This time, Jael didn't sneak away. He waited until just before the watches started and pulled Dred aside. He began, "I'm telling you this as a courtesy, not asking permission."

"You're going after Silence," she said softly.

"Everything changes with her out of the picture. Her

minions become easier to kill, less dedicated to wiping us out."

"I don't think you realize how well protected she is. She's like the queen at the center of the hive. Drones will die in droves to keep you from her."

"And I don't think *you* realize how much experience I have hunting hard targets."

It wasn't an idle boast, either. Back in his days as a merc, his commanders never blinked at aiming him at some impossible task. *Of course, you're only half as effective as you used to be.* But this wouldn't be like assassinating a general behind enemy lines; there was no razor wire, no electrified perimeter, no minefield. At worst, there would be some traps and a lot of tongueless assholes to carve a path through.

"Fine," she said. "I can't send anyone with you, but I suspect you knew that."

He nodded. "This is a solo mission. I'll be back soon."

Jael leaned in for a kiss, and she met him more than halfway, such a change from the frozen princess in chains who glared anytime he stretched out a hand. Until meeting her, he'd lost hope that anyone could accept him as he was and not constantly see a failed experiment instead of a person. Gratitude certainly ringed his feelings for Dred, but at the heart of it, there was so much more.

Everything, in fact.

"Be careful," she said.

"You went there once, right? With the Speaker."

Dred nodded. "I don't know if they're still in the same place, but let me map it for you."

He memorized the route she drew and discarded it. The others didn't notice when he slipped out. This reminded him of when he'd gone out to snipe mercs, not expecting to make it back in one piece. At least this time, he'd kept his promise and not simply disappeared.

There was no laser rifle, either. Weapons would only slow him down and make it difficult to move silently. No, if he succeeded in taking Silence out, it would be with his bare hands.

This shit has gone on long enough.

When he went out with Hex, he had to worry about how well the alien could fight. The same with Dred since she abandoned her chains in favor of stealth. *But I'm sodding tired of being hunted.* He was careful in moving to the center of the station, where Silence had holed up like a spider. Jael half expected to find the place deserted since Dred knew where they were, but from the smell on approach, Death was thriving.

He stilled, listening to their movements. Since it was down cycle, he didn't hear many of her trained killers roaming around. *That'll make my job easier.* Though he'd love to execute the lot of them, that wouldn't cut the head off the snake. *Then again, if I thin the herd, she can't replenish her numbers.*

There was no point in speculating until he actually got inside. Dred didn't know the back way into the territory, as she'd followed the Speaker in through the front door, so to speak. There were two sentries on watch, both painted with the disconcerting death art that made it impossible to read their expressions. Even from this distance, he could tell that they were awake if not alert. Most of the lights had been disabled, leaving only a flickering overhead here and there, and a miasma of smoke hung heavy in the air. It smelled like every village he'd ever burned, all the corpses he'd ever flung on an open fire.

He found a scrap of metal and chucked it between two watchmen. That instant of distraction was all he needed to race up and snap their necks, two clean twists. Jael grabbed their arms and guided their bodies down to avoid the thud. Surely others must be nearby, and they'd recognize that sound. Then he stepped into Silence's domain, ready to end her.

Like a shadow, he prowled amid piles of dried skin and bones, heaps of rotting meat. Though he'd seen countless wartime atrocities, never anything like this, and more than once, he had to choke down the bile pooling in his throat. Breathing the fetid air alone felt like it might kill him. He skirted a pair of bodies writhing together in the blood and filth, playing some unholy game with their blades. Honest to Mary, it felt like a mercy when he snatched up a discarded knife and cut the woman's throat cleanly, only her partner didn't seem to notice. He kept moving on her, transported with grotesque, inhuman ecstasy. So Jael killed him, too.

It's like these daft buggers are stoned out of their minds.

As soon as the thought registered, it rang true. There was no other explanation for how completely Silence controlled her minions. *But what's she feeding them? How do they make it?* If he could find her chem and torch it, Death's sodding Handmaiden would find herself at the mercy of deviants in withdrawal. While he'd much prefer to stick a blade in her neck, he didn't *see* her. He found the massive bone chair that she presumably used when she was in residence, holding court over madmen and junkies, but it sat empty while her followers humped and moaned, oblivious to his presence.

This doesn't make sense. How can they have the presence of mind to patrol? So maybe this is their off-duty reward? His skin crawled. Before he went after the drugs, he had a score to settle on behalf of all the Queenslanders who had died in their sleep.

Jael's blade gleamed in the half-light. *Payback's a bitch, innit?*

◄8►

Truths Writ in Blood

As the hours wore on, it became clear that Redmond wouldn't rally.

While she and Jael might've fought through most of Silence's toxins, the merc didn't have their augmented immune systems. There was no antidote, either. Each of Redmond's breaths sounded wet, a sign that his body was shutting down. He thrashed and moaned, sweat beading on his brow.

"Get the droid," Duran said hoarsely.

Calypso laced their fingers together and, with some surprise, Dred noticed that he didn't pull away. It was strange how fast bonds could form in this place. Maybe it was even as simple as the fact that the mistress of the circle had chosen him. Saying *You belong to me* was enough to change everything.

Silently, Vost powered it up, and the medical bot confirmed that Redmond's lungs were filling with water, but it didn't have the capacity to help with his wounds. Duran cut Dred an accusing look, one that said, *He's dying because we treated you instead.*

She couldn't deny it.

Hours passed, and he only got worse. His breath came in gurgled, choking rasps, and his lips held a blue tinge. Redmond tried to say something, but he fell into a coughing fit. Vost knelt beside him.

"We both know how this ends, sir. Make it quick."

"I'll do it," Dred said.

Judging by the intensity of Duran's glare, that might've been a mistake. Vost shook his head. "This is *my* responsibility."

With a quick twist of his blade, he ended Redmond's life. Duran dropped to his knees beside his commander and stared into his comrade's face. Dred didn't do their grief the dishonor of looking away. For long moments, the two soldiers said a silent farewell; and then, Duran closed Redmond's eyes.

"Right," Duran said, wiping his cheeks. "That bitch is dying. Point me at her."

"Jael's doing some recon. He'll be back soon."

Calypso put a hand on Duran's shoulder. "Sorry for your loss."

Keelah, Tam, and Martine echoed the sentiment, then the spymaster gave Dred a significant look. She nodded slightly, aware that he'd registered the trouble, too. Though she didn't say so, dealing with the remains created another problem. Getting Redmond to the recyclers would be risky, yet they couldn't leave him here. Hygiene and contamination issues aside, his body would also attract scavengers in droves. Without the aliens hunting them to keep numbers down, soon Perdition would be overrun by the mutated beasts.

And that's the least of our worries.

"I'll lay him to rest," she offered.

"You can't manage alone." Vost didn't seem open to discussion on the topic, and she thought it best not to reveal her hidden strength just now.

"Then come on. You should be there to see him off."

She expected Duran to protest, but he apparently knew

that the more people went to attend the funerary rites, the more chances they'd be spotted and attacked. Taking more casualties wouldn't bring Redmond back. *So he's a soldier first, a friend second. Good to know.*

"Be careful," Tam said.

There was a lot more unspoken in the long glance they exchanged. He was the only one who had believed in her even *before* she killed Artan. Tam had whispered ideas and scenarios until she internalized his faith. With Einar's help, he'd also helped her solidify her reign afterward. Though she wouldn't have imagined she could make any friends in a place like this, there were people she missed, Einar and Ike chief among them.

"I will be," she promised.

They wrapped the body in rags, an indignity that made Duran clench both fists. But it was that or leave a blood trail. Once the corpse was prepared for transport, Vost popped open the wall access, so Dred could hand Redmond through, then she followed, taking up the legs for the haul to the recyclers. It was a long way down, nearly to Ike's cache, and they didn't speak more than necessary. Now and then, she heard Silence's men outside the ducts, but they were *running* toward something, not patrolling.

"Seems like your man's got them plenty riled," Vost said softly.

She nodded. "He has a talent for it."

"You reckon he's safe?"

"As much as anyone in here." Truth was, she wasn't so certain, but she'd rather be roasted on a spit than admit any doubt aloud. Superstitiously, Dred felt like that would be tantamount to jinxing him.

"When he gets back and we're done with Redmond, we need to start the diaspora."

"Agreed."

Reluctant admiration flickered to life in her, partly because he *knew* that word and also because he didn't dumb it down. She'd run across so many do-gooders who assumed she must be an ignorant meat-lump, considering the heinous nature of her crimes. But in fact, it was the opposite. Her crimes weren't driven by deviance, passion, or bloodlust; no, they were coolly conceived and coldly executed. And as they died, she always thought the same thing:

It's for the greater good.

Hours later, she didn't feel the same as she shoved Redmond's body down the chute.

"Ashes to ashes," Vost murmured. "You'll be missed, my friend."

What an abbreviated service. The more people die, the less we have to say. Soon it'll be, "See you, pal. Ker-thunk." It was hard *not* to envision a future where there was nobody left to do her the same courtesy. Which meant she'd rot where she fell or be eaten by station rats. Either way, it likely wouldn't end with her in a ship, putting this place behind her.

"Don't give up," Vost said. "If you do, we've already lost."

"What?" She'd almost forgotten he was there.

"You think I haven't noticed that you're the heart and soul of this group? If *you* secretly think it can't be done, they'll sense it. But all great feats are deemed impossible until someone proves otherwise."

His determined optimism pried a reluctant smile out of her. "All right, Captain Brightside. I'll keep my chin up."

As they turned to leave the recycling room, footfalls outside alerted them to enemies nearby. She mouthed at Vost, *Fight or hide?*

He cocked his head, as if trying to estimate the number of opponents, but before he could reply, the opening door took the choice away from them.

JAEL skidded into the recycling room and locked the door behind him. The blood covering him startled a curse out of Dred, who he hadn't expected to find here. Vost stepped out from behind her, pissing him off profoundly. It wasn't that he was jealous, but . . . *Oh, frag it. Obviously I am.* There was no point in being coy inside his own screwed-up head.

"Trouble?" Dred asked.

"I stirred up a bit of a hornet's nest. Just about every able-bodied murderer on board is hunting for me now, and like twenty of them are right outside."

"How many did you take out along the way?" Vost wondered.

"Twenty, twenty-five. I lost count after a while." That made it sound like a mighty battle but it was more of a slaughter. He didn't mention that the ones he'd killed had been so zoned that they couldn't tell a real threat from their chem-induced dreams.

"Did you get Silence?" Dred came toward him, apparently listening to the thump of bodies against the door. It was solid metal, so they wouldn't be breaking it down anytime soon. Yet the way Silence's minions crawled around the ship, they could probably find a hidden route.

And we don't have the food or water to wait them out. Sooner or later, we'll be fighting.

Jael shook his head. "Mary knows where she is, but *I* didn't find her. Did for her new Speaker, though."

Dred smirked. "Now there's a job with short life span."

"She probably can't replace him either unless she maintains a small pool of unmutilated subjects, just in case." That was Vost.

"Somehow, I don't think talking to us will rank high on her list of things to do," Jael said.

"I suppose not."

Kill or be killed. Now it's down to the most basic conflict of all.

"Hm," Dred said. "I wonder why she had someone ready to step in before. It's oddly forward thinking."

"That means she's capable of planning," Vost murmured.

Jael eyed the merc with irritation. "We already knew that, thanks. My odds of surviving this contretemps have gone up, though. I didn't expect to find anyone in here, I was just leading them a merry chase before picking a few more off."

"You can't go on like that indefinitely," Dred said.

"Worried about me, love?"

Once she would've denied it, but now she only nodded.

The resultant pleasure eradicated the residual bitterness at finding her roving the station with Vost. "I culled their numbers for sure, and I learned something that we can use against her."

Vost tilted his head. "You have my attention."

Jael summarized what he'd found out about the method she used to keep her minions docile.

Dred frowned. "If we can find her lab—"

"Then we cripple her mobility," he finished.

"I wonder what she's making. It has to be an organic compound, something that can be produced with human organs."

"Or waste," Dred pointed out.

While that was disgusting, it was also accurate. "If she's brainwashed them enough, they might actually believe she's death incarnate."

"Yeah, I don't see us reasoning with any of her people," Vost said.

"That has to wait." Dred put her ear to the door. "We need to rush before they summon reinforcements. Otherwise, getting out of here may be impossible."

"Depends on how many he left alive. But the odds are not in our favor."

"They never are," she muttered.

"If it's any consolation, our squad should've exterminated the lot of you and yet . . ." Vost trailed off, raising his brows in implicit acknowledgment of defeat.

"Not much, no. But you know better than anyone that I don't roll over." Dred flashed the merc commander a toothy smile.

Meanwhile, Jael was prowling around the room, looking for something that would help him kill a lot of people. He grinned when the solution occurred to him. "Help me pull the cables from the recycler closest to the door."

"Then we'll only have two functioning machines," Dred noted.

"I'm aware. But we won't be around long enough for that to matter." *I hope.*

Vost switched the machine off, opened it up, and started unspooling the wires, then they stretched them across the room, and Jael affixed them to the metal handles. He heard the telltale thump of artless killers adding weight in the hope of getting to them faster. *The human body is conductive, right? Let's see how much.*

Once he got a safe distance away, he said, "Fire it up."

Dred hit the button and the next time Silence's assassins ran at the door, their screams were gratifying. She powered down the machine, so they could check out the damage. The one who hit first smoldered with flash burns all over his face and arm, while three more lay on the ground twitching. More still seemed to be dazed, stumbling around with shaking hands.

Only then. This will be easy.

"Take their weapons," Dred ordered. "Don't even let them scratch you."

But Vost was already on it, snatching blades right and left, even as Jael cut strips of wire to bind their hands. It might be an unnecessary precaution, but he wouldn't put it past them to attack even when they were lying on the ground. Because Silence's people didn't fight to win; they only existed to kill. Once they were all disarmed, Vost cut their throats, a messy-as-hell way to die, and one that left a bloody message for Silence.

We will fight you to the last man, to our last breath. Numbers are not *enough.* In case she was stupid as well as mad as a crack-shelled Ithtorian, Jael dipped a poison blade into the blood of the fallen and wrote it on the wall.

You cannot win.

◄9►

Dead Man Walking

The trip back took a while, and Dred found the rest on edge when they slipped out of the panel. Vost filled them in on the plan while she tended to Jael as best she could. Fortunately, his wounds weren't deep, already sealing to what would look like a full day of healing in anyone else. Taking a seat, she waited for the first objection.

"Bullshit," Duran said, irate at the idea of everyone's moving together.

Dred suspected he was also mourning his fallen comrade, but nothing would bring Redmond back. She sighed and tried to be patient. "I know it's a risk, but we can't afford to lose supplies. Once we get to the repair bay, we'll settle in and get the force fields up. We shouldn't need to leave again."

The merc's eyes sparked with hate. "Mary, that figures. You don't care if we lose more people. But the gear—"

"That's enough," Vost cut in.

"Right, because let's not talk about Redmond. Following her lead got the poor bastard killed. But sure, let's keep following her orders."

The commander spoke quietly. "As it happens, I agree. Splitting up would be a poor move. Yes, we're more easily tracked as a larger group, but if they pick us off, we won't be able to survive long enough to assemble our means of escape. This is my last word."

"Fine," Duran muttered.

But Dred could tell he wasn't satisfied. There would be trouble from him down the line, dissent they could scarcely afford. Yet the clock was ticking. Silence wouldn't sit still long, not after all the havoc Jael had wreaked on her followers. Yesterday, after the carnage, they'd collected everything they needed from Ike's surviving caches. The one Tam and Martine had visited had been blown to smithereens, and at some point, Silence's people had raided the stash she and Vost found. That pissed her off, but there was nothing she could do about it. If the ship couldn't be completed without the converter—

Well, best not to worry about it now.

A little later, Keelah led the exodus from their hiding spot. It was a tense journey, and nobody said much as Dred crept through the ducts, hardly daring to breathe. This was the point where they were most vulnerable and the plan most likely to fall apart. Loaded down this way, arms full, it would be tough to defend against an ambush. Each scrape of feet against metal flooring seemed to echo, and her pulse pounded in her ears, not enough to block out enhanced hearing, so every hum and reverberation sent frissons of alarm through her.

Freezing, Keelah held up a hand, just before they had to leave the ducts for the last stage. The docking bay had come to feel like the Promised Land. *We'll find out soon enough if Vost has the codes like he promised.* Because without the override codes, they wouldn't be able to bypass the current security measures. While a bot 17's size might be able to get through the cracks somewhere, they couldn't without lowering the force fields.

Or maybe he only has departure codes for the external

doors? She wasn't sure how the station security worked or how much info he'd gotten when he hacked the Monsanto mainframe.

She held still, listening as well. Keelah's eyes met hers as if asking for confirmation, and Dred shook her head. *No, I don't hear anything.* She looked at Jael, who answered in the negative.

"Let's move," Keelah whispered.

They followed her into the main corridor, long unused. There were no bot tracks this deep into the station, no tread marks in the dust on the rusted-metal flooring. It was colder here as well, making Dred wonder if there was a problem with climate control. She shifted the box in her arms and kept one eye on the space behind them, as she was guarding their rear.

"So far, so good," Calypso breathed.

Duran nudged her. "Don't hex us."

"My name's a verb," the alien quipped. "Who knew?"

Though she was tense as a steel spike, they made it to the hallway shielded by a force field without encountering any opposition from Silence. That didn't comfort Dred any; it wasn't like the lunatic would give up if they killed enough of her people. Jael's message might even exacerbate the situation; though with Death's Handmaiden, it was hard to tell.

"I have to find the nearest wall access panel." Vost turned to Jael, who was currently packing RC-17 on his back, as the unit was powered down. "Does this thing have access to schematics?"

"I'm not sure if its uplink is still working," Dred said.

Jael added, "But theoretically, yes."

From Duran's expression, he was barely restraining the complaint. She sympathized with his state of mind, but they couldn't waste time placating him. Every moment he made them divert toward settling him down was another where they were exposed with all their assets at risk. *If he keeps whining, I'll kill him myself.* Cold thought, but the

Dread Queen was part of her now, even if she wasn't the whole of her personality.

"I know where it is," Hex said into the tense silence.

All swiveled as the alien moved off down the corridor to the right. "What? I know every millimeter of this place. I survived by staying mobile."

Its glib assertion troubled her. There had to be a reason Silence had hunted Hex down and taken it alive. But the gray guy wasn't talking.

Not that I blame him. I don't trust these people with my secrets either. If they knew I had the potential in my blood to save Redmond, Vost might've opened me up like a ripe melon and drained me dry. Yeah, she wouldn't be revealing her hidden talent anytime soon.

Jael was the first to move, rushing after the alien with predatory grace. Sometimes, his beauty in a place like this struck her like a fist to the chest, as improbable as finding a perfect flower growing in a refuse pile. *The universe threw us both away. How did we find each other?* But emotional questions had to wait.

Vost shouldered past the small group to get to the access panel. "This could take some time. If I had all my equipment, it would be simple, but a bunch of assholes stole my stuff."

Martine smirked. "That's too bad."

"For us it is," Tam said. "And if we had your gear, we'd give it back."

"If one of the other groups looted your camp, it should be somewhere on station," Calypso pointed out.

"That pisses me off," Vost muttered, peering at the wires.

"I could look for it," Hex offered.

"I'll go with you." The offer came from Jael.

Dred nodded, and the two split from the main group. She watched them go, wondering why she felt so uneasy. It wasn't like the alien posed any threat to a man who could kill so many of Silence's assassins single-handed.

Right?

* * *

"DO you have some idea where Vost's equipment ended up?" Jael asked, after a while.

"Nope." The alien's tone was cheerful. "I mostly didn't want to stand around the hallway waiting for them to bypass the security. We'll be safer away from them."

"Sod me. That's why you volunteered?"

"Wasn't that your reason, too? I'm positive it's not because you like the cut of my jib."

"If we're being candid, I wanted to be sure you weren't reporting back to Silence."

"You think I'm a double agent?" Hex appeared surprised though Jael wasn't sure he could actually interpret the alien's expressions correctly. The facial alignment was different than a human's and the side-set dark eyes didn't give anything away. In fact, he could only see himself reflected in them.

"Nothing would shock me at this point."

"I don't know if I'm flattered or offended. It takes a special kind of crazy to agree to let a homicidal maniac bind you and put you in a sack as part of some nefarious plan."

Jael shrugged. "Call it caution."

"Trust me, I'm watching your knife hand, too."

"Then I'll double your workload . . . and tell you that I'm ambidextrous."

Hex made a sound like a sigh and aimed a look over one shoulder. "I hate talented assholes. You make my life *so* much more difficult."

"Noted. I won't apologize. Where are we headed?"

"Priest's old stomping grounds. If we don't find anything there, we'll try Grigor next. I have no idea who did the looting. I was hunkered down during the worst of the carnage riots."

"Good idea."

"You don't stay alive unaffiliated in Perdition without being a clever bastard." Hex tossed the comment as he skimmed up the shaft ladder. The sucker pads on his fingertips let him climb with preternatural prowess, and his feet seemed to be almost as dexterous as his hands.

Priest's old zone had been picked over pretty thoroughly. Now it was just a festering corpse pile. The bodies had rotted where they fell, some of them gnawed by station scavengers. Yet others had been maimed and dismembered, so Jael had to step over piles of entrails and puddles of dried black blood. The smell was indescribable, especially to his acute olfaction, and he almost lost the packet of paste he'd sucked down earlier.

"Sounds like your self-esteem didn't suffer while you were in solitary."

"Self-elected," Hex pointed out.

"What did you do to end up in here?" Jael knew he was breaking Perdition etiquette and didn't fragging care.

What's the point of rules now anyway? Plus he'd never been big on following them in the first place.

"I could claim I'm innocent. Aren't we all?"

"Not me," Jael said. "The lie would probably choke me to death."

"So you're a murderous monster but not a liar?" Hex sounded amused. "Yes, definitely take pride and satisfaction in that."

Jael laughed quietly. Maybe he couldn't trust this alien, but damned if he didn't rather like it. "Right. So you're not talking?"

"I could claim I was caught up in the xenophobic purges on New Terra."

"That's the story I heard from most of Katur and Keelah's crew," he allowed.

"Well, they *would*, wouldn't they? It's always better for people to think you're harmless."

The tone sent a shiver down Jael's spine. But the alien didn't push it, so Jael followed, deeper into Priest's territory. Suddenly, he felt eyes on him, but he couldn't tell where the feeling was coming from. Over his turns as a merc, he'd learned not to underestimate his instincts.

"Something's wrong," he said.

Hex paused. "You heard something?"

"Not exactly."

"Well, don't stand there waiting to be attacked. Keep moving."

The walls were stained dark, evidence of Priest's perversions, and the torture implements reminded Jael uncomfortably of the lab though the techs had called it science instead of sadism. A few minutes later, they found what must've been Priest's throne room, but Jael didn't see anything that resembled Vost's missing tech gear. Instead, it was all bones and rubbish, creating a heinous stench, worsened by the rodent droppings and acrid stink of old urine. In the chaos, there was no telling where the missing kit ended up, and though Dred had snagged some of it, she couldn't be the only faction leader who'd led a successful run.

He sighed. "Damn, we came all this way for nothing." Spare rations, more functional weapons and any gadgets they could recover would certainly increase their chances of survival.

"If they hid it somewhere, we might never recover it," Hex said.

"You're right about that."

"Should we call it, or do you want to check out Grigor's shit hole? Vost might've gotten through without the tech assist by now."

"Let's head back to check in. While it would help down the line, maybe even with the ship, there's no point in wasting time. We can always go back out."

"That's a logical assumption," Hex said.

The alien reached out and set a hand on Jael's arm. At first he thought it was a warning, so he quieted. But then a sharp pain pierced his skin, like thousands of minute needles pricking at once. The sucker pads locked down and something flooded his bloodstream. Everything went hazy, and his body locked. Jael toppled sideways. He could only see the filthy floor and part of the corridor.

"It's safe," Hex called.

In answer, five of Silence's minions melted from the shadows. Jael stared at their bloodstained shoes, unable to blink. His eyes burned, and it hurt to breathe. In fact, it was almost impossible; that was how tight his chest felt. His vision went black and red, spangled with prickles of light. *I'm not getting enough oxygen.*

As hard hands lifted his body, the last thing Jael saw was Hex's face melting into a perfect facsimile of his own.

◀ 10 ▶

Monsters and Darkness

The energy flickered and faded. "It's down," Dred called.

A chorus of relieved noises came from farther along the hall. Everyone came at a run, and she raced inside. Inside the docking bay, it seemed cavernous compared to the tiny junk room where they'd retreated. High ceilings were crisscrossed by beams that provided support to the vaulted space. Some of them offered a good vantage point for defense; they'd brought the surviving rifles, plus all the ammo packs that would still take a charge.

A couple of big machines had been left behind, but they were external maintenance rigs, nothing deep-space worthy. There were some spare parts, old rags, piles of cables. Pretty much what you'd expect to find in a derelict docking bay. Since the place had been sealed off from the rest of Perdition for countless turns, it wasn't as grimy and rusted as the rest of the station. The air smelled a little better, too.

She let out a slow breath as Vost went to the control panel inside and switched the force field back on. Though she shouldn't let her guard down, Dred felt measurably safer with that energy flickering between her and the people trying to kill them. Then the mercenary commander lowered the blast doors for good measure. Calypso whooped and gave Duran a long celebratory kiss. The merc seemed way less pissy when she moved off. Martine and Tam touched hands lightly, a subtle gesture that spoke of their bond. Keelah was watching, and the alien female moved away from the group; Dred didn't need to read the room to know that there were layers of relief and sorrow here.

"Let's stack the supplies over there," Vost said.

Dred nodded and carried her crate to the wall, then she divided the stores according to mechanical and organic. They had enough paste to last several weeks though nobody would be in a good mood by the time it ran out. There was also the risk of someone's developing sensitivity to the enzymes after eating too much of it in a short span. The bad feeling she had before hadn't let up, but it probably didn't have anything to do with lack of food choices.

It's this place.

"Hope is a waking dream," Jael had said. *And it's the last thing to go. It torments you like a bird killing itself slowly against the glass.*

In some ways, she wished she could go back to the flat acceptance that she'd die here. When he came, Jael's mad insistence that they could achieve the impossible—somehow, he'd infected her with it. Now she had only a handful of people left, limited supplies, and she was low on faith. If Silence didn't get them, then more Conglomerate-hired goons would.

Time's running out.

If hope was like a bird, then hers was molting and diseased, on the floor in its death throes. Yet she couldn't give up. She'd committed and made everyone think this crazy idea might possibly work. *Better to go out big, right?*

"I'll take inventory," Tam said. "We might find something we can use."

"There's a side door over here," Calypso called.

"Check it out," Dred yelled.

"We should have RC-17 test for toxins. It's possible they

left some chemicals in storage that might have contaminated the site," Vost added.

Yeah, we wouldn't want to die of secondary poisoning when we could have our throats cut. But she kept her mouth shut and activated the bot's scan protocol.

A bit later, Calypso came to get her. "You should see this."

Dred couldn't tell if this was a good surprise or a bad one. "Coming."

As it turned out, the docking-bay techs and engineers had it pretty sweet. The side door led to a small, six-bunk dormitory with an ancient but still-functional Kitchen-mate, toilet, sink, and a tiny san-shower. While they'd have to sleep in shifts, it was still more comfort than she'd expected.

"I found some stuff." Calypso nudged the nearest mattress and dust wafted from it though not as much as she'd have expected for the number of turns since anyone lived or worked here.

Dred picked up the antique handheld, long since drained of power. "I wonder what's on this."

"Might have some useful information about the station," the other woman suggested.

"I'll give it to Vost, see what he can figure out. Maybe we can charge it using RC-17's battery?"

Calypso smirked. "Don't ask me, I'm not tech support. You can tell by looking that I'm the eye candy, right?"

"And here I thought you were muscle, too."

The woman's smile widened into a grin. "You're not wrong. I *am* the mistress of multitasking."

She left Calypso poking around in the dorm and went to find the merc commander. He was working on the computer in the control room when she located him. Vost looked up, and she noticed for the first time how tired and ill he looked. *Frag me. If he dies before we get this thing built—*

"What are you hiding?" she demanded.

"Pardon me?"

"I can tell by looking that something's wrong." She stepped a little closer, and the faint whisper of putrefaction reached her. "Take that shirt off, right now."

He stilled. From Vost's careful lack of response, she knew she was on the right track. Before she saw, she knew. The bandages beneath his tattered uniform were filthy and obviously hadn't been changed in a while. She steeled herself for the worst, but it was horrific when she peeled them away from his infected wounds. Red rays fanned out over his gaunt chest, and the burns themselves were yellow and seeping pus. The smell nearly knocked her down.

"Are you insane?" she demanded. "You're our only way out, and you let yourself get this bad?"

"There wasn't enough antibiotic to treat me fully. Oddly, the minuscule amounts worked just fine for you. Maybe we should talk about *that*."

Before she could reply, the monitor in the control room flickered, likely activated by motion sensors. When the picture resolved, it showed Jael outside the blast doors, alone, and covered in blood.

MONSTERS took JL489 back to the labs.

Scientists in white coats strapped him back into the suspension rig that made it easier to get at him from all sides and prevented pressure sores from forming. It was hell on his joints, but they didn't care if he was in pain. Even his reaction to prolonged unpleasant stimuli could be useful, all data for the file, and some kernel of information might help them to perfect the technological fluke that led to his creation.

"Subject 489, can you hear me?" He'd recognize Landau's voice anywhere.

He managed a jerky nod because Dr. Landau liked his scalpels. He'd once peeled off JL489's face because he spat on an assistant. The skin took three full days to grow back. Nausea swelled and bile rose in his throat, but if he spewed, he'd only get it all over himself, and there was no telling how long it would take for them to hose him down. Somehow, he sucked in the sickness and waited. He'd watched them haul four more corpses out of the lab yesterday.

We're meat to them, nothing more.

"Good. You've been chosen to participate in a special program, 489. I expect full cooperation."

With arms chained and legs shackled, it wasn't like he had a choice. He didn't make a sound, just hung quiescent. While they'd checked to be sure he could *produce* language, they weren't interested in his words. Compliance was enough. Being malleable would be better, but he couldn't seem to check out as so many other subjects had. Their eyes showed that pain had long since won—that they were broken.

His silence didn't please the scientist. He wanted the same dead blankness he got from the others. JL489 had only hate.

Landau's eyes narrowed. "You have no will of your own, you're a thing. I *made* you."

He dropped his eyes, and the scientist left his field of vision and pressed the call button. "Send her in, please."

The woman who entered had black hair and bronze skin. The lab lights caught her from behind, filling her dark hair with blue lights. Her skin was spotted, too, in a way he hadn't seen before, tiny darker dots all over her cheeks and shoulders. Wide brown eyes studied him from across the room; like the others, she wore a lab coat, but he hadn't seen her before.

"This is inhumane," the woman said to Landau. Her voice held a snappish edge that he'd never heard directed at another person.

Only test subjects. Only things. *Like me.*

Her apparent anger on his behalf eased the tightness in his chest though pain had become so familiar by now that he couldn't imagine existing without it. Then she moved toward him, and he smelled something other than astringent bitterness. A sweetness came from her skin and hair that tightened him from head to toe with a pleasure he hadn't known before. He breathed in deep, then deeper, and it was like he had some of her goodness inside of him.

The world become utterly inexplicable when she said gently, "I'm getting you out of there. Can you stand up? Can you walk?"

He had no idea. It had been a long time since they let him move around. In the early days, when he first came out of the tank, workers would take him to a small room and show him things, say words, let him watch moving pictures, and one scientist had taught him to read to see if he could learn. But they soon lost interest in his mental capacity, as he was supposed to be fashioned into a thing that followed orders unquestioningly. So he went back into the restraints while they tried to figure out why he was so intractable and why he was still alive when so many of his pod mates crashed out.

Yet he gave a tiny nod. Because to follow her, he'd crawl.

"I'm Dr. Indra Parvati. Do you understand?"

Another tilt of his head.

His gut told him she was different than the rest though he wasn't sure why she was here or why Landau was letting this happen. Smiling, she turned off the suspension system, and he thumped to the floor. It took a few minutes for the feeling to return to his arms and legs; she waited patiently until he stumbled to his feet.

"I'm from the Sapient Rights Coalition. We're investigating Sci-Corp for possible ethical violations and to determine your status."

"My what?" His voice sounded strange to his own ears, hoarse and choked.

"There's a proposal on the docket, exploring the rights of bioengineered individuals." She didn't say creature or monster, he noticed.

Definitely different.

"I don't understand."

"They're considering your people for citizenship. That would give you full human rights though you'd have to check 'other' on certain government forms." She smiled at him, and his heart did something strange, beating extra hard for a few seconds.

"Oh."

In all honesty, he still didn't entirely understand what

she was saying, but Dr. Landau was furious. JL489 smelled the rage all over him.

He quivered a little as Dr. Parvati put a hand on his arm. "Let's find a quiet place to talk."

"Aren't you afraid of me?" he whispered.

She shook her head and led the way toward the main exit. The scientists *let him go*. When he stepped out of the lab and into the unfamiliar hallway, he had no context for what might happen next.

"You must be hungry. I can tell they've been feeding you intravenously for some time."

Her kindness hurt in ways he hadn't felt before, a blooming tenderness that filled him with a different kind of fear. She took him to a room with a table, then she pressed a button to order food. When it arrived, he drooled at the rich, complex smells wafting from the covered dishes.

"Now then," she said, smiling. "Don't be afraid to tell me everything, JL."

JL. Jael. It was the closest he'd ever come to a name. It felt right, even if it sprang from the loathsome Dr. Landau. She lifted the first lid to reveal—

Then she was gone, leaving him to monsters and darkness.

And pain.

◄ 11 ►

The Knife of Failure

Dred raced for the front doors. Vost must have fixed his bandages and clothing, then followed because he was at the control panel not long after. He powered down the force field and opened the blast doors, then Jael stumbled inside. The smell struck her first, totally wrong, *not* Jael, and it overpowered even the reek from the merc's wounds.

But first she needed to close off retreat options, if it turned out she was right. "Lock us down. Quickly."

He complied, likely because he suspected there might be enemies on Jael's six. She took Vost's arm and pulled him away from the still unsteady Jael. Even if his scent *wasn't* all wrong, she'd never seen him react this way to being hurt. He was too used to pain.

"Get back," she said.

Vost glanced at her, a frown furrowing his brow. "He needs medical attention. We can bandage him up at least."

"Do you smell the blood on him?" she asked.

The merc tilted his head as Keelah came a few paces closer, her nose twitching. "She's right. There's no scent of injury. And he smells completely off. More like—"

"Hex," Dred finished.

The illusion flickered and went off, revealing the alien. Her bad feeling intensified. If this thing had tried to trick them, there couldn't be an innocent reason. *It didn't want us to know Jael was missing, at least not right away.* That probably meant that its mandate was infiltration.

It was supposed to make us think Hex was dead, Jael was safe, then turn off our security so Silence could finish us.

"Get it in restraints," she said. "But be careful, I don't know anything about Azhvarians."

"They have the ability to project whatever appearance they choose," Tam said quietly. "Similar to a hologram. And they have poison spines hidden in the suckers on their fingertips."

"You bastard," she breathed.

That's how it took Jael down.

"Then I won't get close," Duran said. And shot the alien in the chest.

Then he walked over to make sure Hex was dead. The body looked so small and fragile, and the wound was violent, a red black hole in the torso. Part of her wanted to scream at the merc; they should have questioned it before execution. But really, what did it matter? It had to be allied with Silence, so nothing else mattered. There was no one else who could have taken Jael.

"Space it," Vost said.

Calypso lifted the corpse and carried it over to the chute near the docking-bay doors. This asshole didn't deserve any kind of a service and certainly wasn't worth a trip to the recyclers. In seconds, the machinery hummed and sucked the dead alien out into vacuum. Dred dropped into a crouch, metering her breath until she felt less frantic. Knowing Death's Handmaiden, the things she might do? With his reduced healing capacity, she could actually kill Jael. She couldn't hear for the terror careening in her veins and the cacophony of her heartbeat.

"Not all aliens are good and gentle," Keelah said.

Martine knelt beside her. "We'll get him back, don't worry."

"No matter how you look at it, this is a win for the crazy bitch," Duran muttered. "We go after his ass, and she's drawn us out, bait for the trap."

She let herself have these seconds of weakness, then she locked it away. Fear wouldn't save her man. Only decisive action could. Dred touched Martine's arm in silent gratitude over her attempt at consolation, then she reveled in the rage building behind her eyes. Now her pulse didn't drum with fear; instead, it pounded out a message, no, an edict.

Kill. Kill. Kill.

"We need a plan," she bit out. "Ideas?"

Tam said, "I've spied on Silence *many* times. I'll do some recon and find out where she's holding him. If possible, I'll also take a head count though it may not be fully accurate, depending on how many she's sent on patrol."

"I'll go with you," Martine offered.

Tam shook his head. "This is a solo run."

"We've had this conversation before," she said with more than a hint of bite. "Have you forgotten how this works? Just in case, here's a refresher. *I* decide, and *you* obey." She flashed her sharp teeth in what Dred couldn't properly call a smile.

Something sparked in Tam's dark eyes. And then he nodded. "Let's get moving."

After checking the monitor to make sure the area was clear, Vost let them out with minimal drama. "Be careful," he said as he locked the bay down again.

Dred straightened her shoulders. "There's nothing we can do for Jael until they get back with intel. So let's get started on our primary objective."

Keelah patted her shoulder and moved off to check out the external maintenance rigs. Calypso went with her, and the low hum of their voices echoed slightly in the vast space. Vost lingered, probably because he felt some sense of responsibility, even though he wasn't really in charge. Funny how command became an imperative after a while.

"Two things. First, you let me deal with the heinous mess on your chest. Then I need you to look at the handheld we found."

"Do I have a choice?"

"Not remotely. Come with me." She led the way to the dorm and cracked open the first-aid kit. The antiseptic was beyond expired, but the bandages were still sealed. "How long does Nu-Skin stay good?"

"Not sure. Isn't there a date on it?" He watched her with an inscrutable expression.

Dred turned the package over in her hands and shook her head. "Should we risk it?"

"You're too calm," he said.

"Why?"

"It's unnerving. I thought you cared about him."

The words sank in deep, but she didn't show it. *Who cares if Vost thinks I'm an unfeeling bitch?* "Panic won't save him. Until there's something I can do for Jael, I have to keep moving. Inertia is death."

Instead, something like admiration flashed in his face, there and gone, then he peeled off his shirt. "True. Don't kill me, all right? I have so much to live for."

Dred almost smiled and pulled out her knife. "Hold still, this will hurt."

WHEN he couldn't stand the agony, Jael retreated. The monsters yielded to his tormentors, to old ghosts and sorrows.

"Is it good?" Dr. Parvati asked.

Jael had cleaned three plates, and his mouth was too full to answer. This dish had meat and noodles; he couldn't stop eating even though his stomach was starting to hurt. The pain was mild and bearable compared to how he usually felt, but when this fourth dish was empty, he sat back and rubbed his belly.

"Yes." He really didn't know what she wanted from him.

Dr. Landau had said this was a special program, but she'd used the word "investigation." Jael didn't know what an ethics violation was, either. Maybe he should ask?

"If you're feeling better, I have some questions."

"Go ahead."

"I'll be testing you on the following traits, JL: desire, will, consciousness, ethics, personality, insight, humor, and ambition."

He nodded.

"What is it that you want from life?" she asked first.

Confusion built at his temples, flowering into pain. *You're not a person. You're a thing. You will obey.*

"Do I have a life?" That wasn't the answer she wanted, he could tell. But he'd never been allowed to want *anything.* "For the pain to stop, I guess. To be treated better by the scientists."

Somehow, she was frightening him more than the lab techs because her disappointment could hurt him in ways that he couldn't yet imagine. Dr. Parvati made a note on her handheld.

"What would you choose to do if you could do anything?" she asked.

"Be a person," he said without hesitation.

That, she liked. Her smile deepened, and she gave him an approving nod. "That's good, JL. You may find this question disconcerting but . . . who are you?"

That stumped him, so he gave the answer he had. "Subject JL489."

The sadness surfaced again as she leaned forward. "You haven't given yourself a name?"

His eyes widened. "I can do that?"

"Mmm. Subject limited in self-awareness, little actualization." That didn't sound good, whatever it meant.

"I'm Jael," he said then, hoping desperately to show her what she wanted to see.

"That's just an abbreviation of your test-subject identification," she said gently. "And *I'm* the one who shortened it."

Worried, he gripped the edge of the table, all the food he'd eaten roiling in his stomach. *I can't get sick. I can't get sick.*

Then she asked a bunch more questions, and he didn't know the answers. They were . . . situations, more like. *What would you do if . . . All right then, now listen to this and pick option A, B, or C.* Most of the time, he had no idea what she was even talking about.

Finally, he said in frustration, "How could I save anyone? I'm always in the lab. I'm in restraints. I couldn't, I can't—"

"Hm." Her expression seemed to darken as she murmured, "Inability to envision theoretical situations," and made a note on her device. "No ethical awareness."

"You keep using that word," he whispered. "And I don't know what it means."

"Which one?"

"'Ethical.'"

"Oh. It's the ability to distinguish right from wrong."

"It's wrong that they keep me here. It's wrong that they hurt me."

Dr. Parvati sighed softly. "That's what I'm here to determine. Right now, you have no legal status or recourse, JL. None of your counterparts do. I'm trying to establish whether Sci-Corp has the right to continue their research or if you should be released and educated properly so you can contribute to society."

Relatively little of what she said made sense to him. But he sensed that confusion would work against him. So he nodded, and said, "Oh."

Dr. Parvati followed with a long series of questions that seemed to contradict each other. *You are impatient. You find it difficult to talk to others. Dreams are more important than principles. Your mood changes easily. You would break the rules if the situation called for it.* He lost track of his answers, and his head was really aching by the time she stopped.

I don't want to do this anymore, he thought. *I don't like it.* Going back to the lab was the only alternative, though, so he ignored the throbbing in his skull and braced for more.

"Next question. A little boy steals a loaf of bread. Why do you think he does this?"

"Someone told him to," Jael guessed. That was the only reason *he* did anything, after all.

"Ah." Another tap of her device, laden with dissatisfaction.

Her scent was changing, too, less of the sweetness. He didn't know the reason for it, but it troubled him. *Whatever we're doing, I'm failing at it.*

"I'm sorry," he said.

"For what, JL?"

"I think I'm doing this wrong."

"No, your honesty is exactly what we need to come to an accurate conclusion. I appreciate your cooperation and your candor. Only two more areas to address, then we'll be done. What did the fish say when it swam into a cement wall?"

Jael knew what a fish was, but from the books he'd looked at . . . "Fish can't talk."

"The answer is 'dam,'" she said, sighing.

"Oh. The scientists say 'damn' sometimes."

"No concept or recognition of humor. Finally, JL, I need to learn whether you've ever *tried* to do anything."

"Like what?" he asked, blankly.

"Anything. Have you ever done anything other than what you're told?"

What was the right answer? He didn't always comply, and he was usually punished for it. So maybe the truth would work against him? His pulse accelerated.

"I'm good. I do what the scientists ask." He peered at her, desperate, hopeful.

With a slump of her shoulders, she whispered, "No ambition. All right, I'll take you back to Dr. Landau now."

"No, please don't. I thought you were saving me."

"I wanted to." Her sadness was real, her scent bitter.

When she escorted him back to the lab, he screamed. Pain washed over him, and Landau's face seemed strange and distorted. "Thanks for proving what I knew all along, 489. You're not a person. You're something I made. A monster."

Monster.

The knife dug in.

He screamed again.

◄ 12 ►

Confession, Cleansing, Cruciation

"Jael didn't look good," Martine said softly. "How could she *do* that to him?"

Tam nodded, listening. It was clearly a rhetorical question.

They'd completed their recon mission and discovered where Jael was imprisoned, but one of Silence's patrols had them hemmed in, unable to cross the corridor they needed to in order to reach the ladder that led down to the docking bay. So for the moment, they were holed up and waiting for the area to clear. This had been a janitorial closet and was now mostly full of refuse.

"Not good" was an understatement, even from the half glimpse of Jael they'd gotten from a distance and in the shadows. "Dred will take it hard if he doesn't recover."

"Let's not think about that now."

The footfalls came again, passing their hiding spot. *Frustrating.* It was almost like they were circling, searching for Tam and Martine, but he couldn't fathom how they knew. *We were careful. They didn't see or hear us.* And their olfactory sense must be diminished from the filthy abattoir they called home.

"There's something odd about Silence," Tam whispered.

"You're just figuring that out?"

"It's more than her death fetish. Haven't you noticed how well timed and executed her strikes are?"

Sobering, Martine nodded. "It's like she has eyes on us."

"But how . . . ?"

The answer wasn't forthcoming, and, outside, the killers kept circling. He closed his eyes, conscious of a weariness that went soul deep. Never once had he regretted the choices that landed him here, but now it seemed likely that his demise was imminent. A warm hand on his arm made Tam open his eyes, and when he did, Martine pressed close, her cheek against his, then her lips. Not the time or place, but . . . he couldn't deny her. The kiss tasted of sweetness, sorrow, and desperation.

"Tell me your story," she breathed when he pulled back.

"Very well," he said.

There may not be another chance.

Martine nestled her head against his shoulder as he began to speak. "I'm not sure how much you know about Tarnus . . . ?"

"Nothing," she admitted.

"It's core world with a volatile political history, and many turns ago, there was a revolution. A bloody coup put a tertiary branch of the royal family in power. They were corrupt, venal, and vicious. The people suffered." *There, that should suffice for background.* "You're probably wondering what I have to do with such matters."

"You guessed it." She laced their fingers together, and that made it easier to talk.

Odd. He'd almost forgotten the pleasure of confiding in someone. *The spymaster keeps all secrets and spills none.* But it was time to lay that mantle down, for as much as he wished otherwise, Dred was no true queen, and he didn't serve a higher cause here.

"I was raised in the palace . . . and I rose from kitchen help to a position of prominence in the cabinet. My official title was Minister of Intelligence."

"Bullshit."

He flickered a faint smile. "I could relate a very long story, one that would take hours in the telling. But at base, what I did to land myself here? I assassinated a puppet king, his regent, and a good quarter of their courtiers."

She asked a question that surprised him then. "Why?"

"To put the rightful ruler back on the throne." That wasn't everything, but it encapsulated most. He had been fascinated with the beautiful young princess, forced into exile, her homeland stolen via charges of perversion, when she'd only been guilty of loving one of her handmaidens. From poring over early interviews, he had been convinced she would restore order and rule with both compassion and wisdom. So he went to work. And Queen Dina I returned to Tarnus with her consort, Soraya, to cheering and pageantry while he was hauled off in chains.

"Was it worth it?"

Tam thought for a few seconds, remembering how it felt to have the true queen visit him before his trial and offer private thanks. The once-banished queen's face was no longer smooth as it had been in the vids he watched as a boy. In fact, she was quite old by the time his plan came to fruition. Those deaths had been the culmination of turns of scheming and arranging pieces on a galactic game board. And the last sacrifice, *he* had to make.

Even a quiet revolution needed a scapegoat.

"I'd do it again," he said eventually. "It was necessary."

"Then I suppose that's my answer." She tilted her head quietly against his.

VOST almost passed out when Dred heated her knife and opened his wounds. Pain made him grit his teeth until he feared they'd break. She didn't flinch or hesitate when the pus spurted out from beneath the crusty scabs, just cleared it away and pressed for more. That hurt like a bitch. He'd seen field medics with weaker stomachs. Her hands were brisk and efficient; he tried not to look down at the ruined mess that had been his chest. Closing his eyes seemed like the best option, and it seemed like forever since he'd slept.

A cool hand briefly touched his forehead. It surprised him how good it felt, how much he wanted her palm to linger. *I've lost my mind.*

"You're running a fever."

"I know."

"You're also aware that you're pretty damn infected?"

"That's a hard fact to miss."

"Why didn't you keep these wounds clean?"

"You didn't give me a whole lot of time," he muttered. "And then Casto got my whole fragging squad blown up."

"That was your second's name?" she asked.

What does that matter? But he answered anyway. "Bringing him was the dumbest move I made, apart from taking the job in the first place."

"How did this happen, anyway?" Her hands felt icy prodding at his enflamed skin.

"Some asshole chucked an acid grenade at me," he snapped.

"Looks like it worked better than expected. Since we weren't allied at the time, I won't apologize. If someone came into your house with kill orders, you'd do worse."

He thought of Jamal and how unlikely it was that he'd ever see him again weighed against the unspeakable things he'd already done for his son. "You're right."

His head was swimming by the time she finished with his chest and applied Nu-Skin. It was definitely better than dirty bandages, probably better for him, even if it was expired. Gingerly, he shrugged back into his shirt.

"How does that feel?" she asked.

"I'll live," he said with a faint trace of irony.

For now. But I guess that's as much a guarantee as anyone gets.

"Ready to take a look at the handheld?"

"Where is it?"

In reply, she handed it over. As expected, the unit was obsolete compared to the skin tech that had replaced external hardware, and it was completely dead. Not surprising. He'd have been startled and suspicious if the battery retained a charge after all these turns.

"Can you fix it?"

"Maybe. Find me some thin power cables, and we'll see."

Once she left the dormitory, he slumped against the wall. Vost tried to stand and found his legs too shaky to bear weight. *Damn.* He *had* to repair the handheld so he could record a message for Jamal; he believed in contingency plans for the worst scenarios. The last time he saw his son, the boy was too medicated to recognize his own father. And before his illness worsened, he'd *yelled* at him for some idiotic reason. Vost couldn't even remember why, now.

A few minutes later, Dred returned with a few frayed cables. He opened the unit up and took a look at the hardware. It needed a good cleaning, so he grounded himself and went to work. This wasn't his field of expertise, more of a hobby, but he'd always been better with machines than people. If you used the same process on a gadget, you got the same result, whereas different people reacted to the same stimuli in random and baffling ways.

She leaned in close. "How does it look?"

"Shouldn't you be helping the others?" Vost tried not to show his discomfort, but he wished she wouldn't tilt her head toward him that way.

"Fine, I get it. Let me know if you find anything interesting."

"Will do."

SILENCE studied the network of cuts, mapping the man before her as if memorizing alien topography, a luscious perusal of red rivers and blue veins. The scent of copper hung heavy in the air. This one had a capacity for pain the like of which she'd never seen before. In its own way, his tolerance was beautiful, like the darkness when a star winked out. Whether it was dying light or perishing flesh, nothing was more gorgeous than death.

She gestured at the two who flanked her, and they knew what she meant, melting into the dark to leave her the sweet intimacy of getting to know her new love. In agony, he was exquisite, each twist, each writhe of his spine. And this one was so quiet, delicious with it, apart from the panting breaths he couldn't help.

He's only screamed once. I should like to hear it again. But it's hard to find unblemished skin now.

She'd never seen anyone last so long. Most succumbed to death long before now, and she understood the allure. Silence never blamed those who couldn't resist that dark seduction and chose to transcend rather than serve Death's Handmaiden. Leaning close, she scrutinized his body from head to toe. His eyes were closed, but it didn't matter. No matter where he went, he couldn't escape. Silence set her blade to flesh and traced downward. A trickle of red blossomed, bright and beautiful. With trembling, delighted fingertips, she dipped into the blood and tasted it. Pleasure spiraled through her, multiplying and infinite. He twitched. She painted his mouth red and kissed him.

You feel it, too. It's time. Time for you to join the ranks of the silent.

It had been a long time since she took so much joy in a new disciple. With deft hands, she parted his lips and slipped a wafer-thin disc between them. He choked and tried to spit at the bitter flavor, but she sealed a palm over his mouth, leaving him to gasp through his nose. When she tilted his head, the medicine went down.

Give it a moment. You'll understand everything, then.

His frantic thrashing slowed, and his eyes fluttered open. They were dreamy and unfocused, so she knew he was seeing the other side, as she *always* had. This time, when she touched his mouth, his lips opened voluntarily, tasted his own blood on her fingertips. A shiver went through her and she crawled onto the table, each trembling centimeter bringing her closer, blade in hand.

He didn't resist as she hovered above him. There was no need to ask what he wanted. She knew. The knife slipped between his lips and he didn't cry out when she sliced his tongue out in a river of blood. The soft, fleshy muscle flexed when she pressed it between her fingertips, then she swallowed it whole.

You're mine now. Your voice belongs to Death.

Blood filled his mouth and would choke him if she didn't complete the ritual. So she tilted him forward, filled a bowl with it, and cauterized the wound. His breath came in panting moans that sent shivers through her. Once the danger passed, she submerged her hands in the red fluid up to her wrists and she rubbed her palms all over his body. The pleasure in such things had dimmed, but the way he responded to her touch brought it back.

With blood-slick hands, she touched him once, twice. He jerked. Gasped.

Yes, you're the one.

His fingers flexed where his wrists were pinioned as if he wanted to touch her. *Soon enough. Let's finish what we've started.*

◀ 13 ▶

Wickedness Burns Like Fire

In the security room, Dred sprawled before the monitor, watching the corridor feed.

With Hex and Redmond dead, Jael in captivity, Tam and Martine out for recon, they had more than enough beds, so she sent the others to the dorm. No point in everyone losing sleep. She amused herself by fiddling with the handheld. Vost had gotten it running, as promised, and there were all kinds of interesting tidbits.

Skimming through the files, she found a video diary and tapped to play the last entry. This unit, despite its age, had projection, and a holo image appeared in the darkness. The woman looked vaguely familiar though why that would be the case, Dred had no idea. Her translucent features were strong, but she was sad-eyed and staring off into the distance instead of at the handheld recording her commentary.

After a long silence, the woman sighed and spoke. "This is the last time. The decision is final, they're closing the facility. But I won't go. I know this place better than anyone. I don't care what they say about P&L, this is my home."

That was all. The vid ended, and the machine went dark.

She was about to call up the earlier entries for some context when Tam and Martine appeared on-screen. Dred leapt up and raced to let them in. *It's about time, I'm ready to gnaw my own arm off.*

"How is he?" she demanded as soon as the force field went up and the blast doors shut behind it.

Martine let out a huff of breath not quite long enough to be called a sigh. "We need to get him out before Silence kills him."

"So he's alive." Relief surged through her.

"For now," Tam said.

"Then we need to move fast. What intel did you bring back?" Reverting to the Dread Queen was easier than being the woman desperately worried about the man she—

"Even with those Jael killed on his raid last time, she still has at least fifty. The ones we saw were drugged, and we hid from three different teams on patrol, five each."

"You're sure they weren't the same group?"

"Positive," Martine said.

"So we're looking at sixty-five, at least."

Tam nodded. "It could be more or less depending on command structure. The ones roving the station don't seem to be drugged like the ones back at base. But she's increased guards at multiple checkpoints, so that what happened before doesn't happen again."

"Are those guards counted in the fifty you mentioned?"

Martine cocked her head, probably doing the math. "Yeah, fifteen sober guards, thirty-five chem-heads. It's the former that will give us trouble."

"Damn. We can't take Vost with us." She lowered her voice in case anyone else was awake. "He's still pretty jacked up from one of our firefights."

"I thought he was pale." Tam didn't seem surprised.

"Calypso will be on board, not sure about Duran or Keelah."

The alien female slipped from the shadows. "I'll come, of course."

"Anyone else awake?" Dred asked.

Keelah shook her head. "Not yet. Since Katur died, I don't sleep much."

Dred led the way to the control room and checked the time. Hours didn't have much meaning inside Perdition, except for up and down cycle. Without sleep, they'd all go crazy. Some might argue the inmates of such a place didn't have far to go.

"We need to formulate our strategy," she said.

Tam and Martine nodded as Keelah curled up behind the door. Dred noticed the advantage of that location straightaway. While it might look like Keelah was being humble and unobtrusive, she was actually positioning for a guaranteed back strike. And such innate caution spoke of a lifetime of being hunted, survival at any cost.

She's going to make it.

"The way I see it, we need a distraction team and main strike force. Two people can cause big damage near enough to Silence's turf that she'll have to investigate."

"As soon as she does, the rest of us rush in, pushing to Jael, no matter how heavy the resistance is," Tam finished.

Dred nodded. "He may not be able to walk, so I'll need someone to cover me while I carry him. I won't be able to keep up with the rest."

"We should scatter in retreat," Martine added.

"Giving them more targets to chase makes sense. Now that we have a fortified position, we don't have to worry about secrecy as much."

"No, we just have that moment of vulnerability when we're waiting for someone inside to let us in." Which was another reason for Vost to stay here. He'd disabled the external access they'd used—now the only way in came via the control panel inside.

It wasn't long before Duran and Calypso joined them, both bleary-eyed.

"Somebody call a staff meeting?" the merc joked.

"Something like that," Martine answered.

Quickly, Tam filled them in, then Calypso slammed an open palm against the wall. "I'm in. They took one of ours, and *I'm* taking it personal. Dred, count me in on watching your back. I'll kill anyone who gets close."

"I volunteer for the distraction team," Duran said. "Explosions are my specialty, and as long as I don't have to worry about how much damage I cause, how it impacts overall station performance—"

"See, this is why I chose you," Calypso cut in, patting his cheek.

"You like that, huh?"

"I'll go with you," Martine said. "I'm not bad at that myself."

Tam and Calypso shared a look, but Dred didn't get involved. She cared only about saving Jael, not about momentary partner swaps. They had the plan hammered out and fine-tuned when Vost finally got up, looking a little better than he had the day before.

"What's going on?" the merc commander asked.

Dred told him and finished up by saying, "Don't argue. Your role is holding down the fort."

Stretching, Calypso got to her feet. "Then let's do this. Fifteen to five, 3:1. I don't like those odds." She flashed a devilish grin. "For *them*."

JAEL lost track of how long he had been in the suspension rig. He hadn't seen the scientists in a while; the lab was oddly dark. Usually, there were assistants and techs working at all hours. A boom echoed in the distance, then red lights came on, along with the blaring Klaxon of an alarm. Other subjects stirred around him, but he couldn't move.

A completely inflectionless voice announced, "Perimeter breach in sector five, fire detected. Facility emergency protocols in place. Please proceed to the nearest exit in a calm and orderly fashion."

Another explosion, this one much closer, rocked his harness, and one of the straps broke. He was woozy from whatever they'd been feeding him through the tubes, so his head felt weird and fuzzy as he worked his left arm free.

Surely, this couldn't be happening. Dr. Landau or one of the others would be here soon to tell them what to do. But nobody tried to stop him as he wrenched the tubing from his body. The holes stung, and fluid trickled out, but within seconds, the wounds closed. Reaching over, he snapped the fastenings on his right arm, then he only had to lean down to unbuckle. Jael dropped from the suspension rig, unsteady on his feet at first. His surviving pod mates—only three now—stared at him with mute terror. One of them protested as he unstrapped her from the machine.

"We have to go now," he said to JL490. With dark hair, eyes, and skin, she didn't look anything like him though they were pod mates. He wasn't sure why. "Or we'll die here."

At first, he thought she wouldn't move but then she went to the next suspension harness, allowing Jael to free the last subject in the room. The four of them crept toward the main exit, which he'd used exactly one time since his creation. His failure with Dr. Parvati haunted him.

She brought me back, because I'm not a person.

But he ignored that echo in his head as he pushed buttons at random, trying to figure out how the door opened. At last he got the right combo, and they moved into the dark hallway. He heard people screaming, running feet, and he smelled something dark and gritty that burned his throat. The robot voice had said "fire," which meant this was probably smoke. He'd only seen those things on the vids, but he knew they weren't good.

"Where are we going?" 490 asked.

"Out. Away." That seemed to be enough for the others.

But she paused outside Lab B. "Should we set everyone else free, too?"

He nodded. "Split up. We'll check all the labs. Then come back here."

One of the subjects didn't return, but 490 and another did. The male still hadn't spoken, and his eyes were wild. Jael didn't like the look of him, but he didn't know what to say. So he kept moving. The other two followed him. Getting out had become the only thing that mattered.

They pressed on.

Jael stopped outside the room marked LAUNDRY. "If they see us with no clothes, they'll take us back. We have to look like them."

490 nodded and went inside, returning with gray shirts and pants and jackets. Some of them didn't smell good, but he would wear anything—*do* anything—to make this stop. He dressed quickly, along with everyone else. Jael didn't know the facility, but people should be running toward the exit if the situation was dangerous. So he followed their footfalls.

Security doors stood open, overridden due to whatever was going on, and it let them pass all the way outside. There were people everywhere, men in uniforms, voices booming, lights flashing, and the sound of weapons being fired. Someone grabbed his arm and yanked him away from the front doors.

"Get back, there's a bomb inside. Some crazy activist group has decided that the Sapient Rights Coalition didn't investigate properly, so they're protesting our lack of ethics."

"By blowing up the building with everyone inside? How does that help?"

"Exactly." The man laughed, as if Jael hadn't intended it as a serious question. "These people are insane."

As the scientist turned away, the mad-eyed Bred subject went for his throat, screaming at the top of his lungs. Jael's eyes met 490's, and she nodded. Together, they slipped away from the facility. He'd never seen it from the outside, a large, sprawling complex of interconnected silver domes. The stars were beautiful, and the air tasted different outside, both fresher and dirtier at the same time. He sucked in great, gasping lungs full of it.

"Should we have helped?" 490 asked, once they left the chaos behind.

"No. When did they ever help us?"

She had no answer.

And he had no idea where they were. *Lost.* The word floated up from the bottom of his mind, but it wasn't bad, especially when he paired it with *Free*. Jael had no idea how long they walked. The world was so much bigger than he'd ever imagined; vids couldn't convey the vastness of it, such wide spaces and roaring machines.

They hid as they moved, avoiding other people. But, eventually, 490 turned to him. "We should go alone from now on."

"Why?"

"Because two of us will draw too much attention. We're different from them."

I don't care. I don't want to. But he didn't say those words aloud, and she left him.

From there, he stumbled and fell, down, down, all the way down, into that place of stone and chittering echoes. There was never any light, never a human voice or a touch. He lost himself there, a dragon inside an egg threading in and out of a needle. Jael dwelled in darkness forever.

And pain. There was always pain, a crooning sort of anguish, each slice a tapping, tapping, all the way down to the bone and back again. *Something is devouring me, bite by bite.*

He could not scream.

◀ 14 ▶

More Than Life Itself

The teams were in place.

Dred had Tam, Keelah, and Calypso with her; Martine and Duran were set up and ready. When the big boom sounded, that was their cue; a mass exodus followed. From her hidden vantage, Dred counted twenty killers of sound mind heading out to investigate. She signaled the attack phase by circling her hand in the air.

This time she had her chains; she'd risked retrieving them from Queensland on a solo run. Silence had left blood graffiti all over the place, probably in answer to Jael's message. But it didn't change anything. This time, she was fighting for the person who mattered to her most.

She led the strike personally, slamming her chains into the first sentry's skull. Being the Dread Queen wasn't all bad, she thought, as the enemy's head caved in. Lashing out, she disarmed the one next to her, then whipped her chain around his neck. With a twist, she broke it, smiling as she stepped over the body. There were more guards coming, but Keelah had her knife out and was fighting low, as she preferred, going for hamstrings and Achilles tendons. Tam used two blades while Calypso had a massive bludgeon.

Reminds me of Einar.

The other three fought tight, but Dred needed room to swing her chains. She couldn't worry about the rest; the only thing that mattered was cutting a path to Jael. "Where is he?"

Tam pushed forward, spinning away from a garrote from behind. Twin slashes of his blade dropped his opponent. "This way. Stay close."

Silence's stronghold was worse than she'd remembered, and it was bad before. Now, however, it was like the rituals had taken over all semblance of human life. Blood and viscera lay everywhere, more like Priest's and Grigor's realms. *She's devolving.* Before Silence was strict with her followers, demanding utmost skill and sacrifice, but now there was only death.

"This is all kinds of fragged up," Calypso said.

Keelah nodded, glancing over her shoulder for opposition. "The smell is overwhelming."

Eight killers struck as they pushed forward. Dred squared off against three, easy enough with her chains. None of these acolytes showed any sign of being drugged, unlike the others. Which made them a tougher fight. But it didn't matter how many people she had to kill.

She crisscrossed her chains before her to form a defensive perimeter. One of the assassins struck; she broke his arm with a twist that also pulled the knife out of his hands. Dred kicked the blade away with a clatter, conscious of how strange these enemies were. They didn't cry out in pain or even flinch.

It's like they don't feel anything anymore. How's that possible?

There was no chance for theories, however. The next rushed at her, undeterred. Silence's downfall would be the fact that she'd only taught her people how to work in the dark: one strike, one kill. And they had no idea what to do afterward—in actual combat versus assassination. They couldn't analyze a fighter's style or predict movements.

Clumsy, she thought, and killed another one.

Soon they had eight bodies on the ground, and Tam directed them onward. "He's in the center of her territory. She doesn't have a bedroom per se. I'd call it more of a . . . playroom."

Dred's stomach twisted into knots. *Don't feel that right now. Just breathe. He's alive. We're coming.*

After a while, she lost track of how many they killed. Once they cut past the guards with all their faculties, the silent followers were chemmed to the core, as Tam and Martine had said. That wasn't a fight, more of a slaughter. Dred's arms were red to the elbow, her chains sticky with blood and gore, by the time they got to the room where Silence was keeping Jael.

The three sentries posted went down fast. Keelah took one, Tam the second, and Calypso beat the third one to death with a relish that Dred completely understood. *Almost there.* She braced herself, for she already knew it would be bad, but nothing could've prepared her for how utterly ruined Jael was. Fillets of flesh were just . . . missing, and his face was unrecognizable. He barely seemed to be breathing.

Calypso spat several sharp curses. "I was hoping that bitch would be here, so we could end this, once and for all."

"No such luck," Tam muttered.

"She probably went to check the damage," Keelah guessed.

The alien averted her gaze, but Dred couldn't. She took in every wound, done over hours of painstaking cruelty. *She will die screaming, silent no longer. If I have to die making it happen, so be it. Silence will suffer for this.* The others couldn't even look at him, but she went in quick, desperate strides. His skin was red from head to toe, though she couldn't be sure if it was from how grievously he had been tortured, or if Silence was enough of a monster to make him wear his own blood as some kind of badge.

"Help me get him up," she ordered.

Between Calypso and Tam, they draped him over Dred's back, and she took his poor sliced arms, wrapping them around her neck. Though she would've guessed he was too far gone, in too much agony, he held on somehow, as if he recognized her. She reached back and touched his hair, pressed a kiss to his forearm and tasted copper.

"He has such a strong heart," Keelah whispered.

"No shit." Calypso flanked Dred, ready to defend.

Dred said, "Keelah and Tam, you two take point until we get out of here. Then it's a dead sprint to the docking bay."

Tam nodded. "If we get there first, we'll keep the paste warm for you."

Somehow, she managed a reassuring smile, though the odds weren't good since she couldn't crawl into the ducts carrying Jael. She and Calypso would be in the open, taking main corridors, vulnerable all the way back. "Please don't."

"Good luck," said Keelah.

And the race was on.

A gentle touch breached the haze of endless pain. A hand on his head, a kiss. And then he was borne upward. His throat felt too dry to utter a sound, and his mouth was raw meat, but he flexed his fingers in silent thanks. *Someone came for me.*

"You'll be all right," a woman whispered to him.

I know her. Don't I?

The world blurred around him. Sometimes, he was moving; at other moments, the walls were too close or the floor spun up to meet him. Voices came and went, sounds of violence. Then he lost the thread completely.

Jael had no idea how long he'd been out, but opening his eyes meant he had eyelids again. That was positive progress because he remembered clearly the mute horror of seeing Silence slice them off. He shuddered, realized he was naked . . . and clean.

He opened his mouth, but he couldn't speak clearly. His words were a jumble of consonants and vowels, primate noises, not human speech. But it made the woman asleep on the floor beside the bunk jolt upright. Dred had dark circles beneath her eyes, and she smelled like she'd only washed him, not herself.

She had never looked more beautiful.

"Your tongue's still half missing," she said. "It'll be a while."

How long? He mouthed.

At least I came back clear-headed. Looks like I processed the drug too fast for it to permanently scramble my brain.

"Since we raided Silence and got you out?"

He nodded.

"Three days, give or take. It wasn't easy keeping you alive. I had to funnel water and paste down your throat. And you vomited on me more than once when I gave you too much."

Sorry. He didn't know how good she was at lip-reading, but he couldn't bring himself to try to talk. Not when he sounded so bestial.

In response, she cupped his face in her hands and pressed her lips gently to his. It hurt a little, but not enough for him to want it to stop. The goodness of it flooded over him, providing some endorphins to offset the pain. For long moments, he just let her kiss him.

"If you didn't know," she said softly. "*I'd* want to die if you did."

His heart twisted in his chest. Jael had been tortured time and again, first by scientists, then by enemy commanders as a merc. Physical pain had nothing new to teach him. Silence had never cracked the core of his mind, never figured out his Achilles heel. So once his flesh healed, he could step away and not let it haunt him.

Unlike words that had echoed in his head for turns. *You're not human. You're a monster. A thing. I* made *you*.

But he'd never been *saved* before, never had anyone care for him afterward. In the past, he always crawled off to some hole and waited to die. Except his physiology wouldn't permit it. His body burned through fevers and infections, sealed his wounds, and left him strong enough to face more horror.

He could only imagine how monstrous he looked, a raw-meat thing stripped of any pretext at humanity, and yet she was still here, still touching him with exquisite tenderness. *Stop now. Stop. Please, don't ever stop.* Her fingers slid into his hair, and it didn't hurt, not even a twinge. Closing his eyes, he rested his head in her hands.

"I'm so sorry I wasn't more careful about Hex," she whispered.

Jael shook his head without looking up. *I didn't think it was a threat either.*

She went on, "I knew it wasn't you right away, though. One look, one breath, and I was sure. I started making plans immediately to get you out. I wish it was faster."

If he weren't so damn tired, he'd give her a cocky grin, but now that his eyes were shut, he couldn't seem to open them. He winked out, letting his body heal, as it always had.

When Jael roused next, another two days had passed. Curled up on the edge of the mattress, facing him, Dred looked a little better and no longer smelled as if she'd given up hope. All the bunks were occupied by dark shapes, so it must be down cycle. She rolled over and nearly fell off the bed; he reacted instinctively, pulling her against him. Twinges told him that his body still wasn't entirely healed. *Better me than someone else. I can survive it, I have before.* Experience had taught him to retreat, until it felt like it was happening to someone else. The time with Silence paled before what he'd gone through in the labs and over a much longer span. They'd popped both his eyes, stripped all the flesh off his arms, and brought in random subjects to test his reproductive capacity. No matter the horror, he closed his eyes and vanished. But Jael used to worry that he wouldn't come out again, or if he did, it would be in the shape they demanded.

Gently, he kissed Dred on the forehead. She stirred next to him, always a light sleeper, but then he'd known that. He wanted to see her sleepy response to him, had to know if she still looked at him the same way. Her eyes were green as life when they fluttered open.

She smiled. "Feeling better?"

"I hope I didn't sick up again on you, love. Awful for my dignity."

"No, you were quiet. Too much so for the others, they've been afraid that you're putrid and dying, and that I'm cozied up to your soon-to-be corpse."

"Not really your sort of thing, is it?"

"You know me so well." She reached out, stroking his cheek, his jaw, and he lifted his chin, reveling in such a dear moment.

In Perdition, they were few and far between.

"How's the ship coming?"

"Not sure," she admitted. "The others have been working on it without me. Silence has made three or four runs at us, but she can't get inside. It's beyond entertaining to watch her frustration on the monitor."

"You did steal her favorite toy."

"You were mine first. And I'll do whatever it takes to keep you."

She meant it, he knew. And "relief" was too small, too frail a word for what he felt. Nothing about the woman he loved had changed. In his secret heart, he'd feared she would see him as a broken thing, an object of pity. Apart from these sweet and tender emotions, she also offered complete acceptance. Dred kissed him softly on the nose, chin, and next his cheeks. The pleasure was beyond beauty, beyond freedom, beyond any one thing he'd ever known or wanted.

Breathless and aching, Jael tangled a hand in her hair, brought her mouth to his, and whispered the only truth he knew:

"I love you. More than life itself."

A Pretty Web of Scars

Jael's words filled Dred with a deep and incandescent joy, so out of keeping with this place. She dropped her voice low, just in case anyone else was awake. "I've never said it before. But I love you, too."

She didn't mention how difficult the last five days had been, taking care of him in such basic facilities. Tam and Keelah had scrubbed sheets and helped her change the bedding, often more than once a day. At one point, none of the other beds had sheets or blankets because they were all stained with blood or vomit—that or hanging up to dry. *I thought I might lose you . . . that Silence brought you too close to death.*

So she'd whispered to him, threats and promises. And now, he was awake, alert. *Thank you, Mary.* Dred never had much faith—she'd seen too much horror—but Jael's recovery seemed miraculous, even considering his abilities.

"You say it like it's a dirty secret."

"I just don't want to wake everyone else. They've been working hard."

"While I was slacking." The wry amusement in his tone prompted a reluctant smile from her as well.

Hardly able to believe she could, she traced his features lightly with one fingertip. "Do you . . . I mean, I know it was bad. I'll listen if you need to talk."

"Ah, you're worried about my trauma, love? Back in the lab, Landau did terrible things twice before lunch. Sitting alone in a dark pit, nobody touching me, nobody talking, except the endless echo of Bug chitters? *That* was worse. I reckon I can handle pain better than isolation."

Dred had the feeling he might be putting up a cheerful front, but she had no idea what to do about it. Forcing people to confront their true feelings? That wasn't in her skill set. So she only nodded and went in for a soft kiss. Touch was easier than talk anyway.

"You'll have scars," she said.

To her surprise, he let out a relieved sigh. "Finally. It's not right to go through what I have and for it to leave no trace. For your sake, though, I hope she didn't ruin my pretty face."

"Doesn't matter." Her voice was gentle. "As long as you stay with me."

"They couldn't pry me away with a hammer and chisel."

"I'm glad to hear it."

"Can you help me up? I have some pressing business in the san. Sorry to ruin the mood," he added with a half smile.

"No, it's fine. Come on."

They were quiet as they crept past the others; Dred lent him her shoulder because he was still weak. His body had exhausted itself and spent nearly all resources bringing him back from the brink. Since the sanitary was small, she barely fit inside with him once the door closed. Dred turned her back so he could use the facilities, then he squeezed past her to step into the shower. The light was better in here, and she counted over fifty scars, some slim and silver, others thick and purple.

"I can feel you looking," he said. "So wash my back."

His back was relatively unmarked, at least compared

to the rest of him. She dipped her hand in the dry soap and let the water mist over it, just enough to reconstitute, then uncharacteristically, she did exactly as he asked.

"Don't get used to it."

"Wouldn't dream of it."

He was far too lean beneath her hands, no longer whip-cord strong, but simply thin, most of the muscle burned away in the desperate quest to keep body and soul together. Her hands lingered on his shoulder blades, and she silently counted vertebrae with her fingertips, walking downward toward the scant curve of his bum. Jael smiled over his shoulder at her, rinsing off.

"How do you feel?" she asked.

"Like a dead man walking. Mary, I'm knackered. I don't remember recovery making me feel so wretched before."

"That's because of me."

"Worth it," he said, turning off the trickle of water.

When he was dry, she handed him the clothes she'd scavenged. They were as clean as they could be, considering the circumstances, but from his expression at the stains, it was still slightly revolting. Since she'd found them moldering in a closet, she couldn't disagree. Hand washing in a bucket could only do so much.

To console him, she said, "When we get out of here, we'll buy something elegant to wear and eat at the poshest restaurant we can find."

"Promises, promises. How're we affording such luxury?"

"Not through a life of crime, that much is sure."

"Never tell me that Perdition's rehabbed you?" He aimed a look of mock astonishment her way.

"Near enough. I'll never do anything that could land me in a place like this again." She no longer cared if the world was full of monsters. At best, hunting killers had saved a few lives while ruining her own. Now she had someone special to protect.

Jael grinned. "It'd be enough not to get caught."

"You're madder than I thought if you'd risk another prison sentence."

His levity faded, and he cupped her face in his hands. "You might think this is a strange warning, but there will always be danger if you stay with me. Anyone finds out what I am, I'll be rounded up again. I'm never, ever free because I carry the crime of my creation with me."

"Ah," she said. "Well, if they try to take you, then I'll do whatever it takes to stop them."

"Whatever?" he breathed. "There you go again with such violent talk. What should I do? It's turning me on something fierce."

She glanced down, his grubby replacement clothing still in hand. "So it is. But I thought you were tired."

"Funny how it fades when you start talking about blood-letting on my behalf."

"Everyone else is right outside," she said softly. "And we don't have much space."

He leaned in, dusting a kiss over her lower lip. "I can be quiet. Can you?"

She stepped closer. "I'm not sure. Let's find out."

JAEL couldn't believe it when Dred pulled off her shirt. There was hardly room for them to stand, damp sheets piled on the floor. Despite how bad he wanted her, he had no idea how this would work. He wasn't recovered enough to take her against the wall, but she seemed to realize this as she stepped out of her pants. She was deliciously, gloriously naked, and he hurt with wanting her. Need cramped his stomach and made him shake.

"This should work," she whispered.

And draped a sheet across the san facilities, lid down. It wasn't elegant, but he sat eagerly, reaching for her when she took too long. She settled on his lap, all muscled strength and silken heat. Even her scars were beautiful to him. He knotted his hands in her hair, tugging until she let her head fall back to expose her throat. With lips and teeth and tongue, he marked her, first on the side of her neck, then the curve of her shoulder.

Shivers ran through her, but she didn't moan. Pleasure sparked in her green eyes, then her hands were all over him, stroking until he couldn't hide the shudders of sensation; they drove him to buck his hips, trying to get closer still. She answered his unspoken plea by lifting her hips, and it was the sweetest, simplest completion when he glided home. Her weight took them the rest of the way, and for long moments, he just held on to her, shivering with the silent intensity of that exquisite stillness. Then she began to move in tight, slow circles, somehow intuiting that he needed to be passive and that her body could partly eradicate the pain. He breathed in quick, shallow gasps, not even trying to control himself. Jael jerked each time she rolled her hips, enthralled and drowning in delight.

"Just tell me what you need," she breathed right into his ear.

Another shiver wracked him. "Just you. And this."

She still wants me. This isn't sympathy.

For her sake, he wanted to last longer, but he just couldn't. All too soon, he swelled and came, muffling the sound in the side of her neck. She was still soft and aroused, tense atop him, so he touched her with tender fingertips, reveling in how quickly she came undone when there had once been so much resistance to his touch. Now, she was all melting heat, breathless, helpless against him. The downside of that was how much it turned him on.

He was hard again by the time she calmed.

Her eyes widened. "Seriously?"

"It's your fault, love."

"But can you really . . . ?"

"Not sure. Shall we find out?"

In response, she rode him slowly, patiently, as if she didn't believe he had any spark left in him, but she was willing to indulge him for a little while. He traced her cheeks, her lips, then framed her face in his hands. Dred gazed into his eyes as they moved together, the sweetest stare, then he slid his palms downward over her muscled biceps to the divot of her waist and the curve of her hips.

"Lean in a little," he whispered.

She did, tilting forward so he could wrap his arms around her. Her breasts shifted against his chest, so much beautiful heat. His need kicked up a notch from a low thrum to definite drive. And she felt that sharpening inside her. Dred's movements increased on him.

"Good?"

He kissed her, hard. Her tongue moved against his, hungry, starving. She tasted like sunrise, freedom, and forever, maddening him because no matter how much of her he had, she always left him craving more. Her mouth flowered beneath his, becoming soft and swollen from the pressure, mirroring the shift of their bodies.

Give and take, slide and thrust.

"You can't really—" Her question cracked on a moan.

"Don't talk. Just feel me."

Her breath came quicker, and he could tell when she lost the ability to think. She closed her eyes, hands digging into his shoulders. This time he didn't have to use his fingers at all.

His orgasm was more spirit than body, driven by her muffled cries, but it felt no less intense. In fact, it left him even more shaken, realizing that she could coax feats of pleasure from him that he hadn't even known he could experience.

I love you.

But it was too soon to say it again. Jael could hardly stand by the time Dred slipped off his lap. She had to help him dress, and he leaned on her to get back to the dormitory. The others were awake by then, waiting for a turn in the san, and he didn't even care. Their knowing smirks slid right off him as he collapsed on the bunk. She wouldn't let him pass out, however; Dred insisted he drink some water and suck down a serving of protein paste before she let him close his eyes. There were no monsters waiting for him in the dark this time. He only saw her face, uplifted in ecstasy, her mouth soft and open against his, panting her pleasure.

The mattress depressed when she sank down on the side of it; he felt her nearby, even before she touched him. Her hands on his head, stroking his hair gently, sent tingles down his spine. Jael smiled without opening his eyes.

"You should sleep a little more. If you'll be all right, I'll get to work with the others." But she didn't move yet, waiting for his dismissal.

Oddly, it didn't rankle. He didn't care if she thought he was weak. He only cared that she'd offered to stay if he needed her.

"I'm fine," he said.

There would be bad dreams waiting, more fuel for the nightmarish flames. But none of that mattered . . . because Dred loved him.

And he'd gladly walk through the fires of hell if she was waiting on the other side.

◀ 16 ▶

A Different Way to Die

In the days Dred had spent with Jael, the others had made
some progress. Apparently, they had decided to convert
the two maintenance rigs and were disassembling the back
ends with the intent of welding the two together. The life-
support systems would need to be overhauled, and it would
be a tight fit inside—with primitive conditions—as even
with jury-rigging, she couldn't imagine what facilities could
be provided.

"Talk to me," she said to Tam, who was inside one of the
vehicles, banging around.

The spymaster stepped out, tools in hand. "I wish Ike
were here."

"Not what I meant."

"Ah, so you're done with nursing, and you want a progress report?"

"Something like that. Will this thing even fly? It looks
incredibly ungainly."

"The aerodynamics are a problem. Steering will be a
bitch unless I can figure out how to streamline the design.
With the tools we have available, it won't be easy."

Tam went over everything they'd accomplished so far, and it wasn't nearly enough. But with limited supplies and personnel, it was amazing they'd come even this far. She followed him inside the makeshift craft, having to hunch over where the two vehicles connected.

"Are you sure the solder point won't just break apart, the minute we launch?"

Tam proved he had a dark sense of humor. "Only one way to find out."

"That's not funny."

"I've reinforced it with struts here . . . and here. It's the best we can do."

"Then it'll have to suffice. How's the life support coming?"

Vost answered that, sticking his head in through the cargo doors in the back. "I'm working on the computer, but I'm having a hard time overriding the eight-hour limit. Since nobody's supposed to be in here longer than a single work shift—"

"Have you tried a hard reset?" Tam cut in.

"That was the first thing I did." The merc commander sounded disgruntled.

Dred smirked. "What do you think he is, an amateur?"

Tam smiled back. "Well, *I* am. Despite a rather colorful resume, I've never tried to cobble a ship together from this kind of junk."

"This might be a last-resort option," Dred said, "but maybe we could lift one of the life-support modules from the station and make it work?"

Vost shook his head. "It would be too big, even presuming you could cut it loose."

"Then I guess you have to figure out how to change the eight-hour restriction," she said.

"I'm working on it." His scowl as he withdrew suggested he didn't like Dred's tone.

Ignoring Vost, she checked out the progress from stem to stern. In truth, the craft was strange-looking; in front, it was a two-seater, and the middle was completely open, cargo space converted clumsily to let people sprawl on the floor, then there were two seats at the back, from the other maintenance-rig cab. The others had done a credible job of fusing the machinery, but she didn't know if it would hold during launch . . . and there was no way to perform a thorough, rigorous stress test.

"What do you think?" she asked Tam.

"It'll be a miracle if we don't all die," he said.

"That's what I thought."

The spymaster hesitated. "But . . . I'd rather go out a free man than wait to be killed. I don't have that kind of resignation anymore."

She nodded. "And I'd rather die in vacuum than let Silence or another merc team finish me off. So let's keep at it."

Since Dred didn't have any particular skill at shipbuilding, she left the others to it and went to the control room. Outside, there were five of Silence's killers watching the door. What purpose that served, she had no idea, except to establish that Silence knew where they were. *We can definitely take a squad of five, though, so it's not even an impediment to our movements.* As she was trying to figure it out, the men slipped out of camera view like dark shadows. That was somewhat eerie because there might be more—all the surviving assassins, even—hiding nearby.

As long as we can finish up in here, we don't have to leave.

Dred wished she had a better angle, but she couldn't figure out how to tap into station security from here. As far as she could tell, the systems were limited to the docking bay. Sighing, she picked up the handheld and skipped back to the first message. The date on the vid indicated these logs were forty turns old.

The same woman from before appeared, much brighter-faced and practically humming with enthusiasm. "This is my first long assignment. My father swears he had nothing to do with my Monsanto posting, and I hope he's telling the truth. Nepotism is no way to start your career."

Aw, how cute. She's a little idealist.

She watched the rest of that vid, but it was mostly cheerful speculation about what the woman would be doing on a mineral-refinery station. The second log was a little more subdued, talking about the grim atmosphere on station and the lack of amenities. *Yeah, reality has that effect on all of us.* A random person's life probably wouldn't make for thrilling entertainment, so she set the device aside, marveling that it still worked after all this time.

A problem occurred to her then, and she rushed from the control room to the hangar floor. Tam popped his head out of the ship as Dred approached. "Something wrong?"

"Has anyone figured out what we're eating on board?"

"We can make a lot of paste before we take off," he said.

"We can't install the Kitchen-mate?"

Tam shook his head. "It would weigh us down and take up too much space. The bottom line is, we could run out of food before we get out of this system. There's no way to rig this thing with a grimspace drive."

She sighed. "And even if we could, we don't have a jumper."

It was looking more all the time like this "escape" was just a different way to die.

WHEN Jael woke up this time, he felt both recovered and alert. He crawled out of his bunk and staggered to the san. Afterward, he found everyone else working on the ship. He'd seen shuttles, crashed escape pods, ships too beat-up to salvage. And this one was worse than any he'd ever encountered. *There's no way this thing will fly.* Technically, he supposed it didn't have to. Simple propulsion would guide it out of the docking bay, but then what?

He strode toward the work crew, answering their greetings with a raised hand. "How much fuel do we have?"

From their expressions, it seemed like he'd asked an astonishing question. Or maybe they were just shocked to see him back from the dead. On second thought, it was probably that. But none of them interrogated him about it.

Just as well. He wouldn't have answered. It was impossible to trust people with a secret like his, so they could wonder.

Vost answered. "Not much. Sixteen hours in the combined tanks. I haven't been able to find any spare canisters."

Jael nodded. "Makes sense they wouldn't leave much. It's expensive."

"Even at top speed, that doesn't get us very far from Perdition," Martine pointed out.

"Then we rebuild the engines for greater speed and fuel efficiency," Vost said.

Jael cocked his head. "Can you do that?"

"Not without some help. But we're short on a design computer."

"Could this help?" Dred strode toward them carrying the obsolete handheld they'd found in the dormitories.

"Possibly, depending on what programs it has. We can't bounce an uplink for updates, but let's take a look."

Jael wished he'd spent more time studying and less time fighting. In salvage work, he hadn't needed to be good at creating things, only breaking them down into component parts that could then be resold. Over the turns, he'd picked up some skill at demolitions and a little security, but none of that compared to the innate genius Ike could've brought to this project.

We need you, old man. Why'd you die for us?

Vost flipped through the directory, a frown building. "I wonder who this belonged to."

"Why?" Dred leaned in, and Jael restrained the urge to pull her back. Anytime she got within a meter of the merc commander, his nerves went up in flames.

"There are all kinds of notes, as if an audit was ongoing. See here, someone's analyzed the actual cost ratio, which didn't match up with what officials were reporting." Vost flicked the screen, and a green chart appeared in holo form.

Jael studied the numbers, neatly lined up in columns: actual costs versus reported. There was a significant discrepancy in almost every department. But that wouldn't help them rebuild the engines to be more fuel-efficient. He wasn't even sure why Vost had pointed it out.

Calypso rubbed a hand over her face. "Explain why I should care if the Monsanto admins were corrupt however long ago."

"They might have hidden resources that could help us," the merc commander explained.

Dred shook her head. "Unlikely. They would've taken everything with them."

"But we found this handheld," Martine pointed out.

"Have we searched the bay thoroughly?" Duran asked.

Jael couldn't answer that. He'd been unconscious for like a week. So he glanced at the others, waiting to hear what they said.

"I think so," Tam said, thoughtful.

Martine didn't seem so convinced. "But we were looking for ship supplies, not for cred-sticks or hints of corruption. Maybe we overlooked something?"

A hidden cred-stick would feel like . . . a sign, Jael decided. A good omen, even. Because right now, it seemed so unlikely that they'd even get off station, and if they did, they'd probably die in a dead ship. Though he'd asserted otherwise, he didn't have a lot of faith that he could cut free of this place and start a new life. Yet a cred-stick represented a tie to the outside world, where you needed money to survive, not just your wits or a sharp knife.

THEY split up to dig around the docking bay more thoroughly. Jael went to the dormitory and turned all the mattresses, then checked to see if anything was fastened to the bed frames. *Nothing.* It seemed likely that whatever the Monsanto execs had left behind would be in their quarters, not the shift workers' area. Still, he kept looking, just in case.

Next, Jael moved on to the storage units adjacent to each bunk. They had obsolete, analog locks, but this, he could manage. After five minutes of tinkering, he popped the first one open. There wasn't even dust inside, which spoke well of the airtight seal. The next three were the same, but the fifth one he opened still contained *all* the original occupant's personal belongings inside it.

"Well, that's fragging strange," he said aloud.

"What is?" Dred asked.

"Have a look."

She crouched beside him, hands braced on the edge of the footlocker. The interior of the lid still had a personal label affixed: *Property of Rebestah Saren*. Inside, there were three changes of clothing—Monsanto uniforms and spare underwear—along with all the small comforts you'd carry away from home. As a superstitious shiver flickered over him, Jael didn't want to touch anything, but Dred had no such compunction. She rummaged around, coming up with expired snack packets and some kind of portable entertainment console. Next she picked up a framed holo like the one Vost carried of his son. This one showed a young woman hugging an older couple, probably her parents, he guessed. The loop only ran for three seconds, but it gave him chills when she turned to face the camera with her intense, dark stare. Strangely, he felt like he *knew* her . . . but that was impossible.

"THAT'S *her.*" Dred's words came out sharp with surprise.

"What are you talking about?"

"We found her handheld a while back. I don't think you've seen any of her logs."

"Huh." Jael wasn't sure where she was going with this. It definitely wouldn't help with the ship, which was his first concern.

Her eyes widened. "If she was conducting an audit, and all her gear is still here, then—"

"Rebestah Saren probably didn't make it home."

◀ 17 ▶

Competitive Thrust

"It's interesting," Martine said, half an hour later. "It really is. And if we had time to screw around, I'd say, sure, let's look into this old murder. But—"

"She's right," Vost agreed.

Calypso added, "What good would it do? We can't do anything for this woman. Didn't you already get in trouble doing vigilante work?"

Dred sighed. "It's not the same. I wasn't planning to *kill* anyone over her. I'd just like to know what happened."

"That's because you're bored," Duran said.

"Huh?" Dred stared at the merc.

"You're not good at mechanical work. Nobody needs you to boss them around. So you're looking for something to do." This time, the short man didn't even take a step closer to Calypso as he occasionally did when he felt threatened.

Silently, she admitted that might be true. "Then nobody will mind if I go over her logs to see if I can find anything out."

Vost shrugged. "You might learn something useful about the station in her recordings. But probably not."

"You don't need me on construction anyway," she muttered.

She'd already passed out the dead woman's clothing. Martine and Calypso were both happy to get a change of clothes; Dred was pretty chuffed about it, too. These uniforms hadn't been washed in a bucket with minimal soap and hung up to dry in a room that reeked of unwashed bodies. No, this fabric smelled . . . unspoiled in a way that was hard to describe, turns of being safeguarded in an airtight container.

"True," Duran said cheerfully. "So stop interrupting the rest of us."

Keelah followed her away from the bustle of shipbuilding, back into the dormitories. The alien's eyes were bright with interest or sympathy or possibly both. "You're not alone in your fascination. It's rather marvelous that we have the breathing room to . . . care, isn't it?"

Yes.

She didn't even know that was what she felt until Keelah articulated it. "We've done nothing but fight for so long. It feels miraculous that I could take an interest in something else, something—"

"Esoteric. You can't eat it or mate with it, but you'd like the answer to feed your soul."

She shied away from the spiritual response. "My mind, anyway. Rebestah was here, trying to do the right thing. It was her first job, and something awful happened to her."

"You feel moved by her plight, and you'd like to put her ghost to rest."

"When you put it like that, it sounds crazy."

Keelah's whiskers twitched. "Truly? It *only* makes sense when I consider it that way. Otherwise, it's a pointless exercise in curiosity when you have more important matters to attend."

"Like what?" she muttered.

During her time on merc ships, she'd mostly cleaned, so that didn't offer much value in technical work. Beyond that, she was good at hunting and killing. Again, not applicable.

"Precisely." Keelah sounded sympathetic.

"I don't understand."

"If there *is* nothing more pressing, why shouldn't you grant this specter peace? Even if her ghost haunts only you."

She'd almost forgotten the concept of doing something just because she wanted to, but they did have breathing room. *Silence can't get to us. The others don't need me.*

Keelah headed out then, presumably to work on the ship. With a grateful smile, Dred kicked back on the bunk with the handheld and started the third log. It seemed to have been recorded in a different room, definitely not this dormitory. The walls were brighter and the furniture more elegant.

"Something is wrong here," Rebestah said. "I'm supposed to be working with the administrator, but he rarely leaves his quarters, and I can't get his assistant to give me a straight answer. She seems . . . frightened, actually. The vice president of operations does nothing but drink. He hinted he'd be happy to 'show me the ropes,' but then he grabbed my ass, so I kicked him instead of accepting his offer of on-the-job training."

Dred smirked. "Good for you."

The holo went on, "Since they won't cooperate, it's making my job harder. I've been sent as an independent auditor, and once they pass the check, I'm supposed to join the accounting department as a supervisor, two turns in deep space. But so far, I haven't seen one financial document, and I've been here four weeks."

She had the sense that Rebestah had made these logs because she was lonely. If the higher-ups put the word out that nobody should associate with her, she probably ended up in deep isolation without understanding why. To Dred, it seemed obvious. The execs had been stealing from Monsanto for turns, inflating operation costs and pocketing the rest. Now that their theft was being addressed, they were scared shitless.

"But how did a green girl like you end up with this mission?" Regardless of what Rebestah's old man had claimed,

Dred suspected he must've pulled some strings. *Otherwise, wouldn't someone more experienced be assigned?* It only made sense.

"I won't give up," Rebestah was saying. "Even if it's hard."

A man swept into the room, obviously weaving, and Rebestah set down her handheld. Dred couldn't get a good look at his face, but he seemed to be middle-aged, medium height and build. *This must be VP of Operations.* The angle was a little awkward, but the intruder didn't seem to realize he was being recorded. This was the closest thing to actual entertainment she'd known in forever, made more compelling by the fact that it was all true.

"Administrator Levin will see you now."

"Really? That's wonderful."

"I hope you'll be understanding. He has been . . . ill. The medical officer has treated him, and he's no longer contagious, so you shouldn't worry."

"Let's go," Rebestah said brightly.

They went out together, leaving Dred with an empty room and a strange feeling. All her instincts said nothing good would come from this meeting—it was probably a trap—and yet she couldn't warn the girl in the holo. Whatever had happened forty turns ago, the damage was done.

"**SO** how bad was it?" Tam asked quietly.

The others were taking a break, and there wasn't a ton of space inside anyway. Jael didn't look forward to a long haul in here, even if they could reboot life support, address engine performance and fuel-efficiency issues. For a few seconds, he pretended he hadn't heard the question, but he should've known the spymaster wouldn't let it go.

"Jael?"

"It was hell," he said.

Really, what answer was the man expecting? Silence wasn't known for her kind and gentle demeanor. Even in Perdition, she'd earned a certain reputation, so this couldn't come as a complete surprise. And no, he didn't want to talk about it.

"Yet you seem all right. How is that possible?"

"I've had worse." He'd say it again and again, until they believed him. At least it ended quickly, unlike the legal torture in the labs that they called research. "Can we focus on the ship, please?"

"If you're sure."

The other man went back to work, tinkering with the computer panel they'd stripped from something else. It was supposed to interface with the whole ship, linking the separate systems, but so far, it only recognized life support; the engines and nav system, rudimentary as they were, didn't pop on the controls.

"Mary." Jael banged his head against the metal wall, frustrated beyond bearing. "It could take turns to get everything working."

Without waiting for Tam's response, he tried plugging in a different-color wire and got no better result. Vost was better at this sort of thing, but his specialty was hacking. Nobody but Ike had the skills they needed to make this thing foolproof. An angry sound escaped Jael as he slid to the floor and watched Tam try a couple more things.

"I used to think I'd die here," Tam said softly. "Now I'm convinced I won't. Because if nothing else, we'll get this thing working well enough for us to die among the stars."

"That's scant comfort, mate."

"Is it? If it comes down to it, and we run out of food, we can turn off life support and exit peacefully, together."

"Eh." He imagined curling up with Dred for the last time, bodies entwined. "I reckon I can imagine worse ways to go."

"Exactly. So stop complaining and hand me that adapter."

Jael tried two parts before getting it right, more evidence that he was better suited to other work. "Have you thought at all about what you'll do when we get out?"

"You mean when we reach civilization?"

He nodded.

Tam smiled slightly. "Sometimes. But I try not to dwell on it. Impossible dreams make it harder to deal with current reality."

"We need papers," Jael said, pensive. "I'm talking a top-notch fake ID."

Tam seemed to agree with that though he wasn't looking this way. "We all do. As lifers, we'll pop on any routine scan, and all the fugitive alerts will sound."

"Unless we make landfall in the Outskirts. They don't care so much about Conglomerate law, and they don't check databases, either."

"We can't count on being so lucky," Tam muttered.

"No shit. If any of us were blessed with good fortune, we wouldn't be on Perdition."

Before Tam could respond, Vost clambered in the back. "Any luck with the nav? From what I saw, the two engines are competing. They need something to make them work together."

"But what?" Jael wondered aloud.

"Hell if I know," Tam said. "It's not like I ever made a ship out of maintenance rigs."

"We have engines in stern and bow," he mumbled, mostly to himself.

"You going somewhere with this?" Vost wanted to know.

"I'm not sure. But don't most big haulers have engines port and starboard?"

Tam nodded. "That doesn't help us, though."

"We're going to have problems maneuvering because there will be competitive thrust. We need our propulsion facing the same way."

"Let's flip the back engine," Vost said.

"Install it upside down?" Tam didn't look too sure that was a good idea, and it still didn't solve the interface issue.

"More than that, I think we need to wire them together," Jael said. "If it's a hard connection, then it might help the control panel recognize them both."

"Worth a shot," Vost decided. "But it'll be messy as hell

with cables running bow to stern. I'll see what I can find
for casing."

Jael shook his head. "I'm a pro on salvage duty. You
stay here. I'll look around the bay, and if need be, I'll head
up to Repair for a parts run."

Tam stared. "You really think Dred will be all right
with that, after what happened last time you went out?"

Hearing that felt good . . . and awful, the former because
his woman cared, the latter because it turned him into a
victim, a weakling who needed to be protected. Jael lifted
a shoulder in a careless shrug. "Without Hex, they have no
hope of taking me alive."

"I don't think that would make her feel any better," Vost
put in.

He ignored both of them, crawling out the front and
down through the vertical door. Both cabin areas were quite
a squeeze—no surprise since they hadn't been intended for
long-term use. Hopping down, he went over to the pile of
discarded scrap, pieces of the repair rigs that hadn't made
the cut for the integrated vessel. Nothing in the stack
seemed like it would work for shielding the connecting
cables, especially ones that linked two powerful engines.

We can't risk an exterior mount, either. That would
mean compromising hull integrity more than it already
was with more drilling and welding, plus there was always
the chance of free-floating debris around a station like this
one. After so many turns without maintenance, the exterior
of Perdition might be more dangerous than the inside.

I think I saw something we can use in the repair bay . . .

Mind made up, he headed for the force-field control
panel, but Dred intercepted him, wearing a dark look.
"Going somewhere?"

◄ 18 ►

The Chained Queen

"Should we break that up?" Tam asked Martine. From what he could tell, an argument was raging across the bay between Jael and Dred.

She shook her head. "Not on your life. Interference is likely to get one of us shanked. My money's on Dred. Just look at her face."

"It's only because she's worried," Tam said.

"I know." Martine's voice softened. "Look, I don't think I said it before, but . . . thanks for telling me. You know. About Tarnus."

He paused in his work long enough to smile, and her sharp-toothed response was the most beautiful thing he'd ever seen. "I wanted you to know my story. In case—"

"Don't even say it. You never know what evil god might be listening."

"In my experience, they're not malicious, just indifferent, and they leave us to our own tender mercies."

"That might actually be worse," Martine said.

"Agreed. Let's take a break. I'm not getting anywhere with this. I'll treat you to the finest paste credits can buy."

"I knew I made the right move when I latched onto you."

Tam led the way, and they settled against the far wall of the docking bay, not far from the pile of supplies they'd carried in with them. He handed Martine her foil packet, wishing he could offer her something better than the base nutrients necessary to sustain life. Nobody ever got cheerfully plump on the stuff, though, and she could use a few extra kilos.

We all could.

Life in Perdition had never been easy, but lately, they were hanging on by their fingernails. *If this ship doesn't come together, we're done for.* Yet he gave no sign of those dark thoughts as he tore open his own pouch. The taste always struck him as faintly wrong, not vegetable and not meat, nor even a poor synth version, but something thick and gluey that clung to the tongue and palate, as if daring you to actually swallow it. Tam forced it down.

"I'd rather take a pill," Martine muttered.

"Maybe they've perfected them by now. Things have probably changed since we were out there."

"Never as much as you think," she mused. "How long's it been for you?"

"Ten turns, give or take. I've lost track."

"It's easier to let it go." With a grimace, she finished off her meal, then knee-walked over to the crate to count how many packets were left. Tam watched her divide by the number of survivors, and then: "Shit."

"Yeah. We need to get off Perdition ASAP. I checked the Kitchen-mate. It doesn't have much base organic left, either."

The argument across the bay came to a head when Dred grabbed Jael's arm and he hauled her in for a kiss. Tam wondered if that tactic would work on Martine. Who eyed him warily.

"Don't *ever* try it. I will bite off your tongue."

"Noted," he said, properly submissive.

The kiss only lasted a few seconds before Dred shoved Jael away and slammed him into a wall, before going back in on her terms. Tam noticed both Vost and Duran watching as they cut across to the meal station. He nudged Martine, who glared at the mercs.

"You never saw anyone work out relationship issues before?"

"Not like that," Vost said.

Dred called, "Someone lock up behind us. We're making a supply run."

"Hold up." Vost pulled to his feet, moving so slow that Tam realized there must be some kind of problem. "Let me make a shopping list so we don't have to do this again. We're much safer in here."

Calypso came from the dormitory at a run, carrying a pack with some gear in it. "Take weapons and be alert. Silence has been waiting for us."

"That's fine," Dred said with a truly chilling smile. "I'm eager to see her. We have unfinished business."

WHILE the others bantered, Vost tried to think of everything he might need down the line. Frustrating since he couldn't predict all the problems that might arise. This was virgin territory for him, too, even if the others acted like he was the resident expert. He didn't entirely mind their deference, but it was also exhausting when he just wanted to fall onto a bunk and never get up.

Somehow he managed not to rub his chest. His burns felt better, but they still weren't healing like they should.

Sooner or later, he had to make up his mind what to do about the launch codes. If he gave them to one of the convicts, then they'd have the perfect excuse to kill him in his sleep. Hell, he couldn't offer much resistance, even wide-awake, and Duran wasn't enough backup for the two of them to take out everyone else. Plus the other merc showed all signs of going native, beguiled by Calypso as he appeared.

I can't trust anyone. I have to survive.

But he had no idea if he was strong enough to knock out this infection. Vost stopped obsessing over his physical condition and went back to making the list. Finally, when he was sure he'd come up with all possibilities, he gave it to Dred. She took it, still frowning over the argument with Jael.

"Thanks."

"Be careful," he said.

It was surprising how much he'd come to admire her in the short time he'd been on station. Where other people devolved into monsters, she'd tried to build something. He didn't know if he could've been successful at uniting so many hardened killers under his own banner. Hell, his mercs mutinied after a couple of bad weeks, all but Duran . . . and Redmond.

Poor bastard.

"I'll watch her back," Jael told him coolly.

Easy, brother. I'm not after your woman. But he didn't say it aloud. As the other two left, he went back to the supply crates for his daily ration. Tam and Martine were still there, but he couldn't tell what the smaller man was thinking. If he gambled, he'd make a fortune. The woman was more transparent; she didn't like this outing, yet it wasn't like they had a choice.

"Why does it have to be him?" Martine demanded.

"Jael wanted to go," Vost answered.

He could've explained that it was a matter of pride, or maybe "survival" might even be the right word. If you let something spook you, then it became a permanent part of your psyche, a monster you couldn't stare down. So he respected Jael for heading right out to face his demons even if it was dangerous. Sometimes he suspected it was better to die a hero than live as a coward, but he couldn't say for sure because in the end, he'd always walked away, making the expedient choice time and again because of the boy he had waiting back home.

"He's barely out of his sickbed," Calypso snarled. "Any one of you lazy arseholes would've been a more sensible choice." She kicked Duran in the thigh.

"Not so much. I don't even know where Repair is located."

"Then Keelah could've guided you," Martine said.

Tam spoke as the calming influence. "No point in arguing about it now. Once you finish eating, we should get back to work."

Vost glanced around. "Where *is* Keelah anyway?"

Nobody had an answer, so after he sucked down his paste, he went looking and found her in the dormitory, fiddling with the entertainment console Dred had found. But rather than playing games with it, she had deconstructed it to component parts. She glanced up, flinching when she realized he was alone, like she thought he might hurt her.

"You don't like humans much, do you?"

Her teeth clicked. "Are you an idiot?"

"Excuse me?"

"Obviously, the answer is no. I'm here for the crime of being nonhuman. Explain to me how that's right or fair."

"It's not fair to hold me responsible for crimes other humans committed against you."

"I don't *care*," she snarled.

He hadn't seen her display such hostility to anyone else, but she likely associated him with the Conglomerate even if he wasn't working for them anymore. "Sorry to disturb you."

"You must've come in for a reason, so let's hear it."

"First, I want to apologize for the loss of your mate."

"And?" she said without looking at him. He heard *your words are meaningless* in the tone of her voice, the tilt of her head.

"Next, I want to tell you something. It won't make up for your loss, but I think it'll help."

The look she gave him then burned with both incredulity and loathing. "Impossible."

We'll see. Quietly, he gave her the launch codes.

THERE *is a piece missing.*

A missing piece.

Silence passed through the darkened halls of her kingdom, not seeing the way the survivors cowered at her feet.

It was all empty now, everyone was dead or soon would be. She could feel the cool, skeletal fingers on her shoulder, guiding her steps. She was grief made flesh, and there was no solace for her loss. Tears traced down her cheeks in hot rivulets, marring the mask of perfection she wore for her dark lord, and she did not wipe them away.

There was no Speaker any longer. No words to offer the outside world.

There was only before and after.

After was an abyss of longing unanswered. She had never encountered such perfection, such antithesis to death. *He was life incarnate, and I have lost him.* Licking her lips, she imagined she could still taste him, but every trace was long since gone. Her mouth felt dry and cracked beneath her tongue.

One of the Silent rose up from the floor and gestured. *What should we do now?*

Nothing, she replied. *Nothing but wait.*

Apart from sending patrols down to look for her lost love, she had issued no orders in recent days. The fight was over; she had been defeated. Now she could only wait until they would be united once more in death. He must be aching every bit as much at their separation, and that certainty was all that let her survive this parting.

Some of the Silent were dying. There was no more medicine to hold Lord Death at bay, and so he came to reap among the legion devoted to his name. She saw him come in his feathered mantle and prayed that this would be her time; yet, when she dropped to her knees, he swept past and claimed some vomiting wretch on the ground nearby. Her tears came stronger then, but she did not sob. For countless moments, she knelt and wept.

Until someone dared interrupt her sorrow with a touch on her shoulder. With a silent snarl, she glanced up. *What?*

The prisoner is being moved. Shall we save him?

Truly? A spark of hope kindled within her.

The guard is limited, lady, only one.

Who? she demanded.

The chained queen.

Silence ground her teeth. This could only be a taunting gambit, designed to show the other woman's ascendance on station. But Death never surrendered, no matter how dire the odds. She would recover her consort and be made whole in joy and pleasure once more. Picturing his face gave her solace. Pain pierced her head as she tried to remember what sweet words he had offered. There had been some, surely. *But no—I made him silent. His voice is mine. How could I have forgotten?* Those beautiful, intimate moments wherein he gave her the sweetest, most seductive gift. No lover had ever made her feel so desired. Yet that lapse of memory quivered into a frisson of unease, as if she'd mislaid an important thread.

You are at war, Death whispered. Bony fingers delved beneath the seductive tangle of her hair to stroke the nape of her neck. She shivered, but not from pleasure. The grim one would be enraged to learn she loved another with greater passion, now. *I must never show it.*

Pretending to obey his dark demand, she strode from her throne room with the Silent at her heels. *Fret not, beloved, for I am coming.*

◄ 19 ►

Shit, Meet Fan

"We're not going directly to the repair bay?" Dred asked.

In answer, Jael slipped into the ducts. She followed him, accepting that this wasn't the place for explanations. After all, they had been lucky to get out of the docking area without being attacked. But once they got inside, she paused and let her silence establish the fact that she wasn't moving another step until he clarified.

"I know where Silence's drug lab is. If we destroy it, that will weaken her significantly."

"You're hoping she shows up to defend it. So you can kill her." The last part probably could've gone unspoken.

He didn't deny it. "You already said we have unfinished business, so this shouldn't come as a surprise."

"And if I hadn't insisted on coming with you . . . did you plan on doing this on your own?" Anger cracked her tone, and it was all Dred could do to keep from shouting at him.

"If necessary," he said. "But I'm glad you're here. I always am."

"Sweet talk will *not* get you back on my good side."

Sighing, she gestured. "Lead the way. Hope you have a plan because I didn't bring any special gear."

"I'm versatile, don't worry."

Though she was still pissed, she went quiet as they traveled. She had definite reservations about this idea, but Jael seemed committed, and she'd rather accompany him into trouble than let him go alone. The way she'd felt after he was taken, Dred preferred never to experience it again.

Based on the burn in her muscles, they were near the top of the station. She had no idea Silence's operations were so far-reaching. But with all the other factions gone, Death's Handmaiden pretty much had the run of the place, and Dred didn't give a shit. Her current imperative mandated that she get off the station, not rule it. Silence could have this junk heap.

Jael paused, tilting his head, then she smelled it, too. "Mary, what is that?"

"Their chem lab."

"It's . . ." *Revolting. Unspeakable.* She couldn't decide what word worked best, but he got it, based on the face he was making.

"I know. Come on, let's get in and out fast. She's usually got a couple of the Silent working the lab, poor sods."

Dred smirked. "Now that's a shit job."

They came out of the ducts near the foul-smelling room that Jael claimed was Silence's chem lab. She didn't dispute it, but she had no clue what could be processed under such conditions that wouldn't kill a human straight off. While she pondered, Jael got out their last functional laser pistol. There was plenty of garbage in the area, plus what reeked like rotten feces. *Methane?* Even as she speculated, he fired.

The heat melted the synth and set the organic on fire. The flames whooshed with the gas she'd guessed must be present, and an explosion rocked the room. Before the smoke cleared, Jael grabbed her hand and raced away. She ran with him until a stitch formed in her side, feeling oddly like she'd pulled a prank instead of crippled the enemy's operations. Something about his humor was infectious, and she doubled over laughing when they finally paused.

"I feel like I have to make the obligatory joke about the shit hitting the fan," he gasped.

"What the hell . . ." She couldn't even finish the question.

"She feeds that to her minions. From what I can tell, they're fermenting human waste. Don't ask me how she knew you could make a hallucinogen that way."

"No shit," Dred said.

And Jael dissolved into a fresh wave of amusement. "There's another room where they dry it, once it's processed. We could wreck that, too."

"Will it make you feel better?" It was an important question, one with more layers than she let on. Dred understood more clearly than he realized how it felt to be stripped of volition and turned into a plaything by a twisted, deviant mind. Her torment lasted much longer, even if Artan hadn't literally stripped off her skin. In some ways, the way he broke her down mentally and accustomed her to those chains—and her role as his pet—had been worse.

It would hurt more, and I would've died, but maybe physical wounds would've been better. Then I wouldn't be left wondering, even now, if I should have fought harder. The worst part of her time with Artan was that it had turned her from a brave, cold hunter to a woman who questioned her every move . . . and blamed herself for letting it happen.

"I'm not sure. But I intended to do it even before I was taken."

"Then let's finish it."

"All right, love. The next stop isn't far."

"It wouldn't make sense for them to carry the fresh product very far," she agreed.

Plus it must be disgusting to transport.

The storage room was hot and dry, perfect for the last step in the process. But Dred hesitated. These were just dried chips, basically, wafer thin and innocuous-looking.

"Do they actually *eat* these?"

"Definitely. They take them like a religious offering, in fact."

Her stomach churned. "I have no idea how she made her followers so crazy. For that matter, how did she get there?" She stared at the remaining chem chips, pondering.

"No idea," Jael said. "What are you thinking?"

"If we took these with us, could we feed it to the Kitchenmate, let it break this down to base organic and make more paste?"

"I'm not sure how sanitary that would be. The Kitchenmate isn't designed to process refuse on this scale, not like the big station recyclers."

She sighed. "And it might contaminate the machine. Should we take this down to the recyclers, then? It could make the difference between starvation and survival later."

"We blew the door off, remember? So we'd be exposed the whole time we're waiting for the batch to process." Jael didn't look as if he wanted to guard this stuff.

"True. Then let's destroy everything."

THIS time, Jael started a small fire, and the station protocols kicked in. Water sprayed down from the ceiling, and a couple of maintenance units converged to spray the room with flame-retardant chem. Between the wet and the white foam, it would be impossible to salvage anything in here. Given how hard withdrawal hit, soon Silence would be fighting alone.

He smiled.

"Better?" Dred asked.

"Yeah. Let's head for Repair."

But before they made it more than five meters, a Silent patrol rounded the corner. Disappointed, Jael saw that Silence wasn't with them. This wasn't the largest group he'd seen, only five, and they looked . . . hungry. Apparently, she hadn't been taking care of her people. He didn't think she had a Speaker anymore, and maybe that was part of his function—not just talking to other people on station for her but also making sure that she didn't lose sight of mundane necessities.

Like food and water.

To his surprise, the patrol didn't attack immediately. Instead, they signed at him, and Jael cast a look at Dred, silently asking if she knew their tongue. She shook her head slightly.

"Sorry, I don't know what you want," he said.

In response, the apparent leader pointed at Dred, drew his finger across his throat, then beckoned. He didn't like the implication.

"You'll kill her and take me alive? I don't think so."

The communicative one gave him a dead look, then they all drew their weapons. *Well, this is bizarre.*

"Feel like a little bloodletting before our next stop?" Dred asked with a ferocious smile.

"It's good exercise."

As the Silent rushed in, she pulled her chains out of the pack Calypso had sent. Jael took a few steps back; after all this time, he knew exactly how much space she needed for maximum brutality. But it baffled him completely when the Silent acted like he wasn't a hostile combatant and pushed past him trying to get at Dred.

What the hell? I'm on a no-kill list, now?

Part of him wished he could remember what had happened while he was in Silence's hands. The rest of him was glad his brain threw up roadblocks. He only knew she'd messed him up bad, but the particulars? Not so much. And to some degree, the injuries spoke for themselves.

While Dred kept them at bay with her whipping chains, he slashed at the stupid sods from behind. One kidney shot, two. And then there were three. She cracked one in the head; he stumbled but didn't go down. Jael finished him with a sideways slice of his blade. Blood jetted from his carotid, splattering on Dred, but she didn't even blink.

Two left. We're so good at this we could go into business.

But it wasn't even a fair fight. They clearly had orders not to harm him, plus they were weak and hungry, whereas he and Dred had augmented speed and strength. *Not as fast as I used to be, granted, but more than quick enough to make these assholes look like they're standing still.* He stopped playing and broke another's neck as Dred dropped her chains and went after the last one with her bare hands. She pounded the other woman relentlessly in the chest and stomach, ending the fight with a powerful kick that snapped her spine. The final Silent soldier was down but not dead, and Dred finished her with a quick jab of her boot knife.

"Is it me, or was that too easy?"

"There's something wrong with them," he said softly.

She let out a shuddering breath. "That makes it worse. Feels like everything on this station is breaking down, like we're about to be infected with the same mad disease."

"Remember our promise—elegant clothes, posh dinner? We're making it out."

But she didn't seem to hear him. "Silence can't have many troops left. That means she'll be feeling cornered. And trapped creatures are the most dangerous of all."

"She doesn't have the resources to hurt us," Jael said. "And this is our last trip out of the docking bay. Once we have everything on Vost's list, we bunker down and finish the ship."

She shivered. "I wish you wouldn't say things like that."

"Right, you lifers are superstitious."

"You would be, too, if you knew what passed for luck in Perdition."

"Sorry, love."

He got them back in the ducts before she could fixate on gloom-and-doom scenarios. It was a long climb to Repair, but the station—from what he could tell—was deserted. Silence would probably kill herself when the last of her minions keeled over, or hell, they might start murdering each other when they couldn't take the blue-devils from dropping off the chem.

"It's hard to believe everyone is dead," she said softly. "It used to be so hard to move around the station . . ."

"Now we're up here out of habit, pretty much." He didn't

think they needed to be so careful, per se, but it would probably make her nervous if they got cocky.

Pride goeth before a fall, and whatnot.

And maybe she was right. Over the turns, he'd gotten so good at preemptive treachery that he lost sight of the fact that his plans could backfire or go hideously wrong. Thinking that way got him locked up for half a human lifetime in that hellhole on Ithiss-Tor. So he'd play the game by Dred's rules this time and see how that worked out. He'd never trusted anyone enough before to put his or her judgment ahead of his own.

Strange feeling, that.

"We have to get out of here and risk the lift."

The last time they made this trip, they were racing mercs. Now he had no idea what might be lurking. *Damn, her mood's gotten to me.* Trying to shake it off, he popped the access panel and dropped to the floor. Dred came directly after him, freezing as a deep, low rumble sounded nearby.

"What the frag is that?"

◄ 20 ►

Topsy-Turvy

"Hell if I know," Dred said.

She swiveled her head. The emergency lights were on down here, yet another sign that the station was falling apart. Most of the maintenance units had been stolen and disassembled for parts, so without the droids who kept the place running, systems had broken down. In this part of Perdition, it was electrical, so everything had a strange red cast, swimming in shadows. She couldn't make out the color of Jael's eyes in this light, but she could tell he was edgy, too.

"Where's it coming from?"

Dred shrugged. "All over?"

Answering growls came from everywhere, and she heard movement, but not human or even alien footfalls. No, these were claws skittering on the metal floor. She unwrapped her chains from her forearms; she hadn't bothered stashing them in the pack again. Though she wasn't positive that Silence had been rendered toothless, she did agree that stealth was pointless.

At her back, Jael braced for whatever was incoming. When the first one lumbered into sight, her eyes widened.

The aliens had hunted the station scavengers, but they never bothered Queensland. Yet . . . these creatures looked nothing like the smaller carcasses she'd glimpsed occasionally while doing recon.

Not only were these bigger, they also smelled different, rank with decay. Tumors bubbled out from their necks, worse growths on back and belly. The mottled hides shedding fur, extralong yellow teeth, and red eyes made these animals look especially horrifying. And the biggest one came up to her thigh. The lead beast went up on its hind legs and sniffed the air. Two more joined it, and two more again. More claws scratched across the floor.

"How many?" she whispered. They appeared to be surrounded but from this angle she couldn't be sure.

"Twenty? Maybe more. Fragging fast breeders. The Warren hasn't been empty that long, and there are already this many?"

"Looks like they're surviving on carrion. They probably have all manner of diseases."

"They've mutated," Jael said, low.

"Not surprising. There are *so* many spots where we've stripped off casing meant to prevent radiation leakage to repurpose it elsewhere. It's a wonder we're not mutants, too."

"Let's discuss that later," he said. "When giant rodents aren't trying to eat us."

"At least they can be cleared of having a deeper agenda."

He laughed as the first scavenger charged. The rest of the pack followed. With so many lunging mouths, it was hard to keep them all at bay, harder still to keep from being bitten. And these animals weren't trying to kill, either. As one snatched a bite out of her leg, she realized they didn't care. *They're perfectly content to eat us alive.* Nausea roiled in her stomach as she swung her chains. One hit was enough to crack their spines, but it was hard to target with so many grotesque, tumor-riddled bodies frothing around her feet.

Another bite. Another. Blood trickled down both Dred's legs.

"This isn't working," Jael shouted. Each time he lashed out with the blade, he took two or three bites to his arm, and even with his speed, he couldn't kick them fast enough.

"High ground," she panted.

Dred swept a path clear with her chains and used the wall to spring upward toward the vent they'd come out of. The metallic rim sliced her fingertips, but she managed to haul herself up, and she lowered her chain for Jael. He took a running leap, and she hauled him up, biting down on her lip to keep from showing how much her hands hurt. Winded, he landed beside her while the rodents seethed on the floor below.

"How many did we kill?"

She tried to count. "I can't tell. Five, I think."

Sighing, he got out the laser pistol. "I hope the power pack lasts long enough to thin them out. I don't have a recharge."

"Firing that thing might just bring more. Or Silence's people."

Jael grinned. "Then they can duke it out, and we'll take winners."

"Sounds like a plan." She scooted back to the far wall, giving him space.

Jael braced the weapon and took aim. His first shot dropped one, but the power meter flickered. Based on what she knew of such weapons, it looked like he had six shots left. *But maybe* . . . Well, she'd find out if that could work once he was out of options. He killed seven before the pistol went dead. Disgusted he threw it down to the remaining animals, and one of them *ate it*. The beast didn't keep it down long, though. Soon it horked the weapon back up in a pile of fetid bile and half-digested meat.

"Charming," she muttered.

"Right? I'm thinking we should take one with us, keep it as a pet."

"You're mad." But she smiled though they were trapped, had just advertised their location to anything that might be listening, and still had at least fifteen scavengers to kill.

"It's what you love best about me."

"In fact, it is not." Pressing forward, she peered over the edge and found all the rodents staring up at her with hungry red eyes. The bites on her legs stung even more. With a scowl, she touched the holes in her boots. "I can't believe they chewed right through. This is thick hide."

"Hey now, you can't say something like that and leave me hanging."

Aware she was teasing him . . . and enjoying it, she smirked. "Of course I can. Now's not the time. I'll tell you when we're safely back in the docking bay."

"That's cruel and unusual," he complained.

"And this surprises you, why?" To compensate for her reluctance to talk, she leaned over for a light kiss.

Jael turned it into something else. And he was grinning when he sat back. "True. I've always known you for a heartless princess in chains. Luckily, I find your wickedness irresistible."

"Ahem," she said. "Giant rodents? Blocking our path to Repair."

"It is a problem," he agreed.

"Well, I might have a solution."

"THAT'S crazy," Jael said, when she finished explaining her plan.

"How so? You're always saying that you're stronger than you look."

That was certainly true, but it didn't mean he wanted to bet her life on it. Jael tried to frame an argument, but he couldn't think of a better solution. And while he hesitated, more scavengers appeared, scenting a free meal. *Sod it all.*

"Fine. But if I drop you, it's on your head."

She laughed. "Pun intended?"

"*No.* That's not funny."

"Come on, it is a little. Grab my ankles."

Unable to believe he was doing this, he did as she asked and then took the pain as she fell forward with her chains. They were long enough for her to strike the ground while hanging upside down this way, but she couldn't get her usual momentum because of the weird angle. His arms were already hurting, but he only tightened his grip on her. However long it took, he'd hold until she thinned them out. In time, she got the hang of it and smashed five of their skulls.

"Pull me up," she called.

Panting, he did, and once she was safe, he uncurled his hands with a groan. Quietly she took his arm and massaged the muscle, rousing a groan of appreciation from him. Normally he'd pretend it didn't bother him, but if he did, she might stop.

"Are you all right?"

She nodded. "I think we have to do it in shifts. I get dizzy if I hang like that too long, and you look done in, too."

"I'm getting old," he muttered.

"It's my fault. You were much stronger before." Her tone was matter-of-fact, so he didn't see the need to reassure her. "We'll rest a bit, then I'll hold you next, and you can kill a few, whenever you feel ready."

"I'm not letting you dangle me upside down."

Dred raised a brow. "Why not? I did. And I'm stronger than I look, too."

After a moment of contemplation, he realized there was no good reason not to do it. *She's already proved she'll save your ass when it counts.* So he leaned back against the wall and let her rub the soreness out of his forearms. *That's totally so I can use the chains better.*

"You're spoiling me," he mumbled.

"Am I? Well, I expect the same treatment when I haul you up." Her tone was casual.

Eventually, he said, "Let's get this done."

Up top, he had no idea how disorienting it would be to kill things while hanging upside down. It made moving the chains more difficult, plus the pressure in his head was distracting. The way the scavengers leapt at him and shuffled around made it so his strikes clanged against the floor more often than not. He split four skulls once he got the hang of it, and as she hauled him up, he saw that they were eating the corpses.

Even in the shadows, he could tell that she was too pale. "What's wrong? Was I too heavy? I'll go easy on the paste."

She only shook her head, but he noticed how she curled her hands against her chest, unconsciously protective. Carefully he reached for them, demanding that she let him look with a single heated stare. Sighing faintly Dred relented and he pried her fingers open to reveal deep slices, still bleeding slightly. *It must have hurt so much holding me like this. Yet she never let go.*

"Sorry," she whispered, like it was a cause for shame.

"What were you thinking?"

"That I want us to be partners. Equal."

"Yeah, well, sometimes one person needs the other to take up the slack. I'm *not all right* with you hurting over me. Which is admittedly a mad thing to say in a place like this."

A faint smile flickered. "Maybe you do owe me a little. I've lost good days of my life nursing you."

"See? I'm clearly more troublesome. Let's see how bad it is." A preliminary inspection reassured him. "This should close up in a day or so. And I'm not just talking a scab here. We're special, you and I."

It felt so good including her in that statement. He'd been alone for so long, no way of knowing if anyone like him still existed in the universe. Jael suspected not, however, because Sci-Corp was so reluctant to dispose of him entirely. If they hadn't feared they might need samples someday, why send him to Perdition instead of a quick death? *They wouldn't do that if they had access to other Bred specimens.* It'd been a long time since that word popped into his head. *Almost got used to thinking of myself as a person, eh?*

She nodded without looking at him, and he reached out, pulling the woman he loved into his arms. To his satisfaction, she didn't resist. Dred had so few moments of actual vulnerability that this one tasted candy-sweet. It wasn't that he wanted her to be weak, quite the opposite. No, the delight came from what it signified—the fact that she trusted him enough to reveal it.

From below came the hungry snarls of animals fighting over food. "Once they've eaten their fill, they should move off, giving us a clear run to the lift."

"Seems like an accurate assessment. So this time, the smart move is to do nothing."

"I could use a little rest," Jael said.

"Too bad we can't figure out a way to sic those things on Silence. But they can't get up and down too easily."

"There are definite advantages to being bipedal. Like this, for instance." He tightened his arms around her and rested his chin on her hair. She smelled of the strong powdery soap they all used, not delicate or feminine, but the scent was better on *her* skin.

"I'm not doing you in the ducts."

He smiled faintly. "I know. This is enough. Just this."

◀ 21 ▶

A Pox on Their Houses

Eventually, the scavengers finished their feast and scuttled off, leaving three carcasses chewed all the way down to the bone. Dred waited a few minutes longer and jumped down. Her fingers had scabbed over while they were waiting, giving her respite from the throbbing. But she didn't regret taking her turn, no matter what Jael thought.

Not trying to be quiet, she raced down the corridor, with Jael close behind. The lift doors stood open, and she skidded inside, pressing the button that would deliver them to the repair bay. With a groan and a shudder, the mechanism kicked into motion, but as they descended, the box jerked and strained, heaving and dropping in unsteady judders, until the lights went out entirely.

"Shit." She could see in the dark better than most, but . . .

"On second thought, possibly it wasn't the best idea to take the lift when this part of the station is on emergency power," Jael said.

A quiet chuckle escaped her. "If only we'd considered that before getting on. How far down do you think we are?"

"No idea. But this is starting to feel like a heroic quest."

"With all the obstacles between us and the artifact we must retrieve to save the world?" Dred admired his imaginative bent, especially at a time like this.

"Our own hides anyway."

"Close enough. There must be an emergency hatch up top. Boost me up?" In answer he wrapped his arms around her thighs and lifted. "A little higher if you can."

"You know I'm not the big man, right? Any more, and you'll be on my shoulders."

"That could work. Set me down."

Though Jael grumbled, he let her clamber up, then somehow he managed to straighten without them toppling over. Balancing wasn't easy, but now she could reach the ceiling. Dred felt around until she discovered the latch. Flipping it open meant getting conked on the head; she took the hit on her skull, and the impact made them wobble. As Jael stumbled toward the wall, she leapt from his shoulders and grappled for the top of the lift. This time she didn't cut up her fingers worse, but the scabs broke open, making it hard to hold on. Practically tearing out her nails, she scrambled up and flopped over on her side, breathing hard.

"Hey," Jael called. "Still in need of extraction down here, yeah?"

"I wouldn't forget you. It's marvelous how handy these are." She lowered her chains and braced, so he could climb. The resultant burn in her arms echoed in her injured hands, the blood flowing freely. Fortunately, they were small cuts, not enough for the loss to weaken her too much, only make a mess.

"You've got my vote," he said, surveying the area. "Looks like there's a ladder."

"Then let's get moving."

"Not so fast. It's a long way down." Jael tore a strip from his shirt and wrapped Dred's hands with a practiced touch.

"Thanks. That'll help me hold on."

"Let me know if you bleed through, all right?"

"I promise. Doubt I will. As long as I don't have to do

any more stunt jumps, this should scab over again pretty fast. How're your bites feeling?" She was asking because her legs felt sore and hot where the rodents had gouged out her flesh.

"Not great." From him, that was tantamount to admission of a problem. "But it's too dark for me to see the damage, though."

"Likewise. You want to go first, or should I?"

"I will," Jael said.

He made the leap from the top of the lift to the rungs affixed to the side of the wall look graceful and easy. Conscious of how clumsy she could be with makeshift bandages on her hands, Dred hesitated and only moved once she was sure it wouldn't hurt him if she fell. She hit the metal handholds with a clang and almost slipped, but his hand came up, clamping onto her calf with an unshakable resolve.

"I'm fine, you can let go."

Without arguing, he did.

It was a tight squeeze downward; this shaft wasn't meant for normal use. From what she could tell, it had only been included for emergency maintenance; it ran parallel to the lift space and offered floor access every fifty meters or so. She tried counting as they climbed, but Dred soon lost track of where they were.

"How are we supposed to know when we're far enough down?" Jael asked eventually.

Though her arms were tired, that wasn't a good gauge of how long they'd been climbing. It had already been a long-ass day, between the Silent, the scavengers, then complete mechanical failure. So she couldn't trust her own body to estimate distance, and the darkness made it impossible to read any markers that might've been posted for Monsanto workers.

"We should probably get back to the station proper and look for the stairs," she said.

"On it."

She found a hatch, forced it open, then edged into a tiny crawl space that eventually widened to a small landing, blocked by a blast door. There was a security panel, but thanks to the power outage, it was blinking a NO SERVICE alert. She swore.

"With no power, shouldn't this have opened?" she muttered.

"Today's not our lucky day, love."

With no way to cut through this much metal, they retraced their steps back to the emergency ladder. This time Dred went first; they climbed to the next tier and tried again. *Same obstacle.* By then, her arms ached like mad, but she couldn't be the first to complain or ask for quarter. Besides, it wasn't like anybody was coming to save them. So even if she felt strange and dizzy, hot and sick . . . *Well, suck it up, weakling.*

She started to shove past to the crawl space, but Jael pulled her back. "If we're trapped, we still will be in a couple of hours."

"You suck at pep talks. We'll also be hungrier and more dehydrated."

"Did you check the bag Calypso sent with us? We have a packet of paste to share and a bottle of water. When we get back, remind me to thank her."

AT first, Jael didn't think Dred would go for a rest break. But eventually she relaxed and let him draw her against the blast door that was currently blocking their path. Its sturdy presence also meant nobody could get at them, so they could sleep like they were locked up in the docking bay. He didn't actually expect her to close her eyes, but she leaned her head against his shoulder.

More than I thought.

"Give me the paste. Might as well top off if we're taking a breather."

He ripped it open and watched her suck down half of it. Then she passed it over, and he drained the rest. "Water?"

"Thanks."

She was careful with that, he noted, taking only a few swallows. They could both get by much longer without food than fluids. The emergency lights flickered, giving a low-wattage strobe. With a faint sigh, he pulled up his pant leg to survey the damage. As expected, small chunks of flesh were missing, but more disturbing? The damage to surrounding skin; it was already turning black, and yellow ooze trickled out of each wound. His armpits were sore, too, and when he pressed, the glands seemed to be swollen.

Worried, he touched Dred's cheek and found it burning hot, dry and tight. He compared it to his own and tipped his head back to accuse the ceiling. "Seriously?"

She was already a little out of it, or she would've noticed on her own. He checked her over and found hard lumps forming faster, not just in her armpits. That meant her immune system was a few paces behind. That made sense since the abilities he'd shared probably didn't divide neatly down the middle. But it also scared the shit out of him. Cranky, she batted his hands away.

"Hurts," she mumbled.

Not wanting to scare her, he said softly, "Sorry. Get some rest."

"You should sleep, too."

"I will." There was no way in hell.

We caught the damned plague from those mutant sewer beasts. It's probably contagious. Which meant even if they could find their way out—and that was a question, considering how weak they both were—they shouldn't go back and expose the others. *We'll either survive this with a bottle of water and no medicine, or we die together. Right, then.*

At this point, he couldn't remember which mad Queenslander had said it—his head was fuzzy and aching—but he recalled the sentiment well enough. *Sometimes it feels like the station itself is sentient, like it's trying to kill us.* He'd dismissed that as paranoid nonsense but now that Perdition was nearly a lifeless void, and it was still finding ways to test his admittedly superhuman survival skills, it was hard to ignore.

"I never meant to hurt you." Her voice was clear as a bell, but her eyes were shut.

He had the feeling she wasn't talking to him. Yet . . . "Why?"

"You were collateral damage," she whispered.

Despite the pounding in his head, he still snapped to attention. This prickled his nerves as a secret she'd kept to herself, a story she probably wouldn't share if she were in her right mind. Because he was an awful bastard, he encouraged, "Was I?"

She nodded, cheek gliding against the rough cloth of his shirt. Her face looked a little softer, too, as if she wasn't such a hardened killer in these memories. "Nobody believed me about your brother, not even you."

"I should have."

"Yes. You know how many people he hurt?"

"Not really. You should tell me."

"Dead people don't remember anything," she mumbled.

"Remind me." *Yeah, I'll probably burn in hell for this.*

"I'm so sorry, Cedric." For long moments, she was quiet and he thought she'd succumbed to deeper sleep, but then she whispered, "I'm sorry I never loved you—that I pretended. But it was close, you were so kind. Too gentle, truly."

Jael had never been accused of that; his savagery ran bone deep. Maybe he didn't want to hear this story after all. As he registered the misgivings, she slumped against him. A palm against her forehead told him her fever had spiked. He had no idea how long illnesses like this took to reach critical levels, but she was definitely progressing faster than him.

I need to cool her down, but I can't waste our water.

Nothing in his life prepared him for the sheer helplessness and terror of holding Dred's limp body in his arms and having no way to help her. He couldn't call for backup. There was no way out, only an endless descent into darkness, and he couldn't carry her. *Too weak. We'll both fall.* An awful voice whispered, *It would be quicker.*

Shivering, he pulled her into his lap. The fact that he felt cold now instead of hot meant he was getting worse. Jael tilted his head against hers and couldn't tell who was hotter.

She reached for him with fitful hands, moaning as he held her tighter, and something between them burst. One of the lumps, probably, and it carried the stench of the beasts that had bitten them, a putrid syrup that felt sticky on his skin.

He had been to recovery hell so many times, lived through impossible wounds and purified himself of incurable ailments. Yet it didn't matter right then because even if he made it, *she* might not, and in this flashing darkness, that felt like a fate worse than death. If cutting himself open and letting her drink his blood could save her, Jael would've done it. But it probably wouldn't since he was infected, too.

Trembling, he wrapped his arms around her, his whole body, and they toppled sideways before the blast door. His lashes flickered in time to the guttering emergency lights, showing him the same scene, again, again, the rusted gray metal of the floor, the curve of her cheek, painted red with the awful fever, the ragged tumble of her hair over his arm.

His eyes shut.

Don't care, he thought. *Live or die. As long as I'm with you.*

◀ 22 ▶

Mission Impossible

When Dred woke, her lips were like two slashes of leather, and her whole body hurt. Once, not too long after her arrest, she'd incited a riot in gen pop without getting away fast enough. The enraged crowd had knocked her down, trampled her. *And I didn't feel this bad when I woke up in the infirmary two days later.* Now, everything was dark, and at first, she thought she'd gone blind.

Then she realized her eyelids were fused shut with some kind of gluey secretion. With trembling hands, she scraped the gunk away from her eyes until she could open them. The emergency lights were still on, and she had no idea how long she'd been out. Jael was curled up on his side, and the floor seemed to be smeared with . . . something. Since it was dried, she couldn't be sure, but it smelled like blood.

Next, she realized her body was covered in open sores. Some had scabbed over, and others were still oozing. She'd never felt worse in her whole life. Her aching throat demanded water, so she rummaged through the bag until she found the bottle. From the look of it, neither one of them had had anything to drink since they'd eaten the paste. *When was that?* She sipped, then put it down, worried about Jael.

Rolling him over took most of her strength. At first glance, he looked dead. His face was skeletal, eyes sunken with dehydration, and new lines had formed on his dried skin. He, too, had the sores all over him, and she couldn't tell if he was breathing. Dizzily, she leaned down, setting her ear to his chest. The thumps were so slow and faint that it took her a couple of minutes to be certain it wasn't her own pulse echoing in her ears.

Supporting his head, she tipped some water into his mouth and rubbed his throat so he'd swallow instead of choke. At this point, she'd taken care of him more than anyone in the world, but it was mutual. *We just keep saving each other.* This time, however, she couldn't see the way out. They didn't have the supplies for a complete recovery, and climbing down while they were so weak seemed like suicide. Likewise, they weren't strong enough to break through the blast door, either. She couldn't fathom a solution to this problem.

Dred didn't know how long it was before he stirred in her arms. He had the same trouble with his eyes, but once they opened, she could tell he was lucid. Wincing, Jael struggled upright, and she knew too well how sore he felt. Just this much exertion left him shaky, and fury flashed in his blue eyes over the unaccustomed weakness.

"Ridiculous," he muttered. "They're *rodents*."

"The better question is how to get out of this."

He shook his head. "I wish I knew."

"If we pop the panel, will cutting the right wire make the door disengage?"

"Hell if I know," Jael said. "But it's worth a try."

He struggled on his hands and knees, then made it to a standing position. She handed him her boot knife. After a little tinkering, he managed to get into the panel, but it didn't look like she expected it to inside. Beneath, there were no loose wires, just the smooth metal of pressure chips.

Security wasn't her specialty, but she felt fairly sure that they needed current to open the door. Dred stared up at the flickering emergency light.

Jael sighed and rested his head on the wall. "We're stuck."

"We could try pulling the emergency light down and touching the live wires to the inside of the panel."

"Whoever does it will probably be electrocuted."

"It's my idea. I'll—"

"Forget it," he said. "Hand me your chain."

She did as he asked. Maybe she should protest his determination to take all the damage, but since she didn't even know if she could stand up, it seemed wrong to offer false assurances. As Dred watched, he slammed the emergency light, so sparks sprayed out, and the bulb shattered. On the downside, the landing was plunged into complete darkness. Jael cried out.

"Shit, are you all right?" Somehow she was on her feet, wobbling toward him blindly.

"Stay back." The words came from between clenched teeth. "Don't touch me."

She heard him thumping at the wall, then the crackling of a live wire. Electricity sprayed in an arc from the tip of the broken wire, highlighting his features. His mouth was a flat white line, but he kept pulling. *Please don't let the cable break. Please let it stretch far enough.* He pulled and pulled, getting closer to the panel. Then the wire just . . . stopped. Dred just *knew* if he forced it, he'd yank it out entirely, and it wouldn't work.

Without asking his thoughts, she grabbed his arm and pulled it straight. The shock nearly made her open her hands. *No, I'm doing this. If he can take it, I can.* After that first jolt, numbness flooded her, which was probably worse. Her body felt like it was filled with hot metal, and her arm weighed a metric ton. Yet even as her shoulder screamed, she raised it and leaned, leaned, then, at last, she slammed her palm onto the pressure plate.

The door snicked open.

Dred let go, collapsing before the glorious crack, and she bathed her face in the rush of cool, fresh air. Jael fell over next to her, pulling the gap wider. She couldn't tell how badly he was injured, but he must be burned. Reaching out in the dark, she took his hand and got another little shock. His fingers were curled; he couldn't seem to open them. He pulled away before she could explore the extent of the damage.

"Let's go," he said hoarsely. "The others have probably given us up for dead by now."

She picked up the bag and found it almost heavier than she could carry. "They have more faith in us than that." Bravado was all she had as she pushed through the door.

IT took some wandering before they found the stairs. Jael recalled fighting his way down them when the mercs were after them, but now it was as much as he could manage just putting one foot in front of the other. On the next level, a surviving sector directory told them it was another five flights to Repair at the bottom.

"How are we going to carry everything back?" he asked quietly.

Dred didn't answer. Her breath came quick and fast, pained little pants, as she stumbled down the steps after him. His chest hurt, too. Everything did, really. It would be so easy to fall down and not get up. *Tired. Hungry. Thirsty.* The litany of silent complaints occupied him for another flight. There, he took the bag from Dred and dug out the water bottle.

"Rest break," he said, taking a swig.

"Last time you said that, we passed out for Mary knows how long."

"I'll be stricter this time. No lolling around on my watch, Devos."

In the flicker of the emergency lights, he saw her smile flash. "I'm surprised you remember my last name."

"I remember everything when it comes to you." She didn't

seem to realize that he had a hard time forgetting *anything* but for once, his freakish recall made somebody happy. "Right, moving on."

She seemed grateful that he didn't linger over the emotional revelation. *Mary, I don't have the energy.* Pushing forward required all his reserves, and by the time they got down to the level designed for repair, he was shaking all over. Between the residual sickness and the electrocution, Jael couldn't believe he was still upright.

You know this is for you, yeah, love? You're always making me do impossible things.

Jael hoped like hell they didn't run into any of Silence's killers. He didn't have the speed or the strength to drive them off, and Dred was no better off. They both needed a week of good food, clean water, and uninterrupted sleep, but this was Perdition, so they'd be lucky to get a day and a half of rest, a packet of paste, and to escape drinking their own urine. *Which is most assuredly not sterile.*

His vision sparkled with the lights and darks that meant he was close to passing out. So he paused, ostensibly to let Dred catch up. She leaned on the wall for support as they finally left the stairs and stepped into the internal corridors again. The repair bay stood open, courtesy of their last raid. And he doubted anyone else had been down here since the slaughter in the upper reaches of the station.

"I don't even remember what we came for," Dred whispered.

"Glad Vost made a list."

Focus. This is what we need to get off station . . . it's the last step.

The bay seemed cleaner down here, less close than it had been in the ducts and definitely the lift shaft. He fiddled with the circuits and managed to reroute power, so the main lights came up. Dred let out a relieved sigh, but the brightness also let him see just how sick she was. Her lips had cracked with dryness, and she had the look of a living corpse. Open lesions mottled her arms, probably beneath her clothes, too. A quick inspection assured him he didn't fare any better beneath closer scrutiny.

"We look like hell, huh?" she said ruefully.

"More than. On the bright side, by the time we lug all this junk back to the docking bay, we should be past the infectious stage."

Dred touched her forehead, then his. "The fever's broken, along with the lumps. So, hopefully, we already are."

"That would be a bright spot, yeah?" *Seems more likely we'd carry the plague back and watch the others die, given how our luck's been lately.* But apparently he'd internalized Martine's superstition about not predicting awful things out loud because he ate that thought.

She nodded. "I'll take this side of the bay. Anything we locate, call it out, so we'll know to stop looking."

"Sounds good."

What should've taken only a little while stretched into a momentous endeavor because they kept needing to rest. *Sucks when bending over makes you winded.* Dred didn't complain, though, so he didn't, either. Somehow, her opinion of him had become more important than anything else. That should've scared the shit out of him . . . and once it would have. Once, it might've even driven him to betray her to Vost or even to Silence, because Dred could hurt him in ways that superseded the physical. This woman had the power to scorch and salt his soul so that nothing could ever grow.

But she won't.

There was no science to explain his surety. But he would've taken this conviction to the bank for a loan. He caught her eye as she tumbled forward on hands and knees, trying to pick up something Vost needed. An abortive moment—his first instinct was to help, but her icy glare said that would be a mistake. On her own, she struggled and hauled the part to the center of the bay, along with the small pile of junk they'd already identified.

Sod this. How the hell can we get back like this, hauling

gear? The return would be a gauntlet—all those stairs, the corridor they had to cross, then the ducts? *Forget it.* With this much junk, it would be open hallways, the whole way. He was tempted to say frag the whole mission, but then their chances of getting off Perdition went down dramatically. Each time they popped out of the docking bay, they risked Silence's taking them down.

"What the hell is that for?"

She shrugged. "If I knew how to build a shuttle from scrap parts, I wouldn't be doing grunt work to pay for my ride off station, would I?"

He laughed. "I love how honest you are."

"You know what they say—the truth is a weapon too sharp for most."

"I never heard anyone say that."

"Yeah, well, you don't get out much. For the last hundred turns, you've been touring all the best prisons."

Jael was about to joke back when a noise jerked his gaze to the door.

◄ 23 ►

Last Resort

Silence's trained killers stood watching. There was a tentative air about them, and Dred wondered why they'd given up the advantage, showing themselves instead of trying to attack from behind. She glanced around.

Well, we're in the middle of the room, lights up. They probably had no chance of a silent kill. Frag. The only way this could be worse is if Silence steps out from behind them.

Laughable. On her best day, she could take this many on her own. Now she'd be hard-pressed to end one before they disemboweled her or cut her throat with their fine-wire garrotes. *I'm too weak to use my chains.* Jael took two steps forward, putting himself between her and them.

Not again. They take you over my dead body.

"Don't," she said.

"If this is my time, so be it." He offered his sharp, lovely smile. "I'm not even sorry I was sent here when I tally everything I've lost and gained."

"Bullshit." She planted herself beside him, pretending her knees weren't full of water and that a cold sweat hadn't broken out on her brow just from that movement. "Why aren't they attacking?"

"Maybe they have orders to take me alive, like that first group."

"Doesn't explain why they aren't coming after *me*, though." An idea came to her, ridiculous and far-fetched as it could possibly be.

I've never done that before. Never tried.

But physical conflict resolution was out of the question. *And I'm left with the last resort.* Closing her eyes, she called up all her mental reserves. First she read the watching killers and found not the red of rage but the yellow of sickness. Jael shone with it about the edges, blue for calm inside, but at the heart, he'd turned a rosy pink. *Sorry. I didn't mean to invade your privacy.*

But she didn't think he'd mind in the name of survival.

She gathered all the softness, every gentle and tender thought she'd ever entertained. It swelled at the core of her, white-hot with sweetness, then she let it go like a balloon grown too big to hold. Since she'd never used her gift this way before, she had no control and no certainty. But these emotions should broadcast the same as hate and rage.

Right?

She opened her eyes, half expecting to find herself bleeding out and Jael taken.

But, instead, they were all staring at her with wide, glassy eyes, mouths gaping and slack. Her head pounded so hard, she could barely hear herself speak. She had no idea how long this would hold, if it would be enough to get them back safely. But for now . . .

"I could use your help," she said carefully.

The killers all understood universal; she could tell by the way their heads cocked. Dred strangled a half-hysterical laugh. *I've stolen Silence's minions.* Unfortunately, she'd also robbed Jael of his free will, too, because he was gazing at her with that same rapt attention, as if she were a goddess incarnate in human flesh. None of them reacted, however, apart from waiting for her next words.

"I'm looking for some things. If I tell you what they are, would you help me find them?"

All six of the eager acolytes nodded. She listed off the remaining objects, and the killers ran with incredible alacrity to do her bidding. Maybe that wasn't such a surprise, Silence had them conditioned to follow orders. Jael moved slower because he was weak, and she tried to get him to stop but he shook her off with a bright smile.

"I want to help." His eyes were terrifying and blank and shining with something that was definitely not love or joy.

Her stomach churned. *He'll snap out of it. Of course he will. I've seen him shake off tons of damage that would've killed anyone else, and the rioters never had brain damage.*

Well. That I inflicted.

A gloomy voice whispered, *But those were physical wounds. What do you know about his mind anyway?*

"Okay then. We'll work together," she said gently.

His expression lit up like sunrise, but there was an awful emptiness to it. She'd received smiles from him before, and they felt nothing like this. But with so much assistance, it didn't take long at all until they located all the gear. Every minute, she kept waiting for them all to shake it off; and then she'd have to see if she had enough juice to put them under again.

So far, so good.

"I have a lot of things to move. Could you carry them for me?" Keeping her requests, or commands, rather, simple seemed like the best move.

In response, the Silent gathered up all their parts and waited. Jael tried, but she put a hand on his arm, and whispered, "Not you. Just walk with me."

He beamed at her.

So sorry about this, you have no idea.

She'd used her broadcast abilities very little since becoming the Dread Queen, mostly because she couldn't control the rioting. Until meeting Jael, it would've never occurred to her that she could also use it for peaceful ends. Since she'd overwritten their free will, it was still fairly disgusting, but better than ending up with her innards splattered on a wall. Plus, Silence had already wrecked these poor bastards anyway.

Yeah, keep rationalizing.

She took one last look around and couldn't see anything that would be remotely useful. So she said, "Let's go."

They moved out as a unit and started the long march up the stairs. Dred set the pace, so it wouldn't tax Jael too much. And if she was being honest, she had no breath to spare. Her lungs felt tight, and by now, even her hair hurt, like it was too heavy for her scalp.

It made her nervous, leaving the Silent at her back, but if they shook her emotional control, they'd make a hell of a lot of noise dropping all the junk to get at their weapons.

That gives us ten seconds, max.

THE last thing Jael remembered, they were in the repair bay, about to fight a losing battle. Next thing he knew, he was shambling along a hallway with Dred using the Silent as beasts of burden. She wasn't paying him any attention until he said, "What the hell."

"You're back." A long sigh slid out of her. "Sorry about that."

"What?"

"For sapping your free will, mostly."

"Holy shit." The throbbing in his head reminded him of the worst hangover he had ever suffered. Generally, liquor didn't affect him much, but once he'd swilled some crazy alien booze and wound up in a coma for half a day. And when he woke, well, his skull felt about like it did now—as if somebody had scooped out his brain with a spoon, put it in a food mixer, and poured it back in.

"So . . . they're on our side?" He studied the killer closest to them, and the sod did seem to be completely docile. The group marched two by two, with Dred and Jael bringing up the rear.

"Right now they are. I'm not sure how long it'll last. But it got us up the stairs, and from what I can tell, about half-way to the docking bay. I'm not sure the good feelings will survive fighting their cohorts, though."

"You're amazing," Jael said.

"Huh?"

"Why didn't you just enact a bloodless coup all over the station and make the inmates worship you? No fighting, no killing, no territory scuffles."

Her chin dropped. "Before I met you, it never would've occurred to me to try."

"You pick *right now* to tell me I'm the truest love you've ever known?"

"Shut up," she muttered. "You're lucky I said it at all. Ever."

"So what do we do about your pets?"

"I have no idea. The cautious move would be to kill them before they snap out of it, but then I don't know if we can haul the stuff back on our own."

"If it's any help, I don't think Silence has too many more minions. We've thinned them out pretty well."

"A handful then," she said glumly. "Just enough to kill us."

"That's not like you."

"Sorry. I feel like shit."

He couldn't argue that. Jael's body hurt in places even Silence hadn't managed to injure. The sores had formed in the worst possible crevasses, then split, seeped, crusted over, and popped fully, leaving his skin covered with a mess he couldn't wait to wash off. *Forget fancy food and fine clothing. A shower, just a shower would be enough right now.* The promise of it kept him moving, and they didn't speak of killing their pack mules again. If the Silent turned, then they'd fight. Otherwise, it made sense to gamble on getting as close to the docking bay as possible.

"At least the rodents can't get to us up here," Dred muttered.

He considered not mentioning her slip, but if he didn't,

and these assholes opened their throats five meters down the hall, he'd wish he knew the answer as he bled out. So Jael said, "When you were delirious, you called me Cedric."

"Shit. Did I?"

"What was that about?"

Dred sighed. One of the Silent turned to look and she gave him a smile that Jael guessed was meant to be re-assuring, but he found it slightly alarming. "You want that story, huh?"

"You know a lot of mine."

"That's fair. I met Cedric early in my hunting career. He was a good man. Naïve but well-intentioned. I'm sure you've met the type."

"They don't tend to last long," he said.

She nodded, eyes on the floor. "I was hunting his brother. Who was neither gentle nor kind. They came from money, those two. Parents were never around, so they filled the void in various ways. For Cedric, it was philanthropy. He was always trying to free something or save something or—well, you get the gist."

"Sounds like you admired him." He nearly chewed the words in getting them out, so they came out strange and bitter-tasting.

"Reluctantly. I thought he was an idiot but . . ." She trailed off and shook her head. "Anyway, I used him. I got myself invited to a benefit he was hosting because I wanted to get closer to his brother. I'd tried trailing him, but Car-mine was a top-notch predator. Women went missing in his orbit, but he always had an alibi. And he always sensed when I was watching, so I couldn't find his bolt-hole on my own."

"And you thought it was a good idea to get personal?" Equal parts impressed and dismayed, he didn't know what else to say.

"Yeah. As Cedric's love interest, I finally pinged on Carmine's radar as prey. You've no idea how hard that cha-rade was, either."

Jael had the sense there was a lot she wasn't saying. "The pretending?"

"I was faking everything. Background, interests, personality. But it worked. Carmine became obsessed by the idea of taking something precious from his perfect brother."

"You."

"Exactly."

"But it went wrong, didn't it?" She wouldn't have nightmares about it otherwise.

"Impressively so. Cedric showed up at the wrong time, just as Carmine made his move. We fought, and Cedric . . ."

"Was collateral damage."

Dred let out a slow sigh. "I said a lot when I was feverish, huh? There comes a point where pretense and reality overlap. Kneeling there with his blood on my hands, it felt like I'd lost someone I loved though that wasn't true. I was just playing the part. So maybe it hurt because I thought it was supposed to?"

"I'm not the one to explain it," he muttered.

"That was one crime they never added to my sentence. Because I didn't kill Carmine Genaro. His brother did. Poor Cedric had a knife in his gut, and he yanked it out, blood everywhere. Rammed it right through Carmine's heart. Home-security footage caught everything, so I walked." She looked over at him. "I never felt right about that."

The clang of the first Silent dropping his burden cut short whatever Jael might've said.

◀ 24 ▶

The Worm Turns

Everyone but Keelah was assembled in the control room. Tam paced to the door and back, then locked his gaze on the static feed. The force field was still intact while the blast doors offered another layer of protection, so they hadn't been bothered. No sign of Dred or Jael. While their salvage mission ran longer and longer, he'd worked alongside the merc commander on the ship, but they were stalled now. Without the required parts, the provisional craft wouldn't last long out there. While Tam did think it would be better to starve in space than die on Perdition, he still preferred to give any plan a hundred percent, no matter how long the odds.

Vost had managed to hack a few other camera feeds, but so far they hadn't spotted anything. The majority of station surveillance equipment delivered only white noise and a blank screen these days. Still, Vost flicked through the operational units like it was his religious conviction. Tam knew how he felt.

"They're probably dead," Duran mumbled.

Tam was about to punch him in the head, but Calypso

got there first. The former mistress of the circle used her full strength, too, so the merc was rubbing his jaw when he scrambled away. Martine threatened him with an upraised arm, but Tam gave her a look that said, *Save the good stuff for me.* She grinned a little, despite the somber mood.

"I didn't expect it to take this long," Vost said. "They've probably run into trouble."

"Duh," Martine snapped.

Tam went on, "The main question is, what should we do about it? The longer we wait, the more dire the consequences could be."

"Problem is, we have no fragging idea where they are," Calypso said.

"And the station is huge," Duran added.

"Do you think Silence has them?" Vost asked.

"If she does, then they're as good as dead. We should send another team to Repair and say a few words for them." Duran didn't seem to understand how stupid he was being.

Tam looked at Calypso.

"Look, son, you're warm, fairly clean. Not the best I ever had in my bunk, but for right now, you'll do. That said, keep talking that way, and I will twist your head right off your neck. What part of *these two are our friends* do you not understand?" She snarled and flung herself into a chair next to Vost. "And they call *me* a heartless criminal."

"So . . . rescue mission?" Duran tried.

"Someone has to stay to hold down the fort," Martine pointed out.

That was when the session broke down, however, because Duran didn't want to go back out and fight, Vost couldn't, both Calypso and Martine did, but they couldn't agree on where the team should start looking. Tam listened to everyone bicker for a solid ten minutes, then he just got up and left.

The others didn't notice.

He found Keelah in the dormitory, just sitting quietly. She glanced up as he came in. "The war council seems to be going well."

"Funny. You can hear everything from in here?"

She nodded. "If I had something to contribute, I'd be in there, of course."

"Seems like something is bothering you, besides Dred and Jael."

"You're an astute man," she said.

"I have my moments." *Not as many as I used to, however.* Regret was a raw wound in his chest for everyone he'd failed in getting this far. *Ike and Einar were supposed to be here, too.* But he'd lost all ability to predict cause and effect when the mercs showed up. None of his long-term strategies allowed for external interference. He'd eventually planned to hijack a supply ship and get off Perdition, but his schemes would never come to fruition.

Since Vost got here, I'm reacting, not planning. That's a loser's game.

"If you knew something, and it changed everything, would you tell the world? Or would you hug the knowledge to your chest and wait for the right moment to strike?"

"That's too general for me to give you good counsel, Keelah. Some context?" Watching her, Tam tried to gauge if she knew something about Jael and Dred, but he couldn't tell.

"No," she said softly. "I think I'll make this decision on my own."

VOST whirled when Calypso pointed at the monitor, words babbling out of her faster than he could understand. To his astonishment, he saw their lost lambs stumbling down the corridor toward the force field—and they weren't alone. For unknown reasons, they had Silence's killers carrying their gear. As soon as they realized, the others bolted from the control room.

Before he could follow, Keelah slipped inside and closed the door. She paused for a few seconds, studying him. "Why did you give me the codes?"

"Because I owe you some recompense. My arrival intensified the conflict here, and you lost your mate. I admit my culpability."

"You think a gesture can make it right? Because I'm from a civilized culture. We're known to be tolerant and gentle, patient and kind."

"I don't know that much about your society," he admitted.

"Of course not. Why would you? My kind have been banished from New Terra, and when did humans ever learn anything that didn't benefit them in some way?" She crept a little closer, and he recognized the gleam in her eyes.

Pure hate.

"Do you despise the others this much?"

"Sometimes," she said. "Because they're all monsters, that's why they were sent here. Whereas I just look different."

In that moment, Vost suspected he had miscalculated, misread this female badly. He'd thought that by giving her the codes, he could win her trust—make her see him as an ally. The fact that she'd be antagonized by the move? Impossible to predict. And now that she was coldly furious, she had no reason to spare him. He'd whispered away his leverage.

"So kill me," he said then. Opening his shirt, he showed her what he had been keeping secret from everyone but Dred. While the wounds were no longer quite so infected, they weren't healing, either. His stamina was shot, and he spiked fevers on down cycle.

Instinct told him he wouldn't last a long space journey anyway.

Keelah stilled. She'd probably smelled the gangrenous tissue before now. For whatever reason, she hadn't spoken of it.

"I have two requests, however."

"I'm listening."

"First, promise me you'll find my son. He's in a hospital . . ." His voice thickened as he told her where to find the person he loved most in the world. "I can't protect him anymore, so please . . . if there's any kindness left in you, do it for me."

He couldn't allow his thoughts to formulate properly. If he did, his intentions would crystallize for her. Her senses were acute and inhuman. So he made sure his mind was blank as he regarded her. *Say the words. Believe them. This is all true. I'm dying. This is my surrender.*

"Why would you trust an enemy to rear your young?"

"Because I want him to know better. Teach him everything that I don't know. Help him become a better man than his father."

"Are you trying to evoke sympathy, merc? It won't work."

He shook his head. "You can see I'm terminal, right? Smell it, too. I'm dying by centimeters, and I'd rather not go out slow."

"Is that your other request?"

"Yes, please. Make it quick. But first . . ." As she watched warily, he reached into his pocket and pulled out the framed holo. Vost stared at the looping image for several long moments before exhaling in a shuddering sigh. *My son. I'm sorry.* He offered it to her in a slow, careful gesture, and when she reached for it, he let go.

From the way her whiskers twitched, she'd expected him to try something. Keelah studied the face. "He doesn't look much like you."

Vost smiled. "Lucky kid, huh?"

"Is he ill?"

"That's why I ended up in this hellhole." When she frowned, he clarified, "To pay for his treatments. I've been gone so long now, though . . . the hospital may have cut him off."

"Surely even humans couldn't be so cruel," she murmured.

"Remember what you've seen us do here and say it again."

Keelah opened her mouth, but as Vost suspected, she couldn't. Instead, she produced a dagger. "I was saving this for myself. Every morning that I wake up without Katur, I think, is this the day I use it?"

"What's special about it?"

"It's one of Silence's paralyzing poison blades. No pain."

Vost nodded, closing his eyes. "Then I'm honored you're giving it to me."

Listening to the light patter of her approach, he waited until she was on top of him, then he whipped his hand out with lightning reflexes and snagged her wrist. It took no effort at all for a professional merc to disarm her and jab her lightly with the blade. She shuddered and went stiff in his arms. *Nobody will see a tiny cut beneath her fur.*

Sorry, Keelah. I'm not as sick as I pretended. And nothing will keep me from my son.

He dropped her body, and shouted, "Come quickly! Keelah's collapsed."

SILENCE opened her mouth in a voiceless scream. *Too late, I am too late.* Not only had she failed to liberate her lover from the enemy, but Death himself was most displeased. She found five of her Silent murdered, no sign they had even raised their weapons. For such a grievous loss, Death must have abandoned her.

But if I am not Death's Handmaiden, what am I? If I am beloved of no one, who am I?

I am a lowly worm. Entrails. Carrion. Dead things, devoid of spirit.

Silence crumpled to the ground beside the last of her followers. She touched their skin and hair, and there was no joy in it. These deaths were ugly and unconsecrated. Nothing good or righteous could be born from it. She did not want their skin or hair or teeth. They must be left to rot as if their gifts meant nothing.

My beloved has forsaken me. I am nothing.

The enemy had razed her holdings and destroyed the precious medicines that let her survive this infernal place. Now there was only unhallowed death, the small and pitiful kind, beyond her master's sight. She stared at her own hands. Blinked once. Twice.

These are not my hands. SOMEONE HAS STOLEN MY

SKIN AND BONES. But she could not make the cry; she had sworn silence in honor of the grim one, long before she became the word, crawled inside it like a tomb that let out no light. The reality did not change. Her hands were old, somehow, weathered and crepey, lined and spotted, and when she lifted them to touch her cheeks, they felt the same.

No.

The word rose up as she did. *This is some awful trick. Death has granted me eternal youth and beauty.* While she might be alone now, completely unaided, forsaken by love and death alike, there was always a path for the faithful. *I will make this up to you,* she told Death. *I will make an offering unprecedented. Once more you will come to me and stand at my shoulder. I'm sorry, Lord. The bright one turned my head.*

"Show me," Death said.

When Silence turned, she found the master at her shoulder. A sharp smile cut free of her, cracking the peeling paint of her face—or perhaps it was her skin. Only she could walk with the grim one and still feel the steady thump of her heart in her chest. *I need no minions for this.* She knew what to do now, and the idea was sheer perfection. He would forgive her, raise her up.

I will rule beside you forever.

"Will you tell me your plan?" Death whispered.

She shook her head, all giddy delight. It had been so long since she imagined anything so wonderful. *Let them hide like insects. I need not see their faces while they burn.* Now she had the whole station for her own, and she ran down the empty, echoing corridors. Death whispered in her wake, ever present, ever beautiful.

I'll surprise you.

◀ 25 ▶

A Long Silence

Everything happened so fast, Dred could hardly process it.

The others killed their porters, then hauled all the gear into the docking bay while Calypso and Martine asked a hundred questions at the same time, mostly related to how ravaged they looked. When the two acted like they might get close enough to touch, she scrambled back. Jael kept pace beside her, and they moved to the other side of the room.

"Just a precaution," she said

"Are you sick?" Duran looked like he wanted to suggest something awful, but he didn't say anything else.

Mostly because at that moment, Vost shouted, "Come quickly, Keelah's collapsed."

She wanted to go with them, but her scant medical knowledge didn't outweigh the risk of contagion. So she and Jael watched as they ran to the control room. She let out a sigh and slumped against the far wall. Jael collapsed beside her, tilting his head back.

"It's not because of us," he said. "Hell, we didn't get near her."

"I know. Do you believe in omens, though?"

"Shit happens. Usually there's a reason, but often we don't get to know what it is."

"That doesn't make me feel better." Dred gazed toward the control room, wondering if Keelah was all right. Paste was formulated to sustain human life, so maybe the alien female wasn't getting the proper nutrition anymore. Her normal diet had been disrupted when the mercs arrived and impelled the Mungo to attack the Warren.

"Sorry, I didn't realize I was supposed to." He put an arm around her.

That helps. But she didn't say it aloud.

A few minutes later, Tam came out into the main bay wearing a somber expression. Calypso followed, carrying Keelah, and even from this distance, Dred could tell she wouldn't be waking up again. The former mistress of the circle laid Keelah out on the floor, and they all gathered around. Dred hated that she couldn't join them, but it wouldn't be wise to risk the living for the dubious benefit of saying farewell to the dead.

"We'll go after they move off," Jael said.

She couldn't hear what they were saying, but eventually everyone bowed their heads. "What do you think happened?"

Jael lifted a shoulder, as if unwilling to speculate. "Hard to say. But if you want answers, we could use that medical bot. It could run a scan, yeah? Tell us if she hemorrhaged internally or had an aneurysm, whatever did her in."

"I think Vost broke it down again for parts. Martine said not to, but Tam gave him the go-ahead if we needed them."

"Damn. Sorry, love. That's the only idea I had."

"Don't worry about it."

Once the others finished, Tam came close enough to talk. "How contagious is whatever you two have? Could Keelah have been exposed before you left?"

Dred shook her head. "No, we got this way when the scavengers bit us on the lower levels on the way to Repair."

"Hm. Unrelated, then. You two should use the san. I'll keep everyone clear."

"Thank you," she breathed.

"It's more for us," Tam said, grinning. "Have you seen yourselves? Better question, can you smell yourselves?"

"Funny," Jael said.

He hauled to his feet and offered Dred a hand. Though he acted unaffected, she could tell that Keelah's death was bothering him more than he let on. "You clean up first. I'll wait."

"Thanks."

Leaning on each other, they made it to the san facilities, and she went in with him. She didn't have much water to pass, but she took care of it while Jael stepped into the stall. Probably, she should be worried that her urine was so dark and that there was so little of it. Instead, she just sat forward and put her head in her hands. Dred jumped when he touched her shoulder, completely done washing up.

"What the hell," she mumbled.

"Did you seriously nod off just now?"

"I think so. Let me get in there before I pass out again."

"Right then. I need a drink and some paste."

In the steam, it felt like she was sloughing off layers of dead skin. She scrubbed until her body felt raw, and her hair was a knotted mess. Her hands trembled as she tried to untangle it, but she hadn't tended it since they had abandoned Queensland. Probably she should just cut it all off and start over. Hair offered a place for pests and parasites to hide, so . . . before she could think better of it, she got her knife and started hacking. She had just finished stuffing the last of her locks into the waste-disposal unit when Jael stuck his head in to check on her.

To his credit, he didn't say anything about her ragged new do, just handed her a bundle of clothing. "I disposed of what we had on before."

This was the last outfit she possessed. The clothes she'd found in the dorm were now being processed along with her hair. That gave her a strange feeling, as if she'd sheared

away all unnecessary ties and soon she'd leave this place—
equal parts exciting and terrifying. After so many turns,
she might see more than these rusted walls . . . well, there
were no words. Hope fluttered faint as a phantom in her
chest, nearly starved by the monotonous brutality required
to survive Perdition.

For the first time in ages, she swiped her palm across
the glass and stared at herself. The face that stared back
was older than she recalled, lined and drawn with priva-
tion. Without her hair to soften it, her features were stark
and harsh, all cheekbones and chin. Dred ran her fingers
over a healing sore on her cheek. *Wonder if it will scar.*

"You are not a pretty woman," she told her reflection.
"But you're something better. You're tough. You're unbreak-
able."

Jael caught her when she stumbled out of the san.
"Wrong."

"Hm?"

"Sorry for eavesdropping, love. Physiological hazard.
But I must disagree. You are now and always will be the
most beautiful woman I've ever seen."

Closing her eyes, she tipped her head against his shoulder. "Thank you for that."

HOLDING her was the best part of Jael's day, but she
needed sleep. He'd already asked the others for some bedding and crafted a nest in a corner, behind a pile of junk
that had been deemed unsuitable for construction. Yet the
broken gear and uneven wall panels made for great privacy
as he settled in with Dred.

"How long will it be until the ship is done?" she asked.

"No idea. Vost couldn't give me an estimate. They were
all pretty distracted over what happened with Keelah."

She was already out before he finished speaking. Jael
needed less sleep than the average human, roughly half, so
he wasn't ready to doze off. Yet when he thought of moving
away from her . . . *No, I'd rather just lie here.* Tam came

to the edge of their makeshift quarters, and he seemed to be holding something. With his eyes, Jael warned the other man to be quiet. Tam nodded and set the old handheld down within arm's reach, then he backed out of the space.

He probably figured I'd be bored

Jael had seen Dred fiddle with this thing; she'd found some vid logs or something. So with his free hand, he picked up the unit and powered it on. He watched the first few and found it more interesting than he expected. Plus, there was something about the girl . . . he couldn't put a finger on it, but she seemed familiar. *Maybe she has one of those faces.*

He was alarmed when the vid girl went off with a guy who obviously had bad intentions. *And bullshit, the administrator has been sick . . .* The unit ran in the empty room for quite a while, then the log shut off. *Probably on a timer.* Intrigued, he activated the next one.

"I finally met with Levin, and there's something about him that I don't like. He evaded *all* my questions, and when I asked for access to operations reports, he said they're doing server maintenance for the next three days. I'm pretty sure they're stonewalling me."

No shit.

She was too young to be in charge of rooting out corruption on her own. *What were they thinking, sending you?* No matter how confident or capable she was, Rebestah Saren was still one woman. *They should've sent a whole team of auditors.* Which made him think that a Monsanto exec didn't *want* the truth coming to light. She'd mentioned her father, but surely the man wouldn't sacrifice his daughter. *He can't have known. Right?*

The second-to-last log was dated a week later, and it was audio only. A bad feeling shivered through him, so he held Dred a little tighter. She stirred in her sleep, tucking her face against his neck. Pleasure rolled through him in sweet, inexorable waves. He stroked her back, waiting for his heart to calm, then he played the recording.

"I have a meeting with Admin Levin today. The VP will

be there, too. They've promised to grant me access to all files, now that the computer upgrades are complete. But . . . I don't trust them. So I'm bringing this to the meeting. I don't think either one of them know I'm suspicious, so they won't expect me to consider gathering evidence so soon."

Good for you, Rebestah. Maybe the story had a happy ending after all.

Jael listened to her footsteps as she presumably left her quarters and headed for the conference room. Doors swished open and closed, then he heard multiple bodies settling into chairs. At first, it was innocuous, boring discussion about procedure. Then the movement shifted, like someone pouncing, and Rebestah cried out.

"How long will she be out?" a deep voice asked.

That's not the VP. Must be Admin Levin.

"Don't worry about that. Just call the doctor in."

What the hell?

The doors opened and closed, and he heard footfalls. "I don't want to do this," said a lighter voice, not female, but tenor.

"I paid your gambling debts," Deep Voice reminded him. "That means I own you. Of course, if you're really resistant, I can—"

"No, I'm a team player." Defeated tone.

The whirring of equipment came next, rather like a drill, and Rebestah cried out. Whatever they were doing hurt even while she was unconscious. Listening to this made him writhe with the awful recollection of being under someone else's control. Finally, it was done, and the machine stopped.

"You realize this is experimental tech," the doctor said. "This may not turn out the way you hope."

Deep Voice—aka Admin Levin—laughed. "I doubt that. You said these VR fantasy chips can induce mental illness, right?"

"Yes, but—"

"Get him out of here." A pause, some shuffling.

Then the VP said, "You really think this will work? It might be better if we just kill her."

"Murder always leaves a trail," the admin said. "No matter how careful you think you are. This way, everyone on the station will witness her breakdown. Nobody will be surprised when she commits suicide."

"Then we just report her death to her father."

"Pushy bastard," Levin muttered. "Never shuts up about how amazing his little girl is."

So he did get her the job . . . but not to set her up as sacrificial lamb. Jael felt a little better about that, not that it helped poor Rebestah.

"Take her back to her quarters," he added.

"Yes, Administrator."

The audio must be sound-activated because it kept going, presumably through her forcible return and even once she was left alone in her room. Jael listened to her pained mumbling for another five minutes before the log finally cut off. *Mary, what did they do to you?* It wouldn't have surprised him if that was where her story ended, but he tapped the screen and found one more log.

The last.

Recorded two weeks later, this vid reflected a much different woman. Her hair was unkempt, eyes hollow and circled with deep shadows. "They're all against me," she whispered. "All of them. They have sent Death itself after me, but they don't know, they don't know. I've won. This place is mine. I've won. They want me to scream, but I won't. I *never* will. I am Death. I am Silence."

◄ 26 ►

Conspiracy Theory

When Dred woke, she felt as if she had been asleep for at least twenty-four hours. The awful, debilitating weakness had passed, and her skin looked much better. She'd passed the point of deathly pallor and was back to prison pale. Though she had a few scabs left, most of them had healed to the pink of new skin. She stretched and sat up, glancing over to see Jael lounging on his back, arms crossed beneath his head.

"Feeling better?" he asked.

"Much. You?"

"I think we're out of the woods." He rolled onto his side and got the handheld, an expression she couldn't interpret kindling his features. "Watch this."

"Holy shit," Dred said, after Jael played the last two logs.

"Exactly. Rebestah Saren is Silence. I don't think she was ever sentenced here. I think she must've hidden when Monsanto abandoned the place."

A chill went through her. "So she was here alone while they finished covering up their crimes and then the Conglomerate repurposed the facility."

"Yeah. They chipped her, drove her mad, and—"

"Those assholes are responsible for her crimes. So much pain and suffering, just so a couple of rich scumbags could avoid prosecution for embezzlement."

"This changes everything," she said.

"How so?" From his expression, she could tell that Jael hadn't come to the same conclusion.

"Don't you think we should try to save her?"

"What happened to her sucks, but she's not Rebestah anymore. She's been Silence for so many turns . . . her brain's a mess, love. Even if we subdued her, we don't have the equipment to get that chip out of there. And even if we did, that doesn't mean she'd revert."

Unable to argue, Dred sighed. "I doubt the others care why she's here, either. They would never agree to bring her with us."

"She'd probably blow up the ship," Tam said.

Shifting, Dred saw the spymaster hovering on the other side of the junk wall. "I think we're safe if you feel like risking it. Or we can talk from here."

Tam played it safe by taking a seat just inside the perimeter. "You look like you're recovering."

"How's the ship coming?"

"Vost and I nearly have it ready. Well, as much as it can be, given what we have to work with. The problem is . . ." Tam hesitated, lowering his voice.

"Don't be coy," Jael said.

"With Keelah gone, our supplies will last better. But even on subsistence rations, we have too many people. There's also some risk that our production of CO_2 will tax life support."

Sickness roiled her belly. *After everything we've gone through together . . .* "You're saying we have to cull the herd."

Tam nodded. "The fewer people on board, the more likely it is we'll last long enough to get out of the system."

Jael rubbed a hand over his face. "Vost is a lock. We need him to get the doors open."

"Would anyone miss Duran?" Tam asked. "I could do it quietly."

Dred chewed her lip. It wasn't that she cherished Duran especially, but . . . "Vost is a good commander, he wouldn't let us bullshit him. Plus, we're locked in. It's not like we can say Silence did it. He'll know it was one of us."

Tam leaned forward, his expression dark. "You think too highly of him."

"Explain," she said.

"I thought from the beginning that Keelah's death was suspect, but I couldn't investigate while Vost was awake. So I stayed close to him while we worked on the ship. I made sure he didn't include any questionable installations."

"You *really* don't trust him," Jael noted.

"For good reason, as it turns out. Once he went to sleep during down cycle, I checked Keelah's body thoroughly."

"What did you find?" Dred knew it must be bad, from Tam's grim aspect.

"A scratch beneath her fur, just below her rib cage. It wasn't deep enough to cause harm in and of itself, but—"

"If the blade was poisoned, it could've killed her," Jael finished.

"Silence." Dred couldn't believe what she was thinking. "You suspect Vost went to her with the same deal he presented to us?"

"It would be prudent," Tam admitted.

She turned the ramifications of that over in her head. "So he may start picking us off."

"He can try," Jael snarled.

Tam went on with his speculation. "Say he made a bargain with Silence. He gets our help constructing the ship because, let's face it, her followers are not operating at full capacity. Vost knows he needs skilled help."

Dred took up the narrative then. "Accidents happen, people die. He expected our numbers to thin out more, but we're stronger than he knew."

Tam smirked. "You two in particular are almost impossible to kill. Did you see how stunned he was that you made it back in one piece with all those parts? We didn't need half of what he asked you to retrieve, by the way."

Jael curled one hand into a fist and smacked it into his palm. "You've no idea how much I want to kill him. Slowly."

"We can't. He's untouchable," Tam said.

"Only until we get off the station." Dred smiled at their expressions. "What, did you forget I can be ruthless? It's kind of my thing."

Tam steepled his fingers. "I admire that about you. But back to my theory . . . I expect something to 'go wrong' now that we're nearing the end of construction, something we'll have to leave the bay to deal with."

"And we should expect Vost and Duran to strike then, trying to pick us off." Dred wasn't asking; she already saw how it would play out.

Tam confirmed, "Probably an attack coordinated with Silence. Vost is good with computers, they may be communicating."

"If she has poison blades in reserve, they could take out you three pretty fast." By which she meant Calypso, Tam, and Martine.

He nodded, not taking offense to the truth. "They'd have more trouble with you two—"

"But they don't need to kill us directly," Jael said. "Doubling back to the ship and stranding us? Same thing."

"How does this story end?" Dred asked.

Jael was wondering the same thing

"For them?" Tam questioned.

Dred nodded.

"They proceed to the docking bay while you and Jael are elsewhere. Duran and Vost turn on Silence, and the mercs take off with the ship, plenty of food and water on board for two. At least, that's what I'd do in their shoes."

"Remind me again why I trust you?" she joked.

Jael studied the other man's face and decided not to kill him. Tam didn't have to open this discussion. He could've let shit explode and done his best to survive it. Instead, he was helping them prepare for the worst.

"Because he's proven," he said.

Dred nodded at his words. "True enough. So what strategy do you recommend? We can't wait for them to manufacture an emergency."

But something was bothering Jael. He thought of Rebestah's mad-faced desperation in the vid and her long turns of isolation. "Dred, you think she actually *wants* to leave?"

"Silence?"

"Yeah."

Tam glanced between them, and he took the time to show the spymaster the logs. It might alter his hypothesis because for everyone else, Perdition was a life sentence, a place they'd do anything to escape. Once they finished watching, Tam tapped his fingers lightly against his knee.

"I had no idea."

"None of us did."

Then the spymaster came to the same conclusion. "If she accepted Vost's offer, it's only because she wants him to deal with *us*. I suspect she has no intention of ever leaving this place."

JAEL said, "So she'll be prepared for a double cross. You think Silence can take the two mercs?"

"Probably. Vost is injured, and Duran isn't as brave as one might wish."

Kind way of calling him yellow, Jael thought.

Dred appeared to come to a sudden decision. "For now, we pretend we don't know any of this, especially that Vost murdered Keelah."

"He's not getting away with that," Jael said, low.

She nodded. "You can snap his neck as soon as those docking-bay doors open."

"But why Keelah?" Tam asked softly. "What did he stand to gain?"

"Maybe she caught him communicating with Silence?" Jael suggested.

"She was quiet. Easier for her to sneak up on someone and overhear important info." Dred seemed to think that was the probable answer.

Possibly.

In all honesty, he wasn't a big thinker. He'd spent so much time following orders, first in the labs, then as a merc, that analytical thinking didn't come natural to him. Yet he wanted answers as much as they did.

Before he could say anything else, Martine slipped inside, curling up next to Tam. "Private party, or can anybody join?"

Damn. We didn't finish talking. Are we killing Duran or not?

"You're always welcome," Tam said.

His eyes, however, indicated that they were done talking about treachery, murder, and secret bargains. Jael understood why. While Tam might be cold and calculating, Martine was exactly the opposite. Her temper might provoke her to stab Vost in the neck, then nobody was getting off station. Jael took the hint, as silently requested.

"We should help with the ship if we can," Dred said.

"How's it coming?"

"Just a few more pieces. Vost is working on it now."

Shit, Jael thought.

He saw alarm reflected in Tam's and Dred's faces, too. *What if he installs some kind of fail-safe? Like if he doesn't input the code every so often, the ship goes boom. Good way to make sure we keep him around.* Being around Tam was infectious, it seemed; now he had conspiracy theories popping into his head without prompting.

Martine went on, "Once it's done, then we can start running some stress tests, make sure it's strong enough to hold together."

"Let's go take a look," Jael said.

"Aw." Martine mock pouted. "I thought I was settling in for a long chat."

"We'll have plenty of time to talk after launch, bright eyes."

A happy smile lit Martine's features. "You got that right. I'm already planning to get some crowns to cover my prison dentistry, so I don't scare the nice civilians."

"You're making plans for what you'll do outside?" Tam asked.

"Definitely. Aren't you?"

The other three traded looks, then Jael said, "I guess I'm cynical. Though I've been talking escape since I got here, I won't believe it's true until we're actually out."

"Well, lighten up." Martine smacked him on the shoulder as she pushed to her feet and rushed back out to the main part of the bay.

Jael, Dred, and Tam followed at a more leisurely pace, mostly to cover the unease that had taken root. When he got to the ship, it didn't look any different than it ever had, but admittedly it was a hodgepodge mess. He had a hard time believing the thing would actually run, but as he thought that, the engines powered up, firing a jet of super-heated air toward him. Dred tackled him and knocked him away from the stream. She helped him up, wearing a fierce scowl.

"Idiot," Calypso yelled. "You have to give us some warning."

A few seconds later, Duran stumbled out of the shuttle. "Sorry. I thought the area was clear." He protected his face with his arms while Calypso pummeled him.

Did they just try to kill me?

"That's why I installed a comm system," Vost said, stepping out.

It was hard as hell not to react, so Jael totally got why Tam hadn't told Martine. *Bide your time. Wait for the right opportunity.* He even managed a half smile, hoping it looked like his usual sardonic greeting.

"How close are we?"

"Less than eight hours," Vost said.

"We have so many spare parts." Dred paced around the pile of leftovers wearing an innocent, questioning expression. "You overestimated?"

"It's always better to be prepared." The merc commander didn't avoid her gaze or act like he'd done anything wrong.

Keelah's corpse on the other side of the bay testified otherwise.

Instead, he slipped back into the ship, and Tam followed. It might be too late, however; there might already be a trap on board.

◀ 27 ▶

Likelihood of Catastrophic Failure

Dred could hardly bear to look at Vost or Duran. Every instinct demanded that she kill them both, but without Vost, the docking-bay doors wouldn't open. Even if he'd betrayed them all, the mercenary commander had guaranteed safe passage, and killing Duran would only amount to a temper tantrum. With great effort, she quelled the furious throb in her head.

Jael nodded in silent approval.

Just then, the comm system crackled to life. "Warning. Warning. Monsanto systems detect the following: Overload in sectors four, six, and nine. Smoke detected in the fuel cells. Reactor-chamber breach. Emergency maintenance alert—immediate intervention required. Likelihood of catastrophic failure, 94.7%."

Dred's head snapped up. They were just about to begin the stress tests, and now this. "We need to launch," she said icily.

"We can't," Vost snapped back. "It's too soon, I'm not ready."

"Then fragging get there," Jael snarled.

"Would you rather die in vacuum? I'm not inputting the codes until I'm convinced we can survive."

"You heard the computer," Calypso said. "That crazy bitch sabotaged the place. We stay here, and we get blown to shit with her."

"I say let's risk it," Martine added.

"We can do this the easy way or the hard way," Dred added.

"Hey," Duran cut in. "You think he's yanking you about? If the man says we're not ready, then it means the ship might fall to bits in space. Maybe we can shut the problem down."

"Out there?" Dred laughed.

Just like Tam predicted.

"Go ahead," Jael invited.

The merc looked startled. *Yeah, looks like you didn't think you'd be picked to lead the mission.* Then he made his usual excuse. "I don't know the station. How am I supposed to find the fuel cells, whatever sectors, or the reactor?"

"That's your problem," Tam said softly.

"I'm getting a strange vibe." Vost put down the tools he was holding and came toward the others.

"It feels like you're stalling," Calypso told him.

Impeccable instincts, Dred thought, smiling.

The other woman went on, "Sometimes you have to say frag preparation and take a leap. We have *no idea* how long it'll take for shit to go 'catastrophically wrong' and yet your instinct is to send part of our group out to investigate when we should get the hell out."

"Agreed." Martine put a hand on Calypso's shoulder in solidarity.

"Clearly," Vost bit out. "You've never been responsible for other lives. I've done most of the grunt work on this ship, and I *promise* that I need six more hours to check the data. If you prefer to sit in the docking bay while I ensure I'm not killing you all by taking this heap into deep space, so be it. Honest to Mary, I thought better of you lot. If I could be two places at once, I'd damn sure go see if there was anything I could do to buy us the time we need."

Good speech. If I didn't know why you were so hot to drive us out.

"Then it seems like we should help you," Tam said.

"The work will go faster if it's not just you," Martine added.

Calypso was nodding. "Sure, we may not be experts, but we can take orders, boss man. Let's buckle down and get this done while the station explodes. It's pretty big. If the trouble's down by the fuel cells, it should take a while until we feel the damage."

Duran stared at her, mouth open. "What if we lose life support?"

"That'll be a problem," Jael said.

Dred managed to keep from smiling. "Truth. If the gravity well goes down, we'll find it hard as hell to finish. But I'd rather stay here. We have the blast doors, and we're pretty far from the problem area. Like Calypso says, I feel like gambling that the bay will hold long enough."

Vost and Duran traded looks, but she couldn't tell what they were thinking.

"Fine." The merc commander shrugged. "I'll divide up the trials. Tam and Martine, you oversee this one. Calypso and Duran—" And he snapped out a series of orders.

She noticed that he didn't assign any work to her or Jael.

"I'll check the hardware," Tam volunteered. "I'm not on Ike's level, but I'm good enough to spot anything out of place."

Did Vost look worried? Hard to say. He definitely looked spooked, especially when main power cut out, and they went to the slow red strobe of emergency lights. The floor rocked with what she guessed must be a series of lower-level explosions. *Perdition is literally collapsing beneath us. At what point does he concede his original plan won't work and take us all with him? Or will there be some "accidental" deaths first?*

Not long after she thought that, someone screamed inside the ship. Dred grabbed Jael's hand, making sure they didn't get separated, then she dove through the open door and scrambled over the close-set seats, with him behind her. Pushing through the arch into the cargo space, she found Duran on the ground, Calypso hovering over him. Yet the former mistress of the circle wasn't the hysterical type. With her eyes, she asked, *Did Tam talk to you? Was it you?* But the other woman apparently didn't grasp the silent question.

"What happened?" she demanded.

"We were running the test Vost ordered, and something shorted out. He got blown back, and so far, he's not getting up. I haven't touched him. That's a good way to get electrocuted."

The merc commander shoved his way back from the other side of the ship, and his face whitened. "See, this is exactly why I wanted more time, Mary curse it."

Was that supposed to take Calypso out? She stared at Vost, but he only gazed down at his fallen comrade.

"Looks like you're the last one standing," Jael said.

Vost glanced up, his pale green eyes icy. "Not the first time."

"That means you're a terrible commander," Tam observed.

"Maybe so. Could be I'll retire after this." Then he jerked his head at Duran's body. "Get him off my ship. There's no time to mourn with the station blowing up around us."

Another tremor shook the bay.

She nodded at her people. "You heard him. Be careful, though. Get protective equipment. And Vost, you get that circuit closed off. We don't want to lose anyone else, do we?"

He held her gaze for a few seconds. "Not at all."

THIS is such bullshit. Jael watched that little exchange, wanting nothing more than to pound that asshole merc into paste. *But we need him. Just hold it in a little longer.*

Then he shouldered Martine and Calypso aside. "I can take a little voltage better than you can. Let me."

And he did zing a little from lifting Duran's body, just enough to make his heart skip. It probably would've hurt the other two more. He strode over to where they'd stashed Keelah and dropped the merc beside her.

The comm crackled to life. "Warning. Warning. Fuel cells reaching critical temperatures. Reactor unstable. Chain reaction imminent, point of no return in 143 minutes. Probability of demolition, 96.3%. Please evacuate. Monsanto Station personnel, follow emergency protocols for a safe and orderly departure. Have a nice day."

"Well. Now we know exactly how long we have."

"Less than I expected," Dred said from behind him.

"Silence knows the station. She's been here the longest."

"I guess the place really does belong to her," she mused. "What do you make of the incident with Duran?"

"Calypso's too smart for Vost."

"Or maybe she got lucky. We need to be careful on the ship. Mary only knows what surprises Vost may have rigged up."

"He's got to know his odds aren't good if he takes off with us. Five to one."

Jael stared down at Keelah, remembering how fiercely the alien female had fought after Katur died. She'd made peace with her loss, and she might've built a new life, given the chance. *But Vost took that from her.*

"That's why I think he has something in reserve. He admitted before that he's been the last to walk away."

Her words sparked something to life in him. "Me too. And you don't outlast everyone else without doing some atrocious things."

"Dred, Jael!" Martine called.

He turned. "What's up, bright eyes?"

"We need you inside. Vost says that with the ship counting down, we have to work double time. Otherwise, if we're too close when the station goes up—"

"The shock wave shakes our ship apart, and we're spaced," Dred finished.

Jael shivered. Given her matter-of-fact tone, she'd never felt that icy cold, the pressure and silence, and the burn of oxygen deprivation. It wasn't as dramatic as they showed it in the holos, but it was still an ugly way to die. While wariness occupied the dominant position in his brain, he refused to go out that way. *I've survived everything else. I'll get through this, too.*

A horrifying possibility flickered.

Yeah. You *will. Not her. You think you get a happy ending, JL489?* It was unquestionably Landau's voice, the same scornful tone as when he'd repeated, *You're not a person. You're a thing. You will obey.*

If he looked at his life, it was just one giant random mess. He'd scrambled from one disaster to another, dealing enough death to make Silence envious. Pity panged through him. Those bastards had taken some role-playing scenario and made it her reality. *She was normal once.* But Jael couldn't say the same.

I never had parents who wondered what became of me. Never had anyone at all who gave a shit. Oddly, he remembered when it might've been different—a crew that welcomed him and a woman who treated him as an equal. *Sorry, Jax.* He had felt . . . something. But not love. Not enough to keep him from taking the deal when her mother offered him a substantial payday to betray her. Jael recalled thinking he was better off without a family, if that was how they acted. But now he wondered if Rebestah's father ever recovered from news of his daughter's suicide.

It's all random, right?

There might not be any larger scheme at work—oh, missionaries had tried to convince him otherwise over long turns—but he could never believe it. So accepting that random chance dumped him here and that everything with Dred came from coincidence, not a greater plan . . . in that moment, he made a silent vow.

No matter what it takes, I'm keeping her safe.

Peace stole over him. Always, he'd valued his own life above everything else because it was all he had. But meeting her had taught Jael the one thing that had always escaped him—being human meant weakness. It meant cherishing someone more than yourself. He'd seen those bonds, between lovers, between parents and children. He never understood.

This is what Landau thought I couldn't learn. And maybe he was right in the beginning. I was a thing he made. But not now. Because she taught me how to be more.

The sweetest ache swelled in his chest as he watched Dred quicken her pace in response to Martine's call. Without her hair, she was hard-faced, all sharp edges and hungry eyes, but he hadn't been lying when he said she was beautiful. That loveliness came from the heart of her, and he was determined to make sure she got a fresh start.

With or without me.

He crouched before Keelah, fully understanding how much pain she must've been in for the first time. *She said her people mate for life. And yet she pushed on.* That seemed like real strength. Without even contemplating, he knew he didn't have that fortitude. Now that Dred had cracked him open, there was no way he could live without her. In some ways, she'd stripped him of vital protective armor.

He *cared* about things in a way he never had before. Hell, once he wouldn't have given a shit that a couple of worthless bastards ruined a young girl's life. *Sad story, everybody's got one. So cry me a river.* That indifference had sloughed right off, thanks to Dred.

She made me join the human race. Silently grieving, he touched Keelah's head lightly, saying good-bye. Lost in reverie, for once his instincts let him down.

Jael didn't hear the person slip up behind him.

◀ 28 ▶

All Hands on Deck

Dred stepped into the ship cautiously. Not just because the doors had low clearance, but she also bore in mind that a live, bare wire had fried Duran. Vost couldn't have meant for that to happen. She guessed that was a result of his being rushed instead of dispatching the rest of them to "investigate" the station alarms.

Like we could undo whatever Silence did. If Ike were still around, maybe. But without him, it was just an invitation to divide and conquer.

"Where do you need me?" she called.

"Come aft," Vost answered.

Martine was in the bow pilot's seat, fiddling with the instruments as Dred slid past into the cargo space in the middle of the craft, where Calypso was working to fix the electrical problem. She navigated past the coil of wires and popped her head into the secondary seating area. This vessel was the strangest patchwork monster she'd ever seen, with dueling cockpits and hung together with hope.

"I'm here."

"Hold this for me."

"How's that?" She covered his hands with hers.

Vost pulled back. "Good. We have to get the engines firing in sequence, or we're fragged. I'm nearly there, but it's hard to concentrate knowing the station could blow any minute." The merc's hands shook as he adjusted something.

"We have a couple of hours before the whole station goes boom," she joked.

He cut her a daggered look. "You think that's amusing? I suspect you haven't studied physics, or you'd be worried about the impact of the shrapnel wave on our little raft."

"Like a backdraft, you mean?"

"I hope you don't see it firsthand. We need to put some distance between us and Perdition, ASAP." He raised his voice. "Try it now, Martine!"

A roar came from the front of the ship. The gauges showed numbers Dred couldn't interpret, and Vost studied them before letting out a whoop. The excitement was so boyish that, for a few seconds, he looked utterly unlike himself. "All right, we're golden."

"That means we can take off?"

"This is as ready as we can be. I'll fine-tune once we're out of danger."

"We're just missing Tam and Jael. I'll find them."

"You have five minutes," he said flatly.

"Excuse me?"

"I'm taking off in three hundred seconds. So round up the survivors and get them on board because I'm not dying today." Vost didn't look at Dred as he settled into the pilot's chair.

She ground her teeth as she let go of the lever and whirled to locate the other two. But when she got to midship, she paused by Calypso. "If he tries to leave us, stop him."

The other woman glanced toward Vost. "You got it. Don't care if he's holding our exit pass, he tries to bail, and he can die with us convicts."

"Seems fair," she muttered. "Sit tight, I'll be back soon."

But before she could exit, a boom rocked the whole room. Dred stumbled into Calypso, who caught her and braced both of them against the shuddering walls. "What the hell?"

Dred shook her head, but she was already moving. That explosion sounded way too close to be random station damage. Martine jumped out ahead of her and spun in a slow circle.

"Shit," the smaller woman said. "The blast door's down."

"Force field?" Dred asked, hopping out of the craft.

"Gone, too. We're on emergency power now, all over the station. It won't be long before we lose life support."

"Must be Silence," Calypso yelled. "There's nobody else."

There was smoke everywhere. Whatever Silence had used to take down the blast door, it wasn't clean-burning.

"Where the hell did she get the gear?" Martine asked.

"She raided one of Ike's caches," Dred said, swearing. "I thought she just destroyed it, but she must've taken whatever Ike left and blown the container."

"Mary curse it," Calypso snarled.

"Guard the ship," she told the tall woman. "Martine, help me find Jael and Tam. They have to be in the bay somewhere."

"Let's hope Silence doesn't get to them first."

Dred ignored Calypso's grim mutterings and raced toward the doors. If she knew Jael, he'd have gone to investigate the damage. *Assuming he can.* The smoke was thicker this way, with smoldering piles of rags littering the floor on the way to the exit. She coughed and ran on, covering her face with a forearm. Her heart thumped a warning, telling her to prepare for the worst. *He's gone, he's gone, he's gone.*

And Vost won't wait.

In all honesty, she wouldn't blame Calypso if she made a deal with the merc. Why should she die for some random assholes she met in a max-sec hole? Same with Tam and Martine, really. None of them had anything in common once you removed the fact that they had been sentenced to die in the same place.

"Jael," she shouted, giving up on stealth.

If that crazy bitch comes at me, we'll have it out. Actually, she welcomed that prospect. What the Monsanto bastards had done to Rebestah was beyond wrong, but Silence had hurt Jael in ways that could never be forgiven. *I'd love an hour with her and a really sharp knife.* But with the station disintegrating below them, it looked like Silence would be getting a swift death.

More than she deserves.

"Jael! Where are you, love?" The endearment slipped out.

When a pair of hands grabbed her, she knocked them away and came up in fighting stance, but Martine's face resolved in the smoke, pressing close to hers, and Dred nearly punched her. She let out a breath and was sorry when she sucked in smoke. Dred doubled over, and Martine led her away from the worst of it. She sucked in mouthfuls of clean air with a desperation that gave her some sense how bad it would be to die in vacuum.

"Have you seen Jael?" she gasped out.

"I checked near the bodies, where I saw him last, but I can't find him or Tam. They're not answering when I call, either." The other woman didn't say she was worried, but Dred heard it in her voice, in the flex of her jaw.

Silence.

"**LOVE** is a fearsome thing," Tam said.

Jael stood up and whipped around, his heart pounding like mad. "Good thing you didn't want me dead."

The other man smiled. "I wouldn't live long if I did. Dred's rather fond of you."

"Maybe a bit. I was just . . . saying good-bye. To Keelah, not Duran."

"He wasn't the most endearing soul. I suspect Calypso only bedded him to assert some control."

"I've slept with people for worse reasons," Jael muttered.

"As have I."

"We'll probably be leaving soon. Want to take a last walk,

make sure we didn't leave anything vital in the dormitory or control room?"

"Sounds good."

They left the bay floor and went to the dorm first. He checked the mattresses while Tam peered into the footlockers. In the bottom of one he found the entertainment console that Keelah had taken apart and put back together. He tapped the power button and found that she'd fixed it. *This might make the time pass faster.* Which was probably what Keelah was thinking when she worked on it. Sighing, Jael pocketed the unit.

"Anything?" he asked Tam.

The other man shook his head.

Then a massive detonation rocked everything. He slammed into the bed frame, and the world went sideways. Jael didn't think he was out long; he tended not to lose consciousness, so it was more like being stunned. He shoved to his hands and knees, smelling smoke. Cocking his head, he located Tam by zeroing in on his heartbeat, a feat that required blotting out the rest of the world. He didn't use that selective focus a lot, but time mattered.

When he got to Tam, he found him out cold, blood trickling from a head wound. Cursing, he lifted him and picked a path over the toppled furniture. In the smoke, he could only make out the vague shape of the ship. *There we go.* Jael took two steps in that direction, and a more localized explosion took out part of the ship.

He went down in the back blast, and he threw himself on top of Tam as debris rained down. Shock numbed him. *That was one of the engines.* Silence's plan became transparent then. She didn't need to kill them in combat; it wasn't like she cared about that anyway. All she had to do was harry, sabotage, strike, and retreat. If she delayed them long enough, they'd all die with her, and *that* must be what she wanted. She wanted the grand finale, one last offering to Death.

In hindsight, he wished they'd put guards on the door, as

soon as the force field went down, but then again, that person probably would've been killed outright when she took out the blast door. He strained to see through the smoke and saw a couple of murky shapes trying to put out the fire at the bow of the vessel. Stumbling to his feet, he picked Tam up again and headed in that direction.

It turned out to be Vost and Calypso. The merc had soot smeared all over his face, and he snapped, "Where the hell have you two idiots been? If not for you, we'd already be gone."

He ignored the insult. "How bad is the damage?"

"I can't tell. Can't fragging see."

Calypso produced a light and flashed it across the affected area. "We have to patch the hull. Now."

"Let me put Tam inside, and I'll find the parts. You get the soldering kit."

The other woman nodded. Once he'd strapped Tam into a seat, Jael raced out. *Need a strong panel, something that won't tear loose at the least resistance.* Silence was probably around here, but he wanted to live more than he wanted to kill her. As he laid hands on a scrap of metal the right size, Dred shouted his name, her voice hoarse with smoke inhalation.

"Over here," he yelled back.

It took a few back-and-forth calls for her to locate him, then Dred raced up with Martine hot on her heels. She almost knocked the sheeting out of his hand when she grabbed him around the neck in a death-love strangle-hug. Jael patted her back gently while mouthing, *What's wrong?* at Martine.

"She thought Silence got you."

"Oh." He exhaled slowly. "I'm fine, love. She's slinking around, and it makes my skin crawl. But we have to fix the ship."

Martine let out a string of curses. "Swear to Mary, I can't live in peace until I stick a knife in that woman's eye."

"That makes two of us." Dred's green eyes glinted with

a martial light. "You three work on repairs with Vost. Martine and I are going hunting."

He grabbed her arm before she could take off. "That's a stupid move, queenie."

Jael hadn't called her that in ages, and it registered on Dred with a flare of aggravation. She shook off his hand. "She's got to die. For what she did to you, and now the ship. It's just . . . that's what needs to happen."

Cupping her face in his hands, he shook his head. "That's what she wants. For us to choose revenge over life. She'll ghost around this place, and if you two aren't helping, we might not make it out of here. Choose me instead. Choose life."

For a long moment, she held his gaze, trying to stare him down. But Jael didn't waver. He gave two fucks for Silence. *She'll die anyway. She'll die alone.* He intended to rob her of what she wanted most; that would be the most awful penance. Even now, a small part of him wished he could save the hopeful, idealistic girl Silence had been.

Sorry, Rebestah. If any of those bastards are still alive, I'll hunt them down for you.

Dred snarled. "Fine. Let's go. But you understand, I'm doing this for you, no other reason. My knife hand is so stabby right now."

"Mine too," Martine muttered. "But all hands on deck and whatnot. Let's fix our piece of shit and get gone before it's too late."

A distant explosion shook the docking bay; the comm issued another polite alert.

Frag. We have to hurry.

◄ 29 ►

Fly or Die

Dred held the metal in place while Jael did the soldering. Calypso was inside helping Vost add struts to the damaged part of the ship. Martine had gone to see if Tam was awake, but they didn't have time to administer first aid. Jael had said he wasn't gushing blood, so hopefully it wasn't serious.

"How's it coming?" Vost yelled.

"Halfway," she called back.

Wild laughter echoed all around them, and all the hair stood up on the back of her neck. Jael paused to check the area, but when he didn't see Silence, he went right back to work. She'd never heard of Death's Handmaiden uttering a sound before, but desperate times called for desperate measures apparently. Her arms ached with the weight of the panel, but she couldn't falter. If she slipped, Jael might burn one of them with the kit. The scent of hot metal blazed into her sinuses, mingling with the low-grade irritation already bothering her from the fires earlier.

Throat hurts. So tired. But she wouldn't let Perdition—or Silence—win.

"If she goes after the ship again, I'll kill her," Jael said quietly. "You keep working. We're running out of time."

He wasn't exaggerating. The air didn't seem to be filtering anymore, so the smoke wasn't clearing out. It hung in the bay, polluting the air and making it hard to get enough oxygen. A station the size of Perdition took a while to blow itself to pieces; it only remained to be seen if Silence had crippled them as completely as she intended.

Jael worked the welder to the other side, and Dred slid over, trying to stay out of his way. The inside of the ship vibrated from whatever Calypso and Vost were doing. Finally, he finished the first circuit, but it needed time to cool and lock together. Time they didn't have. Jael revealed his awareness of how half-assed this patch job was as he lowered his tools.

"Let's get inside. That's all we can do out here."

With a quiet nod, she followed him into the craft. This shit bucket literally had a shit bucket, nothing like even the basic amenities they were leaving behind, but when those bay doors opened, all kinds of possibilities did, too. *Finally. We're down to the wire, fly or die.* Instead of fear, the strongest exultation rocketed through her. Dred slammed an open palm against the ceiling.

"Are we doing this or what?" There was no time to think about Silence now, or why Vost had killed Keelah.

Everything else can wait. But there will *be a reckoning.*

"Ready on my end," Vost said.

He was already strapped into the pilot's chair on the damaged end. Martine headed aft; presumably she had some experience flying, too. *Not the time to ask for a license.* Tam was conscious in the seat next to Vost, so Calypso went with the other woman, leaving Dred and Jael to scramble into the cargo space in the middle. The area was piled with all of their supplies—all the water they could find containers for and every last packet of paste. For one or two people, this would last a very long time. Six, however, might make for a chancy voyage. But there were more immediate dangers than dehydration or malnourishment.

We don't have suits. Hull breach means instant death.

"We don't have seat belts," she said ridiculously.

Jael smirked. "Here. This is my handiwork. Didn't I tell you I'd build us a love nest?"

"You never said that."

He pulled down some netting and wrapped them both in it, then reattached it to the wall. It was like being trapped in a web, but since he was close enough to hold her, there was comfort in it as well. She put her arms around his waist and leaned, breathing him in. *We're alive. We're together. And we're leaving.* From her vantage, she could see the bow cockpit while Jael was looking to the back, and she watched Vost adjust the instruments.

Then he shouted at Martine, "Time to go!"

Both engines fired simultaneously, but Dred could tell that there was a problem in the one Vost was manning; it alternately roared and dropped, unlike the steady purr coming from the aft section. Silence hadn't taken it out entirely, but it was no longer running at peak efficiency. *Nothing we can do now. There's no time to replace parts or make a salvage run.* Something slammed the outside of the ship, and Dred jumped.

"Easy," Jael whispered. "She's just a sad, crazy woman. She can't pull this thing apart with her bare hands."

"No, but she could blow the ship with us in it. You know she wouldn't care if she got caught in the blast radius."

"True." Jael raised his voice. "Move! We've got incoming."

Vost yelled back, "On it. Silence is circling, four o'clock. Not letting her mess with my ride again. Martine, can you take us out while I input the codes?" His hands moved furiously on the control panel.

"Roger that," she said.

The ship juddered. Calypso shouted something, but Dred couldn't make it out. Martine yelled, "I never said I was *good* at this. I just said I've done some flying."

"Shit," Tam mumbled.

A red light flashed. Vost spat a curse and went at the

console again, slower this time. The silent prayer formed without her volition. *Please, Mary. Guide his hands. He wants out, too.*

"If you don't know the codes," Tam said icily, "I will cut your throat myself."

"They'll work," Vost snapped.

The craft bucked, distracting her. It had been so damn long since she'd been in a moving vehicle. At first, Dred thought this one would crack apart just lifting off, but it wobbled, then Martine seemed to get the hang of the stabilizers. A couple of test swoops, and they were off. *Mary, dear holy Mary, we're actually moving.* Dred swiveled her head and saw the back wall receding behind her.

Jael tightened his arms around her. "Here's to freedom, love."

THE small craft raced toward the bay doors, and just when Jael thought they'd slam into them, the huge slabs of metal shifted upward in a slow grind of long-untended machinery. *Thank Mary, they aren't fused shut, and Vost wasn't lying.* Since they'd taken no safety precautions, loose debris slammed past, thumping along the hull and out into the void. The drop off the platform was a little rocky, but Martine leveled them out.

Then the ship headed away from Perdition at full speed. Jael wasn't sure, but it seemed to be safe enough to unstrap. Reaching up, he unfastened the netting, so Dred could step away and stretch. She went aft, crouching behind the other women to stare out the maintenance rig's view screen. A little gasp escaped her; he understood that reaction. He choked up a bit too, staring at the stars all around them. Darkness and light, some faint and others in white-hot clusters. Even in an empty system like this one, there was beauty if you'd been starved of it long enough.

"So far, so good," Calypso whooped.

She launched out of her seat and grabbed Dred in a tight hug, one arm about her neck, and Jael stepped back in reflex.

So he was surprised when the tall woman grabbed him with her free arm and hauled him in, openly affectionate. Squished between the two of them, his heart did a strange awkward two-step, back and forth. It was hard enough to accept that Dred loved him, but in that moment, he realized he mattered to the others, too. Calypso would probably fight for him; Martine already had. And Tam . . . hell, he could probably call him a friend, too.

He let out a slow breath and disengaged with a pat for both of them. *That should do it.* To his amusement, Calypso actually kissed his ear and stroked his head like he was a kid.

Never was, actually. But he didn't mind the gesture.

"We probably spaced Silence," Dred said softly.

Probably. Possibly.

After everything that woman had survived and accomplished, it was hard to write her off. He imagined her standing alone in Perdition, even now. *Hell, maybe she* is *Death's Handmaiden.* For her sake, he wished it was true—that she was about to achieve something instead of just reaching the terminus of a sad, atrocious life.

"I was wondering," she added.

Jael cocked his head. "What's that?"

"If Rebestah was an auditor, why did we find her handheld in the docking-bay area. That dormitory wasn't designated for white-collar workers."

Excellent question.

"There's no way to be sure . . . but I suspect she must've lived there for a while. After everyone else pulled out, before Monsanto locked the place down."

Dred looked thoughtful. "That makes sense. It's kind of sad, though . . . she was still wearing the Monsanto uniform."

"Maybe she knew it was important. She just couldn't make the pieces fit with the VR running constantly in her head."

"Poor Silence," she whispered.

Jael couldn't believe he agreed. Gently, he kissed her cheek, eyes full of apology. "Some things can't be changed."

"I know. And I'm *not* sorry we left her. I only wish I'd ended her personally."

Yeah, that's enough talk about people we didn't kill.

"How's your head?" he asked, turning to what had become the main side of the ship.

"Hurts like hell," Tam answered. "But it's not debilitating."

"That's good. Would suck if you dozed off and never woke up."

Tam's mouth twisted in amusement. "More for me than you."

"Show of hands, who thought we'd die before we got this thing out?" Martine called.

Nobody put their arms up, Jael suspected because they didn't want to admit to such private doubts. He wanted to run and scream, but there was no space. If people left their seats, there wasn't even room for everyone to stand in the hold. *If the air refreshers burn out . . . but no. It's too early to list all the ways this can go horribly wrong.*

Leaning over, he saw the shallow nick on Tam's scalp. Not serious, like he said. Surprise fluttered through him at how relieved he was. Some of the tension seeped away as he straightened, leaning on Tam's seat. Vost glanced back like he didn't like having someone right behind him, but Jael gave two fucks for the merc's comfort zone.

He's got to know he's on the razor's edge now. The asshole just cashed in his value.

Setting aside the question of whether he should execute Vost, he peered out the screen. The transport he'd arrived on didn't have a viewer, so he'd only seen the station from the inside, where it looked like a maze and felt like hell, but it was hard to get a sense from the internal schematics. For a few seconds, he just soaked it in.

Perdition was a massive, steely structure, H-shaped, with levels that rotated slowly to create their own gravity.

He had no idea what the center level had been used for during the place's mineral-refining days, but based on the central location, it seemed likely the executives had apartments there. Currently, dark spots and jagged holes pocked the surface, and blinding flashes popped all over, hinting at more explosions.

"It's collapsing," he said.

"And that's a problem for us," Vost replied.

"Yeah." Dred came up behind them, rested her head on Jael's shoulder, and stared at the station they all hated. "Before, you mentioned a shrapnel wave . . . ?"

"When Perdition blows completely, there won't be a shock wave like there would be with grav, but we still have to worry about light-energy displacement and the debris field." Vost always sounded cranky when he explained things.

"What does that even mean?" Calypso demanded.

"That the farther we are," Tam said, "the less likely it is that we'll be smashed apart when Perdition goes boom."

The tall woman made a face. "Ah. So . . . can this heap go any faster?"

◀ 30 ▶

Nice Knowing You

Tam tapped away on the handheld, ignoring the laughter coming from the central hold. While he needed more than estimates, the craft didn't have the equipment, so there was no way to gather more data. Martine had yielded the pilot honors to Vost, and now they were hauling top speed away from the station. The fuel reactor hadn't blown yet; if it had, Perdition would be disintegrating at a much faster rate. He couldn't remember what the computer had said before or even how long it had been since the first warning.

Chain reaction imminent.

He didn't want to alarm everyone else. They didn't seem to realize how serious the danger, despite the comments Vost had made. But the merc commander obviously knew a fair bit about physics because tension flattened his mouth into a pale line, and his shoulders were hunched as he worked the control panel, trying to coax more speed out of the damaged engine.

"How does it look?" he asked quietly.

"Honestly? Not good. All my calculations indicate that we'll still be in range when the station goes critical."

"And the debris field will crack us open." That was the probability the handheld kept predicting, too, no matter how he ran the numbers.

"We're just not fast enough." Vost slammed a hand against the arm of his chair, a muscle ticking in his jaw.

"Would lightening the load help?"

The merc cut him a look. "Don't think I forgot you offering to open my throat, little man. Don't get any bright ideas. You can't space my corpse without endangering everyone on board."

"True. We don't have an airlock." His disappointment was only partially feigned.

"Would it be better if we level with them?" Vost asked. It seemed to be a sincere question.

Tam listened to the others talking. While he couldn't make out individual threads of conversation, he caught the bright spark of Martine's laughter and the lower rumble of Jael's voice, teasing her. Dred wasn't saying much, but Calypso took up the slack. *They're so fragging happy. We beat the odds.*

He sighed. "No. It's not as if they can do anything. We're already worrying enough for everyone, don't you think?"

"I'm working the angles, like I always do. I'm not thinking about anything but getting out of range right now. I can't promise we'll live . . . but if we *don't*, it won't be because I gave up."

"It's good to be in the cockpit with you." To his surprise, he meant it. "But . . . I have a question."

"As long as it doesn't take much concentration, I'll answer." Vost adjusted a setting and the engine whined.

"Don't kill it."

"I won't. What's on your mind?"

"What happened with Keelah?"

A long silence.

"You say that like I know something."

"Vost, you may be many reprehensible things, but I *never* imagined you were a man who murdered females for no reason."

"Will you believe me if I tell you the truth?"

"I guess we won't know unless you try."

So while he ran hopeless numbers, he listened to Vost's side of the story. Once the merc finished, he weighed the facts. "What did you hope to accomplish by giving her the codes?"

"I didn't think she hated me so much . . . she never gave any sign of it. So one, I thought she could be my backup. If something happened to me—other than one of you lot sticking a shiv in me—you could still get off station. Honest to Mary, I thought she was the least likely to turn on me, so I gave up the info."

"But she decided she'd rather end you."

"Yeah. She'd scavenged a poison blade from Silence. Ask yourself, how the hell would I get my hands on something like that? All I did was turn it on her. And I didn't enjoy doing it."

"No more than you enjoyed inciting mass murder over the comm. Because it didn't matter what we did to each other, correct?"

The merc's uncomfortable silence told Tam he was right.

VOST had a thousand reasons to feel guilty, but Keelah's death bothered him more than most. Because she never snarled at him, he hadn't realized her true feelings. *And because of that error in judgment, she died.* If they survived, he could wallow in regret.

For now, though . . .

"You have kids?" he asked Tam.

"None that I know of."

"Then I don't expect you to get it. But if you had any, you'd understand."

"What?"

"That I'm prepared to do anything to see his face again."

Wordless, the other man nodded. He might not feel it in his heart, but maybe this was a starting point. *If not, well, there's nothing else I can say.* Vost knew he was riding hard on the *end justifies the means* argument. He tapped the console.

Frag. Can't go faster. Our time's almost up.

Pushing the engines meant running out of fuel sooner, and as it was, they wouldn't make it out of the system. Which had been chosen as the site for the prison because there was nothing else here. In passing through, he'd come across a satellite and rubble field, junk that Monsanto likely jettisoned ages ago, plus five or six depleted planetoids, none of which could sustain life and had been deemed unfeasible for terraforming. If there had been any more profit to be wrung from the area, the corporation would've done it.

In that moment, he felt incredibly small with the stars surrounding him . . . and trapped on a piecemeal junker with people who'd rather see him dead. Tam had said nothing after his confession, so he might have a knife with his name on it the minute he closed his eyes. Vost was prepared for that contingency, however.

If I live to make another deal with them.

He glanced out, and the brightest of lights practically blinded him. As Perdition died behind them, the big boom rayed out from the station in a widening sphere, a ghostly fireball with fluorescent echoes. The supercharged particles created a corona, shining through the ship even at this remove. Vost braced for the others to notice—to ask difficult questions.

"Why's it so bright?" Martine yelled on cue.

Aiming a look, Vost let the other man field it. He kept quiet.

After a few seconds of reflection, Tam said, "Station fireworks. Enjoy the ride."

Calypso cheered. *Mary.* The sound of palms slapping in back reached him. He didn't feel good about keeping them in the dark, figuratively, since the whole ship was suffused with wild, potentially lethal illumination. *When all that energy catches up to us . . .*

"The reactor just went up," he murmured.

More and more flashes, no sound. It was an impressive light show, even as the station crumbled. Whole sections whirled away. What had been an H turned into twin vertical axes, then they fell apart. Fear laced through him in a way he'd never known. He checked the readings, and sure enough, energy levels were rising outside and closing fast. The debris would be moving too fast for him to track it, let alone dodge it, and it wasn't like this thing had any maneuverability. He tensed, listening to the moan of the engines; they were already giving a hundred percent. The cockpit was loud, and the cabin might not even be radiation-proof.

Yet another test I didn't have time to do because these idiots thought I was more dangerous than the demented demolitionist running amok.

But he understood why now, at least.

So much fragging energy harnessed to keep that thing running. And now it's unleashed.

Tam plugged the handheld into the console, then a holo appeared, prompting him to enter certain figures. "This'll help me do the math."

"Velocity, hull density and integrity versus solar wind and the debris field . . . did you factor for everything?"

"You know it's not *really* solar wind, right?"

"Like verbiage matters right now." Tense, he watched the numbers ticking away.

The other man sighed. "Fine, then. Yes, I input all the data we possess. Happy?"

"Not really."

The simulation ran for precious moments; and then their likelihood of survival appeared. The bottom of Vost's stomach dropped out.

"Nice knowing you," Tam said.

AN icy wind ripped everything in two. *The grim one comes.* Death took her up in his arms and carried her up into infinity. For endless moments, she spun in his embrace, perfectly at peace. Then the burning began. It choked out her sense of him, and suddenly, she cut free.

Rebestah. I am Rebestah Saren.

She opened her eyes. The universe was bright and cold, nothing but stars. She could not breathe, but she had a name. *A name, I have a name.* It felt like awakening from a long, terrible dream. One blink, another, then it was all frost. Something burst and gave in her head.

Red. The reddest red.

Color. This is color.

Scarlet resolved into a lovely, slender woman's skirt, blowing in a warm, flower-scented breeze. The sun shone like molten gold overhead, and the flowers had no end. *Mother,* she tried to call, but she was small, and the delicate white petals tickled her cheeks as she ran.

Laughter.

"Come and find me, Reba! Come and find me."

She ran, smiling. The red skirt sparkled with threads of silver. On the summer wind, she smelled her father's pipe, a sweet and savory smell that meant Mama had banished him from the house. She called it a filthy habit, smiling as she did so, and there were always hugs, afterward. She also smelled a sweetness, lovely yellow cake. The sky was so, so . . . what? She'd forgotten colors existed like this. They had names.

Blue.

Lemon yellow.

Green grass.

"Where are you?" No sound came out, but somehow her mother heard.

"I'm close, Rebestah. Come and find me."

Someone had set tea and cakes out for her. She gobbled them down, and her father came running then. He twirled her up into his arms. And somehow, she fit against the curve of his hip. Other memories cascaded through her brain. It . . . hurt.

Remembering hurt.

Darkness flashed.

Skin.

Bone.

Stars.

It's all broken.

"My darling girl," her father whispered. "Come home."

Then he dissolved into blood mist and his tongue flopped on the lovely clean grass. Tears burned her cheeks. *It hurts. Why does coming home hurt?*

She ran, and the flowers ate her. Their green stems grew tiny razor-fangs, each one snapping at her skin until there were divots missing. *Why can't I weep?* Rebestah had no breath, nothing but pain.

I had a brother. Where are you, Duval?

And then he was there, so young and fresh. He tossed her in the air, once, twice, as he had in the days before. When she came down for the third time, his face peeled away, and a skull snapped its teeth, until she couldn't bear it. She fled into the flowers though they gnawed at her, more, more. In the midst of the field, a tall tree grew, spreading branches and shade. *Shelter, shelter me.* For a few precious seconds she leaned against its trunk. The tree lowered its boughs and rammed a branch through her chest, then cord woven of human skin dropped from the sky and looped about her throat.

She couldn't breathe.

No air.

No voice.

No more.

The rope broke.

Rebestah ran, but she had no strength. *Beauty lies. It lies.* The flowers ended in a crystalline pool with bright rocks sparkling beneath the water. Her mother, impossibly, waved to her from the bottom. Through the flickering surface, she saw the pretty furniture from their sitting room, the rug she used to sleep upon.

The pond sang, "Come and find me, Reba."

She smiled and dove.

The dark let her go when she sank beneath the blue, floating, floating. When she sucked the water deep into her lungs, the red of her mother's skirt spread around her.

Everything in the world washed clean.

———

◄ 31 ►

Mercenary Behavior

Dred couldn't take her eyes off Perdition's destruction, still visible behind them.

Then something slammed into the craft, an impact that rocked them and spun the tiny ship. The electrical fluctuated, sparks popped from the panel that had killed Duran. Dred ducked away from the short and hoped like hell life support didn't fail. When she thought about the rushed way they'd thrown this together, it was frankly terrifying that they'd taken it out into space.

Vost fought with the controls while Dred tumbled around back. She wished there was something she could do, but she wasn't a pilot. Jacl reached out and grabbed her hand, not to keep from falling but in solidarity. *Whatever happens,* his eyes said, *you're not alone.*

An alarm went off as Vost struggled; and then he seemed to find a pocket of calm in all the chaos. She glanced out the view screen and saw that they were . . . riding, for want of a better word just before a giant piece of shrapnel from the station. *If he can hold this position, then we should make it.* The mercenary commander input a series of commands, but she knew they didn't even have a nav computer, so he had to keep them on track manually.

Everyone fell silent.

The celebratory mood died as the others realized they weren't out of danger yet. One by one, they joined hands, Calypso with Dred, whose fingers were already entwined with Jael's. Martine took his other hand, and Dred bit her lower lip until it bled. Nobody spoke in case it disrupted Vost's concentration. Tam seemed to be frantically calculating trajectory on the handheld. She closed her eyes and offered a plea to Mary.

I've done a lot of terrible things. But please. Give us a second chance.

It was impossible to say how long they sat in tense silence, but at last Vost said to Tam, "That's it. The wave's dissipating." He jogged the craft, getting them out of the shadow of the slab they'd been surfing, then slowed, so the metal zinged past.

Dred didn't see anything else nearby. Which made sense since all of the debris spread in a roughly spherical blast radius. It would've been strange if everything converged on one spot.

"Then we're clear?"

"Looks that way."

"How much fuel do we have left?"

"Fourteen hours."

That wouldn't get them far, Dred knew. But she still cheered along with everyone else, hugging Calypso and Martine, then Jael. In escaping, she felt light as a feather, as if she'd chucked the burdens of her old life in leaving Perdition behind. A few minutes later, Tam left the cockpit and came for his share of the heroic accolades. He collapsed next to Martine, and she put her arms around him.

"Good work," Martine said.

"We're out," Calypso mumbled. "But now we're stuck in a ship that doesn't even have san facilities."

"Sure we do." Dred thumbed in the direction of the buckets in the corner.

Calypso scowled at her. "Those will fill up fast. And we have no way to empty them."

It's definitely not ideal. But it's a stepping-stone to better things.

Vost spoke for the first time since the situation got dicey. "I'm aware that you know what happened with Keelah. Tam asked for my side of it, and I hope you'll listen to him."

"We don't have a choice," Jael said. "For now, we need you."

"And that'll continue until we reach civilization, where we can amicably part ways."

The way Jael's eyes flashed made Dred think he wasn't on board with that, but he didn't say anything else. Dred squeezed his hand. *Now's not the time.*

In a low voice, Tam shared what he'd learned about Keelah's death. The others rumbled, and, finally, Martine muttered, "Of course he'd say that. We can't prove otherwise."

That revelation didn't materially change what they had to do. Survival came first.

Vost seemed to realize they were done conferring because he spoke again. "I'm plotting a course to the nearest beacon. If I conserve fuel, I can get us within bounce range. It'll take time, but with this signal, I can attract a ride."

"Before the food runs out?" Dred asked.

Vost glanced over his shoulder. "We may have to tighten our belts. Martine, I won't be able to stay at the helm twenty-four/seven. Can you keep us on course?"

"I think so. I've stolen a few ships in my day."

"Crashed them, too, I bet," Calypso said, grinning.

Martine pretended to be indignant. "But there's nothing out here for me to hit."

Vost ignored their jokes, and Dred wondered if he was worried about being killed in his sleep. "You won't be able to replicate the signal without me, by the way. It's unique to Ronin Group, my guild."

"Ah, so that's why you expect someone to check it out," Jael noted.

She released a slow breath, leaning her head against the wall. Dred didn't mean to fall asleep, but the stress of the past however many days caught up to her. Unknown hours later, she woke to find the ship dead quiet. *Huh. That's probably not a good sign.*

Everyone was asleep but Vost, who was still in the pilot seat. The merc looked like hell, though, with circles deep enough to swallow his eyes. He hadn't bathed or shaved in a week, it seemed. From his pallor, his wounds hadn't healed completely either. She pushed to her feet, wishing they had better facilities. But everyone would stink soon. Perdition had definitely been worse. Vost glanced up as she sat beside him.

"Why's the ship so quiet?"

"We ran through our fuel."

"I was out fourteen hours?"

His mouth twisted. "Guess you were tired."

So we're adrift. When power drains from all the cells, life support will falter.

Dred crossed her fingers, quietly terrified that this was how their story ended. "Are we close enough for the signal to make it on the bounce?"

JAEL covered his mouth with a palm. They had been drifting for five days. The heap smelled indescribable, comparable to the Bug prison. Everyone was angry and scared, tired of each other's faces, but there was no privacy. As tempers frayed, and the paste ran low, fights broke out. Dred played peacemaker, keeping a bunch of violent felons from increasing their odds of survival. *The center can't hold.*

On day six, the water ran out.

His lips burned. His throat felt tight. On the plus side, he didn't need to piss anymore. *Maybe it would've been better to die in battle.* The air was getting thin, too, as the power cells burned out. They were running the most basic functions, just life support and the signal.

It won't be enough. We need a miracle.

On day seven, the console finally lit up with a faint response signal. Vost shouted in excitement and picked up the comm. "This is 9824, who is this?"

A woman's voice responded, sharp with surprise. "8729. Vost, is that you? Everyone's given you up for dead."

"I could use a lift," Vost said. "My ship's DOA."

"How many for transport?" the other merc asked.

"Six."

"That's a light load. Sounds like a job went south on you."

"You have no idea. How far out are you?"

"Two hours, we just came out of grimspace. Lucky for you, we caught your signal."

"See you soon," Vost said.

Jael could tell from glancing at the others that they were afraid to celebrate yet. He wouldn't be doing the victory dance until they were actually on board the other vessel. Through those last two hours, he just held Dred's hand quietly, until he actually saw the lights on the view screen. Calypso teared up—the only time he'd ever seen her cry—and Martine buried her face in Tam's shoulder. Tense, they held on to each other as their craft banged into the other vessel's cargo hold.

When the merc commander turned, Jael said, "We'll call it square for the ride."

"What happens on Perdition stays on Perdition?" the other man said with a weary half smile.

Martine choked out a rough laugh. "Something like that. I'm not starting shit when it's your mates getting us out of trouble."

Jael glanced around to make sure the others agreed. A consensus of nods came back. Guilt pricked at him because he'd promised Keelah that her death wouldn't go unanswered, but since they were riding on Vost's credit, he'd get everyone else killed if he started something on the merc ship. So he made the offer of peace while thinking about breaking it as soon as they hit civilization. Yet that didn't feel quite right either. On Perdition, he'd cast off the person who used to crack promises like knuckles and think nothing of it.

Huh. Seems like my word means something now.

Vost opened the front hatch as Martine popped the back, and they all fell out onto metal flooring that didn't belong to the station or the craft that almost killed them. *Freedom. So close.* His knees buckled because he'd stopped eating four days ago, knowing the others could take less physical deprivation than he could. But the container bay was swimming now.

"Vost, you son of a bitch, it *is* you." The booming voice came from behind him, and Jael angled his head to take in their rescuer.

She was a big woman, both large and tall, and most of it was muscle though she had a generously padded gut that spoke of success. Snug trousers were tucked into thick-soled boots that brought her up to eye level with Vost; she slapped his shoulder in a hearty greeting. Jael could tell she wasn't vain since her garb was utilitarian, shirt and vest in gray and brown respectively, the latter loaded down with tools. She also had short red hair streaked through with white, and her weathered face had smile lines, giving Jael some hope that this would be a soft landing. Really, though, it all depended how Vost played it. If he admitted they were inmates, the mercs might try to turn them in for the bounty.

And then it's a bloodbath. We take the ship or die trying.

His nerves prickled tight. Vost glanced over and beckoned them forward. "This is what's left of my unit," he said.

"Phew." The ship's captain took a step back. "You won't be getting a warm welcome until you hit the san. That includes you, Vost."

The merc nodded. "Appreciate it. We were out of water and almost through our paste."

"You owe me big then."

"You can sell our junker for scrap to cover the cost of our passage," Vost said. "Plus I'll throw in some credits to sweeten the deal."

"We'll talk compensation later, brother. I can see you're

all unsteady on your pins. Especially you, handsome." She threw a wink at Jael. "I'm Ernestine Holland. If I like you better than I do Vost, you can call me Ernie. Time will tell. Now let's get you lot inside."

On Vost's say-so alone, she opened the main doors leading from the hold into the ship. Which was a good size, well maintained, and impressively laid out, especially for a merc vessel. He'd served on a lot of them, and they usually smelled about as bad as the heap they'd just left. But these hallways were clean, with all the areas divided by function, and there were even separate living quarters.

"You've made some upgrades," Vost said.

"Don't hate me because my ship's beautiful," Ernie answered, smirking.

Vost patted her shoulder. "That couldn't be further from the truth."

Grinning, she escorted them down the hall to the san. "There's one here, one there. Form a line and be quick. I'll leave clean gear in a pile. When you're done, head to the mess, which is that way. I'll have some grub waiting, listen to your sad story, and decide how much I'm charging to save your asses."

◄ 32 ►

Down-Cycle Mutiny

Dred waited until everyone else was done in the san, so she could take her time. She scrubbed until her skin hurt, the mist washing away the longest week of her life. In fact, the only reason she came out was for the promise of food. She didn't like going into debt with a bunch of strangers, but there was no other solution.

Unable to believe Vost didn't plan to turn on them, she closed her eyes and scanned the ship. The moods all looked normal enough, nothing extreme or alarming. *Apparently, Perdition made you paranoid. Not surprising.* Seven days without adequate food and water left her weak as hell, so that effort drained her dry. Shaking, she turned off the san and pulled on her borrowed clothing, plain gray pants and shirt, obviously from the lowest wardrober setting. Still, nobody else had ever worn it—the clothing had been generated especially for her. *That* felt like luxury.

Most of the merc crew were waiting in the mess, along with all of her mates. Her gaze found Jael, who lifted a hand as if reaching for her across distance. Her heart pinged, a strange and lovely feeling. Dred skirted everyone else and took a chair beside him.

Bowls of food were waiting—meat or a good synth version, Kitchen-mate veggies and bread. *Damn, it feels weird having a proper meal.* She remembered when she had to guard her bowl and cup because they didn't have many of them, and unlike the freaks, her people didn't fashion eating implements out of skulls and femurs.

"Looks good," Calypso said. "Thank you very much."

Martine added her voice, as did they all. Tam was quiet, but Dred guessed he was weighing the others and taking their measure. What she'd seen with her Psi ability was good enough, however. Her stomach growled as the captain started passing the dishes around.

"Let them eat first," she instructed. "You can tell by looking they've had a worse run than you lot ever dreamt of. Care to tell me about it?"

"We tried to clean out Perdition," Vost said.

Ernie's eyes widened. "Mary's tits, never say you took that job? A drunken Rodeisian would know better. When the pay's too good to be true—"

"I know, I know."

"Well, I understand why there's so few of you left. Say no more."

"I didn't plan to," Vost said with a certain grim amusement.

"If it's any consolation," Calypso said, eating a bite of something orange and delicious-looking, "we left the place in pieces."

Ernie burst out laughing. "I gather those weren't the mission parameters?"

"Nope. Somebody wanted to repurpose. Looks like they have to find a better site for whatever off-the-books black op they wanted to run."

The redhead grinned. "Sad day to be a bureaucrat, eh?"

Tam smiled for the first time, apparently coming to the conclusion that it was best to be affable, and raised his glass.

"Here's to our charming savior. If there's any way we can make ourselves useful until we make port, please don't hesitate to ask."

"How are you at bunk sports?" Ernie asked, deadpan.

That reminded Dred so much of Calypso's approach to Duran that she was smiling before she realized it. Part of her expected Martine to object, so she was amused when the smaller woman said, "He takes orders beautifully. That's usually my purview, but in light of recent events, I don't mind sharing at all." From her expression, that seemed to be true.

Fascinated, Dred propped her chin on her hand and waited to see how this would play out. Below the table, Jael squeezed her knee, and she glanced over at him. *Don't get any ideas,* he mouthed. She grinned more.

"Hm. I don't like coming between a happy couple unless they enjoy that sort of thing." When Ernie chuckled out loud, she revealed a gold tooth. "So how about it?"

"I'm not averse," Tam said.

The captain patted his leg, then Martine's. "Let's finish eating, shall we? I don't want either of you pretty birds to faint before the fun's through."

"I never get invited to the best parties," Calypso muttered.

"Darling, you'd be welcome, but even the captain's quarters have a capacity limit. If you still feel that way when we hit Gehenna . . ." Ernie trailed off with a cheerful wink.

Dred wasn't sure if the woman was truly so lusty or if it was a role she played to get others to let their guard down. She'd noticed that if people thought you were laser-focused on your libido, they tended to discount you otherwise, so she made a mental note *not* to do that with Ernie Holland.

"It stings being second choice," Calypso said, "but I'll take it as an invitation to an extended private affair."

"You were en route to Gehenna?" Vost cut in.

"So we were. You pulled us off course with your message,

but . . ." She pretended to consult her crew. "His life's worth the cost of fuel, right?"

"Might be," said a dark-skinned man with golden eyes. "Shall we auction him to find out?"

"Funny, Higgins." Vost threw a crust of bread across the table. "Which reminds me. I haven't introduced all you jokers."

Dred promptly forgot the fifteen names the merc rattled off. There was a mix of aliens and humans of varying geno-type. They seemed to be a cheerful, prosperous lot, much better than the ones who offered her a berth when she fled the colony she was born on. They'd done mostly scut work, jobs no respectable crew would take on. From what she could recall, they hadn't even been guilded.

But I was too naïve to realize that they were complete scum. Until it was too late.

Once dinner ended, Ernie asked their specialties, an awkward moment. Vost filled in, "Tam is my recon expert. Martine specializes in demolitions and difficult extractions. Calypso handles all of our interrogations. Jael is a hitter with some security know-how."

"And Dred?" Ernie asked.

"Special teams."

She couldn't remember what that meant in merc terms, but Ernie studied her with all-new respect. "Good to know. Your accommodations won't be private, I'm afraid. We don't haul many passengers, so I only have one spare room with limited bunk space."

"It's fine," Jael said. "Perdition wasn't exactly hospi-table."

"I guess not. How long were you there?"

Martine smirked. "Felt like forever."

"Well, maybe I can help you forget. Shall we have that drink now?"

AS Jael watched, the captain took Tam and Martine to her cabin. He hoped they weren't trading sex for safe passage, but surely they'd have spoken up if they didn't want to. From what he knew of the other man, Tam would probably enjoy being bossed around by two women, and Martine wasn't known for holding her tongue.

It's fine.

Soon after Ernie's departure, her crew headed back to their duties or rec periods, depending on the schedule. Which left him sitting with Dred, Calypso, and Vost in the empty mess hall. The space was *so clean*, all metallic surfaces bright enough that he could see a distorted reflection of his face. Glastique like he hadn't seen in a hundred turns brightened the décor, etched with abstract designs and filled with light.

"I love this ship," Calypso breathed. "You know I can walk right over here . . . and this Kitchen-mate is *voice-operated*. One sweet berry swirl, please." The machine whirred to life and soon she had a little cup with a creamy layered dessert in it. "Heaven. We're in heaven."

"Thanks for covering for us," Dred whispered to Vost.

His eyes cut left and right. "What? You're the last of my team. I won't be hiring you on for the next mission unfortunately."

That was smart, Jael decided. Poor conspirators would sometimes discuss the truth without realizing that it only took one witness to make it all fall apart. Dred seemed to realize that, and she said nothing further on that topic as Calypso blissfully ate her whatever it was. It looked pretty good, though. The food on the table called to him, but his stomach was already hurting. Too well he knew that if he overate after near starvation, he'd just vomit everything up anyway. *Have to take it a little at a time.*

Vost rubbed his chest. "I'm heading to Medical. Damned if I'll be the idiot that saves everyone else, then dies heroically of his wounds because he was too stupid to seek treatment."

"I don't find you heroic," Calypso said, smirking. "But you *are* stupid. So accept half a loaf as better than none and go take your medicine."

"First time that woman's smiled at me," he muttered, heading out of the mess.

"We should find the bunk room. Sleep for a while. It won't be long until we're in Gehenna, if they have a good navigator and pilot." Jael stood up and waved to Calypso.

"This is a great break for us," Dred said, a few minutes later.

"What is?"

"Gehenna. If they were going to New Terra . . ."

We'd be so fragged. But he didn't say so, respecting her reasons for not completing that sentence. Even after they got into the spare room, which was four small bunks built into opposite walls, he didn't say anything that could be used against them. *Always assume they're watching and listening.* Life in the lab had taught him that.

"Yeah, it's been a while since I've been there." The memories weren't all good, but he'd build new ones. *With you, love.*

"We should be able to find work." *It's a good place to disappear,* her eyes said.

It was also a lucky break because Gehenna—as a smuggler's paradise—didn't demand papers. They gave two shits if you were wanted by the Conglomerate, as long as you could pay the per-head levy to enter the dome. And Jael had a plan.

"So tired," she mumbled.

Amazing how exhausting it had been, cooped up in that junker and waiting to die. Part of him wondered how much the parts would sell for because those credits, divided by six, that would be the cost of their collective survival. *Maybe I'll ask Ernie later,* he mused. Dred rolled into a bunk, and he squeezed in behind her.

"You're crowding me."

"If we don't share, there won't be enough beds."

"Tam and Martine probably won't sleep here tonight, unless they're a lot more boring in bed than I imagine."

"Would you like to find out?" That wasn't his particular kink, but if she wanted it—well. *Maybe. Once. In all* honesty, however, it would be tough for him. Nobody but her had ever loved him. *And I never learned to share.*

"Not really," she said sleepily. "I love them both, but that many bodies in a bed must be confusing. Plus, I'd probably be pissed if someone else got more attention."

Before he could tease her about that, she was out, making that low, buzzing sound. Jael wrapped himself around her and winked out, too. Nothing kept him from sleeping and sleeping, until he woke up with his bladder about to burst. He couldn't tell what time it was, but the room was still dark. Calypso was in one bunk, Vost another, and as Dred had predicted, the last was empty.

Jael slipped from bed and went out into the hall. *The san is this way.* By the low lighting, the ship was on down cycle, so he tried to be quiet as he passed the rest of the crew quarters. He used the facilities and was about to step out when he heard a door swish open. Innate caution made him freeze. *It's one of the crew. You're not in Perdition anymore. Nobody wants to kill you.* But he couldn't convince the throbbing in his head that he was safe.

"What're we doing with our bounty?" a low voice asked. *Shit.*

"Make sure they don't suspect anything, dipshit." *Really not good.*

"I can't believe Vost thought Cap wouldn't check his story. She told me to scan everyone as soon as they fell asleep, see what popped."

"That guy . . ." A quiet laugh. "He tried to put one over on us, huh? Asshole."

"How much are they paying for real-live Bred specimens anyway?"

They passed out of earshot before he heard the answer. The figure was probably astronomical. Not from Sci-Corp, of course, but rival bioengineering companies who thought they could improve on the original experiment if they only had access to some private data. Getting ahold of him would be a dream come true for a whole new generation of monsters—eh, scientists. *Right. Scientists.* He needed to scrub his brain.

The only way to keep his secret? Killing everyone on board. That was a shitty way to repay them for his life. Yet the alternative was being sold as soon as they hit Gehenna.

"What the hell do I do?" he whispered.

◄ 33 ►

Negotiation Failure

Dred was having an awesome dream. Sunlight on her skin for the first time in turns, an open sky. *Did the wind always feel this good?* But an insect kept landing on her face, buzz, buzz, so insistent. She tried to brush it away but it started shaking her instead— *Hey, this isn't a dream.* Her eyes opened.

"Wake up," Jael whispered. "We have a situation."

"Space pirates? Hijackers? Conglomerate tax collectors? Wait, no, deep-space tentacle beast." He was so serious she couldn't help messing with him.

"What? No. Worse."

"That is a problem. Talk to me."

Vost and Calypso both rolled over and glared at them, but Jael didn't seem to care. He took her by the shoulders, his face a study in concern. "They know what I am. They're planning to sell me as soon as we make port."

"Wait, what *are* you?" Calypso asked, snapping awake.

"He's a person," Dred snapped at the same time Vost quietly replied, "Bred."

Jael wheeled to stare hard at the merc. "How long have you known?"

"It's the only thing that explains why you survive things that would kill *me*. And I'm augmented as much as a human can be. I've got reinforced bones, upgraded autoimmune functions, reflexes, pretty much the whole package. But you . . . nobody should've been able to survive what Silence did to you."

Nobody human. Those were the words Vost didn't say, but Dred heard them in the stillness, and she imagined Jael did, too. Calypso just looked blank.

"What the frag does 'Bred' mean? Some crazy eugenics programs?"

"Once we deal with the immediate threat, I'll explain everything, I promise." Jael perched on the edge of the mattress. "I turned off the audio in here. Not sure if they're monitoring, but if so, they'll probably find and repair the hack soon. We don't have much time."

"What's your solution?" Vost demanded.

"Kill everyone. Dead people don't talk." Dred didn't think the merc would go along with it, however.

"It's a nice ship," Calypso said, thoughtful.

"This is *exactly* the behavior that got you sentenced to Perdition," Vost snapped.

The former mistress of the circle bared her teeth. "Look, I didn't start this. I planned to enjoy the ride, be pleasant and appreciative, but if those people are about to sell my friend like livestock, I'm gonna throw down. You never fought for somebody you love, tight-ass?"

"You make a compelling point," Vost whispered.

"There's no bloodless way out of this," Dred pointed out.

If she were stronger, she might be able to induce a temporary love/obey state in the crew, but there was no guarantee it would hold long enough for them to get off the ship. It wouldn't stop them from talking about Jael afterward either or prevent them from hunting him. *Plus, there's no way the pilot and navigator could function like that, and I don't have any fine control of that ability.* Since she couldn't even read anyone right now without excruciating pain, it was a moot point. Shakes set in for five minutes after her failure.

Need to build up my strength before I can do that again.

Taking the ship while the others thought they were unaware of the plan seemed like the best move. *So tired of killing. When does it end?* She didn't realize she'd spoken aloud until Jael tipped his brow to hers.

"Sorry, love. If I let them have me, you can have a fresh start."

"No way," she said. "If you expect me to say a lot of stupid romantic shit, that isn't happening. But no. I'll never let you go. Did you forget what I said back on Perdition? You belong to me."

"That's revolting," Calypso said.

Vost added, "And vaguely alarming on the personal-liberty front as well."

She scowled at them. "You two are not helping. We have to decide on a plan."

Vost looked like he wanted to stand and pace, but that would give the game away to anyone who might be watching without audio right now, so he scrubbed his hand across his face. "It occurs to me that we should be concerned about Tam and Martine."

Dred contemplated that for a few seconds, then cursed. "She probably didn't want bed partners after all."

"Hostages," Jael said grimly.

"That is just wrong," Calypso said, shaking her head. "She's defiled the sacred threesome. How shady can a villain get?"

Despite the situation, Dred laughed. "In her shoes, I'd have drugged their wine. If Vost was telling the truth about my passengers, they go their way unharmed. If not, I have collateral to keep the enemy from making a move."

"Remind me never to drink anything you pour," Calypso muttered.

"That sounds like Ernie," Vost agreed.

"We could take a couple of her men," Dred suggested.

Jael had been quiet, head bowed since she said the stuff about his belonging to her. At that he looked up with a shake of his head. "That would just create an impasse. We need a dramatic statement."

Calypso frowned. "Like what?"

"I can wipe them all out. Wouldn't be the first time. Even with cameras posted, it's doable. I just need a distraction."

She could tell that he didn't want to, though. *There has to be another solution.* "If we had enough credits, we might be able to pay her off." Dred glanced at Vost. "Would Captain Holland honor a deal if we offered it?"

"You mean not double back to hunt Jael later or tell other mercs of his existence?" The merc shrugged. "Honestly I can't say. We were never close, just in the same guild."

"None of us know what that means," Calypso said testily.

"It's like working for the same company. Sometimes you form tight bonds. Sometimes you can't stand the guy at the next desk. But mostly you just . . . cross paths, you know?"

"It's a moot point," Dred said. "We don't have anything to offer."

"That's not exactly true." Jael stood up. "You three stay here. If anyone tries anything, resist. I'll be back soon, love."

JAEL strode down the hall to the captain's cabin. He didn't need to bang on the door before it opened. Captain Holland stood there, still dressed, and it didn't look like any partying had taken place. Peering past her, he saw Tam and Martine unconscious trussed up on the bed.

"Most people prefer their partners a little more alert."

"Variety is the spice of life. Come in, handsome. I thought I might see you. My crew have big mouths and tiny brains, not a great combination."

"Hard to get good help these days."

"Exactly what I said to Vost earlier. It's strange he took

up with a bunch of felons and a Bred specimen. Not your usual crack merc unit." Her gray eyes were flat and hard, belying her cheerful tone. And the woman's hand lingered near the blaster on her hip.

Won't help you if I go. Three seconds. For a silent moment he pictured it, hands wrapping around her neck. Lunge and twist. *Yeah. Three seconds.*

"You did us a good turn," he murmured. "So I'm giving you a way out. I'll match the highest offer on me. In return, you drop us at Gehenna as planned. We go our separate ways, and you don't tell anyone, ever, that we crossed paths."

"Mary's tits, that's a fine counteroffer, but you know it won't work. Even if I keep my promise, one of these knuckle-heads will booze it up and let slip. Then you'll have some-body on your trail again. Sad for me, I thought I'd keep you happy with hospitality until it was too late for you to get out of the trap springing shut."

I'm sorry, he thought.

She died as fast as he'd known she would, still struggling to get the gun off her belt. He laid her down gently and untied Tam and Martine. Since the captain had private san facilities, he dragged them both in there and turned it on. The rain of cold water eventually brought them to, groggy and angry as hell.

Martine came up on her knees, spluttering. "What'd she give us? Are we dying?"

"I think you were drugged, not poisoned. But once we clear the ship, it might not be a bad idea to have a medical bot check you out. If there is one."

"Dammit," Tam mumbled.

"We have to kill everyone? All right then." Martine didn't even ask why; that was how good a friend she was.

Touched, Jael touched the top of her head lightly. "When you feel up to it, join the fight. If we're careful, it'll be over quick. Until then, rest up and watch your backs."

"Don't kill the pilot or jumper," Tam said.

"I won't. Otherwise, we're in the same predicament as before and probably won't get lucky a second time."

"Let's hope they can perform under duress," Martine muttered.

"One problem at a time," Jael said, grabbing the gun from Holland's body and slipping out of the cabin.

Dark hall. So far so good.

The other three were still in the guest bunk waiting for him. Dred stood, grabbing his shirtfront. "What's wrong with you? What happened?"

"Negotiations did not go well."

"Then it looks like we're getting a new ship," Calypso said brightly. "Did I mention how much I like the Kitchen-mate on this thing?"

Vost replied in a dry tone, "Perhaps in passing."

Damn. Maybe it was just habituation, but Jael was actually starting to like the merc. Then he immediately remembered Keelah and felt guilty about it.

"Will this get you in trouble with the guild?" Dred asked.

"Yes." It was a simple answer, but the merc didn't seem like he wanted to back away from hijacking this vessel.

Hell, maybe if you pushed a person to the wall, anybody was capable of crimes that would get them thrown away in Perdition.

Calypso stood, stretched, and pulled a shiv out from under her pillow. "What? Old habits die hard. I'm sure I'll grow out of this. Someday."

"Since you have a blade, you check their quarters. Kill anyone you find sleeping." Dred gave the orders like a Dread Queen, and Jael saw the echo of that person in her sharp green eyes.

She's part of you. Not all. And she always will be. I can live with that.

With all his heart, he wished things had worked out different. That Ernie had not only seemed kind and trusting—that she had been. Because then she wouldn't have double-checked Vost's story, and she wouldn't be dead on her cabin floor right now. He wouldn't be plotting mass murder. Again.

How many people have to die so I can live? A hundred?

A thousand. The number was already too high. Before, he hadn't even realized it was wrong, just scrapping for survival like an animal, all hunger and instinct. Dred touched his arm, as if she knew what he was thinking, and she shook her head slightly.

The woman's a witch.

They were all still in their simple gray wardrober clothes, thin and soft, almost like being naked. Armor would be nice, but they couldn't waste time wishing. A quick search turned up nothing in the bunk room that could double as a weapon, so he handed the laser pistol to Vost. *Wonder how combat capable this crew is.* The two he'd overheard didn't seem like dangerous men, but judging by appearances was often a mistake.

"How would you rank this lot, compared to us?" he asked Vost.

"Lambs in the field," the other man said with a scary smile.

Yeah, Perdition left a mark on him.

"Don't waste time." Calypso twirled her shiv, demonstrating why inmates all over Queensland had both loved and feared her. "Let the bloodbath begin."

◄ 34 ►

To Live or Die

There were two men in medical, one being treated for an embarrassing social ailment, and the doc, who was laughing about it. Dred slipped up behind them, picked up a scalpel and killed the patient while Jael broke the doctor's neck. She sighed, staring at the bodies. If everyone had played their parts, that should be the last of them, apart from the pilot and jumper.

In the hall, Tam and Martine were waiting. He was clean, but the other woman had blood spattered on her shirt. She looked down with a rueful expression. "I know. It's brand-new."

Which wasn't what Dred was thinking, but she laughed. She did a walk-through and found Calypso and Vost completing their circuit of the other half of the ship. Calypso nodded in response to the silent inquiry.

Great. The mutiny is complete.

"The jumper's asleep," Calypso said. "And the pilot's playing some kind of VR game in his quarters."

"They're resting before making the jump to Gehenna," Jael guessed.

That seemed likely to Dred, too. It had been a while since she'd traveled this way, but if they'd made an unexpected side trip to this system on top of other travel, they must need recovery time. Otherwise, the ship would already be docking in port and they'd have no clue about the plans for Jael. *We owe his life to their frailty.*

"It takes more out of the navigator than the pilot," Tam said.

"So we should let him . . . her? Sleep until we come to an agreement with the pilot."

"To be honest, I couldn't tell," Calypso admitted.

"Whether the jumper's a man or a woman?" Jael sounded surprised.

"Well, you look. It's one of those big flipping froggers. They haven't been traveling the space lanes very long."

"Oh. Yeah, I don't remember what they're called, either." Dred glanced around, but everyone was shaking their heads.

Tam seemed to be wracking his brain, as keeping up with up-and-coming alien races must've ranked high on his to-do list when he was a government official. Eventually, he snapped his fingers. "Mareq."

"That's right. I don't think I ever met one," Martine said.

"Well, he or she's asleep right there." Calypso pointed to the room two doors down.

"I'll guard the door," Tam volunteered.

Dred nodded. "Then the rest of us will go chat with the pilot."

She didn't look forward to this conversation because if these two were deeply loyal to their crew, they might choose death rather than offer assistance to their murderers. And really, they had no leverage, apart from sparing their lives. But she gave away none of that trepidation as she stepped back and let Jael override the personal lock on the door. Calypso had been right about the pilot's immersion; with a blank stare, he was jacked into his entertainment console and didn't even notice them come in.

"I feel bad," Martine said. "He's so trusting."

Vost strode over and pulled the plug. The pilot rocked backward, clawing at his eyes. His head twitched on his neck, once, twice, then he managed to focus on the room. It took him a little longer to realize there was a problem because he wore a confused smile. Then his gaze zeroed in on the dark stains flecking Martine's shirt.

"What're you doing here?"

"Taking the ship," Vost replied. "We found out about your plan to sell one of us."

Dred nodded. "It's done. You and your navigator are the only ones left. So now you have a decision to make. You can resist and die. Or you can make one final jump on this vessel."

Jael cut in, "We'll compensate you appropriately, of course. Then you sign on with another ship and continue breathing."

"I don't know how Gazel will feel," the pilot whispered. "Can I talk to her?"

"Nope," Martine said cheerfully.

Vost was nodding. "I agree. Currently, we have her under guard, and it's best if you make your decision independently. She might be impelled to throw her life away in solidarity if you're the reckless type."

"I'll stay with him," Jael offered.

Calypso was already halfway out the door. "Let's go wake the navigator. I bet she's had enough sleep at this point to get us to Gehenna."

Dred followed the others out with a quiet look at Jael as he propped himself by the door. Hopefully, things wouldn't escalate. The pilot looked too bewildered and cowed to try anything, but people's behavior could be hard to predict. It would be helpful if she could read him, but the last attempt left her leery. She'd prefer to put a few days of uninterrupted sleep and solid nutrition behind her before she tried that again. They found the Mareq's quarters without trouble.

The navigator hadn't even secured her door, just passed out on her bunk. Which spoke of exhaustion or a trusting nature. But camaraderie developed on a ship where people felt safe. She'd never traveled with mercs who wouldn't prefer raping a woman in her sleep to consensual sex, however.

"I'll do the honors," Calypso said.

The tall woman went over, but before she could touch the jumper, the Mareq female rolled out of range, crouching in the corner of her bunk as shivers rolled over her. Her abdomen changed color, probably indicating her emotional state. Dred could tell she was scared without reading her. Guilt flared. *Mary, I'm glad Jael isn't here to see this.* The pilot was more restrained, at least.

This will take a delicate touch. Without the jumper's agreement, the pilot would dig in, too. Killing them both would leave them stranded, something the pilot and jumper had to know. But this was a good ship, plenty of fuel. It was possible they had sufficient stores to make a slow haul to the nearest port. *Tam would need to run the numbers.* No question they were better off in this ship than they had been the junker; that had been the space equivalent of a life raft.

"These people are like my family," she began quietly.

JAEL lost track of how long he watched the pilot. The man didn't speak, just sat in his chair looking nervous and ineffectual. His wispy little moustache didn't do much to amend the impression. In the VR he was playing, he was probably an action-hero type, shooting people with impunity. In his room, though, he jumped anytime Jael exhaled too loud.

"So what's your name?" he asked.

The man acted like it was a trap. "Why do you care?"

"Because I'm hoping we don't have to kill you. I didn't want trouble, believe me. If the stubborn woman had taken my offer, there wouldn't have been any."

"Huh?"

"I offered her whatever the top bounty's paying to drop us off safe and sound."

"Stupid move on her part. I'm Anjon, Benivar Anjon. You . . . can call me whatever you want, I guess."

Jael didn't explain that the captain had been trying to be honorable in her way. It would've been beyond shady to take his money, then let her crew blab his whereabouts over bottles of hooch. If she had, however, she could've saved her ship. *Is it better to die honestly than to live on a lie?* He wasn't qualified to judge.

"I'm Jael. Just Jael."

That did it for conversation.

Finally, the door slid open, and the Mareq jumper came in, flanked by the rest of his group. He couldn't recall ever talking to one, so he had zero background in reading their expressions. So like the pilot, he had to wait for the news.

"This is not my time to die," the jumper said clearly.

Jael thought Anjon looked relieved. "What did they tell you?"

The Mareq perched on the edge of the pilot's bunk. "Did you know that Captain Holland promised aid, then secretly made plans to sell one of their number into slavery?"

"I heard something about a bounty," he admitted. "Did *you* hear that these folks offered the same amount to go about their business?"

The navigator shook her head, her chest flushing a peculiarly attractive shade of Gehenna red. Jael hoped it was a sign. "I'm not dying today. I hope you won't either."

A slow sigh slid out of the pilot. "To be honest, I was thinking the same. It's not like the mercs give us a full cut anyway since all we do is drive. So that bounty they decided to collect, they wouldn't have paid us from the pool."

"That's a poor choice," Vost said. "I always give my transport officers a full share even if they don't see combat. Because getting out in a hurry can make all the difference."

"See, I tried to explain that to Holland, but she wouldn't listen." To Jael's amusement, the pilot aired some work grievances then, probably to rationalize his decision.

"I don't care about credits." Gazel truly looked as if she didn't. "I do care about my life. It's my responsibility to see as much of the universe as I can and go home with my observations."

"Like a life quest?" Tam asked, obviously interested.

"Something like that." The jumper's expression seemed open and friendly, from what Tam could tell. That seemed strange under the circumstances. "Most of us have the J-gene, but only a small portion choose to train as navigators. My people don't live long, and so when we leave Marakeq, we're tasked with enriching the body of knowledge available to everyone. The Mareq tend not to trust what we haven't seen or experienced for ourselves, so . . ." She trailed off. "But this isn't relevant. If Ben agrees, I'll accept your offer to pay for passage."

"You can have the ship, too," Vost said.

Anjon and Gazel shared a look, then they both shook their heads. Gazel spoke for the pair of them. "This vessel will have bad . . . energy now. You're welcome to it."

"We could sell it and split the credits. Then the bad juju is somebody else's problem." Calypso glanced around, seeming pleased with the solution.

"Sounds good to me," Martine said.

The pilot and jumper were the last to agree, but when they thought about how much even an eighth of a ship would likely amount to, they finally nodded. Then Anjon got down to business. "Captain Holland gave us orders not to jump until we heard from her."

"Is that why we're still puttering along on auto in straight space?" Dred asked.

Gazel nodded. "I can take us to Gehenna whenever you wish."

"We need to scrub this vessel first." Vost glanced around, as if gathering consensus.

Jael agreed it was a good idea. Fifteen bodies and blood spatter wasn't a good way to make port, even in a smuggler's haven. So he said, "Go for it."

Martine put in, "Don't take this the wrong way, but I'm keeping these two company, on the off chance they're telling us what we want to hear right now."

Tam's mouth flattened into a line. "That would be most unwise. You can take us wherever you wish, true, but your lives won't last long thereafter. And if you try anything in grimspace, you'll perish *with* us."

"I understand your concern," Gazel said. "And I don't mind if she waits here while you . . . tidy up the ship."

"Can I go back to my VR?" Anjon asked.

Martine shrugged. "Knock yourself out."

With everyone else on sanitation detail, it didn't take long to jettison the corpses and clean up the traces. An hour later, after Tam had himself checked by the med droid—that only found traces of a strong sedative—they reconvened in the pilot's quarters. Anjon was playing his game, as requested, while Martine kept an eye on Gazel.

"Ready to jump?" Jael asked.

The navigator bounded to her feet. "It's my favorite thing in the world."

◀ 35 ▶

The Fun Never Ends

Since this was a good-sized ship, there were plenty of seats in the hub. Dred's nerves screamed as she strapped into the safety harness. This gear was supposed to keep your brain from frying as the vessel slid in and out of grimspace. But brain damage aside, there were so many ways this could go wrong. For these moments, they were completely dependent on Gazel and Anjon.

And people lie.

She didn't realize she was frowning until Jael reached over and touched the pleat between her brows. "Hey, we're out of Perdition. This is the last step, right?"

"Big, massive leap, more like."

"Still. We can do it."

"Listen to the man," Calypso called.

Jael wrapped his fingers around hers, and she tried to relax. Martine was whispering to Tam, while Vost sat quiet, likely thinking of a reunion with his son. The engines roared, signaling that they were gathering the power to make the leap. This was such an odd feeling, being completely powerless. If Anjon and Gazel wanted to, they could kill everyone on board and turn this into a ghost ship.

Her stomach knotted. Some ships had view ports, so passengers could watch the difference in light between grimspace and straight, but this one didn't. Just as well, it always made her feel queasy. The jump didn't seem to take long, but it probably felt different to those in the cockpit. As soon as they shifted back, Tam unstrapped. Dred and Jael followed suit, and they all headed up front.

She waited for Tam to read the star charts over Anjon's shoulders, poised to put these two down. But then he smiled, relief visible in his dark eyes. "Good work."

"It's not my best." Gazel sounded apologetic.

"True. She's gotten us within half an hour of a target before. But forty-five minutes isn't bad," he added hastily, like they might be executed for a sloppy jump.

"No, this is good." Jael patted his shoulder, prompting a subtle release of tension. "If you have a working handheld, we should be close enough for me to transfer credits."

"Handheld?"

They both looked puzzled, and Anjon produced his wrist. "I have this?"

Oh. Skin-tech had been in beta testing when Dred was locked up. *Looks like it's in mass production now.* From what she recalled, the customer had a processor implanted in his wrist, and the skin became the screen. You could do business, watch holos, anything the old handhelds used to offer. Jael hesitated, then took hold of Anjon's hand.

"This is awkward."

The pilot laughed. "A little. But you should be able to move funds this way."

With some trial and error, as Dred watched, Jael pulled up an account. She wouldn't have guessed he had money socked away, but he had an account with the oldest independent financial consortium, where they didn't use any citizenship markers, only numerical codes and biometric readings. The number of zeroes astounded her.

"Huh," he said. "Looks like Ramona Jax sent the credits, as promised. Not that I got the chance to spend any of it. And Mary bless interest-bearing accounts."

"Holy shit," Anjon breathed. "You're seriously loaded."

"Whoever said crime doesn't pay," Dred said, deadpan.

"So how much for the ride?" Jael asked.

Gazel glanced at Anjon. "What should we charge for a single jump?" The Mareq seemed not to realize she could ask whatever she wanted; there was a sweetness about her that made Dred feel protective.

But Anjon wasn't a strong, decisive type either. In fact, she'd never met a gentler, more passive pair. Which might be why Holland had hired them. These two weren't likely to argue or question orders. Gazel only wanted to travel, and Anjon seemed unnaturally attached to his VR unit, odd considering his own life could be chock-full of adventure. The two discussed the price for a bit, then settled on a number that was half what Dred would've said.

Jael added twenty percent when he made the transfer, and the funds popped up in Anjon's account. "I can trust you to share with her, right?"

"Absolutely. We're a team."

"Then take us into Gehenna."

So close. We're so close now.

Before long, the others were gathered just outside, making Anjon nervous. But she couldn't blame them. It would be impossible not to want to see freedom get closer and closer on the screen. When the world popped into visual range, Dred took a deep breath.

Stunning.

From this distance, the world was a titian swirl, sunset orange and blood red, mingled with a softness that made the place glow with apparent warmth. They came in fast, so Dred's focus shifted from the abstract patterns of color to being able to make out the tops of tall buildings through the transparent haven of the dome. Anjon flew smoothly, no sign that his ship had been hijacked.

Let's hope he's calm on the comm.

"*Stargazer*, this is control one. What's your purpose in port?"

Before the pilot could answer, Tam leaned in. "Pleasure, of course."

The docking agent laughed. "That's the best reason to come. Are you carrying cargo?"

"That's a negative, control. We have eight passengers, ready to pay the leisure tax and enjoy your finest hospitality." There was a smile fixed on his face, conveyed properly in his tone, and she admired Tam's aptitude for management.

"You make me wish I had time off, *Stargazer*. Sounds like you're ready to cut loose."

"It's been a long time coming," Tam said.

"Proceed to the first checkpoint and wait for further instructions."

Dred had almost forgotten that part. There was a system of complex locks to protect the atmosphere in the dome, so it took a while for Anjon to pass through all of the safeguards.

But eventually, they were on the ground in the hangar. *Free, thank Mary. Finally.*

THANKS to a swift deployment of cleaning bots, the ship didn't smell like blood. There was no overt sign that a mutiny had occurred hours before, nothing to alarm the dock authority. Jael escorted the pilot and navigator to the exit, then he stepped past, beckoning his people.

"Good luck," Jael said to Anjon and Gazel.

The two nodded, but they didn't seem to want to leave the ship first. He didn't blame them. Whatever they did now, they'd kept their part of the bargain, so he beckoned the others.

"Let's get out of here."

"Can't come soon enough for me," Martine mumbled.

"The things I'm going to eat . . ." Calypso practically ran for the hatch doors.

Maybe they should've planned this better, but Jael stuck

close to Dred as they exited. He paid the entry fee for everyone, then they had the green light to do whatever they
wanted. Credits could solve anything on Gehenna.

The smell of engine oil and unwashed bodies swept over
him, in some ways similar to Perdition, but in others, it was
completely different. Because these people had the choice
to bathe or not. They could pack up and go on a whim. He
breathed in the chemical tang, then cut a path across the
hangar to the public exit. Things had changed a little in so
many turns, even inside the dome. There was a moving
walkway now, so he grabbed Dred's hand and hopped on
it. The speed whisked them away from the others, and Dred
glanced over her shoulder, as if alarmed.

"Don't worry, we'll find them later."

"If you say so." From her expression, she was a little
overwhelmed.

Gehenna could hit you like that. Neon everywhere, half-
naked people roaming about, signs promising all manner
of exotic pleasure. The walkway dumped them off in the
market just outside the spaceport. And this, this hadn't
changed much. The stalls were still small and close together,
selling fresh food, chem, slaves, weapons, and now, alien
tech. Hawkers tried to attract his attention with fast patter,
but Jael kept his head down.

"Where are we going?" Dred demanded.

"Quiet, you."

"Are you showing off right now?"

"No, I'm taking care of business."

That did settle her down, but her narrow-eyed look said
he'd pay for it later. *Worth it.* Jael stopped at a stall that sold
encrypted cred sticks. From what he could tell, most people
used wrist-pay, but he wasn't in a hurry to have something
like that implanted. There was no telling how his physiology would impact the integrated tech, plus the tech doc
who did the install would notice anomalies.

"You prefer the old way, eh?" the old man said.

Jael nodded. "Nothing like the classics."

The vendor spat on the floor. "Between you and me, son,

you're smart not to have that junk in your body. I think they use it to track your movements. And plus, I heard it gives you health problems. I knew this guy whose son had one of the first units put in. Two turns later, his nervous system is shot, and he can't hold a job. Coincidence? I don't think so."

He got three in total and loaded credits on all of them. Though he didn't explain, he planned to give them to Tam, who would presumably share with Martine and Calypso. He had money to burn these days, and nothing would make him happier than giving his fellow convicts a leg up out in the world.

"You meet the most interesting people," Dred said, as they walked away.

"Don't I?"

The other three caught up with them as they walked back toward the spaceport. Calypso slapped Jael on the shoulder. "Were you trying to drop us at the first opportunity?"

He grinned. "Not a chance. I'm offering you a chance to party. On me." Then he handed out the cred sticks. "You two share, don't worry, I gave you each the same amount as Calypso."

"Are you sure about this?" Tam asked.

He probably suspected it wasn't a trivial amount, based on what he'd seen on Anjon's skin unit. Jael only nodded.

"Then let's meet up tomorrow," Martine said.

"Hidden Rue," he said.

But before they could make concrete plans, a commotion started on the other side of the market promenade. Jael glimpsed a handful of men in uniforms, never a good sign. They seemed to be private security, and since Gehenna had ten different companies striving for control on any given day, that didn't automatically mean trouble. But he'd had shit blow up in his face often enough that Jael knew to run.

He was already moving, Dred's hand in his, when someone shouted, "That's him!"

The other three scattered. Maybe he should let Dred go, too, but he couldn't. He just couldn't. She didn't seem to want him to, either. Her hold tightened on his hand as they ran, dodging around stalls, leaping over piles of merchandise, and ducking under shelving. On the last, he miscalculated on purpose and slammed his skull straight through a display of jarred creepy crawlies that hit the floor running and caused mayhem behind them.

"Who are they?" Dred gasped out.

"Not sure. Guessing Holland bounced a message, and they're working for the new consortium that wants to run new and exciting experiments on me."

"Then we should kill them."

Jael wished he could pause to kiss her. "While I love your problem-solving instincts, that won't work. It'll only raise our profile and get us in trouble. Right now, we haven't done anything, so we can expect some protection. We've paid our docking fee and hadn't violated any laws when they gave chase."

"You think they'll offer sanctuary?"

"When they find out how much money I plan to spend here? Probably. But first we have to talk to someone in power."

"Who the hell runs this place?" she wondered.

"That, love, is the billion-credit question."

Guttural swearing mingled with shrill screams while they dealt with the beasties he'd unleashed. Now he had a reason to do things right, no more careless carnage. It was past time for the universe to forget about him and leave him be.

And everything *on Gehenna has a price.*

◄ 36 ►

Give Me This Much

Tam and Martine ran until they couldn't anymore. The scenery had changed by the time Tam paused. The buildings were squat and run-down, and the pedestrians were careful not to make eye contact. Since Martine was still wearing a bloodstained shirt, he understood why. The first order of business had to be new clothes, whatever would help them blend in best.

"That was novel," Martine said, breathless.

"What was?"

"Fleeing from men in uniform and having them chase someone else." She flashed a sharp grin that made Tam want to kiss her.

He'd had his own plan for getting off Perdition, but it went nothing like this. Since Einar had died, his whole life was one huge digression. And . . . he didn't mind. Sometimes it felt good to set aside all of the calculations and just be. He offered his hand to Martine.

Who took it with an almost shy smile. "So what should we do first?"

"Shopping, I think. But if you'd rather do something else,

we can just grab you a shirt." He indicated one of the auto-kiosks that sold GEHENNA FOREVER gear. Snagging the cred stick, Martine promptly bought it and pulled it out of the machine.

She shrugged into it quickly. "What do you think? Am I pulling it off?"

"Totally."

"So what now?" she asked.

"That's up to you. I'm happy just breathing as a free man."

Her look turned pensive as she gazed down the narrow street, teeming with people who suspected nothing. "We can never tell anyone, you know."

"That we escaped?" Tam didn't even say the name of the place aloud.

"Exactly."

"You'll find that I'm quite adept at keeping secrets."

"I'm counting on that." Martine leaned over and whispered in his ear.

His smile widened quite without his volition. "I hate to disillusion you, mistress, but that's not a secret."

Martine leaned over casually and bit his shoulder. The twinned pleasure and pain of it stole his breath even in the busy thoroughfare. He could hardly wait to get her alone. *Those teeth* . . . He'd be sorry when and if she had them capped.

"We all thought you were her pet, you know."

"Who?"

"Dred."

"I've never been anyone's pet," he said.

"Oh *really*?"

"I prefer the word 'plaything.' As you well know." A teasing glance.

She grinned, but she didn't press on that topic. Instead, her expression sobered as she took in the dazzling attractions. "Part of me wants to do nothing but eat delicious food and roll around in bed with you."

"I'm waiting for the downside of that plan," Tam said.

"Well, we'd be wasting Jael's money, for one. And . . . I don't want to act like an escaped convict, living like my freedom could be taken away from me at any moment. I want . . . to make plans, I guess. Are we staying on Gehenna? If not, where? Do we need new papers to travel? And more importantly—"

"Are we staying together?" he cut in.

"That's not what I was going to ask." She seemed not to realize he was.

"I know. That's *my* question. Because it impacts every-thing else. We got together in a dark place at a dark time. I would understand if you wanted to cut loose and start again."

White teeth sank into her lower lip. "Damn. That's deep for a walking conversation."

"Should we talk about it over a meal?" His heart con-tracted into a hard, thorny knot in anticipation of her response.

Yes, Tam. It was fun while it lasted. But . . .

"No, let's just find a place to sit." Martine led the way to a bench out of the foot traffic; it had a good view of the vendors across the way.

The rich and powerful smell of incense wafted to him. A woman in a veil was tending a brazier not far away. He watched her instead of looking at Martine.

"Well?" he prompted.

"I never once thought I'd get out of there. You might've had schemes, but I ended up feeling like, well, this is it. No matter how bad it gets, I won't let it break me."

"It didn't."

"There's somebody I love, someone I made a deal to protect. I used to lay awake thinking about her, hoping she was happy. If she was, I thought it was worth it, right? No matter who I slept with inside, she was always the brightest part of my heart."

This hurts . . . more than I expected.

Tam nodded. "Do you plan to search for her now?"

"Just let me finish, you idiot." She seemed impatient for

some reason, angling to gaze at him intensely. "So I didn't even notice when the game I was playing with you got real."

"Excuse me?"

"We're not just sexually compatible, I'm in love with you. So yeah. It'd be good for me if you stuck around." Her eyes were liquid warmth, and her hand on his knee made his heart pound like he was fifteen turns again. "It doesn't matter to me where we met, though I warn you, if people ask how, I'll make up a different story each time."

"That works for me. Because I'm mad about you."

"Back to my original questions, then."

"For what it's worth, I agree with you about not living like convicts. I'd rather start as we mean to go on, as people of great worth."

"You know what they say, the future starts now," she said, and drew him in for a kiss.

VOST went straight to the guild building from the spaceport. With any luck, he should be able to cash out and get a ship out before anyone realized what he had done to Holland. There would be a reckoning, but not before he kept his promise. He played it cool, nodding here and there at mercs who recognized him.

The offices were open twenty-four/seven on a hub like Gehenna, a point in his favor. The Pretty Robotics model working the front desk gave him a facsimile of a smile. "Good to see you again, Commander Vost. What brings you to Ronin headquarters?"

"I need to empty my account."

All assets would be frozen when the guild found out he'd sided with a bunch of felons and a Bred monster over a fellow merc. True, technically, Holland stepped on his toes first since Jael was in his company. That made the Bred bastard his catch. But they would've fined her for that; the matter wouldn't have ended with the whole crew ghosted.

Her face froze as her fact-finding protocol kicked in. "Is there a problem?"

"My son is sick. It's going to clean me out to pay for his next treatment."

The Perdition payday should've gotten him the operation that would save his life, but there was no more money coming in. So he'd liquidate. He had some property to sell, too. Maybe he'd end up a destitute fugitive, but it would all be worth it. *Soon, I'll be there soon.*

"Sorry to hear that. But you realize there is a penalty—"

"It's fine. Cash it out. Put every available credit here." He held out his wrist.

There was some risk of being jacked. Occasionally, junkies would just take your money at the wrist, but unless the mark was an idiot, it was usually pretty hard to tell who had enough credits to be worth the violence. Pickpockets were pretty much out of luck, but thieves always figured out another way. *Only matters how far you'll go.*

He fought the urge to break out in a cold sweat while she ran the numbers and eventually gave him a figure, lower than he hoped, but it was all he could raise. *This will have to do.* Probably, he should be drinking his guilt away. Redmond. Duran. Everyone on the *Stargazer*, but he only straightened his shoulders, accepted the deposit, and strode out.

Back to the spaceport.

Vost paid for a private hire ride back. He'd taken public transport, but time mattered as much as money. Trying not to look desperate, he scanned the various kiosks. Twelve different transport companies ran ships out of Gehenna, and none of them were particularly aboveboard. Finally, he went up to the one with the slogan: "Where you go is your business and nobody else's." Quantifiable bullshit, of course, as secrets were always for sale, but better than, "We'll get you there. Probably," with a smiley face dripping blood.

Somebody's got a dark sense of humor.

The electronic face on the screen brightened when he stepped up. "Name your destination, we can get you there. If it's not on our regular route, ask about a charter deal!"

Awesome. The perky VI package.

"I need to get to Ankaraj as soon as possible. When's the next ship out?"

"Tomorrow morning. We have four berths available. Would you like to purchase one?"

Swearing, he said, "Maybe" and left the kiosk hanging. As luck would have it, the only ship leaving tonight came from Bloody Good Shipping aka "We'll get you there. Probably."

But their vessel was heading out in four hours, and they had one ticket left.

"I'll take it," he said, holding out his wrist.

I'm coming, he told the orange sky. *Hang on for me. I'll keep this promise if it's the last thing I do.*

Once he had his documents, Vost headed to the lounge to wait. The other passengers were shady as frag, shifty-eyed, and one had a bag that seemed to be . . . oozing. A woman strode in, surveyed the lot of them, then turned around. Maybe she reconsidered her travel plans. He didn't speak to anyone. *I'm not here to make friends. I just need those Bloody Good bastards not to crash the transport.*

And for the guild not to learn anything before my ship leaves.

Come on, universe. Give me this much.

◄ 37 ►

If Dreams Come True

Once they lost their pursuers, Dred went with Jael on public transport, away from the spaceport. The security team searching for him wouldn't give up easily, but there were countless places to lose yourself in Gehenna. Jael seemed to know the city, so she trusted him and got off in a seedy-looking district. She hadn't spent much time in the dome, only one stop on a merc ship, long ago. She'd stayed near the spaceport, just done a little drinking before shipping out the next day.

They ended up on a narrow street lined with bars. Some of them were little more than stalls, open-faced shops with plastique tables and chairs and in some cases, buckets and crates, where people could drown their sorrows. A woman in a dirty apron tried to convince them to sample her soup, boiling away on an open fire. Jael shook his head politely as they strolled by.

Right, we're not in a hurry.

"Are we looking for something in particular?" she asked.

He appeared to be scanning each building with an

assessing eye. Jael turned to her with a faint smile. "It's driving you crazy for me to be in charge, isn't it?"

"Maybe a little."

"In payment for your honesty, yes, there's a club where we should be able to make contact with some players. I haven't been here in turns, though, so I don't remember exactly—aha. Here we are."

Glancing past him she read HIDDEN RUE in blue, flashing letters. The building looked ancient, but it also showed some signs of recent renovation. A few scruffy bastards loitered outside, one of them smoking, and herbal-scented puffs scented the air as they passed by. She got a slight rush just from the secondhand inhalation, so whatever chem he had, it must be good. One of them aimed a smile and a wink at her. Dred laughed.

Holy shit. I'm in Gehenna. He has no idea who I am. He's hitting on me.

It was hard to control the wave of hysterical euphoria that rose up in her chest. *I have no idea how to act or what to do.* But Jael had ahold of her hand, so she went into the club. Inside, everything was dark and red-tinted. An elevated stage ran across the back of the bar, with cages hung high on either side. Right now, they were empty, and there weren't too many people drinking or watching the heavily scarred woman undulate; she wore nothing but crisscrossed straps with judiciously placed buckles and a pair of lethal-looking shoes.

"This is our first stop? Really?"

"Contacts, love." Jael went over to the bar, where an old man was nursing a drink. "Who owns the place now?"

"Who wants to know?"

"What matters is that I knew Domina," he said.

The man made a sound that was one part burp, one part raucous laughter. "Tell me another one. She's been dead for forty turns."

Dred scanned the room, looking for a better source of information. She focused on a large, well-muscled man in a dark suit. Before him, he only had a glass of water. In most places, they had the public bouncer and quiet backup in case things got out of hand. The bouncer standing by the back wall wouldn't make conversation, but his partner might.

"Try that table."

Jael followed her gaze and nodded. "Good eye. Let's go."

He went over with a purposeful air. The other man looked up, revealing clear eyes and a speculative air. Dred guessed he must stand over two meters, probably 120 kilos. His arms were no joke, either. He'd shorn his hair, and she suspected that was to give no handholds in a fight.

"Can I help you two?" he asked.

"Maybe. I'd like to talk to the owner."

"What about?"

"Domina always knew the major players. I'm thinking of sticking around . . . and making some local investments, but I could use a hand settling some business first."

"Ah. Why don't you take a seat?"

Dred raised a brow at Jael, but he'd already accepted the invitation. *Maybe he's not the backup bouncer?* On closer inspection, she reevaluated the cost of his suit, adding another thousand credits based on the fabric and the cut. It looked as if it had been hand-tailored, nearly unheard of these days. Most men just input their measurements into their wardrobers. She took the seat next to Jael, both opposite their host.

"Thanks," she said.

"As I'm sure you've worked out, I'm the current owner of Hidden Rue, Domingo Pace. But I'm not sure you'll find me as useful as my grandmother."

"Nice to meet you." She hesitated, wondering if she should give her full name. Coverage of her crimes had been plastered all over the bounce. It had been long enough, however, that she'd probably been forgotten by the general populace. "I'm Dred."

"Jael." He reached over to shake the proprietor's hand.

Domingo Pace signaled one of his human servers, a

quaint affectation for a bar. "Bring me some wine." He named a vintage and turn that meant nothing to Dred. "Now then . . . what do you think I can do for you?"

"Possibly put us in touch with the appropriate party . . . for a finder's fee, of course." Jael seemed at ease though his request must seem odd to the other man. "There's an uncrowned king or queen of every city like Gehenna. If I can make his or her acquaintance, I have no doubt my problems will disappear."

Dred suspected he meant literally.

"Is it a legal matter?" Pace didn't act like he'd mind if it was.

"Not exactly. Some businessmen want me for a project I have no interest in. They've had no compunction about issuing a private-pay bounty and trying to force my compliance."

"How rude," Pace said.

"My thoughts exactly."

The other man steepled his hands, prepared to do business. "As I'm sure you know, anything can be had for a price. Do you have a skin unit?"

Jael smiled. "I prefer the old ways. May I borrow a handheld?"

"Of course." The owner signaled again and murmured to his server, who returned momentarily with the old tech Jael preferred. Dred guessed Jael was flashing his account balance to prove he wasn't a con artist. Pace's smile warmed by five degrees. "Please, keep it for your own use. I'll have Vienna show you to the suite upstairs while I make some calls."

JAEL followed the waitress through the club and up the back stairs. Upstairs, he heard the giggle of happy toddlers. *They must have a crèche on-site for the dancers.* Vienna took another flight and another, until they reached the second-highest floor in the building. She keyed something on the security pad, then turned to him.

"Put your palm here, please, sir. This will key the flat to you, no need for a card or code."

Quietly he did as instructed, then she bowed and hurried off the way she'd come. For some reason, Vienna seemed nervous. He watched her go.

Dred cleared her throat. "See something you like?"

"No, it's nothing." *I hope*.

He palmed open the doors and stepped inside; the suite was an opulent dream—lush fabrics, ornate furnishings in black and white. Accents came in red and gold, sparks of color. The far wall had an elegant frieze, and the bed was enormous, piled with cushions. Across the room, a row of cupboards hid myriad amenities like a Kitchen-mate and personal wardrober.

"How the hell do you have so much money?" Dred demanded.

"I didn't spend much of what I made as a merc, then later on, salvage. Before everything went wrong, I did one last job, and it had a *huge* payday. Then I got locked up, and it just sat there earning interest. It's a high percent account, too."

"So sitting in prison made you rich," she said, grinning.

It also drove me mad.

"That's one way to look at it."

"Do you think we can trust Pace?"

"Not really. But I think he's more interested in getting what he can out of me. He must know I'll pay more over time than the company trying to collect me like a specimen."

"I noticed you were cagey about why they're after you."

He nodded. "Better if he thinks they want my brain figuratively, love."

"So what now?"

"We wait. But while we do, I can think of a number of fantasies we could fulfill. Fine food, elegant clothes?" He tilted his head. "Interested?"

"It feels . . . silly, after everything we've been through."

"Why? I want to see you as gorgeous as nature allows. I want to eat something delicious while imagining how I'll peel you out of a pretty dress."

A shaky breath slipped out, and he could hear the unsteady skip of her heart. *Love knowing that you want me.* "You've talked me into it. But let's wash up first."

It had been ages since he'd stepped into a san so luxurious. In fact, apart from the recycling function on the water system, there was no efficiency to it all. A huge tub dominated the room, a waterfall on the far wall, gilded spigots and impossibly thick, lush robes waiting for use on golden hooks. Dred stopped in the doorway, eyes wide.

"I feel like such a yokel right now."

"You came from a backwater colony, rode around in dirty merc ships, then moved on to hunting killers. No time to live it up?"

"I couldn't afford it," she admitted. "I spent my money on travel and weapons. The only taste of the good life I had came from Cedric, and he was all about philanthropy."

"So opera and charity benefits?"

Dred nodded, looking sheepish. "He wasn't one to indulge like this."

"I'm glad to hear that. Because it might take the shine off if you were comparing my lavish generosity with someone else's." Though he kept his tone light, he didn't want to talk about Cedric Genaro, even if he'd died tragically. Maybe *especially* because he did.

He stopped the tub and turned on the water. There was a dazzling array of bath products lined up along the edge of the tub: ruby red, sapphire blue, gold, and silver. Jael smelled a number of them and decided on a rosy pink, then he scattered the kernels into the water. They burst into fizzing life, tinting the water with romance. Maybe it was ridiculous to do this when he should be planning, but he'd never been able to shake the taint of his heritage on his own. Now that he had Dred to protect, the problem had to be solved, one way or another.

She was already naked, slipping into the bath with a delightfully innocent pleasure. So odd to use that word in correlation with the Dread Queen, but her life had been stunted by her Psi ability, just as being Bred had marked him. He shucked the gray garb and stepped into the tub with her. The water burbled white at the spout and blushed pink deep down.

Rolling her shoulders, she settled in, eyes falling half-closed. "I don't even care if this is a politic move anymore."

Jael shifted closer and pulled her against him. The water slicked her skin, so she felt like wet s-silk in his arms. "It's the best we can do, trust me. Without powerful backers, they hound us all over Gehenna. We can kill them, but they'll send more. Sooner or later, the authorities will intervene, and they won't care *why* we fought, only that everywhere we go, dead bodies pile up."

"I'd prefer to stay out of prison," she said.

"Don't worry. I have a plan." He smiled at her, trying to look reassuring.

That was mostly true. It would be more accurate to say he had a dream. Since he'd never had one before, there was nothing he wouldn't do to make it come true.

◄ 38 ►

Future Perfect

After a long luxuriant bath, Dred put on the white robe and went out to see what kind of dress she could design. Pace's hospitality was top-notch because he didn't limit the cuts or fabrics she could access. In the distant past, she recalled staying in hotels that required a credit stick to unlock the better options.

She took this mission seriously, every bit as much as any murderer she'd ever hunted. It was about more than creating a gown; it was also directly linked to reclaiming her identity as a person, as a woman, completely apart from the Dread Queen. She input ideas, discarding them almost as fast. Dred lost track of how long she was at it, but eventually she entered the production code and waited for her dress to be finished.

When it was done, the style came to a round collar in front and left most of her back bare. This couldn't be worn with anything beneath it, but Perdition had left her more than lean enough. In fact, as she slipped into it, she wished she had more curves. She touched her shorn hair and peeped in the mirror. The result was . . . beautiful, sleek, and slightly dangerous.

Jael had gone first since suits didn't take nearly as long. He was waiting in the other room, so she called out to him. "I'm ready."

He came to the doorway and stopped, wearing an inscrutable look. "Words fail me."

"I hope that's a good thing."

"You've no idea. Let me . . ." Jael pulled out her chair, and she sat, oddly shy.

In the real world, there had been no romance for her. With Cedric, it was pretense, one that made her feel guilty the whole time. So she didn't know how to act. Part of her wanted to rip the gown off, but they'd promised each other elegant clothes and a posh meal. So even if things went hideously awry later, that pledge should be kept.

"Thank you."

"I'll get the food. I already programmed the menu."

Maybe someone else would've preferred a fancy restaurant, but other people would've just made Dred more anxious at a time like this. Quietly, she watched him set out dishes in rich-smelling sauce, noodles, bright fruits and vegetables, plates of creamy sweets. Then Jael joined her and took up his cutlery. For the first time she noticed that his hands were trembling.

He's nervous, too.

That helped. She had no confidence that she knew how to live as a free woman and as half of a working romantic partnership. It was one thing in Perdition, where all the rules were clear, and survival always took precedence over emotional entanglements. This felt like a series of traps and snares waiting to trip the unwary. Trying to hide her tension, she served a little of everything on the fine china plate.

"What's wrong?" he asked.

She ate a bit, marveling at the quality of the food. "We'll probably make ourselves sick. Apart from the meal on the *Stargazer*, we haven't had anything but paste in forever."

"*That's* what you're worried about?" From his expression, he didn't believe her.

Fine, I shouldn't lie.

"I don't know how to do this."

"What, eat?"

"Be a real person. I've no idea what role I can play in a future with you. I mean, you have plenty of credits. And I'm not good at anything besides killing."

"So protect me."

Dred laughed. "You don't need me for that."

"Sure I do. You think I can watch my own back all the time? I have to sleep occasionally. And you're the one person I trust above all others." He ate a few bites, seeming unconcerned with her existential crisis. "I intend to offer jobs to Calypso, Tam, and Martine if they're interested."

"Doing what?"

"Tam's a natural analyst. Calypso and Martine would make the perfect security team. They can decide who's in charge." Jael grinned in abdicating the decision.

"But . . . what business are you contemplating?"

"Venture capital. I'm particularly interested in biotech for obvious reasons. The way I figure it, if I can't get away from what I am, I might as well embrace it."

"So . . . you'll fund your own bioengineering research?"

Jael smiled. "Life will get easier if I'm not the only one, don't you think? I'd also like to look for survivors who might need a safe haven."

"Why didn't you do this before?" she asked.

"Lack of resources. Which I have, now. If you're worried about pulling your weight—and I suspect you are—tell me what training you want. We'll get it for you."

Suddenly, it occurred to Dred what she could do, beyond sex or violence. "Could . . . would my talent come in handy? I can read people. That might help screen out bad investments."

"Definitely. I'll want your opinion after every presentation. Don't worry so much, love. I have a sense for these things, and . . . Gehenna will treat us right."

"If you say so."

Relaxing, she ate the rest of her dinner. Jael was quiet, watching her more than his food. Her heart thudded wildly. Finally, he took away their plates and stacked them in the cleaner. After that, he drew her to her feet and cupped her face in his hands.

"Do you trust me?" he whispered.

Normally, that question preceded horrific betrayal, but he was the one being hunted. The injustice of it made her feel frankly murderous. But if he could be cool and consider their course, she could keep from hunting those assholes down. Dred nodded.

"That's all I needed to hear."

In a bold move, he swept her into his arms and carried her to the bed, which was all romance, all the way, down to the red flower petals scattered on the white coverlet. Happiness poked tiny pinholes in the skeptical armor that kept her from living in the moment.

Dred circled his neck with her arms, then touched his cheek. "You did all this for me?"

"I do everything for you," he said softly.

AS Jael set Dred on her feet, he half expected private security goons to kick the door in. But the suite was quiet. He unfastened the high collar of her gown, so the top fell away. Things had never been so clear between them. She wasn't staying because she needed to; this was pure, heady choice. The minute the *Stargazer* touched down, she could've gone her own way.

"It's been a while," she whispered.

"Not as long as it has been." Those long turns where he didn't even hear a human voice, for instance.

"Let's not waste any time." With eager hands, she pulled at his jacket.

Jael blessed his speed as he got out of the rest of his

clothes in seconds. And then he rolled with her onto the mattress in a flutter of perfumed petals. The linens felt incredible against his bare skin, a level of comfort and indulgence that he barely remembered. Surely, there had been nights before, with the occasional paid companion, but he couldn't recall now.

There was only her. Now.

She kissed him first, a little surprising, because she usually went straight to sex. The preliminaries were welcome, though, and he touched her, relearning the shape of her body. She was leaner than she ever had been, the curves of her breasts shallow, her ribs more prominent. But she was probably thinking the same thing.

The wide bay of windows threw rosy light across their twined bodies. Hunger burned in a low, banked fire in the pit of his stomach. For the moment, it was enough just to touch and kiss. There was no need to rush, no emergency calling for their intervention, no risk of imminent bodily harm. So Jael took his time, kissing and stroking, until she stirred, restless, and clutched at his shoulders.

But he should've known she wouldn't take without giving. Soon her hands were all over him, touching his new scars. The raised, puckered flesh made him self-conscious in the best possible way each time she brushed her mouth back and forth. It changed how everything felt, frissons of pleasure breaking like waves over him. Her nails bit into his back as he kissed just beneath the delicate line of her jaw.

"How's that?" he teased.

"Not bad. But I could use a little more."

"Too slow?"

In answer, she wrapped one bare leg across his hip and drew him fully against her. She took his mouth in a deep, lush kiss, moving with each dart of her tongue. His lungs went crazy, and he forgot how to talk. One shift, another, and he pushed into her. This way, curved together, it had to be sweet and slow. The need for restraint maddened him, but with her green eyes so close, lashes fluttering, clouded with pleasure . . .

He rolled, bringing her on top, but he didn't let her sit upright. Still joined, she could only move in tiny increments, not enough to drive either of them over, but he could touch her, feel all of her, while still watching her face. Sheer joy kindled in her expression, and he hoped she was seeing it back but he couldn't think straight. Jael forgot why he was going slow and moved with her, faster, more, harder. Her breath skipped. She bit her lower lip, and he pulled her down for a long kiss as they lost control together. Long moments later, she tumbled sideways and bounced on the mattress beside him.

Reluctant to let go, he drew her in, smiling lazily as she drew circles on his chest with idle fingertips. "That was . . ."

"It was," he agreed.

"How's sex as a free man?"

"Perfect. I may get a doctor's note establishing it as necessary for survival."

Dred kissed his shoulder. "You don't need a prescription for this, love."

"*What* did you call me?"

"Don't make a big thing of it," she mumbled, "or you may never hear it again."

Jael closed his eyes as incredible sweetness swept over him. But he couldn't revel in the feeling long. A few minutes later, the bell rang, signaling a visitor. Dred was out cold beside him, so he pulled up the covers and put on a shirt and trousers.

Checking the view screen revealed Domingo Pace, quite alone, so he opened the door. The other man couldn't be a match for them, even if his partner was currently dead to the world. He stepped back with an inviting gesture.

"I take it your efforts bore fruit?"

Pace nodded, moving past him. "I've explained your circumstances and set up an introduction tomorrow morning if that's convenient."

"Excellent. I'd prefer to conclude this matter in a timely fashion."

"I'm always interested in making potentially helpful

connections." Pace was good at saying the right thing without revealing his agenda.

Could be, it's that simple. He went over to the Kitchenmate and ordered a carafe of wine, the same kind the man had offered them in the club. *That should appeal to him and establish my acuity.*

"A business like this one could always use a little more cash flow," he observed.

"Indeed. You might have noticed the half-completed renovations outside. A silent investor would make my life easier." Pace accepted a glass of wine.

Jael smiled. "If this meeting proves helpful, we'll talk terms. What can you tell me?"

"Fatima Sorush has a finger in most of the pies in Gehenna. If you need intervention or protection, she's your best bet."

"That's a good start. Anything specific I should know about her?"

"Be courteous. Don't rush the niceties. Her family is one of the original settlers of the dome, so she takes such things seriously."

"Got it. I won't insult her."

"Please don't. My reputation is riding on your finesse."

At that he raised a brow. "Why take that risk for a stranger?"

Pace offered a faint smile, lifting his glass for a toast. "Old Gehenna tradition, my friend. Your bank balance attests to your good character. Obviously."

Not in the Stars but in Ourselves

Jael was prepping with Domingo Pace for his meeting. He'd told Dred it was a big deal, and if he brought anyone with him, it might offend his tetchy hostess. So she slipped out to see a little more of the neighborhood, wearing a casual outfit that she'd chosen and the wardrober produced fresh this morning. *Small pleasures,* she thought, heading downstairs.

The club was in full swing, despite the hour. Of course, with no sunrise and no sunset, time was arbitrary on Gehenna. So people could sleep whenever the hell they wanted, really. Therefore, the men who were drinking, complaining about their lives, and watching the dancer on stage didn't seem so odd, on second thought. She passed through the bar and out onto the street, where she drew up short, astonished.

Tam, Martine, and Calypso were coming down the street toward her. It felt like much longer than a day. Pleased, she ran toward them. They'd all bathed and changed clothes, and from the looks of it, they'd had a relaxing night.

"How did you find us?"

Tam smirked. "I have my ways."

Then she remembered Jael shouting the name of the club as they ran from the security team. "Whatever. You just want me to think you're amazing." He shrugged, belying the twinkle in his dark eyes, and drawled the reply, elongating the single word into multiple syllables. "Maybe."

"Have you had any trouble from those goons at the spaceport?" Calypso cut in.

Dred shook her head. "Not so far. Jael's talking to someone this morning about some potential business."

"Sounds shady," Martine said.

"This is Gehenna. Wouldn't you be surprised if it wasn't?" Tam said.

Calypso slung an arm across Dred's shoulder. "I'm down for whatever as long as we don't get locked up again."

"Credits are power here. We should be all right," Martine said.

"So what should we do today?" Tam asked, taking Martine's hand.

Dred took a minute to soak it in. Her friends were walking down a street outside Perdition in new clothes, all healthy and safe. *This feels like a dream.* Like, it was all too good, and suddenly her hands were shaking. She pinched her own arm, hard.

"It's real." Martine smiled at her. "Don't feel bad, I kept doing that yesterday. But look . . ." She flashed a smile and Dred saw that her teeth had been capped. No more terrifying smile, just a pretty, brown-skinned woman with bright eyes.

"You always said you'd do that first chance."

The smaller woman nodded. "I had my reasons for doing it, but I'm ready to let that part of my past go."

"Our destinies lie not in the stars but in ourselves." Calypso sounded like she was quoting something, but Dred couldn't place it.

No matter.

"If you don't mind, I'd like to head to the market outside the spaceport." She glanced at the others with a tentative expression.

"What, you're asking?" Martine grinned to allay the sting. "Queenie."

"Don't even. I'm not the boss of you. Hell, I never was."

Tam seemed thoughtful. "Let me guess, you'd like to ask around. Find out about who's chasing Jael."

"Got it in one."

Calypso nodded. "Questions aren't illegal. Any information we can gather will probably help him later."

"Let's try not to cause trouble," she said in a cautioning tone.

Martine grinned guiltily. "Are you talking to me?"

"Maybe."

That settled, she hurried down the street to the stop she and Jael had used to get here. She scanned the credit stick she'd borrowed from Jael for the fare—and damn, that rankled. Dred had never been a kept woman in her life. Privately she doubted her Psi sense would be worth much, certainly not enough to warrant a full paycheck and damned if she'd let anyone own her.

Not even you, love.

The others hopped on behind her. At this hour, there was plenty of room on the vehicle though public mass transit couldn't take you to the expensive aeries in the best part of the city. For that you had to hire a private car. Transport had tiers in Gehenna; the cheapest ran on the ground, mid-level hovers could take you to industrial and business districts, and only the priciest ones got access to the highest altitude, where there was little traffic.

Eventually, they jumped off near the port market, bustling as it had been the day before. They'd also cleaned up the damage created by the chase.

Dred beelined for the stall Jael had destroyed. It looked like only half the creatures had been rounded up, a definite loss to the tired, dispirited man running the place. He looked up, hopeful, as they approached. She bowed her head in quiet apology.

"I'm sorry, sir. I'm partially responsible for the losses you suffered yesterday."

"What?" He leapt to his feet with an angry shout.

"If you'll add up the cost of the merchandise, I'm happy to compensate you."

His outrage drained away into stunned silence. Martine grabbed her arm, and whispered, "Are you crazy?"

Tam added, "Please make sure to give us an official item list as well, in addition to the verifiable credit value. If there are any discrepancies—"

"No problem, none at all," the vendor assured him.

While Dred waited, the merchant tallied and named all the wee beasties that Jael had unleashed on the market. "Some of them were poisonous," he confided. "So the guards just stomped on them instead of helping me. How was any of that my fault?" He appealed to Calypso with a sad look.

"It's not, that's why we're paying you for the trouble," the tall woman said.

"You have no idea how much I appreciate your honesty. It's rare on Gehenna."

Once he had the credits, he was even more talkative, exactly what Dred had hoped to accomplish—all the benefits of a bribe with the added perk of taking the moral high ground. "So . . . what can you tell me about the guards you mentioned before? Who do they work for?"

Now a couple thousand credits richer, the merchant happily spilled everything he knew.

THIS house loomed impressive even amid the others in the aerie, adorned with stately columns and a terraced approach. Jael climbed like a hundred stairs before they reached the front doors. A manicured garden sat to the side, a luxury of both botanical achievement and space. Buildings were incredibly close together in the dome, so dominating this much territory told him everything he needed to know about Fatima Sorush.

A real human servant led them to an expensively appointed antechamber, where Jael straightened his jacket and squared his shoulders. Pace gave an approving glance, and nodded at the glossy, lacquered double doors before them. Jael preceded the other man, as requested, and stepped into a lavish temple of femininity. With his acute senses, the sweetness of the perfumed air felt like an assault, and he struggled not to let his eyes water.

A woman with a fall of dark hair rose from a white chair, clad in a red robe. Everything about her was dramatic, from her beringed hands to the pattern painted on her right cheek. Her lashes were too long to be real, but she used them to good effect. He couldn't even guess how old she was, but Rejuvenex had been kind to her. Broad, pleasant features belied the sharpness of her dark, deep-set eyes, and her wide mouth was painted with a crimson shine.

So I don't forget she'd happily eat my heart.

Jael bowed deeply at the waist as Pacc murmured a greeting and ducked out. He waited for Madame Sorush to acknowledge him, counting to thirty in his head.

At last, she said, "Please, sit. It's always a pleasure to receive a visitor that dear Domingo deems worthy of my attention."

That sounds like a threat. Disappoint me, and it's his head.

"Thank you. It's only good manners to pay your respects when you move."

"Ah. Should I welcome you to Gehenna, then?"

"I hope that you will be so kind," he murmured.

"Domingo gave me to understand that you knew his grandmother. How is that possible?"

"I'm older than I look," he said, smiling.

"As am I. Domina and I were . . . friends, of a sort." She reminisced a little, and her stories were amusing, so it was no hardship to laugh at the right times.

They made polite talk for half an hour more with Jael doing his best to keep up on the topic of arts and fine wine. Eventually, Madame Sorush tired of the pleasantries. Her smile sharpened as she set down her fine china cup. "Shall we be a little more precise?"

That had to be an invitation to set his cards on the table.

So he explained the situation without coming right out and saying that he was Bred. By her expression, she understood more than he'd articulated. *She probably looked into me.*

"You could apply for citizenship," she said, studying him.

"That tends to be time-consuming."

And it's not nearly enough protection.

"There are ways to cut through the red tape. Gehenna has a soft spot for investors. Someone who feeds the local economy with his credits, for instance, is eligible for immediate citizenship with all benefits. From what Domingo said, you're certainly a candidate."

"That would be an excellent start," he replied. "But I suspect you already know, I need more of an ironclad guarantee. I want to live and work here. There are those who have made my life difficult in the past."

"You want me to take care of them for you and seal our borders." Her dark eyes didn't reveal how she felt about such presumption.

"Simply make it clear that I'm not to be touched. In return, I'll happily support any cause you advise." In time, he could build his own empire. Right now, he needed her.

"I'll think about your proposition," she said.

There was nothing more he could say to sweeten the deal. Credits only went so far, even in Gehenna. But he could prove he wouldn't be a weight around her neck. "Then I'll get started on the citizenship investment. I suspect Mr. Pace can assist me with that."

A faint smile curved her mouth. "I do enjoy nothing so much as initiative. Thank you for calling. My people will be in touch."

Pace was waiting outside in the car on the platform. "Did it go well? You're ambulatory, so that's a good sign." When Jael raised his brows, Pace said, "She broke somebody's kneecaps once for being uncouth."

"I need someone like her backing me."

"You certainly do."

"How much do I need to put into the bar to qualify for citizenship?"

When the other man named the figure, relief spiked strong enough in Jael's temples for it to feel like a headache, something he ordinarily didn't suffer from. *I can afford to set everyone up.* The others could pick their own properties, but the sooner they all qualified for Gehenna's protection, the better it would be. As a real person with papers, he'd have legal means for the first time to drive the consortia back, and if they sent extraction teams after him onto private property, he'd have the legal right to defend himself.

Funny how much status mattered.

"You must feel like I'm a windfall straight from Mary's arms," Jael said then.

"Somewhat. But my mother always said living right is its own reward." The serious expression sold the joke.

"Gehenna's one of the few colonies that doesn't have any qualifications to its citizenship eligibility, did you know that?"

That mattered more than anything. To live with Dred as an equal, he had to achieve personhood officially. Otherwise, it wouldn't matter how many credits his account contained. The threat would never end.

"Can't say I did. Did *you* know we have more prostitutes than any other settlement?"

Jael grinned. "I did not."

"Happy to educate the newcomers. Let's get back to Hidden Rue. Unless I miss my guess, you intend to give me a lot of money today." Rapping the roof, he signaled to the driver to take them off the platform.

Hover cars upset Jael's stomach, but the vertical drop was worse. "That's first on my to-do list. If I transfer funds today, will you start the paperwork with dome administration?"

Pace was much friendlier now that they'd passed the Madame Sorush gauntlet without bodily harm. "It would be my pleasure. I know a solicitor who can file everything for you before the end of business."

◄ 40 ►

Unchecked Momentum

"So now we know *who* is after Jael," Calypso said.

They had paused for lunch at a café near the port market, and the remnants of the meal still littered the table. It was such a novelty to order a meal from the serv-bot and have it delivered. Freedoms that others took for granted seemed marvelous to her. Hopefully that appreciation wouldn't fade.

I don't want to take this fresh start for granted.

"Now we should decide what to do about it." Martine sipped her kaf, eyes slitted in appreciation.

"We shouldn't take action without discussing it with Jael first," Tam cautioned.

"And our first instincts probably shouldn't be indulged." Calypso sounded glum.

Dred smiled. "We'll learn to solve problems with something other than a hammer."

"But it won't be as much fun," Martine muttered.

Tam finished his drink and stood. "Let's learn what we can about the Quintel Consortium. There should be information available, we just have to find it."

"I think I'll leave that in your hands," Dred said. "I'm heading back to Hidden Rue to see how the meeting went."

The others stood as well. Martine and Calypso went off together, looking secretive, while Tam was bound for research. She paid for their meal and went to the tran stop, waiting along with a handful of other people. None of them looked twice at her. Anonymity was a strange and wonderful thing. During the trial, people spat on Dred when they saw her in public. They threw bottles and rotten food, and the officers never attempted to shield her.

We hate vigilantes. You're scum, Devos, nothing but a cold-blooded killer.

She hopped on a transport along with everyone else and reveled in the snippets of conversation. One man was whining about long hours at his job while a woman boasted to her friend of the present she'd just gotten from her boyfriend. There was nothing portentous or vital about any of it, but no violence or danger, either. The trip ended when she hopped off a couple of blocks from Hidden Rue.

Dred took her time, watching the way other people moved. In Perdition, she always had one eye over her shoulder, and a few people walked that way in Gehenna as well. But most of them seemed to be driven by time instead, if they were running late or not.

Music thrummed from Hidden Rue, but then in the short time she had been here, it always did. From what she'd seen, it never closed. There was always a dancer onstage, always at least a few drinkers watching or doing business. She passed through and headed up to their suite. Jael was inside already, poring over something on his handheld. A frown furrowed his brows, and he didn't seem to notice her. Dred closed the distance to peer over his shoulder.

"What's wrong?"

He started. "Didn't hear you come in, love. Where have you been?"

"Checking on some things with the others."

"Ah, so they found the place. That's good." He was so distracted.

"Didn't the meeting go well?"

"Hm? No, it went fine. That is, I'm still waiting to hear. This is something else."

"Is there a problem?" Dred tried not to sound impatient, but she was used to being in charge and having all the information before anyone else.

"Not exactly," he hedged. Then he seemed to focus on her expression and apparently realized she wanted details. "Sorry. I think I made a good impression on Madame Sorush, but she's not rushing into an alliance. Not that I blame her." Then he told her about the citizenship requirements and how he'd already invested the necessary funds in Hidden Rue. Jael concluded, "Now I have the forms to submit, but I've hit a small hitch."

"What is it?" Concerned, she leaned closer.

With a faint sigh, he tapped the screen, zooming in. She saw that the "surname" space was blank. All at once it hit her. *He doesn't have a last name.* At one point, he'd told her that even his first name came from the initials of the scientist that had created him.

"I'm not sure what to do about that," he admitted quietly.

The words came out before she properly processed them. "Use Devos."

His eyes widened. "What?"

"Unless you don't want to. It's a pretty notorious name, now."

"Are you proposing to me?"

A hot flush washed her cheeks. *Mary, how long's it been since I blushed? This is ridiculous.* "No. I was just offering a solution to a problem."

"You sure that's all?"

"I'll let you know if I change my mind," she muttered.

He touched the handheld, then hesitated. "The same surname will definitely foster the impression that we're a married couple. You all right with that, love?"

"It won't bother me."

With no further hesitation, he entered Devos into the

field and flew through the rest of the document. Happiness
didn't begin to describe his expression when he transmitted
the final forms; it was more like pure radiance or incandescent joy. Dred felt weird using those phrases even mentally, but they both applied.

"It only takes twenty-four hours," he said, smiling. "As
long as Pace's solicitor files everything as promised."

"So that means you'll be a full citizen of Gehenna, this
time tomorrow. Congratulations." While she couldn't pretend to understand how much it meant to him, she could
guess. For the longest time, he'd been a thing in the eyes
of the law.

He nodded, eyes overbright. "I can vote. Run for office.
Own property."

Dred perched on the arm of his chair and wrapped an
arm around his neck. It was impossible not to kiss his forehead in silent gratitude. Now Jael would have legal recourse;
he wouldn't need to resort to carnage that resulted in his
inevitable capture.

"I like the ring of Senator Devos. Is that what you want?"

"I'm not sure. Never thought about it. Before, I was
always running, just trying to stay alive. Now I have time
to breathe."

And live, she thought.

THE next day, Jael stared at the courier package. Pace's
solicitor had been as good as his word, so he unwrapped
it. The documents he held proclaimed his citizenship in
black and white, red stamp, gold foil. He hadn't expected
it would feel like this, but after so many turns, it was . . .
overwhelming. For long moments, he held on to his desk.

The long wait is over.

Soon thereafter, Tam rang at the suite door and came
in with an information packet on the Quintel Consortium.
He made his presentation efficiently, then said, "My
advice is to proceed with whatever business plans you're
making, solidify your position before taking action. It will

be better if you can respond to their offense from a place of strength."

Jael nodded. "Dred is out with Pace right now, looking at real estate. We can't stay at Hidden Rue forever."

"What do you have in mind?"

"A ten-story building. The bottom floors will serve as our corporate offices. Then we'll remodel for flats on the top levels. I meant to ask you about that, actually. I reckon we need one for Dred and me, another for you and Martine, then one for Calypso. Or do we need four?"

Tam smiled. "Three would be fine. I'm just a little surprised you want to keep us all so close. Don't you want separate houses, a normal life?"

Jael set down his precious citizenship papers. "No, I really don't. I don't think I'd sleep well if we were spread all over the city. What if something happened, and I couldn't get there fast enough?" It was more honesty than he usually offered but the other man had asked. "Maybe it's trauma talking or habituation, but . . ."

You're family to me, all of you.

Tam was quiet.

"If I'm presuming too much—"

"No, I think a private flat will be fine, though I'll need to check with Martine, of course. If you haven't guessed, I'm rather at loose ends. My plans never extended to what I'd do, should I survive an escape attempt."

"There's a job for you here," Jael said. "Analyze data for me, the way you always have. I've got credits, now I plan to found an empire. But the right people are critical for any start-up."

"Make me an offer."

They talked terms for close to an hour, and, at the end of that time, Jael signed a contract with Tam. He'd never put his name on anything before; there would've been no weight, no meaning. For a few seconds, he stared at the signature: *Jael Devos.* Tam watched him, wearing a faint smile. The smaller man seldom gave away his thoughts, but he seemed pleased by the agreement.

"Do you think your better half will be willing to sign on?"

"I'll talk to Martine and get back to you, but I can't imagine she won't be interested."

Just then, his handheld buzzed with a message from Dred. *Found a likely locale. Come and see?*

He sent back, *On my way.*

There was no need for a jacket. Gehenna climate didn't change. "Did you want to scout the property with me?"

Tam shook his head. "I need to find out what Calypso and Martine are plotting."

"Then I'll see you later."

The building they had found was exactly ten stories, as he'd requested. It wasn't located in the aerie, so the premiums weren't as high as they might have been. Yet property in Gehenna was *always* expensive because of limited space. A sales agent chewed Jael's ear off, explaining that the area was a "bridge," whatever that meant, and that it was becoming gentrified. He shot Pace a look, who read it correctly and led the woman away so he could talk to Dred.

"What do you think?"

"She said it intersects a fair number of communities." That wasn't really an answer.

He stood gazing up at the façade, a sort of neoclassical design. The style wasn't modern, and someone had leased one side to augment failing revenues, so there were a series of flashing advertisements for other businesses. Those would have to go.

"You don't sound enthusiastic. Shall we head in?"

The foyer had clearly been grand at one time, but it was grungy now, a little worn-down, with scuffs on the floor and dings in the walls. The structure would require an external facelift, much like Hidden Rue, plus a full remodel on every floor. Jael didn't have the skill set to estimate how much all of that would cost. There were few mod-cons; the two lifts were dated and creaky when he and Dred inspected the place floor by floor.

She was oddly silent, venturing no opinion, even after the lift doors opened onto the final stop, a single open space.

Instead, she paced to the windows that flooded the room with light. Clearly, this had been the penthouse office of some failed business. He could still make out divots in the ancient carpet where the desk legs had dug in. But he could envision the room transformed; there was already a kitchenette and executive san. It wouldn't take much doing to turn this into a home. Mentally, he mapped it out, placing furniture and choosing the décor.

"I don't want to hire someone," she said unexpectedly.

"What?"

"If we buy this place, I want us to fix it together. It will slow your plans somewhat, but . . . this is the only way I'll feel part of it, not just tagging along on your goodwill. I think they call it sweat equity." Dred let out a nervous laugh. "Anything we don't know how to do, we'll learn." She was watching him in the glass, apparently unable to face him, as she whispered, "I want to build a home with you."

In that moment, he wanted it too, more than anything.

◄ 41 ►

Calm Before the Storm

Dred lifted her drink to toast everyone gathered around the table. Pace had shut down Hidden Rue in celebration, both because of Jael's investment in the club and purchase of the building that would serve as corporate headquarters. Since Jael was a new stockholder, Pace had also invited the dancers to get to know the new silent partner, so it felt like a real party. Loud music streamed from the walls, the clink of glasses mingling with the scrape of cutlery.

"We may be in the suite upstairs longer than expected," Jael was saying to Pace.

"Oh?" The club owner raised his brows.

Jael explained their plan to renovate the acquisition themselves. Calypso seemed excited by the news. "I can get on board with this. You know I'm great with my hands?"

One of the performers glanced over at her. "Are you now?"

Calypso grinned and got up to dance. With the club empty, there was plenty of space. Dred couldn't help but feel that this was the calm before the storm. While she wanted to celebrate, in her heart, she was waiting for the next explosion. The Quintel Consortium still loomed over Jael, the Ronin mercenary group might retaliate, their own citizenship issues were up in the air, and the silence from Madame Sorush bothered her. *How hard is it to make a decision, yes or no?* She loathed powerful people who got off on jerking others around. Maybe that wasn't what Sorush was doing; she might be looking into Jael but while they waited, Dred hated feeling vulnerable.

Martine elaborated with palpable excitement about her plans to install a state-of-the-art security system. Since she'd specialized in circumventing them, that sounded right up her alley. Meanwhile, Jael was all about business, making plans with Domingo Pace. Dred didn't realize her discontent was obvious until Tam leaned over.

"You'll find your place," he said.

"That's not . . ."

"Something else?" He paused, thoughtful. "Let me guess. You feel strange. Displaced. He needed you before . . . and now it seems like he doesn't."

I wouldn't admit it even if it was true.

It was natural for things to change once they left Perdition, but he clearly had more than an inchoate idea of what he wanted to accomplish if they got out. Because she'd learned to fear dreaming, she hadn't allowed herself more than the occasional stolen glimpse of sky or the remembered wonder of luxuries no longer available to her. *Now I have to catch up . . . or risk being left behind.*

"I'm fine," she said, mustering a smile.

Tam surprised her by saying, "I expect the grim foreboding to fade sooner or later. We've been living in the midst of a crisis for so long . . . it's impossible for us to stand down all at once."

"He seems all right." She watched Jael from across the table.

"I suspect life has forced him to become more adaptable than most. Set aside your worries for a night, Dred. The sky won't fall on us." That was such unusual advice, coming from the perennially cautious Tam, that she figured he must be right.

Ronin Group doesn't know where we are. Neither does the Quintel Consortium. It'll take time to track us down, so I might as well cut loose.

The party raged late, and she woke in the morning with no memory of why she was asleep under a table with a strange woman curled up against her. She crawled away, eyes gluey, and found Jael sprawled on a bench, facedown. His fair hair stood on end, and his cheeks were creased from the synth. She stood by him for a few seconds, just smiling, as the others stirred.

"What a night," Calypso moaned.

Pace clapped his hands. "Everyone up and out. I have a crew coming in to fumigate the place. I need the club open in an hour."

"We don't have to go home, but we can't stay here?" Trust Martine to manage a quip even as dry heaves wracked her.

Somehow, Dred rounded her group up while Pace dealt with the hungover dancers. She herded them to the guest suite, mostly because they all needed food and a bath before she'd unleash them on the world. *Mary, this is a strange job for the Dread Queen.*

Once everyone had eaten, they showed no signs of being in a hurry to clear out. Tam and Jael holed up to talk strategy while Calypso was skimming on the handheld, comparing prices on the supplies they'd need to reno the building, and Martine kept trying to take it because she wanted to check out the latest security developments.

"My knowledge is no longer cutting-edge," she complained to Calypso. "You're actively sabotaging me right now."

That word reminded Dred of Silence. *No. Rebestah Saren.*

Fortunately, she still had the one they'd found on Perdition. It was even older than Jael's, but it still connected on the bounce. Dred ran a search, scanned her cred stick to pay for the background check, and came up with the information she wanted a few minutes later.

I didn't think it would be that simple.

Quietly, she read, *Rebestah Saren, aged 25, died on Monsanto Station. Parents deceased. Survived by one brother, Duval Saren.* For an additional fee, she could acquire his personal data. Did she want it? Dred hesitated only a few seconds, then she touched her cred stick to the screen again. The bounce code followed, along with his address, date of birth, and other information that she was faintly alarmed to acquire so easily.

There was more privacy in Perdition.

"What are you so focused on?" Jael asked.

"Following the clues Rebestah left us."

Chagrin and guilt flashed in his blue eyes. "I can't believe I forgot."

"It's all right. I didn't." She told him about locating the woman's brother. "I'm wondering if I should send a message."

"And say what? That she didn't die all those turns ago?"

She sighed. "True. We can't tell him that Monsanto turned her into a madwoman."

"In this case, love, it's best if we leave the man's scars alone. Our energies are best directed elsewhere."

"Like . . . where?"

Jael told her.

WITH the dirt they already had on the Monsanto executives, Jael set Tam to digging.

Soon he had the answers he needed. While the VP had died in a shuttle crush only two turns after the station closed, Administrator Levin had enjoyed a meteoric rise. Now eighty-eight turns and robust with Rejuvenex, he was currently CEO of a luxury travel company with offices on Venice Minor.

"How's this?" Tam asked.

Jael scanned the data. "You were very thorough."

"That's why you pay me the big bucks," the other said.

"That reminds me. Have you decided where to invest your credits? I can't write an official indemnity policy for you until you take care of your citizenship. We're fudging the work permits, as is."

A laugh escaped Tam, and he shook his head. "Never thought I'd hear the Dread Queen's champion talk like that."

Jael grinned. "Isn't it grand?"

Once Tam left, Jael went looking for Dred. The others had taken temporary lodgings nearby, and he couldn't wait for the materials Calypso had ordered to arrive. But until then, this mission was just as important as anything he might achieve in his lifetime. Dred was studying the forwarded files on her handheld when he found her. She was a serious person, more than he'd realized at first in Perdition. But he liked getting to know this side of her and finding that she wasn't just sardonic humor and a yen for violence.

"What do you want to do?" he asked.

"About what?"

"Administrator Levin. He turned Rebestah into Silence, and look at him now." Countless features on the news net showcased his lavish lifestyle.

She watched a few more minutes of garden parties and yachts, glittering galas and extravagance, before saying, "Let's crush him."

That decided, Jael contacted Madame Sorush because he thought she might benefit from the fall somehow. And if he proved he could be useful, she was more likely to come down favorably as his patron. So he left word with her assistant and waited for a call back. Several hours later, her comm code pinged on the handheld.

He activated the chat. "You must be wondering why I've gotten in touch."

"People usually wait," she admitted. "But your message was . . . intriguing."

Dred made a face on the other side of the unit, but Jael

didn't dare glance at her. If he started laughing during the call, it could ruin multiple layers of plans. "I have some life-changing news on Nial Levin. You might find it relevant for a number of reasons."

"The CEO of Diamond Tours?"

"That's him."

"Tell me everything," she ordered.

Tam had done all the legwork, so Jael *knew* Gehenna tourism was suffering in comparison to Venice Minor, so anything she learned about Levin would help boost the economy. If Diamond Tours went down, another travel company could snap up all the lovely tourist credits. Travelers might well choose to come to Gehenna and gamble instead.

Sad as Silence's story was, it didn't take long to summarize it for Madame Sorush, whose expression darkened as she listened until her eyes practically sparked electrical. Without comment, he played the audio that proved what the administrator had done, in conjunction with the vice president, on Monsanto Station so long ago.

"It's proof," she said in disbelief. "There are tests that can verify it is his voice."

"This might not hold up legally," Jael reminded her.

Madame Sorush chuckled. "Dear boy, we're going after him in the court of public opinion. I don't care about prison. With this record, we can turn the entire universe against him. I'll create a sympathetic portrait of the young auditor. His stock will plummet, nobody will want to purchase timeshares or cruise tickets from a monster who built his empire on the blood and bones of an innocent girl."

"So I take it you're interested in this information?"

"Beam me a copy of the audio and any pertinent information on Rebestah Saren. If this turns out as I hope, I'll back you, Mr. Devos. And if *I* stand behind you, there will be no stumbling blocks to your company's economic growth." With most people, that line would come across as pure arrogance; somehow, Madame Sorush delivered it with elegant confidence.

"She's impressive," Dred said, after the other woman hung up.

"There's a reason Pace pointed me in her direction. She's not involved in government, but I wouldn't be surprised if all the major players owed her, one way or another."

"The power behind the throne, then. Like Tam." Dred shot him a rueful look.

"That wasn't true at the end."

"Eh, I'm not hankering to start that nonsense again. I've had enough political jockeying to last me a lifetime."

By the time they sat down for the third meal of the day, the news was all over the bounce: *Nial Levin's Fall from Grace. Dark Deeds from the Diamond CEO.* Jael wondered privately if this would make a difference to Rebestah. *Probably not,* he guessed. But it made him feel better, and it also brought him one step closer to his endgame.

That night, however, Jael dreamt of blood and knives and a dark figure devouring him bite by bite. That was new. Before, he'd only dreamt of the labs. When he woke in a cold sweat, he rolled over in search of Dred. She wasn't in bed, which might explain the nightmares. Something about her kept the bad things at bay.

She makes me better. Stronger.

He rolled out of bed and searched for her. Not hard since their suite wasn't enormous. As expected, she was sitting near the Kitchen-mate with a steaming mug.

"Can't sleep?" he asked.

She shook her head. "Just thinking of what I want to do next."

"Citizenship?"

"I'm investing in your company. That's allowed, right?"

Startled, he stared for a few seconds. "It's your money, don't give it back to me because you feel beholden."

"I don't. But there's no other way for me to go on the books as a partner, much as I don't feel entitled to it since the money came from you initially."

"Is that still bothering you?" he asked.

"Yes."

"Creds are nothing. They never saved my life or made me feel like I was worth anything. Anyone can earn credits, whereas nobody but me gets to be with you."

"You say that like it's special."

In answer he carried her back to bed and proved that it was.

◀ 42 ▶

Loose Ends, Frayed Knot

Tam sat down at his temporary desk and checked messages.

The name on one leapt out at him, freezing him in place. Though he'd sent word that first night, he hadn't expected a reply at all, let alone that fast. For long seconds, he just stared at the screen that was integrated with his desk. And then he activated it.

A strong face appeared, framed in silver hair. Time had been kind, or she'd used Rejuvenex strategically. Either way, she didn't look measurably older than when he'd completed his mission and taken the punishment appropriate for crimes such as his.

"I wish I could come to you in person, but unfortunately, affairs of state prevent me from traveling to Gehenna. It would invite speculation that I can ill afford at this stage in some critical negotiations." She sighed faintly. "I am not as free as I once was. You've no idea how often Soraya and I have thought of you, Tameron. The magnitude of your devotion to Tarnus . . . I have no words to express it. It never set right with me that you gave so much and paid so high a price to see justice done."

He paused the feed. After all this time, it rocked him that she knew who he was.

I'm nobody. I'm a kitchen boy.

But from the first time he reached out to her in exile, she had never treated him like a lesser being. She didn't mock his plans. Instead, she had listened, and said, "It's impossible."

Nothing is impossible, he'd replied.

It took months to convince her to see multiple doctors and scientists, until someone said he could help. On her end, all she had to do was find a nonlethal extraction method for the implant in her skull. He promised to handle the rest.

And I did.

Tam let out an unsteady breath, surprised to find tears standing in his eyes as he listened to Tarnus's true queen. "You did your part. I never doubted that you'd be worth the sacrifice."

That first night on Gehenna, after Martine fell asleep, he'd scanned the news feeds, catching up on Tarnus history, quietly fearing that nothing would have changed for his people. But she had repealed restrictive laws, lightened the burden of taxation on the poor, and reduced the nobility's privilege. Later, policies had been dedicated to improving trade and creating a strong economy. Ten turns ago, the queen and her consort had adopted a little girl, who was known as the People's Princess. One day, a commoner would govern from the Tarnus throne, a feat made possible only because Dina had returned from exile.

The message was only half-complete, so he played the rest.

"I am beyond relief that you have risen from that place. It was my deepest sorrow that I couldn't intervene. I wanted to. So hearing that you're safe and free . . . it gives my heart peace. While I can't see you in person, I can finally remunerate you as you deserve. I've opened an account, here are the particulars . . ." She spoke a series of numbers and Tam committed them to memory. "Don't worry. There's no tracing the funds, and I used an intermediary. No one will know that I've finally rewarded you for unparalleled service to your country. One day, the history books will show you, not as a monster but a patriot. I will endure long enough to make it so, this I swear. I've told my daughter about you, and she will pass the truth along to her children as well. Live well, Tameron, and know that you are ever in our hearts and minds." The queen of Tarnus wiped the tears from her cheeks, and the message ended.

"I didn't need credits," he told the dark screen.

This . . . this is more than I ever hoped or imagined. Finally, it felt as if that door had closed, freeing him to look to the future. He had expected to be executed and once he was sentenced to Perdition, he started scheming. Because *not* to plan meant accepting that his life was essentially over. On Tarnus, he had made few friendships, so it was rather astonishing that he'd come out of the worst place in the universe with the best people he'd ever known.

I have a future. I am needed. And there's work here to be done.

"You all right?" Martine asked.

She paused in the doorway, tilting her head. Hurriedly he swiped at his eyes and went to her. "Better than. I've just had an unexpected windfall."

"Ooh. Are we rich now?"

"Yes," he said softly. "We are."

VOST didn't bathe or shave after he got off the hellish transport to New Terra. He passed through all the checkpoints with no problem, which meant the guild hadn't flagged him yet. Relieved, he called for a car and went straight to the hospital. He was braced for the worst—that the private-pay assholes might've cut his son's treatments—but when he checked the registry, Jamal was still listed. With shaking hands, he emptied all his accounts and received a BALANCE PAID flicker from the screen.

Tension seeped out of muscles he hadn't even known

were cramped. He closed his eyes, trying to dial down his fading panic so it wouldn't register when he got to the room. But as he headed that way, someone stepped out of a cross corridor, blocking his path. His heart went cold and dark. Vost lifted his gaze and recognized the Ronin enforcer in full battle armor.

"Did you think Anjon and Gazel wouldn't report your treachery? You hijacked a guild vessel and murdered the crew. If you provide the names of your accomplices, we might be persuaded to show mercy."

That seemed unlikely. It was an execution-worthy offense, not one that could be mitigated by information. While mercs might double-cross each other, there were lines that could not be crossed, and according to guild policy, what Holland had intended to do didn't warrant how they had responded.

Here at the end of his life, he chose defiance. "I'm not helping you track anyone down. Find them on your own, if you can. But I suspect you won't profit if you do."

Don't underestimate them. It'll be the last mistake you ever make.

Part of him hoped they did go after the convicts because it wouldn't surprise Vost at all if they somehow managed to burn Ronin Group down and piss on the ashes. The thought amused him though that obviously infuriated the enforcer.

"This is funny to you?"

"Not really."

"You going to step outside with me, or should I gun you down right here?"

That sobered him quick enough. "I know there's no reason for you to acquiesce but . . . will you give me ten minutes? I'd like to say good-bye."

That's why I came. To see my boy. To keep my promise.

The Ronin goon hesitated, and since he had on a helmet, Vost couldn't see his expression. Finally, the merc said, "Fine. I'll go with you to the boy's room and wait outside.

But if you try anything, I will splatter you all over the walls. And that'll be pretty traumatic for a sick kid, huh?"

"I got it. That won't be necessary."

He fell silent then, his boots lined with lead as he made his final visit to Jamal's room. His chest hurt, and breathing felt like too much work as he stepped inside. The boy was asleep, but he stirred when he heard footsteps. Bright blue eyes shone in his pale, thin face, and spindly arms reached out for a hug, despite all the tubes and wires.

The enforcer jerked a nod, averting his eyes.

Five minutes.

Gently, Vost sank down on the mattress and wrapped Jamal in his arms, burying his face in the boy's hair. "I'm back, buddy."

"I was worried, you were gone so long."

"Yeah, well. The job took longer than expected."

His eyes found his partner across the room, dozing in the chair. Breck was scruffy and unshaven; it looked like he had been basically living in Jamal's room. *Do I wake him? Do I tell him?* Sometimes there were no good answers. This was the last time he would ever hold this kid in his arms. Vost fought tears.

"You stink, Daddy." Jamal pulled back, wrinkling his nose.

"I know. Sorry about that. You . . . take care of Papa, okay? I know you're going to grow up to be an amazing man."

Until this moment, he hadn't known how to solve this problem. Treatment alone couldn't save Jamal, only transplant surgery or a cloned organ could, and so far, they hadn't found a tissue match, plus they didn't have the credits. *Indemnity will pay out if the guild kills me.* Between his life savings and the death benefits, his son would be fine. Now he knew why everything had worked out this way. Breck might not agree, but Vost had no regrets.

He touched his son's head. *My life for yours. That's how it's supposed to be.*

"I love you," he whispered. "More than you will ever know. Now be a good boy and get some sleep."

Smiling, Jamal settled into his pillows, and Vost went over to his sleeping husband. From the hall, it looked like he was brushing a kiss across Breck's forehead. Which he did, but he also tucked the credit stick into his pocket as well.

"You ready?" the Ronin thug demanded.

"I am," he said.

Vost was smiling when he died.

◀ 43 ▶

Strange Days

Dred spent the next two weeks doing manual labor.

The first part of the remodeling project was depressingly like janitorial work. On the plus side, she definitely felt like she was pulling her weight. Alongside the others, she scrubbed and scoured, scraped turns of neglect off the floor and walls. They hauled junk away by the bin, while Jael complained that he had more than enough creds to pay people.

She threw a dirty rag at him. "This is a good team-building exercise. Probably."

"The minute you start spouting corporate jargon, I'm burying you in a dark hole."

She smirked. "Liar. You'd die without me."

"Possibly."

Tam interrupted, "How soon can you take my credits?"

Apparently, he'd come into some money, though he wouldn't explain where it came from. Maybe he'd shared the truth with Martine, but she wasn't talking.

Jael glanced over in surprise. "You're investing, too?"

"It only makes sense. I'll diversify later. If I'm to be

involved in building this business, we might as well use private capital. That way, we needn't share the dividends."

"I heard blah blah blah, we keep all the money." Calypso perked up visibly. "Does it still count if you gave me the money and I give it back to you? For citizenship."

Jael seemed unsure, so Dred buzzed a message to the solicitor. Who responded right away. *Nobody cares where the credits come from, as long as the documentation is filed under the right person's name.*

Elated, she shared that info, and Jael dropped his brush in a bucket of water. "You four carry on. I have to take care of incorporation right away."

"You haven't filed yet?" Dred scowled at him.

Grinning, he held up both hands defensively. "I bought the building under my name. None of you told me you were considering dumping all your money into . . ."

"You don't even have a name," Martine accused.

"Devos Interstellar." Dred shooed him toward the door. "Now go put it all together. Get the nice attorney to help you."

"You'll be sorry when I'm rich and powerful." Jael made his escape as two buckets were emptied in his direction.

"Damn. I was going to call it Five Convicts or maybe Prison Break Unlimited," Calypso said with a smirk.

Tam laughed. "Considering our goals, that might limit our potential."

"Time for a break." Martine threw down her cloth and fell backward.

The only purchase they'd made for the building so far was a portable entertainment console since Tam liked watching while they worked. Dred appreciated the new tech; it was so tiny that it could be stuck right on the wall; any flat surface morphed into an awesome vid screen with size adjustment and everything. Calypso switched channels, flipping from entertainment to drama to sports, and, finally, Tam locked it on the news net.

A perky, dark-skinned woman told them, "Stocks for Diamond Tours have hit an all-time low. Creditors are calling for immediate loan repayment, and whispers of bankruptcy cannot be far behind. The latest update . . ." She went on to talk about how the board was calling for Levin's immediate resignation and that Venice Minor had hinted they would prefer it if he relocated, as they didn't want their tropical charm tainted by scandal.

Jael had been right about Levin avoiding criminal charges since there was no other evidence for the prosecution to examine, but Rebestah's brother Duval took up the cause and started a virtual takedown campaign, demanding sanctions and boycotts in his sister's name. Sometimes, Dred wondered if they should tell the man that his sister hadn't been immediately driven to suicide as the media presumed. But since it would only make things worse, Levin certainly wasn't talking about the way he'd abandoned the young auditor on Monsanto Station.

The presenter covered the protest rallies on New Terra next, and Tam switched the unit off. "Even Silence had people who loved her. Missed her. That's . . . sobering."

Martine nodded. "I wish we'd known sooner."

With a snort, Calypso said, "What would you have done? Kidnapped her and done amateur brain surgery?"

"Maybe."

Dred laughed. "Get back to work, you lot. When Jael gets back, this will be our official headquarters, and we'll all be equal partners, whatever comes."

"Just like . . ." Tam didn't say Perdition.

Nobody ever did. It felt like an invitation for hell to reach out and drag them back. The mood was a little dimmer when they went back to scrubbing. With elbow grease and plenty of sweat, they finished the last room on the second floor before Jael got back. Dred's shoulders were sore, and her hands were blistered, but this felt right in a way she couldn't explain.

"It's shaping up." Calypso stretched and groaned. "Damn, I'm starving. Whose turn is it to get food?"

"Mine, I think." Dred didn't say she'd heard a noise downstairs, and that was why she'd volunteered to go out.

Jael's probably here. He can go with me.

"Get noodles," Martine called.

"Grilled meat." From Tam.

"I want some fruit," Calypso yelled.

"Fine, I'm on it." She couldn't have imagined she'd be such a jack-of-all-trades in the real world: sanitation worker, builder, courier, server.

But keeping busy felt better than sitting around, and going to bed with her back sore from honest work, well, it wasn't a feeling she'd known in a long time. Dred ran down the stairs, noting all the places they needed to be repaired. *One thing at a time.* She expected to find the man she loved coming toward her.

Instead, she nearly slammed into six men in armor, all bearing the Ronin Group insignia. *Shit. I let my guard down.* But she pulled her Dread Queen façade in place and didn't let them know she was worried. That lesson had been hammered home—fear was weakness and weakness? Death.

I'm fine. The others are upstairs. Jael will be back soon. Stay calm.

Dred made up her mind then. She wouldn't start trouble here though she'd finish it if push came to shove. "Can I help you?"

WHEN Jael saw Dred pinned on the stairs, his first instinct was to break all their necks. He even took a step toward the mercs, but with great effort, he stomped his instincts to silence. Instead, he silently activated the emergency signal on his handheld. If Dred had hers handy, she might've done the same.

"Where are the rest?" a merc demanded.

Dred's gaze met his over their shoulders, but the Dread Queen expression gave the goons nothing but icy disdain. "I asked you a question first."

"Don't screw with me," the man snarled. "I'll kill you where you stand."

"Then you'll be incarcerated." Dred seemed to enjoy telling him that. "See, I'm unarmed. I'm not attacking. You're on private property. Mind you, I *could* execute all of you right now. But I choose not to. I'm trying to cut down on the butchery."

At first, the mercs didn't seem to know how to respond. Thinking probably wasn't their strong point. Mooks like this generally excelled at mouthing threats and shooting off their guns, though not very accurately, from the ones Jael had encountered. Since Dred wasn't cowering or trying to negotiate for her life, they had no idea what to do. Likely, they had orders to round everyone up and deliver them to Ronin leadership for judgment.

Since he'd paid for premium service, sirens screamed toward the building within a few minutes. Jael wondered when the mercs would realize they were the offenders the authorities were coming to collect. They didn't seem to have put it together since the leader tried another threat to get Dred to cooperate.

Jael crept back down the stairs to greet the officers, the only time he'd ever done so willingly. Usually, they were hauling *him* off. In a whisper he explained the situation, and the four guards accompanied him to the stairwell. They'd come in full riot gear with heavy weapons. *Yeah, premium service is totally worth it.* Law enforcement was privately contracted in Gehenna, but the law was definitely on his side. The novelty of it made him laugh.

"What the hell?" the head merc growled.

"You're trespassing," Dred explained.

"You murdered fifteen of our men," another snapped.

The tallest peace officer tapped his wrist, presumably to activate a recording function. "Where did this alleged crime take place?"

"Uh . . ." The leader of the six didn't look like he wanted to make a formal complaint. "On the *Stargazer.*"

"That's a ship?"

"Yeah."

"And was the ship docked in Gehenna port at the time

of the alleged instance?" Jael had rarely met such a serious hard-ass.

And he's on my side.

"No," a merc muttered.

"Then you need to file a complaint in the appropriate jurisdiction. Per my records, this man is a Gehenna citizen with a clean file."

Fresh start. It's really happening.

All of the officers were laser-focused on the armor and weapons. "Did you pay tariffs on all your gear? Should I check what you declared coming into port? Let's start with your names. Jans, start with those three."

"Frag this." The head merc took a step, like he meant to shove past.

"Lay one finger on me, and I'll put you down. That's six months for assaulting an officer. You came onto private property with hostile intentions. I'm documenting. Repeat offenses will be treated as harassment, which escalates on the third visit to stalking. That gives these folks probable cause to believe their lives may be endangered. You realize that on Gehenna, self-defense isn't a crime."

"Huh?" the merc said.

Jael laughed. "It means if you come twice more, we're legally allowed to kill you."

"Like you'd survive a second visit." The merc raised his weapon, but his buddies didn't follow suit.

The four peace officers reacted as a unit, leveling their guns. "You want to escalate? I guarantee my gear's better than yours. I'll bet my life that you shitbags don't walk away."

To his amusement, the mercs slunk off like whipped beasts. And then the guards inclined their heads politely. The one that had spoken before added, "Sorry about the inconvenience. Madame Sorush put a star on your contract to ensure we knew you're VIPs. I'll put extra patrols on this place for a while in case they're as stupid as they look."

"I'll let you know," Jael said.

"If they reach strike three, do what you have to. Some

dumb-asses are unteachable." With that, the guards turned and withdrew.

"So that's what it feels like on the other side," Dred marveled. "It's . . . nice."

"Did you hear how they talked to me?" Respect. That was the word, and it rushed through him stronger than any chem. It made him want to do the right thing and keep doing it. No more brute force, no more pain.

"Madame did say you're a VIP," she teased.

They went back upstairs together, and for some reason, Martine threw a rag at Dred. "Damn, woman. Did this pretty lad distract you? Where's my dinner?"

"It's my fault." Quickly he told them about the mercs and about how perfectly local law enforcement had performed. Jael finished, "We should stay sharp, but—"

"That whole security company's running backup for us." Calypso shook her head in wondering amusement.

"Strange days," Martine muttered.

That pretty much summed it up for everyone.

◄ 44 ►

We Have People for That

Dred's office was perfect.

From picking out the furniture to the art on the walls and the plush rug, everything was her choice. The windows gave the room an airy feel, despite being on the fifth floor and hermetically sealed against the scent-rich dome air. While the technicians were meticulous about oxygen flow, they usually couldn't do anything about the pervasive cocktail of smells, intensified by her enhanced olfactory sense.

I can't believe this belongs to me. But she no longer felt as if it had all been handed to her undeserving. She'd even tacked the carpet in place herself. Dred adjusted the crystal thingamabob Jael had given her to celebrate their official opening and let out a happy sigh. Glancing down, she took in the tailored suit. *I look good.* There was already a backlog of inventors hoping to acquire venture capital from Devos Interstellar. After lengthy discussion, they'd decided to split the liquid funding between in-house and external projects. Tam had screened the list down to the top ten; now they were ready for the presentations to begin. Applicants had flown in from all over and were now gathered downstairs waiting for the Pretty Robotics receptionist to sort them out.

She tugged on her jacket one last time and went to the meeting room, where Jael, Martine, Tam, and Calypso were already waiting. Jael and Tam wore business clothes with consummate elegance whereas Martine went for quirky charm with a short-cut jacket and swirly skirt. Calypso was lean as a knife in trousers and a tunic designed to conceal multiple weapons. Six months after breakout, the former mistress of the circle was probably still sleeping with a shiv beneath her pillow.

Not that Pace seems to mind.

"So . . . is everyone ready?"

"This is . . . unbelievable. You're really paying me to listen and rate crazy ideas?" Martine grinned.

"That and turning our HQ into a fortress," Tam added.

"Let's do this." Jael pressed a button, spoke briefly to the PR receptionist, and a few minutes later, the first candidate came in.

"I'm Amali Cervantez." The young woman bowed as if she were meeting royalty.

Dred kept her composure, knowing that if she smiled it might be taken for mockery. Best not to upset a young scientist who had passed the first cut.

At first, Cervantez seemed hesitant, but as she spoke, she warmed to her theme. "I'm sure you're all familiar with the portal technology that led to the great La'heng cure."

"Pretend we don't know anything," Jael said.

Some of us were . . . preoccupied, Dred thought.

Cervantez went into lecture mode. "Well, some turns back, a couple of travelers stumbled through an ancient portal on Marakeq. They were stranded on a strange world where time moves differently. They also brought back terabytes of schematics, technology so advanced that we're still working to understand it, forty-odd turns later. In scientific circles, it's widely theorized that the original inhabitants are the antediluvian race that first built the grimspace beacons we use today for navigation."

"Interesting," Tam said. "How does that relate to your research?"

"My interest is in the portals," the scientist said. "First I intend to chart them. Marakeq isn't the only one, just the only functional gate we've discovered so far. Perhaps they lead to other worlds . . . or even different times. There's no telling what we might learn if we explore, resources that could be retrieved . . ."

Essentially, you want us to fund your treasure hunt.

But she found the idea fascinating. In her younger days, if she hadn't gone after killers, she might have eagerly signed on for such a dangerous adventure. Now, staying on Gehenna and *not* murdering anyone sounded like paradise. Amali Cervantez finished her presentation with a series of holos showing research trips she'd already taken, along with data she had collected on the portals.

The scientist concluded, "The company that currently owns all exploratory rights to the Marakeq portal has released four tech innovations in the last ten turns. Coincidence? I think not. If you give me the funding I need, I'm confident I can deliver similar results."

"Thanks for your time," Calypso said.

In Dred's opinion, that was actually the best pitch of the day. The others were far less interesting: clinical trials, money for prototypes that were just a rehashed version of something else. By the end of the ten sessions, she had a hard time hiding her yawns. When the last applicant departed, she vaulted from her chair.

"Finally."

"I had no idea work was so boring," Martine grumbled. "I thought about picking that last guy's pocket just to make things more interesting."

Tam kissed her forehead. "Let's not rob the people who come to *us* for money."

Calypso snickered. "That'd be rich, actually."

"Brief consensus. What does everyone think? We agreed to fund two projects, maximum, while we're developing our own labs." As usual, Tam was all about efficiency.

Like he was inside.

Perdition might have carved deep channels in her soul, but the chains fell away from her heart. Dred listened to the others debating the merits of each opportunity. Finally, she said, "I only liked the portals."

"All in favor?" Jael called for a vote.

There was no dissent.

"Excellent. Here's hoping it's always this straightforward." Calypso popped her neck and headed for the door.

It won't be, Dred thought. But she looked forward to the arguments and the struggles, the pulling together, and cheering up afterward. All the lovely normal things she'd never known.

"Shall we get dinner?" Jael asked.

"Sounds good. I haven't fully figured out the new Kitchenmate yet." Dred felt like an imbecile admitting that, but Jael had purchased top-of-the-line everything for the penthouse, and the stuff they'd had on Perdition was outdated twenty turns before the first inmates arrived.

Since none of them had the latest implants, she figured they wouldn't judge.

"Me either," Martine admitted.

"Then it's settled," Tam said.

They headed out together.

NEAR the lifts, a light cage framed around them. Jael grinned at Martine. "After-hours security, eh, bright eyes?"

"You know it. Just hold still. It'll verify that we belong here, and—" The lasers switched off, allowing Martine to call an elevator with a swipe of her palm.

"You wired this building to kill us, didn't you?" Calypso said. "Then you'll keep everything the company earns."

"Don't be silly." Martine got on the lift and waited until everyone joined her to add, "I'll keep Tam. He's endlessly entertaining."

The world was all sunset glamour when Jael passed through the newly gilded lobby and stepped onto the street.

Laser fire bounced across his shoulder, and the pain fired through him before the nerves died. Instinct took over.

He rolled for cover while shouting, "Ambush!"

Even here I'm not safe. I'll never be safe. Worse, I'm a danger to others.

When Ronin Group had heeded the warning and didn't come again, he'd thought they must've cut their losses. *Should've known better. It's really not merc style to be smart.*

Might be Quintel, too. They've been ominously quiet.

He couldn't see if it was Ronin or Quintel Consortium but from the shots coming in hot, there must be fifteen or more, converging on their location. Tracking the trajectory, some were street level, while others covered from the upper stories of the building across the way. Another rain of energy sizzled the pavement. Pedestrians and people who lived in the neighborhood screamed as they ran. A stray shot winged an elderly woman who wasn't fast enough to get out of range. It hit her leg, so she tried to crawl to safety.

"See, this is why I don't like roving around unequipped," Calypso snarled.

"Cowards." Like Jael, Tam was bare-handed.

He activated the emergency code, but there might be more collateral damage before the cavalry arrived. If his neighbors hated his guts, they'd make sure the business suffered, and even Madame Sorush couldn't protect him from public opinion.

You're not killing my dreams. I'd rather die.

Straightening, he ignored Dred's cautionary shout and ducked his head, using his preternatural speed to dodge the shots striking sparks at his feet. The heat singed his legs, and his shoulder felt weak, though it didn't hurt at least. He didn't think about killing the men perched high with his death first in their minds. The only thing he had to do was get the woman who was whimpering ten meters away: silver hair, blue apron, sensible shoes.

Five meters.

Another shot nailed him, this one in the back. Jael swallowed the scream and pushed on. In a single motion he scooped her up and ran back the way he'd come. He was grateful he'd installed giant planters in front of the building. Funny, it hadn't even occurred to him that the thick stone provided excellent cover while the plants inside were a green riot of camouflage.

Gently, he set the woman down. Her eyes were wide and teary as she gazed up at him. "I . . . I thought I was dead."

"Not on my watch," he said.

Martine snickered.

The housekeeper reacted like that wasn't something only a dumb-ass would say; instead, her expression said he was an Honest-to-Mary hero, not a monster.

And maybe that was the key. When people treated him like a beast, he did his best to live down to their expectations. Then he went to hell and met those who thought he could be better. How . . . improbable.

"Help is on the way," Dred said softly. She touched the old woman's hair with a gentleness that would've surprised him if he hadn't already glimpsed that aspect of her.

With no targets in sight, the action died down. Sirens, flashing lights, and security drones locked down the district a few minutes later. When emergency personnel showed up, Jael let the old woman use his premium pass to get immediate care. Tam watched with a thoughtful expression while the professionals rounded up the criminals.

Calypso frowned. "Wait. So . . . we're not killing anyone again. *Ever?* That wasn't even that many. We could've—"

"Haven't you realized?" Martine cut in. "This is how you know you've arrived, my sweet. We have *people* for that now."

"What?" Jael asked Tam, once the confusion died down a little. The man was staring at him, eyes narrowed, and that look demanded the question.

"Was that real, or was it PR?"

"Excuse me?" He honestly had no clue what Tam meant.

"The heroics. Your kindness."

He shrugged. "Does it matter? Six of one." Then he realized he didn't *want* to stick with the sardonic answer. *That's not who I am anymore.* "Honestly? This is my home, and I was . . . protecting it. Not the old way. The way we are now, the way that leaves people thinking I'm one of the good guys."

"You *are*," Tam murmured.

Talking to the security company and signing off on reports delayed dinner another two hours, so Jael was starving by the time they got to the café. He'd planned on a more expensive place to celebrate Devos Interstellar's first day of operation, but all the good spots were busy at this hour, and nobody wanted to wait. So they ended up at the usual place, ordering the customary meal. Not that routine was a bad thing.

Sometimes, it was downright comforting.

A bit later, his handheld buzzed with a message from Madame Sorush, who had been exceedingly helpful since Diamond Tours went bankrupt. He'd heard that former CEO Levin was dealing cards on some backwater space-cruise casino. *So sorry,* Sorush wrote. *I missed signs of collusion between Quintel and Ronin. I've taken steps. They won't trouble you again.*

I'll be damned. Martine was right. We do have people for that.

Quietly, he raised his glass to toast his friends, no . . . his family. "Here's to us and ten more turns together, each better than the last."

◀ 45 ▶

Gehenna Forever

TEN TURNS LATER

Dresdemona waited at the spaceport, hands white-knuckled at her side. She peered through the crowd of disembarking passengers. Though she didn't have time for personal errands—as Chief Operations Officer she'd normally dispatch an assistant for escort duty, but this visitor was special. *I've been looking for you for so long.*

Devos Interstellar was close to replicating the work Sci-Corp had done, so many turns ago, but without the ethical violations. She was constantly monitoring the projects, taking ownership and oversight so no engineered being would ever suffer as Jael had. There were over a hundred different projects being funded currently, not all related to biotech.

Tam was supposed to give me the updated list this morning.

At last, a dark-haired woman came toward her, wearing a simple black dress. Her face possessed that ageless quality that couldn't be purchased with Rejuvenex. It was, however, exactly as Jael had looked when he arrived on Perdition. *This must be her.*

"Katlin Jenton?" she asked, offering a hand.

The other woman responded with a smile and firm shake. "That's the name I use now. He'd remember me as JL490."

Finally.

"Thank you for coming. He's never given up hope, not for all these turns, that one of his pod mates might've survived, just as he did. I know you've both changed so much, but I hope you'll forgive me saying that you're the closest thing he has to family."

"Besides you?" Katlin fell into step with Dred, who led the way out to the waiting car.

In the last ten turns there had been pressure to relocate to the aerie, particularly as DI became more successful. Tam was excellent at screening investment opportunities and advising which projects were most likely to demonstrate the greatest growth. They had seed funding down to an art, and the returns allowed them to pour credits into their own research departments.

But Jael had been firm. He wanted to keep the money in the neighborhood that welcomed them initially, back when they were still fledglings in the Gehenna business world. She didn't mind the location, and she enjoyed the special dispensation that allowed them to land on the roof instead of dealing with traffic down below.

"Thank you for saying that." She was curious why Katlin hadn't brought a guest, but maybe she was between partners.

As they flew over the city-under-glass, she pointed out a few landmarks. The face of Gehenna was ever changing, a seductive creature of twinkling lights and blood orange magic. Today, the sky beyond the dome was all drama, all slashes of smoky red wrapped around a ginger heart. Apart from the colony where she grew up, this was the longest she'd ever lived in one place. At first, she wasn't sure about the dome—she missed fresh air and weather—but she stayed at first because it was the one spot in the universe where Jael's rights could be guaranteed.

One turn ago, he'd won his suit against the Conglomerate and was awarded citizenship retroactively from the point of his creation, which meant he also had a civil case for rights violations. Their team of barristers expected a weighty settlement though that couldn't make up for the suffering. Others had come forward since, adding their own struggles to Jael's story.

See? You're not alone, love.

Smooth as s-silk, the pilot set the hover car down on the roof. Dred waited for Katlin to alight first, then she climbed out behind her. The party was already in full swing; she could hear the music even through the thick glastique and layers of cement that was supposed to soundproof the penthouse. And for most people, it probably did.

From the tip of her head, Katlin heard it, too. "Is it strange that I'm nervous? I remember so clearly how he looked when I said we should part ways . . . does he honestly want to see me?"

"The answer's definitely yes. Come on."

She headed for the small walled garden they cultivated; Jael still loved fiddling with plants in his spare time as much as he had on Perdition. When she flattened her palm, the metal door sprang open, granting access. As ever, the peace of this space washed over her and smoothed out the kinks. It seemed to have the same effect on Katlin.

Another touch unlocked the door to the stairs that led directly to the penthouse. The music clarified into the orchestral sort that Jael favored when he had important guests coming. When it was a smaller party, he'd crank up the bass, letting Calypso and Martine rock out. *They're probably around, wearing gorgeous gowns and quietly starting some new scandal.*

Dred recognized most of the guests, but she didn't see Jael straightaway. She glanced at Katlin. "Let's mingle a bit. He'll turn up."

Then the crowd parted as if on cue, revealing him over

by the windows. He was lean and gorgeous in a tailored blue suit, chatting with an elderly couple. Since their backs were turned, Dred decided to surprise him. She couldn't wait to savor his reaction. *He has* no *idea*. Over the turns, this had become a competition of sorts—to see who could astonish the other more.

There's no way he can ever match this.

But when she got closer, she stopped walking. Hell, she might've even stopped breathing. Pale blue eyes filled with tears at the sight of her, and a woman with wrinkled hands reached out, before drawing up short. But her eyes swept up and down, so avid that Dred almost turned and ran. *If it's you . . . is it you? You must be so ashamed of what I became.* A sob broke free from the woman, and the man circled her shoulders with a wiry arm, more skeptical, more guarded. She'd received that look countless times during her childhood, as her dad always wanted something proven beyond any shadow of the doubt. It was the scientist in him.

"Mum?" she whispered.

JAEL locked onto the reunion like a happy sniper, so he didn't notice the woman with Dred at first. With an ache in his chest, he watched the hugging and crying. It didn't matter that he wasn't part of it. Seeing her family for the first time in ages, Dred had a lot to say to her parents. It took a couple of minutes before the other guest's nervous shifting caught his eye.

His gaze roved over her, then snapped back. Sharing his abilities meant that he no longer had perfect recall. As he aged, the memories softened, faded, and went fuzzy about the edges. *But I know this face. This is probably stupid, but . . .*

"490?"

"A long time ago," she admitted. "I prefer Katlin now."

His breath went in a rush, and he stumbled toward her. "You made it."

"Not as glamorously as you . . . but yes."

"How . . ." He wasn't even sure what he was trying to ask. But fortunately she took pity on him. "How am I here?"

"That's a good start."

"From what I gathered from our correspondence, your wife has been looking for me ever since you arrived on Gehenna. She seemed to think it would make you happy."

"It does," he whispered.

"I can't imagine why. We might've found life a lot easier if I hadn't been so self-serving. But I was so scared. Back then, I didn't understand the concept of friendship or that burdens are lighter with someone else to help you bear them."

"Nobody taught us. How would you have known?"

"I only came forward after you won your suit. I suppose I'm not much for confrontation. What a defective super-soldier, right?" Her self-deprecating tone made him laugh.

Sensing she was nervous, he led Katlin away from the party, up to the rooftop garden. "Is this any better?"

She perched on a nearby bench, collecting herself enough to nod. "I can forgive myself now, I think. Over the turns I heard of you, mostly when something awful hit the bounce. They talked a lot about discovering you mistakenly incarcerated on Ithiss-Tor."

That seems like a lifetime ago.

"The Ithorians sentenced the wrong person," he said then. "So that was the error, and some entrepreneurial adventurers decided to balance the scales. No hard feelings."

Hell, I don't even call them Bugs anymore.

"Where did you go from there?" she asked.

There were a thousand answers he could have given. But only one felt completely true. Sometimes you had to walk all the way through hell to find your way. "Home," he replied.

Jael chatted with her a little more, but he felt guilty about vanishing from his own party. So he pushed to his feet and gave a quiet bow. "I'd love to talk with you more, but for now, duty calls. I hope you'll stay a few days so we can . . . catch up properly."

"I don't plan to disappear," Katlin said. "After all, you're kind of like my long-lost brother. Right?"

Jael smiled. "Something like that."

When he came back to the penthouse, Dred was holed up with her parents in the corner. Her mother couldn't stop touching, arm, shoulder, knee, and her eyes streamed tears. The other guests were politely ignoring the emotional display. Dred's gaze met his, and she mouthed, *Thank you.* There would be time for more eloquent expressions of mutual appreciation later.

A stream of new guests called his attention, so he dutifully devoted himself to smiling at the right people, laughing at their jokes. He spent a full half hour with Madame Sorush. Protecting his status as her favored protégé occupied a fair amount of his time and attention, not that Dred complained. The older woman sent him to fetch her a drink, and he nearly bumped into a couple entering late.

Jael didn't recall inviting them; there were no Ithorians on his guest list, but they must be VIPs, or they wouldn't have invitations with Madame's personal seal. The woman was small and slight, impossible to guess her age. Though he didn't know her face, her eyes struck a chord and she . . . smelled familiar. Jael took a second look, conscious of the woman's doing the same.

It can't be.

With a flex of his mandibles, the Ithtorian took a protective step closer, a clawed hand settling in the small of her back. The woman's scent was all over him, unmistakable and distinctive. *Definitely lovers. Well, it takes all kinds.* He smiled and stepped back, inviting them in with a friendly smile.

"Did you need something?" he asked.

"For a moment, I thought you were a man I met long ago. But . . . on second glance, definitely not. You're someone entirely new."

"I suppose so," he said, bemused.

With a smile, the woman joined Madame Sorush, who lifted a glass in his direction. Jael scanned the crowd for Tam and Martine; he found them making conversation with a senator who didn't seem to like what he was hearing. Martine glanced his way with an impish grin. Then he sought Calypso, holed up with Domingo Pace, who had given himself up to her three turns ago. Their courtship had seemed two parts loathing and one part violent sex, but they'd reached equilibrium. As he watched, Pace traced a hand down Calypso's back, and she bit him.

Katlin slipped back into the room, donning a polite smile. She seemed ready now to meet new people so he introduced her around.

And at the end of the long night, when Dred's parents had gone to their rented suite—with the promise to return for breakfast in the morning, he drew his beloved into his arms. "This is how I want to end every day," he told her.

"What's stopping you?" She turned and kissed him with the same irresistible sweetness that always reminded him that he'd come home.

If we can build a life like this, then nothing is impossible. Nothing at all.

As long as we're together, we'll never lose the light. In the city-under-glass, the horizon shone with infinite promise, Gehenna red, Gehenna forever.

From *New York Times* bestselling author

ANN AGUIRRE

GRIMSPACE

A Sirantha Jax Novel

As the carrier of a rare gene, Sirantha Jax has the ability to jump ships through grimspace—a talent that makes her a highly prized navigator for the Corp. Then the ship Jax is navigating crash-lands, and she's accused of killing everyone on board, leaving her in a jail cell with no memory of the crash. But her fun's not over. A group of rogue fighters frees her...for a price: her help in overthrowing the established order.

"Sirantha Jax is an unforgettable character, and I can't wait to find out what happens to her next. The world Ann Aguirre has created is a roller-coaster ride to remember."

—Christine Feehan, #1 *New York Times* bestselling author

annaguirre.com
facebook.com/ann.aguirre
penguin.com

M1675AS0415